THE MESSAGE OF BLOOD

THE MESSAGE OF BLOOD

DAVID PENNY

THE THOMAS BERRINGTON HISTORICAL MYSTERIES

The Red Hill

Moorish Spain, 1482. English surgeon Thomas Berrington is asked to investigate a series of brutal murders in the palace of al-Hamra in Granada.

Breaker of Bones

Summoned to Cordoba to heal a Spanish prince, Thomas Berrington and his companion, the eunuch Jorge, pursue a killer who re-makes his victims with his own crazed logic.

The Sin Eater

In Granada Helena, the concubine who once shared Thomas Berrington's bed, is carrying his child, while Thomas tracks a killer exacting revenge on evil men.

The Incubus

A mysterious killer stalks the alleys of Ronda. Thomas Berrington, Jorge and Lubna race to identify the culprit before more victims have their breath stolen.

The Inquisitor

In a Sevilla on the edge of chaos death stalks the streets. Thomas Berrington and his companions tread a dangerous path between the Inquisition, the royal palace, and a killer.

The Fortunate Dead

As a Spanish army gathers outside the walls of Malaga, Thomas Berrington hunts down a killer who threatens more than just strangers.

The Promise of Pain

When revenge is not enough. Thomas Berrington flees to the high mountains, only to be drawn back by those he left behind.

The Message of Blood

When Thomas Berrington is sent to Cordoba on the orders of a man he hates he welcomes the distraction of a murder, but is shocked when the evidence points to the killer being his closest companion.

PLACE NAMES

For many of the Spanish cities and towns which lay beyond the boundary of Andalusia the current Spanish names have been used, except where the town had a significant Moorish past, such as Cordoba and Seville.

I have conducted research on the naming of places within Andalusia but have taken a few liberties to make the names easier to pronounce for a modern day audience. Where I have been unable to find reference to the Moorish name of a place I have made one up.

---

al-Andalus … Andalusia
al-Mariyya … Almeria
Gharnatah … Granada
Ixbilya … Sevilla
Malaka … Malaga
Randonda … Ronda
Qurtuba … Cordoba
Sholayr … Sierra Nevada mountains

SPAIN: 1489

CORDOBA, ANDALUSIA

CHAPTER ONE

"God's teeth, Thomas, is it really you? After all these years?"

Standing in the doorway to a small inner courtyard, Thomas Berrington shrugged. "How many other Moorish Englishmen do you know, my friend?" He examined the face of the man who held the door open. Lawrence looked older, but so, Thomas expected, did he.

"Come in, come in." Lawrence turned and called out toward the house. "Laurita, come and see who is here. And fetch wine. Two jugs. And food. You are hungry, aren't you? Yes, of course you are—you look thinner than I remember." Lawrence's mood changed in an instant and Thomas saw that he knew about Lubna.

A woman appeared in the door of the small house. She showed no expression as she stared at the two men before turning back inside.

"I heard about your wife," said Lawrence. "We were both sad to hear the news." He put his hand on Thomas's shoulder. "How are you bearing up?"

"Better for taking my revenge."

"I heard about that, too. Mandana and his son, the two of them. They deserved to die."

"You have no argument from me on that."

Lawrence patted his shoulder before turning to take a seat at the small metal table that was either unchanged or identical to the one they had sat and talked at five years before. Five years during which Thomas had discovered joy only for it to be torn from him. He tried not to think of either the joy or the pain. It was starting to become a little easier day by day, and he had Jorge to thank for that. The man would not allow him to fester in his own misery. Except Jorge had been scarce of late, which is why Thomas had found his way to this square and this house, unsure if Lawrence would still live here.

He waited as Laurita set a platter of bread, hard cheese, fruit and nuts on the table, then returned to the house.

"She still doesn't like me, I see," Thomas said as he took the seat opposite Lawrence.

"She likes you well enough I think, but Laurita always finds it hard to display her feelings to anyone other than me. Perhaps she thinks I will be jealous." He smiled. "One look at your ugly face should set her mind at rest."

"You are right."

"No, I am wrong. Tell me—" Lawrence broke off as Laurita returned with glass goblets and a jug of wine.

"I will bring another if you manage to finish that one," she said as she turned away.

Thomas and Lawrence both watched her walk to the doorway.

"She hasn't changed at all," Thomas said.

"Kind of you to say so, but we both know she has. Not too much, I admit, and she still has great enthusiasm for the important things in life." Lawrence poured wine for them before holding his glass up. "To the important things in life, Thomas, yes?"

Thomas nodded and touched his glass against the other. "Yes, to the important things."

"What brings you to Córdoba?" Lawrence reached out for a chunk of dark bread and cut a slice of cheese. "Are you tupping the Queen yet?" He grinned. "I hear all the gossip from the palace."

"Does the whole city know?"

Lawrence laughed. "So you are, damn it! I knew it."

"No, I am not. I was merely curious how many other people believe these falsehoods."

"Oh, not so many I expect. You are not of as much interest as you might think to the people of Castile. So if not love, what brings you here? Other than to see me, of course."

"Of course." Thomas looked at the cheese and decided he might have some soon. The air in the small courtyard was warm, scented by the orange tree that offered shade, though something more acrid underlay the scent and he wondered if Laurita had burned their supper. "I am sent on some make-work task by the Sultan."

"I heard about the negotiations," said Lawrence. "They go well, do they?"

Thomas pushed hair back from his face and turned to catch the warmth of the sun. "You and I both know how this war will end, and it will not be through negotiation. It is a pretence, but if I do not turn up at least once a day, it is noticed. No doubt someone takes great pleasure in reporting I am not doing my job."

"Your job? You are no negotiator, Thomas. Jorge I could understand, but not you. Is he with you?"

"He is, somewhere. He has taken to making himself

scarce the last few days. And my job is to keep my mouth shut and make sure everyone knows I am there. I believe everyone overestimates my influence with Isabel."

"Have you seen her?"

"We have been here less than a week and it is not my place to seek her out."

"But she would like you to, wouldn't she?" Lawrence glanced around, sniffed at the air.

"I smell it too." Thomas smiled. "What were you going to have for supper?"

"Laurita has never burned anything to my recall. This is something else." He stood, but the enclosing wall did not allow him to see much beyond it, only that the tower of the church next to the house was not ablaze. Though it seemed something was.

Lawrence went into the square and Thomas followed.

"There," said Lawrence, pointing to where a dark billow of smoke rose into the air. "It looks to be close to the river." He went back inside, but returned in a moment with two leather buckets. He handed one to Thomas. "Come on, with luck we might be able to offer some help."

Thomas knew without Lawrence, he would have become totally lost among the maze of alleys they ran through. They emerged on to a long street that dropped down toward the riverbank of the Guadalquivir to find a horde of people had already formed a line and were passing buckets from hand to hand. Lawrence went to join it, Thomas to the head of the line where he took a bucket of water. Even as he threw it into the blaze, he knew there was little point.

A dozen men stood beside him. Each took a bucket as it

arrived, threw the contents into the blaze, then tossed it away empty to be run down the street by young boys. The heat was intense, but nobody stepped away from it, even if they knew their task was fruitless. In the end they had to let the house burn because there were others to save. They split into two groups, one to either side of the by now almost empty shell. The house to the left-hand side began to smoulder and men were brought to add to the number already there.

Then a man pointed upward to where a gout of flame broke through falling tiles. "Leave it burn," he shouted, and they all moved on to the next house.

Thomas looked along the street, calculating how many more houses might be lost. At the far end a stout woman in a white smock stood with her knuckles pressed into her waist, watching as they worked. No doubt she was wondering the same thing. Wondering if her house would still be standing come nightfall.

Two more houses were lost before the fire eventually came under control. The house where the fire had started was now a smouldering shell which men continued to throw water at, and would keep doing so until they were sure it would not re-ignite. Thomas walked down the slope looking for Lawrence, found him coming up to meet him. They stood side by side, arms and faces dark with soot, and watched as a wall broke apart to fall into the gaping hole inside. A shower of sparks rose and Thomas watched them, but they fell back to the ground without igniting any new flame.

"There is a cellar down there," said the man standing next to him. They stood as close to the remains of the building as they could, so close Thomas feared his robes might begin to smoulder, but still he did not step back.

"It isn't so surprising, is it?"

The man glanced at Thomas, back to the hole. "I have lived here twenty years and never knew any of the houses in this row had cellars."

Thomas didn't think the statement required any response, but the man was warming to his subject.

"Alonso never said he had a cellar, not to any of us."

"Is that who lives here?"

"Alonso Cortez," said the man. "Keeps himself to himself. Doesn't mix much."

Which would explain the lack of mention of his cellar. "Where does he work, this Alonso?" Thomas asked.

The man nodded at the ruins of the house. "He works here. He's a scribe."

Thomas began to get a bad feeling. Scribes dealt in words and contracts, both of which required ink and, more importantly in this instance, paper and vellum. Both of which burned hot.

"Has anyone seen him today?"

The man shook his head. "Not me. I don't know about anyone else."

Thomas moved away to question those who remained. Some had already returned to their homes to check for damage, others milled around the street as some kind of perverse party atmosphere began to set in. No doubt most were grateful their houses had been spared.

Nobody had seen Alonso Cortez and the feeling of dread settled deeper into Thomas. He looked around, searching for Lawrence, saw him at the end of the street talking with the woman who had watched events as though unconcerned the fire would ever reach her establishment. Thomas walked up the slope to join them. When he arrived, the woman handed him a pie, still warm against his palm.

"Do you know Alonso Cortez?" he asked the woman. Now he was closer, he saw her white smock was some kind of apron dusted with flour and smears of dried pastry.

"Of course I know him. Where else would he buy his bread? Was that his house that burned down?"

"According to a neighbour."

"Is he all right?"

"That is why I am asking. Have you seen him today?"

"He came early, as usual, but I have not seen him since." She peered around Thomas at the smoking ruin. "Do you think he was inside?"

"There is no indication either way. I am asking is all." He looked at Lawrence. "Is there a Hermandos' office nearby?"

Lawrence nodded. "The old one is still open this side of the river. It's not far. Do you want me to fetch someone?" He glanced at the woman, though she appeared unconcerned. "Just in case?"

"Yes, fetch someone," Thomas said.

"If they will come."

As Thomas watched Lawrence stride away, he considered the fact that the Hermandos set up by Isabel to police the cities of Castile had clearly not improved since he last had occasion to deal with them. As with all such organisations, there was a surfeit of bad men and a paucity of the good. He took a bite of the pie and instantly regretted it.

"I didn't like Alonso, but I would wish him no ill," said the woman. "I hope he was off on one of his jaunts."

"Jaunts? I thought he was a scribe."

"Oh, he is, but he often travels out of the city. He is always going somewhere or other. Always having people come to him." She smiled. "He often sends them to me for sweet pastries and fine rolls, so he was not all bad."

"Did you see anyone else at his house today?" Thomas

was unsure why he asked the question. The burning of a house was an unusual, but not a suspicious event. He supposed his mind had grown used to suspicion over the years.

"Not going into his house, but coming away from it." She gave a grin of pure lechery. "A man I will not forget in a long while."

"He came out of Cortez's house?"

"I did not see him do so, only that he came from that direction."

"Was he running?"

"He did not look the kind of man who would run. He moved like a cat, with such grace I could not take my eyes from him."

"Really. How was this paragon of a man dressed?" Questions had become a habit to Thomas, but the longer he remained with the woman, the longer he was away from the heat of the fire. The day was hot enough without flames adding to it.

"In silk and fine linen. He was as handsome as the devil and looked like he possessed double the mischief."

"Did he speak?"

"He bought two pastries. I tried to sell him a pie for he looked too thin for my taste, but he refused."

Sensible man, Thomas thought. An edge of unease had settled through him for no reason he could define.

"Can you describe him? How tall was he? What colour was his hair? Was it long or short? Did he have a beard?"

"Tall, light, neither and no. What are all the questions for? Do you think he harmed Alonso? He did not look like a man who would harm anyone, despite his size."

"Taller than me?" Thomas asked, and the woman looked him up and down.

"By a few inches, I would say. And as I said, well dressed." Her meaning was clear.

"You said he spoke to you?"

"He asked for pastries, so of course he spoke to me."

"In the tongue of Castile?"

"What else would he use in Córdoba? Though now you mention it his accent was different. Softer. I would say be might have come from beyond the borders of Spain."

"Indeed. Did he offer a name?"

"Unfortunately we did not get to know each other that well." She glanced at Thomas's hand. "How do you like the pie?"

"Good. I may have more questions for you."

"I am always here. And if you see this man, for there can be none other like him in the whole of Christendom, send him to me. He can avail himself of my pastries any time he wants."

By this time Lawrence had returned, and the woman's coarse laugh followed them down the road

"Are you not going to eat that pie?" asked Lawrence.

Thomas handed it to him. Lawrence took a bite, spat it out and tossed the pie away.

"What were all the questions about?"

"Only me being me. Did you go to the Hermandos? What did they say?"

"That they would send someone when they could find the time." Lawrence's eyes tracked Thomas's face. "You think there is more to it than a simple fire, don't you? I can tell. You change when you get a sniff of something suspicious. You suspect Cortez lies dead in his house, don't you? And this well-dressed man, do you suspect him of killing him?"

"I am trying not to," Thomas said. "You know as well as I

that her description fits only one man in this city, and I am equally sure that Jorge did not commit a murder today."

Even as he spoke the words, Thomas wondered where Jorge had been today, and where he had been for the last several days.

CHAPTER TWO

Thomas stripped to the waist and began to help the inhabitants of the street, throwing himself into the work as a distraction from his thoughts. It was a thankless task. Alonso Cortez's house, which had to be where the fire had started, was too hot to approach closer than a dozen feet. The house to the right was also a shell, though the one beyond that appeared relatively unharmed. To the left the house still stood, though most of the windows had exploded outward. Peering inside, Thomas saw wood panelling had burned away, but panelling could be replaced. He wondered if it was worth it.

When Lawrence ambled across to join him, Thomas glanced at the Hermandos constable, who was talking with some of the neighbours.

"Is he the best you could find?"

"He is the best they would send. Constable Miguel Sánchez." Lawrence glanced over to where the man was taking tiny steps as he tried to get closer to the house. "I am not sure he has started shaving yet."

"He looks keen enough."

Lawrence laughed. "He looks like he might burst into flame at any moment."

"It's not so bad now," Thomas said. "By nightfall we can probably go in there and take a look around."

"Why would we want to do that?" Lawrence stared at Thomas, then nodded. "Of course. You want to, don't you? You believe it was no accident."

"I believe nothing yet, but nobody has seen the man who lives here since morning. At the least I want to know if his body lies somewhere among the ashes." Thomas looked at the house and frowned. "There are many ashes."

Lawrence followed his gaze. "Indeed there are." He glanced at the houses on either side. "Two levels, like the others. A good sized house, no doubt with fine furniture, which would account for the ashes. This Cortez must have had money. This is a nice neighbourhood."

A gust of wind came along the street. It picked at the ashes Lawrence was explaining away and curled a plume of them into the air. Thomas watched them rise then drift downward. He took three paces and picked up a curled remnant and showed it to Lawrence.

"Paper, do you think?"

Lawrence examined it without touching, though his hands and face were already dark from the smoke.

"Could be."

"You are the man to know, aren't you?"

"If you say so. Yes, it looks like paper." He glanced at Thomas. "Burned paper. A man is allowed to have paper in his house, isn't he?"

Thomas let the scrap fall to the cobbles where it broke apart. He walked across to the Hermandos constable. The ashes were cooling faster than he had estimated and he found he could now stand close to where the doorway once stood. The door, however, had gone. A blackened shape lying within showed what it had once been, but the stone surround remained. Thomas leaned closer to look into the cellar that was not meant to be there and wondered why it had been. Was it so curious the neighbours had not known of it? What did it matter if a man wanted to dig a cellar to store … what? Papers? The baker woman had told Thomas the man was a scribe, and paper was their stock-in-trade.

Thomas looked left, right. The cellar appeared to run in both directions, under the neighbouring houses. It was nobody's business if Cortez wanted to build a cellar under his own floorboards … but under those of his neighbours?

"Did you help quench the fire?" asked the young constable standing beside Thomas.

"We were too late. It was well alight by the time we arrived, but we helped save the rest of the row, other than the houses to either side." Thomas glanced at the man, at his immaculate uniform, and wondered how long he had been a member of the Hermandos. "Lawrence and I didn't do so much. It was those who live nearby, those who live in this road, who did most of the work."

"As would be expected." The man nodded toward Lawrence, who was talking with two men. "They knew your friend in the barracks. Is he important?"

"He is known to the King," Thomas said, "so I expect he is."

"And you?"

"Am I important, or known to the King?"

"Either."

"Is who I am known by relevant to why the house burned down?"

"No, I expect not. I apologise." The man offered a

crooked smile. "I have only been a constable a few months and am never sure what questions need to be asked and what do not. I am sorry if I offended you."

"You didn't."

"What is your name?"

Thomas considered if this was also an inappropriate question and believed it probably was, but saw no harm in answering anyway.

"I am Thomas Berrington."

The constable's eyes widened a little. "The physician?"

"I am a physician. Whether I am *the* physician is another matter."

"I have heard it said you are indeed friend to both King and Queen."

"Perhaps." Thomas began to wish he had never come to examine the remnants of the house. Most of the time he could pass as any other man, until people heard his name. He wondered who might have spread it so widely and glanced toward Lawrence. Fortunately the constable did not appear to be as impressed as others might be.

"Do you think the man who lives here is dead?" he asked.

"Alonso Cortez?" Thomas said.

"Your friend told me that was his name. It is not one I know, but I have not lived in Córdoba long."

Long enough to know who I am, Thomas thought. *Why is that?* He realised he had not answered the man's question.

"Yes, I think Cortez is dead."

Thomas glanced at Miguel Sánchez to see how he took the information, but he could not tell if he had even heard. He was leaning into the ruined doorway in an effort to see better into the jumble of stone, burned wood and paper. He reached out a hand to steady himself and cursed. The stone held on as tightly to the heat as a miser to gold. Thomas reached out and grabbed Sánchez's arm to stop him tumbling into the gaping cellar.

"I see no sign of a body."

"I'm not surprised." Thomas put his palm close to the stone Sánchez had recently touched. Yes, still hot. "It will be morning before we have a chance to search for him, I think."

"We?"

"I am sorry. You and your companions."

"I would rather it was we. I am unsure if I made the right decision when I joined the ranks of the Hermandos. They do not seem to like me."

"Are you venal, dishonest, or a bully? Are you lazy?"

"Of course not."

"That is probably why then. Perhaps you should try acquiring a few of those traits."

Sánchez said nothing, and Thomas suspected he had come to the same conclusion himself.

"I can help perhaps, if you will accept it," he said.

"Do you know of such matters? You are a physician, of course, so I expect you see a lot of dead bodies."

"I try to save most of my patients."

"Of course. I meant … no matter. Yes, I would welcome your advice, though I cannot pay anything. I can ask my captain, but I know what he will say."

"I need no payment."

"Are you wealthy?"

"No—I am bored."

An hour of light remained when, sooner than he expected,

Thomas judged the ashes were cool enough to risk examining what might lie beneath. The fire had burned hot but fast, and appeared to have cooled as quickly as it flamed. Thomas had spent his time questioning those who lived in the street. Most knew Cortez and most appeared not to like him. None would say exactly why, but listening to them talk, Thomas suspected the man had kept to himself. Rumour and wild speculation ran up and down the street as people spun their own theories concerning Cortez's death. For the moment, Thomas considered keeping his own to himself the better option. He had learned several things and made a mental note to write them down when he returned to the small tent he shared with Jorge on the banks of the Guadalquivir. Cortez was wealthy, but the neighbours were unsure how, unless he had inherited his money. None had known of the cellar running beneath the houses to either side, nor heard evidence of its construction. It made Thomas wonder if it had not been there since the house was built. Which then made him wonder if Cortez had bought the house because of the cellar. To store what? Only a search might offer an answer to that question.

Lawrence and Miguel Sánchez stood at Thomas's side, all three staring into the ashes, which continued to smoke. Miguel had said little and appeared distracted.

"We should leave any search until tomorrow," said Lawrence.

"There is not so much heat coming off the remains now," Thomas said. "There is a beam over there that is almost whole. We can climb down it. If I judge it too hot, we will return at first light, but I would prefer to conduct a search tonight." He glanced at Miguel. "What is your opinion, constable?"

"I have none."

"If Cortez is down there, he is not going anywhere," said Lawrence. "I doubt you will find him even if he is."

"There will be bones."

"Where is Jorge, by the way? You and he are usually inseparable."

"That, my friend, is a good question. A very good question."

"Jorge?" said Miguel, a frown on his face.

Lawrence cast a glance at him. "A friend of Thomas's."

Thomas was grateful Lawrence said nothing about what the baker woman had said, that Jorge was in this street before the fire started. He reached out.

"Here, hold my hand while I grab that beam."

Lawrence smiled. "As long as you never mention it to Laurita." He gripped Thomas's wrist as he leaned out.

Thomas caught the corner of the charred beam and heaved on it until one end crashed against the edge of the roadway. Dust and fragile ashes rose from the disturbance to hang in the air. Thomas stripped out of his robe and handed one edge to Lawrence.

"Hold on to this in case I need to get out fast."

Lawrence wrapped the cloth around his hand. Thomas gripped the other end and began to climb down the dark beam. The wood continued to hold heat within, but it had cooled enough for Thomas's purpose. He reached the surface of the ashes and probed with his foot. It felt like stepping into hot water. His foot disappeared beneath the roiling surface, which offered no resistance.

Thomas pressed on until he touched stone, the layer of burned ash reaching his knee. He let go of his robe. The ashes were warm, but he was not going to burst into flames. He began to wade through the ashes. He found a length of wood which looked as if it had once formed part of a shelf and used it to part the ashes to reveal the stone floor.

He glanced up at Lawrence outlined against the setting sun. "You can come help if you want, it's warm but not hot. It will go quicker with two of us."

"All I can say is it is fortunate I have a place to bathe at my house. What are you going to do, wash in the river?"

Thomas had given little thought to the state of his body. "If I have to. Where did Miguel get to?"

"Wandered off somewhere. I think he is knocking on doors." Lawrence grinned. "You could always ask that pretty companion of the Queen's to scrub your back. She would do it, I wager."

"As would I. Which is why I intend to do no such thing." Thomas handed Lawrence the length of wood he had been using and searched for another. They moved in different directions, probing the floor, working around fallen masonry. Light began to leach from the sky and the brightest stars pricked the velvety dark above.

Thomas was beginning to think either Cortez had not been in the house or had burned so hot nothing remained, not even his bones, when Lawrence called from the far end of the cellar.

"There's something here."

Thomas waded toward him and leaned over to examine what he had found.

"What is it?" Miguel had returned and stood on the roadway. He seemed to be trying to decide whether to risk the descent to join them.

"It looks like a body," Thomas called up to him.

Curled into the corner lay the remains of a man, remarkably intact. Even most of his robe remained, and Thomas suspected Cortez had crawled to this corner in an attempt to protect himself. The stink of roasted flesh caught in Thomas's throat and for a moment he thought he might throw up. He was used to the smell of death, but this was closer to roasted pork than rot, reminding him that the bundle lying on the stones had been a living, breathing man that morning.

He started to use his stick to clear the ashes from around the body, discovering as he did so a small cache of papers which were protected beneath it. Cortez's face had gone, the flesh burned from it, but beneath his robe he had fared better, even if that failed to make him any less dead.

Thomas knelt and rolled the man over, revealing more documents. He wondered if they were important, or no more than whatever had already lain here. He passed them to Lawrence.

"Keep these safe, in case they are evidence of anything."

Lawrence pulled a face as he took them, then took a few steps out of range of the smell. Thomas drew the robes aside to reveal the flesh beneath, mottled, with areas that had burst from the heat. If this was Cortez, then his death had not been easy. Thomas tried to imagine the man's final thoughts as he crawled to this corner, seeking a safety he must have known was false. Were the papers he had gathered beneath him important, or nothing but the meaningless grasping of a dying man?

"Thomas," said Lawrence.

"I am busy."

"There is a document here you need to see."

Thomas turned at the urgency in Lawrence's voice.

"One mentions a name. Two names in fact. One is Olmos and the other is Jorge. They are separated, but both are noted here." He held out a scrap of paper, charred around the edges. "I cannot make out everything, but it certainly mentions the name Jorge, and another name I do not know, Inigo Florentino. The rest of the letter is charred and cannot be read."

Miguel had come to join them. "Jorge Olmos?" he asked. "I was given that name less than an hour since and told to find the man and arrest him."

CHAPTER THREE

"Why?" Thomas said.

"It was an order from my captain. I did not question him as to why, it is not my place. I assume he had information about what happened here. An informer, perhaps. It is why I was puzzled when you mentioned his name, and then when you said his full name, I was sure. Do you know where he is, Thomas?"

"Missing."

Miguel looked around at the ashes, now almost hidden by the coming night. "I have been speaking with the neighbours and the baker and his wife at the end of the street. She claims to have seen a man coming from Cortez's house this morning. Two of the neighbours also saw a tall man outside this house. Is your friend handsome?"

"It has been said of him, yes." Thomas wondered why the Hermandos wanted Jorge arrested. Even if he had been seen, nobody knew who he was. Something didn't sit right with the accusation.

"Could your friend be involved in this man's death?"

It was a question Thomas wanted an answer to as well. "When I find him I will ask him."

"Then find him, and do it quickly. Bring him to me so I can talk to him. My captain was insistent, but I would question a man before arresting him for murder. Bring him to me in the morning."

There was nothing more could be done for Alonso Cortez that night, so they covered his body in the ashes as well as they could, not wanting any passer-by to see him the way he was.

"I take it you are going to talk to Jorge?" Lawrence stood beside Thomas on the dark street. Miguel had gone so both could talk freely once more.

"If he has done what he has been accused of here, it would explain his absences since we arrived."

"Except you do not believe he has done it, do you?"

"How can I? He is closer to me than anyone in this world." Thomas shook his head in frustration. "It would ease my mind if I knew where he has been and what he has been doing."

"Have you been to Daniel's house?" Lawrence spoke of Jorge's brother, a sword-smith.

"I don't even know where Daniel's house is. The last time I came here he lived beyond the city wall, but I doubt he still does."

"Oh, he lives outside the city wall, but not in the same place. He has a works and fine house near the river beyond the old bridge." He slapped Thomas on the shoulder. "Go there. No doubt you will find it is where Jorge has been the whole time."

They parted, Lawrence to return home to the comfort of a bath and a place beside Laurita in their bed once he was clean. Thomas passed through a city starting to come to life, the night offering a myriad of charms. Isabel and Fernando, the Queen and King of Castile, were in residence and their presence attracted those who sought favour, as well as those who offered comfort and solace to the lonely.

The thought of washing in the cold water of the Guadalquivir offered little attraction, so Thomas allowed his footsteps to guide him to the palace set next to the old mosque, now converted to some excuse of a cathedral. The guards nodded him through. Thomas was a familiar figure since arriving in the city a little less than a week before as part of a delegation from Gharnatah. It was also known he was a friend to both the King and Queen, except in this instance he sought someone else.

He had seen Theresa only once since his arrival. She had been pleased to see him. Perhaps too pleased, and Thomas was aware they almost had a past. Whether they had a future was something he did not wish to give thought to. His anguish at losing Lubna remained, but it was beginning to fade, little by little, day by day. There were times Thomas missed it, though he wished no return of the debilitating grief that had almost killed him.

Thomas had spoken with Theresa only the day before, near the royal chambers, and he made his way there now. He glanced into the Courtyard of the Moors, one of the only sections of the old palace to remain after extensive rebuilding. Had he the time, he would have been tempted to enter, for the arched openings offered exquisite views across the gardens which always calmed him, but he needed hot water more than beauty.

He began to turn away, then stopped as five figures appeared, four women and a man who was a stranger to him. They paused beneath an archway, some discussion taking place between them, and Thomas shrank into the shadows.

Two of the women were familiar, while the third sparked a faint memory he could not place. He was surprised nothing came to mind, for she was a handsome woman, close to his own age and someone it would be difficult to forget. The fourth woman was a stranger to him, as was the man dressed in the red robes of a cardinal.

The first two women he knew well: Isabel, Queen of Castile, and Theresa, once a nurse but now far closer to the Queen. The sight of both raised feelings of unease in him. One he loved in a way more complex than even he understood. The other … he smiled before acknowledging that he had once almost tumbled Theresa into bed. As he studied her, he saw she remained a beautiful woman. Older now than she had been when she assisted him in the healing of Prince Juan's injured leg, but maturity could bring a different form of beauty. In the case of Theresa, this was doubly true. Thomas waited, though he had no intention of approaching the group, but intended to follow Theresa when they were finished.

The familiarity of the third woman continued to nag at him, recognition almost forming only to slip away. He wondered if she was one of the ladies-in-waiting who gathered around Isabel. Despite Isabel being Queen of Castile, it was the man who held the attention of all four women. He was tall and handsome. His hands moved as he made his point, whatever it was, and then the group broke apart and Theresa came directly toward where Thomas had believed himself hidden.

"Did you think we could not see you? It was Isabel who saw you first." Theresa gave a laugh. "I think the Countess thought you were a brigand of some kind from the way she paled when your name was mentioned. Your fame precedes you, though I admit with some justification." She offered a smile and reached out to touch his arm before stopping. "I am sorry for what happened to you, Thomas, and glad you avenged Lubna." She looked him up and down. "What have you been doing?" She sniffed and took a step back. "You stink like the fires of hell. If this is how you come to ravish a woman, you need to talk to Jorge about hygiene."

"I intend to, as soon as I can find somewhere to bathe. I thought you could help."

Theresa offered a teasing smile. "Of course I can help, though you look as if you will need two changes of hot water, at least."

"Please."

Theresa took half a step toward him and touched delicate fingers against his wrist. "Only if you promise to ravish me within an inch of my life."

Thomas shook his head, aware she had changed not at all. "I thought you were a married woman."

"Would that make a difference to a rough man such as yourself? Besides, I am single again now, a widow."

"I am sorry to hear your own news."

"No need to be. He was a pig, he was old, and he stank. It had been years since we shared a bed, for which I am profoundly grateful. So now I am yours to do with as you will." She smiled. "Please."

Thomas shook his head. "I am looking for Jorge."

"He was here earlier this morning, just after dawn. I remember being surprised. I was not aware Jorge knew there was such a time of day."

"What was he doing?"

"I don't know, I only saw him in passing." Theresa tilted

her head. "If you are not going to accost me, would you at least take wine with me, for old time's sake?"

"We have old times?"

Theresa tapped her brow. "In here we do, you know we do." She reached up to touch Thomas's brow, then withdrew her hand and looked at the stain on it. "It looks as if I will need to bathe as well, now."

"One day you will tease me once too often and I will take you up on your false promises." He glanced over his shoulder, but the small group had broken up and disappeared. "The other woman with you, who is she? I am sure I recognise her from somewhere, but cannot place her name."

Theresa flicked her fingers as if in dismissal of a rival. "Some Countess, that is all. She is French, come to offer men and gold to assist in the war against Al-Andalus. They come constantly, but I must admit most are men. Besides, she is too old for you. Unlike me."

"She looked to be about my age," Thomas said.

"Exactly."

As Theresa started away, Thomas fell into step beside her, her presence a small comfort he had not experienced in a long time. He had believed he would never think of another woman after Lubna's death, but time had smoothed the edges of his grief. Lubna would not want him to turn his back on what small pleasures he might take. He was no longer young, but not yet dead. He wondered if Theresa's teasing was only that, or was there more? If so, how might she respond if he tried to take advantage of her offer? Not that he could ever promise her anything, for he had vowed never to remarry. It was one more thing Thomas knew he should talk to Jorge about. After he had accused him of murder.

Theresa led the way to a suite of rooms, well-appointed, including a small room in which to bathe.

"I will have someone bring you hot water." She looked him up and down. "Take those rags off and I will burn them. I will send you something more suited to your position."

"I have no position."

"Then it does not matter what I send, does it?" She patted his cheek then wiped her palm on her dress. "Now do as I say." She turned away, stopped. "Oh, and Isabel gave me a message for when I saw you. She wants you to visit her as soon as you can."

"On what matter? I have things to do first, finding Jorge the most important of them."

"She is the Queen of Castile, Thomas, and most people are happy to answer her summons. As you will be once you are clean."

Thomas made no effort to seek out Isabel once he had bathed. Instead he dressed in the clothes Theresa had sent for him and returned to the tent he shared with Jorge, but it lay empty. He turned aside to ask a group of men sitting around a fire if they had seen him, but none had. They invited Thomas to join them, but he thanked them and turned away.

The old bridge took him across the Guadalquivir. He followed Lawrence's instructions and turned left at the first roadway. He had considered Daniel Olmos's house would prove difficult to find, but Thomas had walked barely a hundred paces when he heard the sound of hammers on metal, then shortly after saw the glow of fires. He came into an opening which lay in front of a row of stone buildings set along the bank of the river. At least a dozen fires burned, one and sometimes two men standing beside each as they worked. Sparks flew from heated charcoal and the constant clatter of iron on steel filled the air. Anyone living nearby would be either driven half-mad by the noise or forced to grow used to it.

Thomas studied the men silhouetted against the orange glow, but did not see Daniel. The man should be easy to recognise, unless he had changed greatly. Shorter than Jorge, with a thatch of dark hair and coarse beard. He limped badly—a gift from Jorge when they had been boys.

As Thomas approached, one of the men came out to greet him. "I am sorry, Señor, but we are about to finish work for the day. If you need our services you will have to return in the morning, though I warn you there will be a long wait. The palace has commissioned all our work for the next month at least."

"I am looking for Daniel. Daniel Olmos. He is a friend."

The man nodded, accepting Thomas's word. "He is in the back. Safest way is to go around the side of the fires and you will find a door."

Thomas followed the smith's instructions and entered through a wide door held open with a rusted anvil. A solid stone wall masked off most of the working space, and the noise here was muffled. A man stood with his back to the door as he leant over a wide table. He could be none other than Daniel Olmos, and Thomas approached. He circled to one side, not wanting to surprise Jorge's brother, but Daniel glanced up almost at once. There was a moment of hesitation, then he came across with his swaying walk to embrace Thomas.

"Jorge told me you were here. I said to invite you to eat with us but he must have forgotten to pass the message on."

"Like everything else. Is he here?"

Daniel shook his head. "Not since last night. He said he had something to do today. He is not with you?"

"His bed was empty when I woke."

"That does not sound like Jorge, though he has been distracted since he arrived. Your talks are going well in the palace?"

"Not mine. I have nothing to do with them. I don't even know why I am here."

Daniel laughed. "Then tonight you are here to eat with us. Zanita wants to see you, not to mention the children. We have nine now, did Jorge tell you?"

Thomas shook his head. "I cannot eat with you, I need to find Jorge as soon as I can."

"Is he in trouble?"

"No … not trouble. I hope not."

"At least come and say hello otherwise Zanita will not let me into her bed tonight."

"Nine children, did you say? Perhaps she needs the rest. Does she get any sleep at all?"

"Those are only the ones who survived. You know how it is with birthing, you more than most men. Birth and death, it is the way of life, is it not?"

Thomas saw a realisation of what he had said come to Daniel's face and held up a hand. "There is no need to mention it. It was a long time ago now."

Daniel gripped Thomas's shoulder and squeezed, no words necessary, but he used the grip to draw Thomas through the door and across a wide yard, beyond which sat a substantial house.

"You have come a long way since those days beyond the city wall," Thomas said.

"All thanks to Jorge and you, my friend. A man like me

would never have met the King, and it was that single stroke of luck that changed my fortunes. All of us here are forever grateful to the fates for what happened." Daniel stopped and turned to Thomas. "I hear you killed him, the Abbot?"

Thomas nodded.

"Good. He was evil. You killed the son, too?"

"It was the son who stole Lubna's life."

"A son is forged by his father, so of course you killed them both. They were evil men." Daniel nodded. "You did well. Now come and say hello to Zanita. She might know where Jorge has gone to."

CHAPTER FOUR

"Look who I dragged in off the street." Daniel led the way into a wide room fragrant with the scent of bread and cooking.

Zanita rose from where she was kneeling over a tiny boy, who sat solid like only the very young can, short legs spread, back straight as he moved coloured wooden blocks to create shapes. Zanita's eyes widened as she came toward Thomas, only to stop a pace away, uncertainty showing. Thomas closed the gap and embraced her, as comforted by the touch as he hoped she would be. He glanced over the top of her head at Daniel, who smiled indulgently at them, his strong arms crossed over his broad chest. Thomas broke the embrace first, then kissed Zanita on the brow.

"Jorge didn't tell us you were here, though we thought it odd you would not be together." She took a step back, her hands continuing to hold his.

"You have seen him?"

"Of course."

"Today?"

Zanita frowned. "Not today, no. Why?"

"I need to talk to him."

She smiled. "He is bound to turn up when we least expect. You know how it is with Jorge." She finally released her hold and went to the infant. She picked him up from the floor and brought him back. "Lope, say hello to your uncle Thomas." She lifted the boy's pudgy arm and gave it a wave.

"Hello, Lope—though I'm not really your uncle." Thomas shook his head, wondering why he even bothered, knowing Zanita honoured him with the title. He looked around the comfortable room, a place where real people lived real lives.

Children sat or stood and he tried to count them, but it was like trying to count ants as they kept moving all the time. Two came and hugged his legs, one a girl, the other a boy, and then another figure appeared through the doorway and stopped dead. Thomas recognised her at once, even though he had not seen Adana in almost six years. She was even more beautiful than he recalled. Taller now, willowy, with golden hair that curled in waves to her shoulders. Thomas had shared a cell with Adana all those years ago in what felt like a different life, both of them sure they were about to die. She had been brave then and, he hoped, brave since.

He was surprised to see her in the house. She must have twenty years by now, and he expected her to be married. As he recalled, she had been engaged to a man much older than herself. Perhaps she had married and he'd died, freeing her to return home.

Adana's eyes found something fascinating on the floor and would not rise to meet his, though her cheeks coloured. Thomas was aware she had carried an affection for him once, but dismissed it as a result of what they had gone through together. He had tried to find some way to disappoint her and would do so again if need be, but that could wait until later. Now he crossed the room to embrace her.

"I didn't expect to see you here. I imagined you with children of your own by now."

Adana finally raised her gaze and offered a shy smile. "There are enough children here for me to look after."

"A girl as pretty as you needs her own."

"Perhaps if I find the right man." Her voice lacked emotion and Thomas wondered who had broken her heart.

"The last I knew you were engaged." He noticed Daniel had taken a place at the head of the table as Zanita began rounding up the children. Some sat on chairs, others were dropped into special seats that looked as though Daniel had fashioned them himself. Zanita glanced toward Thomas and Adana, smiled and went to the stove to spoon out some kind of stew.

"I refused him." Adana glanced at her father. "It caused trouble, but I was determined. I will only marry for love. Like you did." She squeezed his arm. "I heard about what happened, but will not mention it again, as none of us will, but know we share your pain and loss."

She moved away to help her mother. The others took up the spaces allotted them, each one inviolable. Thomas decided he would share their food after all, though wondered where he would sit until he saw a vacant seat half way along the table. He almost laughed that he had been placed in the heart of the children arrayed along both sides. Adana took the seat opposite his.

"So, what has my brother been up to?" asked Daniel.

Thomas leaned to one side as Zanita set a roughly cast plate in front of him, the scent of the stew sparking a sudden hunger.

"Nothing, I am merely curious what mischief he is

getting into without me." Thomas didn't want to voice his suspicions until he was more sure of them. Perhaps not even then. Not to this family.

"You know whatever it is will involve a woman. Speaking of women, have you seen the Queen yet?"

"Today, but only from a distance."

"Have you fallen out?" asked Zanita, finally taking her place.

"I don't believe so, but she is a busy woman, and I would not want to intrude."

Daniel barked a laugh. "From what I hear she would more than welcome your intrusion."

Thomas half expected Zanita to scold him for speaking coarsely in front of the children, until he realised they were either too young to understand or, if old enough, more likely to agree.

"Jorge tells us you and he are involved in some kind of negotiations at the palace. Surely that is more than enough excuse to meet her?"

"I have no idea why we were sent," Thomas said. "Certainly not to negotiate. My job, it seems, is to show my face twice a day until I am recognised, and then I can leave. I don't even know what they are talking about."

"War, I expect," said Daniel.

"Almost certainly. War is good for business, is it not?"

"Of course. And thanks to you my business grows daily, as you saw. Though I am saving what comes in now for the day the war ends. Who will want my swords then?"

Thomas laughed. "I don't believe you will have much to worry about. Men always want swords, and there will be another war soon enough, you can be sure of that."

"You should go and tell the Queen to end this war," said

Adana, leaning across the table toward Thomas. "She would do it if you asked her."

"If only I had such power."

"Does she not love you more than her husband? That is what we hear."

"Hear from who?" And then Thomas realised who. "Don't believe everything Jorge tells you." He laughed. "In fact, you are better off not believing anything Jorge tells you."

"And why is that? Am I not the most reasonable, as well as handsome, of men?"

Thomas turned to see Jorge standing in the doorway. Zanita stood and hurried around the table to offer an embrace, bringing him to stand beside Adana while she brought another chair. The children all moved to make a space and Jorge sat, staring across at Thomas, who stared back.

"Here we are, all together again," said Zanita as she set food in front of Jorge.

"Where did you get to?" Thomas watched as Jorge spooned stew into his mouth before smiling blissfully.

"Out and about. Here and there."

"Doing what?" Thomas glanced around, but the others were all talking, apart from Adana, who continued to stare across the table at him while trying not to make it obvious.

"This and that." Jorge set his spoon down and stared at Thomas. "Am I not allowed a life of my own?"

"Of course you are. I was curious, nothing more." Thomas leaned closer and lowered his voice. "But I do need to speak to you as soon as possible. It is important." He could not discuss the accusation in front of Jorge's family, but he needed to explain it before anyone came to arrest him.

Jorge shook his head. "You haven't got yourself involved in some new mystery, have you?"

They stood side by side on the old stone bridge. The waterwheels had been silenced for the night so as not to disturb the Queen. The only sound came from the rushing water between the buttresses and the occasional bark of a dog. It made Thomas think of the dog he had inherited from a dead man. Kin remained in Gharnatah with Will and Amal and Belia, the Gomeres mercenary Usaden looking over them all.

Jorge leaned on the wall and stared down at the silvery rush of water.

"You know where we are, don't you?" he said. "Exactly where we are?"

"The place that changed your life."

"Yes. The place that changed my life."

"For the better or worse?" There were times Thomas wondered if Jorge considered his unmanning of him for the good or not. It had saved his life, certainly, but there had always been the chance he might escape his captors.

"Oh, for the better. Certainly for the better." Jorge glanced at Thomas, his teeth showing white. "I would be dead if not for what you did to me, and I thank you for it."

"You are welcome."

"How many eunuchs have you made over the years, Thomas?" Jorge turned to look again at the water. No doubt this place and its memories called to him.

"A lot."

Jorge laughed without looking up from the river. "I

expect you have the exact number in one of those journals you are forever scribbling in. How many?"

"I would need to check, but a hundred, somewhere around that."

Jorge was silent for a moment before asking, "And how many died?"

"Seven."

"See, you know that exact number, but not the other."

"You remember the ones you lose," Thomas said. "If anyone else had carried out the procedure, the numbers would have been the other way around."

"You told me how it used to be done before you unmanned me. I still remember the conversation we had. The way you put it to me as a choice, even though we both knew it was nothing of the kind." Jorge glanced at Thomas again. "Why did you not unman me completely?"

"Because it pleased me."

Jorge laughed. "My mahood pleased you, and only now you tell me? All these years we could have been pleasuring each other."

Thomas slapped Jorge with the back of his hand. "It pleased me to leave you with at least something is what I meant."

"Of course you did."

"I want you to tell me where you have been today, and what you have been doing."

Jorge finally straightened and turned to face Thomas. "Why?"

"Is it such a secret?"

"You don't usually care what I get up to, thank the gods, for I don't think you could accept it if I told you."

"I may not be able to accept this if you have done what I suspect."

Jorge was silent for a time. Beyond him a man walked on to the stone roadway of the bridge and came toward them. His footsteps grew louder, but Jorge didn't look away from Thomas. The man passed and the sound of him faded into silence. Only then did Jorge speak.

"Tell me what I am meant to have done."

"It would be easier if you told me what you have been up to."

"Tell me!"

"I visited Lawrence today and we went to fight a fire. A man died."

"So you have found a new mystery. Congratulations. Do you want me to help? You know we are a good team."

"There was a witness. A woman. She described a man leaving the scene. A man more beautiful than any she has ever seen. A man dressed so finely she wanted to drag him through her door there and then to be ravished." Thomas leaned closer to Jorge, his eyes hard across the gap. "Can you think of anyone that description applies to?"

"There are other beautiful men," said Jorge. "Not as beautiful, of course, but a man even half as handsome as me is still a thing of wonder. Not that you would ever know such." Jorge's eyes remained locked on Thomas. "Are you accusing me of killing a man?"

"Did you?"

"What man?"

"How many men have you killed today that you cannot recall?"

Jorge shrugged. "What do you think of me to make such an accusation?"

"It is not only me. There is a Hermandos constable who has been told to arrest you. So tell me what you have been doing!" Thomas's shout carried across the water, echoed back from the palace walls.

"I..." Jorge looked away, looked back. "Am I truly suspected of murder?"

"The evidence is sound and it points to you. I don't believe it, of course, but it would help if I knew what you had been doing if not killing a man."

"I did meet with a man, a stranger. He sent a message he had something I needed to know."

"Did he ask for money?"

"Of course he did. But the information he promised is worth more to me than the small sum I have paid for it."

"You have paid him already? When were you going to tell me this?"

"I planned to tell you tonight, but then you go and accuse me of murder."

"I still haven't heard anything to make me change my mind."

"Except it is me we are talking about, Thomas. Your friend. Your best friend in all this world. Perhaps your only friend."

"Just tell me."

Jorge pushed at him with the flat of his hands and Thomas laughed. "You will have to try harder than that if you want to topple me into the water."

"The man told me he knew the name of my mother. All he wanted was a small sum of money in exchange for the information. He told me where I could find a man to confirm it."

"You know who your mother is. You told me she is dead."

"My real mother." Jorge's breath hitched with a surge of

emotion. "My mother, Thomas. The woman whose blood runs in my veins. Not those disgusting people who failed to raise me, but another . . . perhaps one who still loves me. He said once I pay him, he will tell me her name and where I can find her."

When Jorge came forward, Thomas took him inside his arms and waited while he sobbed against his shoulder, waited until the sobbing eased, then held him at arms' length.

"Then we need to find this man. When and where did you meet him? If the timing is right, he can vouch for your presence away from the murder scene."

"It was beyond the city wall, close to where Daniel used to live, as if the man knew. I left the money for him at first light this morning. I stayed out all night watching the spot in case he went there, but when the sun rose, I took my bag of silver and went to find the other man he told me about, who could offer me proof."

"All he promised was a name?"

"He said he had more information if I was willing to pay for it. I will pay a hundred times what he asks. And he did tell me about the other man who could offer a confirmation, but when I went to see him, he was not at home."

Thomas stared at Jorge for a long time. "Did you happen to talk with a baker woman and buy some pastries from her?"

Jorge shook his head as if he failed to understand. "How did you know that? And she told me no payment was required." He smiled. "The pastries were not good, but I told her they were."

"You are fortunate not to have tried her pies."

"How do you know all this, Thomas?"

"Because the burning house we went to is near her bakery. She described you well, and you are right, there are few others who would match your description. Why were you there?"

"You said a man is dead," said Jorge. "Is his name Cortez?"

"Alonso Cortez."

"I was only given the last name."

Thomas gripped Jorge's shoulder. "Have you already left the money for this man?"

Jorge nodded. "It is done. That was where I was before I came to Daniel's house. I returned to the place he asked me to leave it in and placed the bag beneath a stone."

"Then take me there, it might not yet be too late to clear your name."

"It is the middle of the night," said Jorge. "I will never find the place again in the dark."

"Then at first light, for your life may depend on it."

CHAPTER FIVE

The sun had not yet risen when Thomas and Jorge passed through the northern gate and climbed a low slope beyond which distant hills rose.

"This is where Daniel used to live, isn't it?" Thomas said.

"The very place," said Jorge.

"Did you not think it strange?"

"It's an isolated house, not too far beyond the city walls. It made sense to me."

Thomas saw the house ahead, nestled in a fold of ground. He recalled the first time he had seen it, before Jorge knew his brother still lived. So many years, and so many changes, had occurred since.

"How did this man approach you?"

"On the street. He came up and asked if I was Jorge Olmos and I said yes. I asked him what he wanted and he told me he had information for me. Valuable information. He said if I wanted to know more to meet him at Daniel's old house."

"He said that? At Daniel's old house?"

"He said at the house Daniel Olmos used to live in before he got lucky."

"Those were his exact words?"

"As far as I remember them, yes."

"When did you meet him?"

"Late in the afternoon two days ago, then I left the money last night, as I told you."

"Why did you sit out all night yesterday waiting for him?"

"I was suspicious, of course. He might have been making up a tale to steal my silver, but as I waited in the dark, I realised he knew my name, knew about Daniel and the family I was raised in. It made me think what he was offering could be genuine."

"Then let's hope there is something here that will allow us to find this man. What did he say when you met him?"

"Two things. First that he had information about who my true mother was. That I told you last night. The other that a scribe by the name of Cortez could prove his claim if I went to him with a name."

"He gave you Cortez's name. Did he tell you who your mother was as well?"

"He promised me her name today, once I had left the silver."

"So why did you go to visit Cortez without a name?"

"I thought he would probably have it and tell me."

"You're an idiot," Thomas said.

Jorge stopped walking. "What would you have done? If a man came to you and said he knew who your real mother was, when you had been raised by someone else? Not that the woman I thought my mother did much in the way of raising me. My sister did all that. I always knew I was different to everyone else in my family. It made sense, Thomas. It made a lot of sense."

Thomas knew Jorge was right, but he still thought him an idiot, and his money lost with nothing in return. What he didn't know was how the man had discovered who Jorge was, and how he knew of his hunger for an explanation for his difference.

They were almost at the ruins of Daniel's old house. Off to the left a stand of almond trees stood where Thomas had first spoken with Zanita. A narrow stream cut a channel in the dry soil.

Jorge went on, slowed and went to one knee. "This is the stone I left the silver under." He pushed at it, tipping the stone until it fell backward with a thump. Nothing lay beneath.

"What time did you leave this silver?"

"I told you, at sunset yesterday."

Thomas came and stood over the hole revealed by the stone.

"Well it's empty now."

"I can see that."

"Are you sure this is the right stone?"

"Of course I am." Jorge made no effort to hide his annoyance.

"Then your silver is gone, and so is the man. You have been taken for a fool."

"Not for the first time, as I am sure you will be happy to point out."

Thomas knelt and examined the stone, the hole the bag of silver had been left in, but neither offered any help. He rose and brushed his knees down, walked toward the ruined house, curious to see if he could remember any of it, or if time and neglect meant the house carried no memories anymore.

The door had fallen off its leather hinges and lay outside. Within, the layout of the house sparked a faint memory. The body of the man lying in the middle of the floor sparked none. Thomas held a hand up as Jorge started to enter.

"Your mysterious thief is inside. You might want to stay out there for the moment."

"If he is there I want to talk to him."

"He won't be doing much talking. I know you hate dead bodies so stay where you are. Better still, go back to the city and fetch the Hermandos. There is one by the name of Miguel Sánchez who is dealing with the death of Cortez. Fetch him if you can." Thomas hesitated, changed his mind. Sánchez had said Jorge was wanted for murder. "Better still, go to Lawrence and have him fetch Sánchez."

Jorge hovered beyond the empty doorway. "What if whoever killed him comes back?"

"Then I will take care of them. Now go. Unless you want to help me examine this man to find out how he died?"

"No, no, I'll leave that kind of thing up to you. Sánchez, you said?"

Once Jorge had gone, Thomas started to examine the body, but it was clear how the man had died. The side of his skull was caved in where it had met one of the square stones littering the floor. Did it meet the rock by accident or deliberately? Thomas wondered. A fight? An argument? An accident?

The body lay on its back, arms at the sides, legs straight. It was not the way a man who had tripped would lie, indicating the body must have been arranged this way. Which meant his death was no doubt deliberate. Thomas opened the clothing

—of poor quality and well overdue for replacement—but found no weapon, nor any bag of silver coin. He touched the flesh to discover it cold. Rigor had come and gone so the man had most likely been dead some time. He had probably lain in watch as Jorge left the money, waited for him to leave and retrieved it immediately. Had the man any intention of making good on the information he had sold or not? Thomas thought not, but had been proved wrong in the past. Jorge was a far better judge of character than him.

A brief check confirmed there was no bag of coin on the body, beneath it or anywhere else. Thomas rose and checked what few hiding places remained without any expectation. The silver was not inside the house, no doubt stolen by whoever had killed the man. Disappointed, Thomas returned to the body and checked the clothing again. He was rewarded with a crumpled note he found pushed into the sole of the man's boot.

He began to remove all his clothing and found another two items. One was a second note, the other an ornate cross fashioned from base metal which hung around the dead man's neck on a leather thong. The cross was too well made for the material it was constructed from. It deserved to be silver at least, if not gold. Thomas raised it, let it turn in the rays of the rising sun that came through an empty window-frame. The more closely he examined it, the more puzzled he became.

The cross showed Christ in his final agony, each limb perfectly crafted, the spear-thrust in his side clearly fashioned. Base metal it might be, but the skill needed to create it would have attracted a price. Did the cross belong to the man, or was it something else he had stolen? Thomas shook his head. Either way it proved nothing. There was no link to who he was or where he had come from, so Thomas turned to the notes.

For a moment, he stared at them without comprehension, then, slowly, it came to him. They were written in a bastard form of Latin, one he had seen before. It was often used in Roma and the Papal states of Italia, which were trying to introduce some standardisation of law and language across the disparate principalities. From what Thomas heard, they were having little success.

He tried to read the words, but could make out only half, and half was not enough to impart meaning, so he folded the notes and put them in his robe to show to Lawrence. If anyone in Qurtuba would be able to make sense of the notes, it was Lawrence.

Lawrence's head popped through the window on the first floor of his small house. "You do realise what time of day it is, don't you, and what a red-blooded Englishman is meant to be doing when he wakes?"

"I have found something," Thomas said.

"So had Laurita. Which is more important?" Lawrence waved a hand. "All right, all right, I know the answer. Give me ten minutes."

Thomas sat at the small table beneath the single orange tree and waited. Lawrence arrived sooner than promised, a satisfied smile showing on his face.

"Laurita will bring us coffee in a while, once she has recovered. Show me what you have."

Thomas handed over the two documents, then drew the base metal cross from around his own neck, which had seemed the simplest way of carrying it.

Lawrence looked at the cross, turning it over before handing it back.

"Where did you get these?"

"Off a dead man."

"Who was he? Was he anything to do with Cortez?"

"That I don't know. They might be connected, might not. The man was Jorge's alibi."

"Then perhaps these are something to do with Cortez." Lawrence examined the objects. "The cross is interesting, but not my field." He pushed it away before tapping the documents. "These, however, are, but they will take me a while to translate. It has been some time since I saw this bastard of a language." He looked at Thomas and grinned. "While you have been enjoying yourself, I have also made some progress. I managed to work out what was in the documents Cortez was clutching. Wait here."

Lawrence rose and went into the house. Thomas stretched out his legs. He turned his face up to the sun and closed his eyes so its light glowed orange on his eyelids. A sound caused him to sit up and he saw Laurita placing a steaming jug and two cups on the table.

"I thank you for helping Lawrence," she said.

Thomas tried to remember whether she had ever spoken to him before, and could not recollect if she had.

"It is the other way around—he is helping me."

Laurita smiled. "He was bored two days ago, now he is a man sparked with new life." Her smile broadened. "He is the Lawrence of old."

Thomas took the opportunity to ask a question he had always wondered about. "Can you tell me, is Lawrence his first or family name?"

Laurita laughed. "It is no good asking me that, for I have no idea. To me he has always been Lawrence. No more, no less." She started to turn away. "I hope the coffee is strong enough, you look as though you need it."

The coffee was both strong and good. When Lawrence returned, Thomas was on his second cup and hoped he had left enough for him.

Lawrence placed the charred documents they had taken from beneath Cortez on one side of the table, then laid out fresh sheets he had written himself. He tapped one of them with a long finger.

"This is the most interesting and relevant, I think." He pushed it toward Thomas. "Here, you read it. I left it in Spanish rather than translate into English."

"My thanks. I am not sure I could read my native tongue anymore."

Thomas scanned the page, looked up to meet Lawrence's amused gaze.

"Is this what I think it is?"

"I don't know what you think, but I know it is part of a contract between one party and another regarding the adoption of a child. A baby, I would say. It's possibly an older child, though I think not."

"The name Jorge is stated here, as is the name Olmos, but I assume it is not an Olmos giving the child away, is it?"

"It is not. I have seen such contracts before and know their wording. The child being given away is our Jorge, of course. The family he is being given to has the name of Olmos. It all makes sense so far. What is not stated which should be there are two other names, and what is stated that should *not* be there is a number. The number first: I cannot read all of it, but it shows a sum for the care of the child. A legal adoption would not require the handing over of any money."

"And the names?" Thomas asked, though he had a bad

feeling he already knew the answer and the document, while interesting, was a dead-end.

"The most important name missing is the person who drew up the document. The other, clearly, is who gave Jorge away."

"Surely that is more important than the name of a scribe?"

"If I knew who wrote this I could look it up in the city archives. Every scribe must lodge a copy of whatever he produces with the city. It is law. People break the law occasionally, but most do not if they want to continue working."

"There is no hint, no style you recognise?"

"Scribes do not have a style. It is considered bad form to add embellishments of any kind."

"So we are no further forward," Thomas said.

"We know Jorge was given away—that's progress, isn't it?"

"I suppose so. Do the other documents offer us anything?"

"I believe Cortez was in the last throes of life when he grabbed these. They relate to local land and property purchases, nothing more. One even has his own signature on it, which means he worked as a scribe as well as a blackmailer."

Thomas jerked so hard as he sat up, he spilled coffee from his clay cup. "A blackmailer? Are you sure?"

Lawrence smiled. "It makes sense, doesn't it? The grand house. The cellar extending under the houses of his neighbours. The quantity of documents stored there. A simple scribe could never afford to live as Cortez did."

"But why accuse him of blackmail?"

"Perhaps he came by his money in some other way, but it explains what we have found. The man collected documents and knew enough about what they contained, and the law, to tease out secrets people might want kept private."

Thomas let his breath go and set his empty cup on the table. "Is the document relating to Jorge one of those someone would want kept a secret?"

"It would explain why he has been set up as the killer, wouldn't it?"

"Set up by who?"

"Ah, now that is a question I do not have an answer for. You are the better man to discover that, Thomas. Do what you have done before and find the real killer of Cortez."

"And more than likely the same person who killed the man I saw this morning. You will continue to look for information?"

"Of course. Come back regularly, you know you are always welcome. If I discover anything in the meantime, I will send a message. Are you staying in the palace?"

"In a tent."

"A tent?"

"With Jorge."

"Then I will send a message to Daniel's house." Lawrence rubbed his hands together. "Now, to work. You can stay and help me if you wish. By which I mean watch, and touch nothing."

CHAPTER SIX

It was late afternoon by the time Thomas approached the palace. He had spent the day—or rather, Lawrence had spent the day while Thomas sat and watched—searching for references to documents created by Alonso Cortez and held by the city. Not, as Lawrence explained, that the documents would be to hand. The extensive space where he held his index contained only a reference to where a document was stored. Even so, Thomas was impressed at the organisation. Lawrence was able to find Cortez quickly, but time was taken in transcribing the references on to several sheets of paper, which in turn would link to the actual documents. Thomas did not bother asking for a copy because he knew only Lawrence would be granted access to where they were stored.

As Thomas approached the palace, the last of the sunlight caught the upper storeys of the houses and cast a soft glow over everything, but the beauty of the light did little to alleviate his anxiety. He had detoured to the camp the negotiating party had pitched along the banks of the river to see if Jorge had returned, but was disappointed.

Thomas hoped he was with Daniel and his family again, but knew he had been wrong before.

Difficult as it was to believe Jorge guilty of what he was accused, there was as yet no proof of his innocence. Thomas knew they would have to sit down together and work out where Jorge had been, and what he had been doing the day before. He also needed to make some effort to discover who the mysterious dead man was, though he suspected it a fruitless task. The more he thought of it, the more he became convinced the meeting with the dead man had been set up to ensure Jorge had no alibi. Even less of one now the man who had sent him to Cortez's house was dead. Thomas was also keenly aware Isabel had asked to see him—a summons he would rather avoid at the moment, but knew he could not. He might as well get that done, he decided, so he could concentrate on Jorge.

Approaching the main entrance to the palace, Thomas saw a familiar figure emerge, stocky, head down, his gait rolling. It was too late to turn away. Cristof Columb was known to him, and Thomas known in return. Thomas slowed, aware the man regarded him as some kind of kindred spirit, with no idea how he had come to such a conclusion. He prepared himself to brush him off, but there was no need. Columb continued past without raising his head, preoccupied in his own thoughts.

Once inside the palace, Thomas was unsure where to go next. He decided to make for the wide room where he had seen the Queen with Theresa and the woman she claimed was a Countess. The woman whose appearance continued to nag at him. He knew eventually a name or memory would pop into his head, and no doubt when it did, the answer would be boringly mundane.

He entered the room to find it empty. Beyond, dusk

filled the manicured gardens with shadow, and birds swooped and chittered through the thick air to feast on insects. Thomas walked out on to the stone slabs which offered a view of fountains, rills, beyond them a wall and distant hills. There was no sign of Isabel and no Theresa.

In the distance, beneath a hanging lamp, two gardeners were trying to heave an almost full-grown tree out of a pot and into a hole they had dug, without much success. Thomas turned away, deciding he would have to ask one of the servants where he could find Isabel, only to discover Theresa standing a dozen feet away, arms crossed, a smile on her pretty face.

"You looked so wrapped up in the view, I thought it better not to disturb you. I take it you are here for the Queen? Or would you prefer to ravish me first? I am sure she will be happy to wait an hour if you explain the reason for your tardiness."

Once again, Thomas was undecided how to react to Theresa's teasing. He was sure she meant nothing by it, but her words sparked a want in him he'd thought he would never again experience. He had not lain with a woman since Lubna—had vowed never to lie with any woman ever again, but recently he had started to think some promises are made to be broken. He knew Jorge would tell him to stop being stupid ... and sometimes Jorge was right, much as it irritated him to accept the fact.

"Be careful, one day I may take you up on your offer. What will you do then?"

Theresa approached, as usual coming closer than was comfortable. "What do you think I will do?"

He smiled. "If I knew that, I would not have the need of asking, and likely not make the offer. Is she available?"

"For you, always. Except … not at the moment. She is with the King and her advisors. Religious men. The mariner has been here again pressing for a decision."

"Do you know how long they will be? I have things to do if she is going to be a while."

"I do not know." Theresa turned and started to walk away, leaving Thomas to catch her up. "They are debating Columb's request so may be some time yet. Come, Thomas, I will find somewhere we can sit and talk while you wait. Unless your business is more pressing than the Queen of Castile?"

"It may be."

Theresa stopped and turned to him. "You are teasing me, surely?"

"I wish I was."

"Then even more reason for us to sit, so you can tell me what is so important as to disappoint her. By the time you have finished, perhaps she will be available."

Theresa led them to an intimate room hung with tapestries depicting hunting scenes. Through the tall windows, the Guadalquivir was fading into the approaching darkness. Theresa indicated a chair before turning to leave, abandoning Thomas to the view. He stared across the water, watching as workmen carried out the dangerous task of bringing the water wheels to a standstill for the night, as ordered by Isabel so her sleep was not disturbed. He became so engrossed with their task, he didn't hear Theresa return until she laid a hand on his wrist.

"I asked for wine to be brought, and some small plates of food." She sat, staring up at Thomas, who was unable to read whatever might lie behind her eyes. With a sigh, he took the chair across from her.

"Now tell me," she said, "what is so important as to distract you from Isabel?"

Thomas considered making up some tale until he realised he would welcome a chance to unburden himself.

"Jorge."

"Is he in love again?"

"If only it was that simple. He is accused of murder."

Theresa's face showed shock, and then she laughed as though Thomas had told the funniest joke ever. "Jorge? Murder?" She shook her head. "No, it is not possible."

"The evidence points directly to him."

Theresa's amusement drained away as quickly as it had come. "You cannot believe it."

"Of course not, but there are others who might. I have to prove his innocence. Not that he is helping, as usual. I wanted to talk to him, but he has disappeared again."

"He will be with his brother on the other side of the river."

"How do you know about Daniel?"

"I know everything." Theresa smiled. "Jorge told me, of course. He grew bored with those make-work discussions and found me in the gardens the day you arrived."

"What did he want?" Thomas wondered if the reason was related to Jorge's current predicament.

"He asked if you and he could be found a room in the palace, as you are such important men involved in vital discussions." She laughed. "He told me you were both sleeping in a tent."

"It's true. What did you tell him?" The thought of a comfortable bed appealed, and Thomas knew he could have as easily done the asking, probably with more chance of success.

Theresa pursed her lips. "I told him I would see what I

could do. At least he came to see me. It took five days for you to come, and then only by chance." She waited while a servant placed glasses, wine and a variety of small plates of food on the low table between them. Theresa held up a hand as the servant backed away. "Send a message to the Queen that Thomas Berrington is here. He awaits an audience with her. Come tell me at once when she is free." She waited until the man had left the room before leaning forward and pouring wine for them both. "Do you know what Isabel said when she saw you that day?"

"How could I? You were forty paces away."

Theresa smiled as she sat back. "She said: 'Ahh … Thomas'."

"Is that meant to be intriguing?"

"It is meant to be the truth. It was the way she said it. 'Ahh … Thomas'. There was such longing in those two words. I wish someone would speak my name in such a way."

"No doubt you misheard. Was that when I saw you all together—Isabel, you, that Countess and the other woman, and the Cardinal?"

"The Countess is too old for you," said Theresa.

Thomas smiled. Theresa was not much younger than he was, but she appeared to have shed years from her age since they first met six years before.

"And no doubt too married," Thomas said.

"Since when did that prevent a dalliance? But no, I believe her husband died some years ago and she never remarried. I hear tales she yearns for someone else, an old love."

"What is her name? Sight of her sparked a vague memory in me, but I couldn't place it."

Theresa laughed. "Are you saying you know so many good-looking women you cannot recall their names?"

"It is an itch I cannot scratch. You know how it is when something hovers like a fly you can't quite touch?" He waved a hand as if trying to swat a fly, then reached out to pick up his wine. "No matter, it will come to me when I least expect. Columb looked upset when he left here. I used to think him mad, but less so of late. I looked into his claims and they contain some truth, though I believe his calculations to be wrong. What does Isabel say?"

"She rarely mentions him. Unlike you."

"I was curious, that is all. I give the man barely any thought."

"I mean Isabel. She rarely mentions Columb, but she talks of you often."

"It must be dull in the extreme being a queen if I am the best she can talk of."

"Tell me who accuses Jorge of murder, and on what evidence? I still refuse to believe him capable."

"He was seen close to a house that burned down, and met with a man who claimed to know who his mother is, and then turned up dead. Jorge was told of another man who could provide proof of his adoption. A man who is also dead, burned to death in his cellar. The timing of all this could not be worse."

"That man Lawrence should be able to find out if the claim is true. The adoption of a child must be registered by law."

"Lawrence is already working on it, but Jorge's parents—the ones he thought were his parents—were not the kind to worry about breaking a law or two."

"Why can he simply not go and ask them?"

"Because they have disappeared from the face of the earth. Jorge says they were a bad lot anyway, and probably drank themselves to death, or were killed in some pointless argument."

"What if they are still alive? Have you asked Lawrence to check that? If you can find them, they will be able to answer any questions you and Jorge have."

Thomas cursed himself. Theresa was making more sense than him, but concern about Jorge had driven everything else from his mind. Now here he was talking nonsense with a beautiful woman while Jorge was in danger. He drained his glass of wine and stood.

"I can't stay, pleasant though the company is. Send a message to me if Isabel can see me tonight, though I'm not exactly sure where I will be. Most likely at Daniel's house, or our tent on the riverbank."

Theresa trotted alongside him. "I will send a servant if she finishes her talks in time, otherwise return in the morning. She keeps meetings until after noon if she can." She touched his arm. "And she does want to see you. I think..."

Thomas slowed when Theresa didn't go on.

"You think what?"

Theresa breathed deeply, let the air go. "She has mentioned once or twice she feels some guilt about what happened to your wife. Do not tell her I said anything, for she will know where the information came from. Please, Thomas, speak nothing of it, but you deserve to know her feelings."

"I will see what she has to say, but I put no blame on her. Fernando, perhaps, but not Isabel."

Theresa stared into his eyes for a moment before saying, "You did say you are sleeping in a tent, didn't you?"

"It is quite a large tent." It was a lie, but Theresa would not know that.

"But a tent all the same. When I tell Isabel, I am sure she will find a place for you here. It will make it all the easier for us to have secret assignations."

"I do not wish for any assignations, secret or otherwise." As he spoke the words, Thomas knew they might also be a lie.

Theresa laid a hand on his arm to stop him from moving away. "That woman you asked about, the Countess. She asked about you as well when she saw you, for the same reason. You sparked a memory in her, too."

"Did you tell her my name? Are you going to tell me hers, or keep me in suspense?"

"Oh, suspense I think. I did not say your name, but Isabel did. Well, I told you, 'Ahh … Thomas'." Theresa offered a smile of such mischief, Thomas had to suppress a laugh. "When she spoke your name, the woman blanched. Perhaps she has heard of your reputation for dealing death to enemies." Another smile, this one more sympathetic. "You should ask her yourself. She is staying here in the city. I can tell you where if you ask me nicely. And a kiss would help."

Thomas almost pulled away, then realised it was one small itch he could scratch and forget. So he asked. He even attempted to be nice in the asking, but it was unfamiliar to him.

Theresa spoke the words, unaware of the shock they sent through him. "It will be easy enough to find her, for she is staying in Córdoba at the house of Castellana Lonzal. She was the other woman you saw with us. At one time Castellana was married to Cardinal Rodrigo de Borja, who you also saw. It was a long time ago now, but they remain friends."

"Never mind Castellana whoever, what about the other woman?"

Theresa smiled, clearly pleased to have annoyed Thomas. "She is Eleanor, Countess d'Arreau. And I doubt very much you know her, for she is both powerful and wealthy."

CHAPTER SEVEN

The house sat square to the street. It was imposing, three storeys high with large windows. A metal gate offered a glimpse into an inner courtyard which many of the elegant houses of the city possessed, though this one appeared more ornate than most.

Thomas hesitated, his mind distracted by a swirl of memory. It was impossible to believe the woman Theresa had so glibly named could be the same girl he had once loved. The girl who had been carrying his child when she was stolen from him. They had run wild in the southern lands of France, lovers, friends, conspirators. And then soldiers sent by the man she was betrothed to had come. Three men dragged her away while ten more beat Thomas, cut him, stabbed him. And then, when they thought him dead, they had tossed him into a gorge.

After all the years, it seemed beyond even dreams or nightmares.

Before his rational mind could persuade him to turn away, he climbed the three steps to the iron gate and raised a knocker set in the wall, the sound echoing away through the courtyard. He waited, but as he raised his hand to knock again, he heard footsteps approaching.

A short man, leaner even than Thomas's dog Kin, stopped beyond the iron bars. He said nothing, merely cocking his head to one side in question.

"I am here to see the lady of the house."

"Señora Lonzal is not in residence. If you have business with her, she will be at her estate." The man eyed Thomas up and down, his expression making it clear he could think of no business his employer could possibly have with him.

"I understand she has a guest staying here. I believe she is someone I know."

"Do you have a name, sir?" The man leaned forward and looked both ways along the dark street. "This is a wealthy house, and the Señora's guest is a lady of importance. Should brigands learn she is staying here, they may call on some false pretext. As you are."

Thomas knew he might well look like a brigand. He was about to name Eleanor when a female voice sounded from somewhere within the house.

"Who is there? Send them away, it is too late for visitors."

"Some vagabond, Countess. He is leaving." He turned back to Thomas. "You are leaving, aren't you?"

"Is that Eleanor? Perhaps I can speak with her for a moment. I am a friend. A very old friend."

"We are not an open house. You would do better to leave before I call the Hermandos." The man began to turn away, but as he did so, Thomas saw a woman appear at the far end of the courtyard. She tilted her head to one side so she could see who stood outside. As she did, the small movement triggered a tumult of recognition that flooded through him. He had not believed it could be her, but that instant told him who she was, and he reached a hand out to the bars to steady himself.

She was indeed the woman he had seen at a distance in the palace talking with Isabel and Theresa. The woman who had sparked an uneasy familiarity. A familiarity that now brought a thousand chaotic memories.

"Eleanor?" Thomas's voice came out a croak and he coughed, repeated the name more loudly.

She crossed half the courtyard and held up a hand. "Open the gate. I must see him clearly."

Thomas stood as though rooted. Something coiled within, half pain and half fear. The woman who stood beyond the door should not be here, as he should not be here. It was not possible. And yet…

The servant opened his mouth to object.

"Open the gate, now!" It was the voice of a woman used to giving orders and having them obeyed without question. She came closer, stood just beyond the bars. To Thomas, they represented all the years since he had last seen her, bundled on the back of a cart, screaming his name as soldiers tried to kill him. Which is what she no doubt believed had happened. What he had believed himself until he woke to despair and pain.

He heard the rustle of her clothing. Inhaled a delicate scent that drifted across to touch his senses. He recalled other scents. Sweat. Sex. Mud on her skin when he washed her clean in cold river water. He stared at her, unable to speak, and as he did so, he saw the recognition bloom in her own eyes.

Eleanor gave a single cry and collapsed to the floor.

The servant reacted at once, slamming the bars he had half-opened in Thomas's face.

He stood like a statue, trying to make sense of the

memories flooding through him. And then he came to his senses and pushed at the gate, but it was locked. He hammered on the bars with the flat of his hand. He had to get inside. Had to see if Eleanor was all right.

Eleanor.

His Eleanor.

The name echoed through his mind, together with the memories.

She was the first girl he had truly loved. For a long time, the only woman he had ever loved. Eleanor, who was torn from him. They had been sixteen when they first met, both wild creatures without limits or morals. Eleanor was betrothed to a man four times her age. Thomas was the leader of a band of renegades roaming the southern borderlands of France. Within a day, she had seduced his body. Within a week, she had captured his heart.

They were together half a year before her husband-to-be, the old, sick Count d'Arreau, sent men to tear them apart. On a hot, dry road, the men had found them both and struck, leaving Thomas for dead. Except he had survived. How he did not know, but thanks to an old man in the Pyrenees, he had survived. That old man, like Eleanor, had changed his life.

Thomas heard a voice from out of sight where the servant had carried Eleanor's prone body. He was objecting, Eleanor insisting as she recovered. And then the man returned and unlocked the gate. He swung it open and walked away as if he wanted nothing to do with this madness. Then Eleanor stood before him, and all at once Thomas had no idea what to do next.

She had changed, and he almost laughed at the recognition of such. They had both changed, and he wondered how she could possibly have recognised him in turn. Even as he saw the girl she had once been beneath the woman she had become, she had no doubt seen the boy Thomas had been. Her hair was the same, a deep red, fine and soft. He recalled the scent of it and almost staggered to his knees himself.

"I..." she started. Stopped. Shook her head, a deep frown creasing a brow that had never known lines until the day she was taken from him. She took a breath, her clothing creaking as she did so—the clothing of a wealthy woman.

Thomas waited.

"I was told there was a man in Córdoba by the name of Thomas Berrington." Eleanor's words came fast, as if she needed to release them before she thought better. "I wondered if it might be you, but could not see how. I dreamed it was. Feared it was not. I wanted to see you, but feared your reaction, after all these years."

"I saw you with Isabel. You looked familiar, but I could not remember from where." Thomas shook his head. "How could I forget you?"

"I did not recognise you either, though there was something. But I believed you dead. I dismissed the truth my eyes showed me as impossible." She gave a small laugh, put a hand to her mouth. The hand was the same, the skin older but still smooth. He recalled those fingers touching him...

He shook his head, tossing the memory aside.

"You *were* dead," she said. "I was told you were dead."

"What happened?" Thomas's voice croaked. "Did you marry him?"

She gave a nod, shook her head. "We cannot talk here on the street. Come inside." She offered a smile. "If you trust me, that is."

"I am not sure I trust myself."

"Then don't." She put her hand to her mouth again. "Oh, Thomas. Thomas my love. Come inside, we have to talk.

There is so much to talk about. I want to know about your life, how you survived, and I will tell you of mine, for there is much to tell."

Behind her, the man who had come to the door crossed the courtyard. His head turned to watch them and Eleanor snapped a command.

"Bring wine to the large room at the front." She turned back to Thomas. "And food? Are you hungry, Thomas?"

He shook his head.

"Just wine, then." She stepped back so he could enter the courtyard.

For a moment, Thomas believed himself incapable of movement. He tried to move his legs, but they were rooted to the flagstones. Eleanor smiled, and in it he saw the girl he had known; the girl he had run with, swum with, lain with and loved. He stepped across the threshold and put his arms around her as if they had never been parted.

Time slowed ... stopped ... ran backward to when the world was a simpler place.

He wanted to kiss her, but did not. Instead, he held her in his arms, and after a moment, Eleanor wrapped her own around his waist and rested her head against his chest.

She gave a tiny laugh. "You are a lot bigger than you used to be."

He laughed as well, raw emotion welling through him as he clung to her, not knowing what would happen next.

What did happen was even more of a shock than he had already experienced. Beyond Eleanor, a man emerged from a side door and stopped dead in his tracks.

"Mother—what on earth are you doing?" He took four paces toward them, a hand falling to his waist where a finely-made dagger rested. "Unhand her, sir. Unhand her at once or suffer the consequences!"

Eleanor held on to Thomas a moment longer before twisting from his embrace. She touched a hand to her breast, her hair, as if it had become disarrayed, as if Thomas had touched her as once he had.

"Yves…" She took a breath, and as Thomas watched her steel herself, he all at once knew who the man was, even before Eleanor uttered the words. "Yves, I want you to meet your father."

Yves stared at Thomas, confusion on his face. Thomas said nothing, waiting, aware of a roil of emotions within. This man—and man he was, a strange concept for someone who had been nestled within Eleanor barely two months when last Thomas had seen her—was a total stranger. Though the longer Thomas stared at him, the more there came a sense of familiarity. He could not see himself standing in front of him, but the shadow of another man. A man long dead—his father, John Berrington.

Yves was not as tall as Thomas, stockier, with more muscle, just as John Berrington had possessed. The same attributes Thomas's brother, another John and also dead, had possessed. Thomas wondered if Yves shared other traits with those men—their bullying, their temper, their roughness with women. And then as he waited, his question was answered.

Yves came forward fast. His hand dropped to his waist and drew the dagger there.

"You lie!" The words were meant for his mother, even though his eyes never left Thomas. "I am Count d'Arreau. My father was Count d'Arreau. Who this man is I have no idea, but he is *not* my father. My father is dead. And so will he be in a moment."

He came forward fast, the dagger raised. Thomas waited until the last possible moment before stepping aside. His hand whipped out as fast as the strike of a snake, and before Yves could react, the knife was in Thomas's hand, not his.

"Don't hurt him," said Eleanor. "He does not mean it."

"I take it you didn't bother telling him about me?" Even though it made sense, it still hurt.

She gave a tiny shake of her head. Thomas turned the knife around and held it out toward Yves, who stared at it as if it was some strange object he had never seen before. Then he took the hilt. Thomas waited to see what he would do, but the knife hung loose, the moment of anger past.

"We need to talk," he said.

"Yes," said Eleanor. "With Yves, or…"

Thomas looked at his son, the connection of blood growing stronger. He thought of the strangeness created when a man and woman lay together. It intrigued him, as it had always done. There was something of Eleanor in Yves, a little of Thomas, but a great deal of his father. Yves was a mix of all those who had contributed to his making, stretching back generations into time uncountable to bring this man here, to this moment and this revelation.

"Did you never suspect?" Thomas asked, speaking directly to Yves.

"Why would I? My father—" He stopped, dropped his gaze. "He was always my father. I was his son. Why would I doubt it?" When he raised his eyes, he looked at his mother. "Is it true, Maman?"

She nodded. "It is true, my sweet."

"How?"

"How do you think?"

An expression of distaste crossed Yves's face and Thomas tried not to smile. Yves was more than old enough to have lain with a woman, more than likely several women if he had inherited anything from his grandfather, but no doubt the idea of his mother lying with a stranger was too much to accept.

"With *him*?" He was barely able to get the words out.

"Leave us, my sweet. I need to talk with Thomas alone."

"And if I do not want to leave you alone with him? What if he tries to attack you?"

"Don't be stupid."

Yves stood rigid, a faint tremble in the hand that still held the knife, and Thomas watched in case he tried another attack. But Yves turned away and ran up a set of stairs to a gallery that ran around three sides of the courtyard. Once he was gone, Eleanor surprised Thomas by twining her fingers through his.

"Come, we can talk privately in the back room."

Thomas had no choice but to let her lead him, a tumult of emotion raging through him. Eleanor drew him to a couch and sat, offering no choice but for him to sit next to her, his hand still grasped in hers.

"How old is he?"

She laughed. "Surely you can work it out, can't you? You used to be the cleverest boy I knew. Have you changed so much?"

Thomas calculated. He had seventeen years when Eleanor was taken from him, which would make Yves thirty-one or thirty-two. Most likely thirty-one.

"I expect I have changed in other ways, too," he said. "What did you tell the man you married?"

"That Yves came early, and he believed me. Why would he not? I had missed barely two bleedings when we married, and such things happen. I know I have changed, Thomas. Are you disappointed?"

From her tone, he wished he had Jorge's skill with women. The girl he had loved remained, but now she was cloaked within another woman. Eleanor had been lithe, slim, her breasts barely showing beneath the shirts she wore. This Eleanor possessed breasts, hips, all the female attributes men lusted after in a woman. Thomas knew he was not most men, and wondered if he had ever been. He studied her face, saw lines around her eyes, fine creases at the corners of her mouth, but through them all he still saw the girl he had once loved.

"No," he said, "you have barely changed at all."

Eleanor laughed and clutched his hand between her breasts, holding it there so he might discover their fresh promise. "Oh, but you have learned to flatter since I knew you last. You would never have had the wit to do such then." Slowly she raised his hand and kissed it, then settled it back between her breasts. There was something bright and sharp in her eyes.

"Did you ever remarry?" Thomas asked.

"I am the Countess d'Arreau. There were many suitors, of course, but finding a suitable husband, one I would want to take, would have been difficult." Her fingers tightened against his. "I looked for you when my husband died."

"How old was Yves then?"

"He had nine years. He might have accepted a new father at that age. He barely knew the man he considered his father. My husband was old and set in his ways when he took me, and he only grew worse. He did not like children."

"He must have lain with you to believe Yves was his." Thomas examined his own thoughts, searching for some hint of jealousy and finding none.

"Of course he did. On our wedding night I made sure he did. And then, when he saw my body change, I also made sure he never touched me again. And you, Thomas, there must have been other women. Did you ever marry?"

"I did."

"Are you still married?"

"She died."

"I am sorry."

"No, you are not, why should you be? She died less than two years ago, and I killed the men who took her from me."

Eleanor stared into his eyes and he saw she understood. "You are still the Thomas I knew. My Thomas. I saw that by how easily you took the knife from Yves. You are as fast as ever. You should have abandoned me and run."

Thomas thought she might be about to cry, but her eyes remained dry.

"If you thought me dead, why did you look for me?"

"Because my heart," she drew his hand tighter against herself, "told me you lived."

"And when you found nothing?"

"I still believed. And I was right, was I not? What are we going to do, Thomas?"

"About what?"

"About us, of course. You and me."

"The us we were is long in the past. Now you are Countess d'Arreau and I am nothing but a poor physician."

"You are a physician?" It was as if she had taken no heed of his words and Thomas feared this encounter was already beyond his control. He stared at Eleanor's face. Felt the warmth of her breast against his hand. He wanted her. Despite the years, the women in between, he wanted her as badly as he had ever done. He knew it was impossible to reclaim their youth, but that didn't matter. He ached for the certainty he had once possessed as a youth of seventeen years. Invulnerable. Certain of himself. But for now, all that mattered was the two of them, together in this place, with darkness kissing the windows.

He turned his hand so it lay against Eleanor's breast and she smiled.

"I should show you around the house. It is impressive. My bed chamber is particularly impressive."

"Yes, I would like you to do that." In that moment, an inevitability washed through him, taking away all his doubts, for the moment at least.

Thomas allowed her to lead him. Allowed her to remove his clothes, then he lay on her bed with the door locked and watched as she revealed to him the changes of her body, and despite them all he saw only the girl he had loved restored to him in all her glory.

Eleanor lay next to him, her fingers tracing the scars on his body, asking questions Thomas was unwilling to answer. Each scar was personal. Lubna had traced them, just as Eleanor did now, and the answers to her questions belonged to Lubna. But the arousal he felt belonged to this woman beside him. Belonged in the scented bed and the magical room which excluded the rest of the world and all its concerns, for this one night.

CHAPTER EIGHT

Thomas crossed the Guadalquivir in the dark, using the ancient bridge. He walked in a daze, barely aware of the world around him, which was underlaid by images of the past and present. He wondered if he would have fallen into Eleanor's bed so easily had he not been worried about Jorge. Had he been seeking distraction from those worries?

When he arrived at Daniel's house he found the source of them kneeling on the floor. He was playing with the smallest children despite the lateness of the hour, while Adana helped her mother tidy away the detritus of their evening meal. Daniel sat at the table, watching Jorge with an indulgent smile—or at least what could be seen of the smile beneath his thick beard. The domesticity of the scene and the danger Jorge was in hit Thomas like a slap across the face, and he tumbled back to earth.

Zanita turned as Thomas took a seat. "I can find you something to eat if you want, there will be a little left in the pot."

"Nothing, but my thanks." Thomas turned to Daniel. "Has Jorge told you what he is accused of?"

"I am here," said Jorge.

"And I am talking to Daniel." Thomas continued to stare at the smith—though no longer a simple smith. Daniel had become a man of substance, his house large enough to have many rooms.

"Not the detail," said Daniel. "Something about an accusation, but he made it sound like some foolishness."

Thomas glanced toward Jorge, who had stopped playing, except two-year-old Graçia had other ideas and clung to his hair as she tried to climb his body.

"If only it was," Thomas said. "So he has not told you what happened?"

"I told you he has not." Daniel looked toward his wife. "Has he told you? Or you, Adana?"

Both shook their heads.

"It should be you who tells them," Thomas said to Jorge, who had started to play with the children again, as if seeking their distraction.

"You know more of it than I do." Jorge would not look at Thomas.

"It is you who is accused."

"Then tell them of what I am accused."

Zanita and Adana came to the table and sat. "What has Uncle Jorge done?" Adana's pretty face showed concern.

Thomas sighed and ran a hand across his head. He knew he had to reveal the facts before he could explain the reason he was here. He would have preferred it if Jorge hadn't been present, but he could not change that.

"He is accused of killing a man."

"Uncle Jorge? No!"

Daniel laughed. "You know as well as I he is not capable. Oh, in battle perhaps, but in cold blood?" He shook his head.

Zanita turned to Jorge. "Is what Thomas says true?"

Jorge would not meet her eyes, but offered a brief nod of his head.

"Who?" Daniel asked.

"A scribe by the name of Alonso Cortez." Thomas made no mention of the other dead man.

"I know him. I have used his services in the past. He drew up the contract when I bought this house and the land next to it to build the works." Daniel leaned across the table. "Who brings the accusation?"

"The Hermandos have only one suspect. A baker woman claims she saw a man running away from Cortez's house. His neighbours identified a tall, handsome man standing outside the house before it burned down."

"Who makes these accusations?"

"I have been helping a young constable by the name of Miguel Sánchez. It is he who has been told to arrest Jorge on a charge of murder, though the order must come from far higher. I am surprised nobody has come here asking for him. They must know he's your brother." Thomas sighed. "The evidence isn't strong, but there are witnesses and we both know most times an accusation is enough. What puzzles me is why the Hermandos want him arrested on such weak evidence. Someone must be behind it. If I knew who, it might point to the person who killed Cortez."

Daniel sat straight. He turned to look at Jorge, who had finally given up his pretence at play and gotten to his feet, though his eyes remained downcast.

"Jorge no longer lives in Córdoba, why would someone want to make him look guilty of murder? What if it is me they are trying to damage? I have a reputation these days, someone who can call the King a friend. Men are jealous of my position. They would like it for themselves. You know both the King and Queen, Thomas. Can you not go to them and have this accusation put aside?"

"You know how Isabel is. For her the law is everything." What he didn't want to say was what if Jorge was guilty of the charges against him? Thomas wanted to think not, but, as always, required proof. Which he did not yet have.

"But you could ask, for my brother?"

Thomas glanced from Daniel to Jorge, back again. "Yes, I will ask, as soon as I can see her. She wants me to visit her, but there are many calls on her time and I am the least of them. I would talk with you alone, if I can."

Daniel's stare met Thomas's. "There are no secrets in this house. None between me and my brother, none amongst our family."

"It will be easier if it is only you and I," Thomas said. "I will tell Jorge everything later, but you know how he is. It will go better man to man, without interruption."

"I never interrupt," said Jorge. "Only when I believe you are wrong. Which is often enough."

"Exactly." Thomas watched Daniel until he saw an acceptance settle through him.

"Let us go to the workshop, then. We will not be overheard there."

"And I will make up a room for you both," said Zanita. "Jorge tells me you are sleeping in a tent beside the river. There is no need for that. From now on you must stay here."

"It is further from the palace," Thomas said. He also wondered if he might be sleeping in Eleanor's bed again. The hours he had spent with her were already fading like some dream, even as an unease grew that he had made a mistake in submitting to her. And it had been a submitting, he knew.

"Not much further, and you both need looking after."

She stood and slapped Thomas on the back of the head. "Go have your talk, man to man, then come back here." She turned and pointed at Jorge as he too started for the door. "You, do as Thomas says. Stay here."

Jorge came to a halt, his body tense. Daniel rose and patted him on the shoulder as he passed. Thomas followed, no sign of affection from him even though he was aware Jorge was now the closest person in the world to him. They were closer than brothers.

It was a short walk to Daniel's works, but neither of them spoke, as if they knew the conversation had to wait until they were inside. As they approached, Thomas was surprised to see the furnaces still glowing white and sparks flying as a team of smiths worked iron and steel.

"We are busy," Daniel said, as though aware of an unspoken question.

"Why?"

"You should know why. You are the man talking terms with the palace. How is that going, by the way?"

"It is not me doing the talking. In fact I only turn up once a day because they think my presence will soften the King and Queen. The rest of the time I have been sleeping half the afternoon away. Apart from the last two days."

Daniel nodded to several of the workers, stopped briefly to check on a sword being fashioned before offering his approval. A small office with a door was set toward the rear and he entered it, waiting until Thomas was inside before closing the door. Not because they would be overheard, but because the constant clash of hammer on metal made conversation impossible.

Daniel nodded to a wooden chair, then took one himself. Thomas glanced around, impressed at the neatness and organisation on display.

"So what is this all about?" asked Daniel. "Is Jorge really suspected of murder?"

"He is. Like you, I don't believe him guilty, but I need to prove it to myself as well as others. So to start: did you see him early yesterday? Say between dawn and noon?"

Daniel took his time answering, as if he had to think about his response. "No, but then I started here early and did not leave until well after noon. It is Zanita you should ask. What does Jorge claim?"

"That he met with a man who claimed to know who his mother is."

Daniel laughed. "We both have the misfortune of knowing who our mother was. That is no mystery, much as I might wish it."

"Jorge says the woman he thought his mother was not the woman who gave birth to him. This man he met said he knows who his true mother is."

"Did he say who?"

"He told him he would do so in exchange for money. Jorge left the money, but when he took me there the money was gone, and the man dead."

Daniel gave a shake of his head. "Do you think Jorge killed him?"

"I have no reason to, and why take me to the place if he had done so?"

"He has always been a fool with money. I would not have done what he did, not without some promise first. A small exchange of information, at least."

"The man gave him Cortez's name, which is what sent Jorge to his house. Which in turn resulted in the accusation against him."

Daniel nodded, then something seemed to occur to him.

"Do you think I am the child of someone else as well, or only Jorge?"

"The man didn't mention the rest of you. How many were there?"

"God knows. Some died. Some moved away. Others came and went—not my parents' children, but treated the same way as the rest of us. By that I mean badly. Has Jorge not told you how we were raised?"

"He has."

"Then you know. Beaten. Starved. The girls whored out, the boys as well if they could make them. Jorge fought back. So did I."

"And your mother?"

"She sold her body to anyone with the smallest coin."

"Your father?"

"A bully, a braggart, and no doubt a killer in his own right."

"You are sure they are both dead?"

"More than likely. Dead to me in any case. I haven't seen them since I fell from that bridge. Since my leg was made this shape."

"Do you truly believe them dead? Could they be behind this in some way?"

"Oh, they are dead sure enough. I haven't seen their bodies, nor heard how they died, but trust me, they are dead. They could be nothing but dead. They drank and fought and whored. They either killed themselves or someone else did them the favour."

"Do you believe Jorge might be another woman's son?"

Daniel shrugged. He held his arms out from his sides. "We are not exactly twins, are we? If he is, she cannot have loved him much to give him away to our family."

"Do you recall him coming to the house?"

"I was too young. There were many of us, and too much chaos to notice a new baby." Daniel stood, walked to the door and opened it. He looked out at the working men for a while before turning back. "I have never given the idea much thought before. Why would I? But now I think back we had a sister, a sweet girl, who was only a few months younger than Jorge. She was beautiful. An angel." Daniel shook his head. "Now she is truly an angel."

"She died?"

Daniel nodded. "Years ago. I must have been eight or nine, Jorge had no more than five years." Daniel offered a short laugh devoid of any humour. "And now I am trying to think of her name and cannot." He looked up to meet Thomas's gaze, the brightness of grief in his own. "How can I forget my own sister's name?"

"If what you say is true and this sister was born of your mother, then Jorge cannot have been. How much younger was she than Jorge?"

"No more than three or four months. I never thought of it that way before."

"It's not the kind of thing you do, as a child."

"I expect not. Did you know your brothers and sisters, Thomas? I do not know, did you have any?"

"A brother and a sister."

"There you go." As if this was answer enough, when they both knew it was not. "There is someone you could ask who might know, but where she is now is another mystery."

Thomas waited. There was little he could say, and he knew eventually Daniel would tell him.

Daniel returned to his chair. He reached out and picked up a piece of paper, read it and put it back, but Thomas knew it was nothing but a distraction.

"We had a sister who was more of a mother to both of us

than our own, despite her age. Beatriz. She must have had nine or ten years when Jorge was born, more than twenty when I broke my leg and believed Jorge had perished in the river. Beatriz..." Daniel repeated the name, his voice soft, his mind distant in time. He looked up. "She was no beauty, but a hard worker. Clever, too. Far cleverer than the rest of us. She married a mariner and left home, but we were older then and could take care of ourselves. I was strong and our father stopped beating us after I hit him back. Once was enough. He was a coward. You should ask Beatriz about Jorge ... she would know, if anyone does. You will have to find her first, of course."

"Beatriz," said Jorge. "I haven't thought of her in years. Not since I was carried away to my new life. Even before then. She left our house before I thought I had killed Daniel."

A candle burned beside the bed where he and Thomas lay, a soft mattress beneath them, linen sheets covering their bodies.

Jorge laughed. "I could get used to this comfort. Perhaps we can stay here instead of that stupid tent."

"I don't see why not. What do you remember of your sister?"

It was clear by the softness of Jorge's features he was thinking of the past. "She was mother to us both, and could be stern sometimes. She married..." He shook his head. "Someone. I don't remember who, though I have a recollection I thought the name strange. Not Spanish."

"Daniel said she married a mariner."

"That is my recollection too, though all I remember is an older man, very handsome. Older than Beatriz. She would have had eighteen or nineteen years by then." Jorge rolled on to his side and stared at Thomas. "Do you think we can find her? Would she know the truth about where I came from?"

"If there is a truth to be found."

"It makes sense. I am nothing like Daniel, and when I think back, nothing like any of my brothers or sisters, though whether they were all the children of my parents is another thing I don't know. There are too many things I don't know, Thomas. It is why I rely on you."

Jorge rolled on to his back and went silent.

"We ought to think about taking two horses and riding away from the city." Thomas stared at the wavering candle-light on the ceiling. From somewhere in the house footsteps sounded on wooden boards and a female voice called out. Adana, Thomas thought, but could not be sure.

"Why?"

"Because this doesn't feel right to me." This time, Thomas lifted himself on one elbow and looked at Jorge. "It is clear someone wants harm to come to you, and it seems more and more like a conspiracy. Even if I can find evidence to the contrary, it might not be accepted. Leaving Qurtuba would be the safest option."

"When have you ever run from a fight?"

"When it was one I couldn't win."

"Then I have never seen it. We stay. There are people here I care about. You too, I expect. We stay, Thomas."

"Do you remember me talking of a girl called Eleanor?"

"Your first love? Of course I do. Why?"

"I..." Thomas stopped, trying to think how to say it. Eventually, when Jorge turned his head to stare at him, he decided there was only one way. "She is here in Qurtuba."

"You have seen her?"

"I saw her tonight."

"And...?"

"I came here fresh from her bed."

Jorge laughed and slapped Thomas on the chest. "Good. It is time you lay with a woman again. Long past time. I thought it would have been Theresa ... but your first love? That is even better. It was meant to be."

"Was it?"

Jorge chuckled and lay his head on his pillow again. After a while his breathing slowed and a soft snore sounded. Thomas stared at the light cast by the guttering candle, then reached out and snuffed the flame out. He was unaware of drifting to sleep, but painfully aware of being pulled awake by the sound of shouting and boots on the stairs. The door to their room crashed open and men swarmed in.

"Jorge Olmos? We seek Jorge Olmos. Which of you is him?"

Jorge sat up, washing hands across his face. "I am."

One of the men drew out a sheet of paper. "I have a warrant from the King for your arrest. You can come peaceably or we can drag you out. The choice is yours." From his expression it looked as if he preferred the idea of the dragging.

Jorge turned to Thomas, who was already out of bed and pulling on his clothes. "What should I do?"

Thomas realised why the Hermandos had not come for Jorge before—they were waiting for the small hours of the night when men were deep asleep.

"Go with them. I will find Fernando and sort it out. You will be out again before nightfall, but go with them for now."

CHAPTER NINE

The first intimations of dawn were starting to lighten the eastern sky as Thomas was turned away from the palace by the night-guard, and he wondered if he was no longer welcome within its walls. Was he tainted by the accusation made against Jorge? Had Fernando really signed the warrant for his arrest? If so, had he been aware of what the document said or not?

Thomas stood in the cool air listening to the whisper of the river as the city came alive like some great creature, slowly at first before gathering pace. Soon everything would be bustle and distraction. Thomas knew he needed more information so made his way toward the Hermandos' office. He asked for Miguel and was told he was on patrol in the city. Most likely he could be found in Calle Melilla. He usually broke his fast there at a street stall.

Thomas found him standing with some kind of wrapped meat in his hand, as if without a care in the world.

"Why was Jorge arrested?"

Miguel looked at him like he wished he could be somewhere else. "I am a constable, Thomas. Men far higher than me made that decision. I heard the warrant was signed by the King, no less."

"Why?"

"Why did the King sign it? Perhaps you can ask him when you see him next, for I do not know."

"Why now? There is no evidence against Jorge."

"In that you are wrong. As soon as it was light, Jorge was taken to the street Cortez's house stood on, where he was identified by several people. They say they saw him standing outside the house, and the baker woman identified him as the man who bought pastries from her." Miguel glanced at the food in his own hand. "How could he eat pastries after killing a man and setting fire to his house?"

"Because he didn't do it."

Miguel looked away.

"You told them, didn't you? You told them his name and that he was a friend of mine. I was honest with you and you betrayed my trust. Did you tell them where his brother lives as well? No wonder they came so quickly for him." Thomas shook his head, disappointed in Miguel.

"I told you two nights ago they already knew his name, but where from I do not know. I had no choice, Thomas. I am new in this city and want to keep my job. They would have found out soon enough, one way or another."

"Do you believe the evidence against him?"

"Even you, his friend, have to agree it is convincing."

"But false. I want you to do something for me." Thomas thought the man might refuse, but perhaps he felt a little guilt at his part in what had happened.

"If I can." Miguel took another bite of his food.

"See what you can find out about the arrest warrant. Who set the chain of events in place. Who was really behind it. The King signs everything put in front of him, but someone else will have set Jorge up for arrest. I want you to find out who spread Jorge's name before they should have known anything about events in that street. And if I get the chance, I will ask Fernando directly why he signed that paper."

Thomas knew it was still too early for Lawrence to be out of bed, but he also knew he could wake him easily enough, even if it sparked his temper. He hammered on the door until a head appeared from the upper window.

"Fuck off, Thomas Berrington."

"Jorge's been arrested."

Lawrence's head disappeared, then returned. "The door is unlocked. Let yourself in."

Thomas declined the offer and walked to the small table beneath the orange tree. He sat, watching as the fast-growing light washed shadows from the stone wall, until it caught at the spire of the church next to the house and flamed it. He recalled the madman who had leapt from that roof, believing he could escape justice by flying. It all seemed so long ago, and as if it had happened to someone else.

Lawrence came from the house but did not sit. "This had better be good, and preferably short. I might still have time to go back upstairs if Laurita stays in bed. She likes it when … well, you don't need to know what she likes."

"They have arrested Jorge."

"You told me that. Why else would I be down here instead of in my bed? What do you want me to do about it?"

"I need to send a message to Gharnatah. Do you know a fast rider?"

"I can do better if you have the money. A pigeon will get there within a day. Write your message and I will make sure it is sent. Make it short, they are not big birds."

"I will write it before I leave. Have you found anything more out?"

"There are a lot of papers to go through, and they are scattered all over the city, but I can tell you one thing. I think I can, anyway. How big was that cellar under Cortez's house?"

"Big." Thomas saw a flare of light in the bedroom window and knew Laurita must also be getting out of bed. Lawrence would be out of luck when he returned. "It stretched under the houses on both sides. I don't think anyone knew it was there other than Cortez himself."

"So thousands of contracts?"

"At least. Tens of thousands possibly. Why?"

"From what I can tell, Cortez was not particularly prolific as a scribe. I have identified the indexes for his documents and there might be a thousand, but I would say less. The question is who did the others belong to, and why did Cortez have them?"

"Do you think he stole them?"

"I don't think anything. I leave the thinking up to you. Why did they arrest Jorge?"

"You know why. Because they believe he killed Cortez."

"Then you need to prove he didn't. Or go down on your knees to the Queen and beg for a pardon. That might work."

"Jorge is innocent."

"Only to people who know him. You need to find out why the Hermandos think he killed Cortez. You say he was seen?"

"By that baker woman and some of the neighbours, and Jorge admits he went to the street. It is where that dead man told him he would find Cortez, that he would confirm the information about his mother."

Lawrence tapped the table, thinking. "This other man, the one you took that cross from—do you still have it, by the way?"

Thomas reached inside his robe and drew the cross out, still strung on its leather thong. Hanging it around his own neck had seemed the simplest way of keeping it safe. He had almost forgotten it was there.

"Do you have any more information about it?"

Lawrence shook his head. "No. I was curious, that was all. But does what you're saying mean we're looking for two murderers now, or were both killed by the same man?"

"The same man would make sense."

"Which means the two dead men must be connected in some way. This man who told Jorge he knew who his mother was, I wonder how he found that information out?"

"It's likely it was no more than a lie to obtain silver."

"Suppose it was not."

Lawrence stared into space for a long time.

Thomas waited for him to work through his thoughts as he pursued his own. Lawrence was right, of course. It made sense two killings on the same day were most likely to be carried out by the same killer. Particularly when both, in some way, were related to Jorge.

"It would explain why Cortez had all those documents," said Lawrence.

"What would?"

"Suppose Cortez was a collector of secrets? He would search the city archives, buy documents from other scribes, or more likely steal them. It always surprises me when people record every detail that damns them. Cortez was using what he obtained to blackmail people." Lawrence nodded, the chain of logic clear in his own head. "Which is almost certainly why he was killed. He blackmailed the wrong person. And it explains the other man's death. Cortez could have sold him information on Jorge's mother which he planned to sell on to Jorge."

"Did you get a chance to look at either of those documents he carried?"

Lawrence nodded. "I did. One is not relevant, a confirmation of a passage from Pisa to Sevilla. The other is more interesting. It's from a man by the name of Inigo Florentino asking the note holder, presumably, to travel to Córdoba and search for a man by the name of Jorge Florentino."

"Is that our Jorge?" said Thomas. "It's not possible, is it?"

"Jorge is a common enough name, but under the circumstances…" Lawrence waited for Thomas to see the logic.

"Agreed. But will we ever know for certain now the man is dead?" Thomas stared into space for a moment. "If the man had been sent to find Jorge, why did he try to extract money from him? And how did he know the name of Jorge's real mother?" He shook his head. "It doesn't make sense and it does make sense. The name can't be a coincidence, it has to be our Jorge. But where are the connections?" Thomas felt like banging his head on the table. "The man said he knew who Jorge's mother was, but what if that letter tells us who his father is?"

"Everything will be in the documents," said Lawrence, tapping the table. "I will follow the documents. I have a list of those produced by Cortez, though there is unlikely to be anything damning in them, but there will be links, and I will follow them."

"How long will it take? Jorge is in prison, remember." Thomas shook his head. "I don't even know where he is."

"He will be across the river. They moved the gaol when

they built new offices for the Hermandos. Ask anyone and they will tell you where it is. That is assuming the men who took him were not Fernando's soldiers."

"They didn't say, but I would recognise soldiers, so Hermandos."

"Then he is in the new gaol. I hear it is better than the old, but not by much."

"It is still a prison. I will go and see if I can see him, then go to Isabel. She wants to talk to me but I would rather she forgot she asked."

Lawrence grinned. "I imagine she won't do that. And while you are doing all these things, I will follow the trail of documents."

"One other thing," Thomas said as he got to his feet. "I am sure some of this must be connected to how Jorge came to be lodged with his family. Daniel told me the name of their older sister, the one who raised them both. She might know something about how he came to their family. Her name is Beatriz, family name Olmos I assume, and Daniel thinks she married a mariner. That is all I know, but I want to talk to her if I can."

"That should be easy enough, particularly if she married here in Córdoba. Come back when you are done and I may have more information. Have you considered Cortez's death may have no bearing on what is happening to Jorge?"

"I don't understand what you mean. The man is dead."

Lawrence rose to his feet. "If someone is trying to blame Jorge for the murder, Cortez might be nothing more than a convenience. The wrong man at the right time."

"It's a stretch," Thomas said. "Doesn't it make our job even harder?"

"Our job?"

"Sorry—my job."

Lawrence laughed and slapped Thomas on the shoulder. "No, our job, though it would be good to have something to do that is not all about musty papers. Gods, I miss the days when we rode after Mandana. Perhaps we can find someone to chase again."

"Perhaps. I want you to send a message to Belia in Gharnatah. Ask her to come here, but don't give a reason. Just tell her Jorge misses her, she might believe that."

When Thomas found the gaol, it was to discover only the smallest of coin was required to gain access to Jorge, who sat in a cell close to the guard station. There was a single cot, with not enough space for another. Jorge's face was bruised, a cut to his cheek, another to his lip. His fine clothes had been stolen to be replaced by others fashioned of coarse hemp that smelled as if another inmate had died in them.

When Thomas entered the cell, Jorge remained where he was, sitting on the cot, his head turned away. Thomas put his fingers beneath Jorge's chin and turned his head so he could examine his wounds. None were serious. They would heal without needing his skills. There would be a small scar from the cut on his cheek, but it might serve to make him look more dangerous.

"Send for Belia," said Jorge.

Thomas nodded. "Already done. I came here expecting to spend whatever was needed to get you into quarters such as this, but here you are. Who beat you?"

"Who do you think beat me? Daniel came while I was being questioned and paid for me to have a room of my own. Zanita and Adana are going to bring me food."

"Tell Daniel to bring it himself, or perhaps someone else, but not those two, not here."

Jorge nodded, but there was little conviction in it. "I can try, but you know how they both are." He looked up. "Have you seen them?"

"Not yet, but I will. What did your questioners want to know?"

"Why I killed Cortez."

"And what did you tell them?"

"That I didn't do it, of course, but they told me they have witnesses."

"I heard that as well, from Miguel. How long did the interrogation last?"

"It felt like a long time, but probably was not." He raised a hand to his face. "These are the wounds you can see, but they hit me everywhere. They wanted a confession to make their lives easier." He gave a brief smile. "One even kicked me in the balls, but he was out of luck there."

"Stand up," Thomas ordered.

"I am all right," said Jorge.

"Let your physician be the judge of that."

Thomas waited and eventually Jorge stood. Thomas stripped the coarse shirt from him and examined the bruises to his body, which were many. He pressed on each rib, but none were broken. Then he felt the bruises, looking for any deeper damage and finding none. He told Jorge to put his shirt back on but to remove his trousers, then checked his legs and thighs.

"All these years and you have never touched me there before," said Jorge.

"All these years and there has never been a need. You are bruised, but I cannot see anything permanent. No doubt Belia will be pleased."

"No doubt." Jorge pulled his trousers up and sat. "When are you getting me out of here?"

"I am going to Isabel and Fernando now to plead your case. I will tell him you are innocent and have to be released."

"What about this Miguel you know—was this his doing?"

"The order came from the palace."

Jorge stared at Thomas. "Who in the palace?"

"Fernando."

"Why?"

"That is what I intend to ask him as soon as I leave here, but it may be the order is only in his name and he knows nothing of it."

"I thought he liked me." Jorge's voice was that of a disappointed child.

"Everyone likes you. This is something else." Thomas let his breath go, reached out and touched Jorge's shoulder. "I wonder if someone is trying to hurt me, and you are nothing but collateral damage."

"Collateral damage?" said Jorge. "Why is everything always about you, Thomas? Am I not important enough to be a threat?"

"Of course you are." Except Thomas didn't believe his words. Jorge was a benign presence, loved by all.

Jorge waved a hand. "Go see Fernando and find out what this is all about. And if that fails get Isabel to free me. Bed her if you have to, unless you have already done so."

"I have never…" Thomas stopped as he realised Jorge knew the truth and was only trying to anger him. "Lawrence is looking into the work Cortez did to see if there is anything there, or links to the dead man. He is also trying to trace your sister Beatriz. If he finds her I may go and talk to her."

"After you free me, then I can come with you. I would like to see Beatriz again."

"Yes, of course. After I free you."

CHAPTER TEN

By the time Thomas approached the palace in the early evening, there were new guards on the entrance and none tried to stop him this time. He had spent the day talking to Cortez's neighbours, who confirmed what they had told the Hermandos, confirmed the man brought before them had been the same man they saw the day Cortez died. Later he had tried finding any clues linked to the dead man who had tried to sell Jorge information about his mother, but that, too, had come to nothing. Now, inside the palace, he considered looking for Theresa, but suspected he knew where Isabel and Fernando might be.

He found both together on the covered terrace overlooking the gardens, where servants were bringing small platters of food. Isabel saw Thomas first and rose. It was clear she wanted to come to him, equally clear she could not. Instead she hovered in indecision. Fernando glanced up and offered a nod. Thomas wondered how much he knew.

Isabel raised a hand for one of the servants to approach. "Lay another place for our friend. You will join us, Sir Thomas?"

He was about to object to her use of his pointless title until he saw it was for the purpose of the servants, to explain why a man with too-long hair and Moorish dress should sit with the King and Queen of Spain.

"I need to talk with you," Thomas said to Fernando.

"Then talk. You know there are no secrets between us, are there, my sweet?"

Thomas tried to work out if there had been an emphasis at the end of Fernando's reply, or was it only in his own mind?

"Jorge has been arrested." Thomas heard a faint gasp from Isabel, which told him she had not known. "The warrant is in your name, Your Grace." Thomas maintained formality, unsure what kind of reception he would receive. He had not spoken with Fernando since the fall of Malaka, where he had watched as the man stole the bulk of the city's gold for his own use in the incessant war against the Moors. He had blamed the man in part for Lubna's death, but had softened his judgement since. As the pain of losing Lubna had softened within his own heart. Something he had once believed impossible. He continued to think of her every day, but now the memory brought a smile rather than tears. And it seemed he must have moved on, as Lubna would have wanted, when he recalled his and Eleanor's sweaty bodies of the night before.

"You are no doubt aware many warrants carry my name. Am I meant to know of every single one?"

"I don't know, Your Grace. What do you know of this specific warrant? Are you saying you know nothing of it?"

Fernando waved a dismissive hand just as a servant brought a chair. Another laid a place at the table for Thomas and poured dark wine into a finely wrought goblet.

"No, I admit I know of what you speak."

"You signed it?" said Isabel, staring hard at Fernando. "You signed a warrant for Jorge's arrest? What were you thinking? We know the man. We like him."

"Everyone likes Jorge," said Fernando with a dismissive wave of his hand. "Does that make him innocent of the crime he is accused of? I was told the evidence is sound and that a quick arrest will set the minds of the city at rest."

"The city barely knows what happened," Thomas said.

"The city knows three houses were burned to the ground. They know the owner of one, an upstanding citizen, is dead. And they know his killer—a man of distinctive appearance—was seen by several reliable witnesses. That is the evidence that was brought to me." Fernando turned from Thomas to his wife. "Was I meant to allow a killer to remain free to kill again? No, I did what was right."

"Jorge is no killer." Isabel continued to stare at her husband.

The food and wine remained ignored on the table until Fernando reached out and tore the leg from a plump capon.

"That is not what was told to me."

"Told by who?" Thomas asked.

"The Hermandos, of course. Do you think I issued a warrant to arrest a man on gossip?"

"We are talking about Jorge," Thomas said. "Do you truly believe him capable of murder? And why would he kill this scribe?"

"What scribe?"

"Gods, you don't even know who the dead man is, do you?"

"I have no need to know the detail, only what was brought to me. And yes, I believe Jorge could kill a man. I have ridden with him and seen him fight. We are all of us capable of murder, Thomas. You more than anyone. If you feel so strongly you should offer yourself up in his place."

"Would you even care if I did?"

"I would," said Isabel, and Fernando cast her a glance of annoyance.

"Let Jorge go," Thomas said.

"I am King of Aragon and Castile," said Fernando. "I will not be dictated to by some ... some heathen Moor."

"You know as well as I that Thomas is a man of England and a good Catholic. Is not our own daughter betrothed to the son of their King? You may not want to do as he asks, but you will do as I ask, husband."

Thomas was unaware the betrothal had been agreed, but it made sense. Two great powers joined by marriage. Treaties signed. Promises made. And Catherine, who he had helped into this world, not even five years of age. The whole thing made him nauseous.

"I will not allow him to be executed," said Fernando. "You have my promise on it. I like Jorge. He, too, is amenable. All he has to do is stay in prison for a month, two perhaps, until everyone forgets about this man. Then you will both leave this city and never trouble us again. Either of us."

Isabel started to speak, but Fernando stilled her with a look of pure hatred. "Leave us," he said, barking the words at her. "Thomas and I have private matters to discuss."

Isabel rose and walked fast from the courtyard, her shoulders hunched with anger.

"Why did you do that? Do you enjoy hurting your wife? Your Queen?" Thomas wanted to remind Fernando who the true ruler of Castile was.

"Are you aware you have become a joke? You are seen as Isabel's pet hound, her plaything, her supplicant. You are her tame Englishman. Oh, I know how you look at her, but I also know she too believes you to be a joke. We laugh about it often when I visit her room. Yes, I go to her still, for a wife needs to be serviced now and again even if her husband does have to look elsewhere for real pleasure."

"If that is true then you are an even bigger fool than I already thought."

"At least I managed to keep my wife alive." Fernando smiled when he saw Thomas's fists bunch. "And I service my mistress often and well." He leaned closer. "Isabel does her duty, but it is only duty. It is not enough for a man with red blood flowing through his veins. But you would not understand such things, Thomas Berrington." He came closer still. "Shall we fight, you and I? Shall we fight here as we have fought before, as I have defeated you every time we have played at killing each other? Do you know how much I would really like to kill you?"

Fernando turned aside and called out for swords to be brought.

"What is it you want from me?" Thomas asked.

"I want you to leave my wife alone. I want you to leave this place and never return. Promise me that and I will have your eunuch friend set free so you can pleasure each other again." He punched Thomas on the chest. "Leave this city. Leave this country. Leave my wife alone!"

A servant approached with the two blades asked for, but Fernando waved him away.

"It is not me who is betraying her," Thomas said. A calm had filled him, and he wondered if the prospect of fighting had brought it or his realisation of how much he hated the man standing in front of him.

Fernando punched Thomas again. "It is not betrayal. A man is expected to take mistresses, a king is expected to take whoever he wants, whenever he wants. Do you think she does not know? Of course she knows."

"Why did you order Jorge arrested?"

"Because it pleased me. Because I knew it would hurt you. Because I could. What do you say, Sir Thomas—will you leave my wife alone now?"

"In your care? What do you think?"

"So Jorge dies because of you?" Fernando snapped his fingers. "That is all it will take." He snapped them again, beneath Thomas's nose. "Less than that."

Thomas looked around, at the guards and servants. All of them studiously ignored the conversation between him and Fernando, but it would take only a nod for them to protect their master.

Fernando laughed and pushed at Thomas. He strode away across the courtyard, snapping his fingers with each step.

Thomas passed a man in the slow process of lighting lamps in a long corridor, the scent of his burning taper sharp in the air. Thomas had told Isabel she needed more guards stationed near her chambers but she had refused, saying it would feel like a prison, not a palace. Now he was glad of the laxity because he wanted to find her and talk. He had much to talk of, but his search became increasingly frantic with the urgency of matters weighing on his mind. Jorge sat in a prison cell at the mercy of a hundred men while a guilty man walked free, perhaps to kill again.

Thomas didn't understand why Fernando was acting as he did. The man had more or less admitted he had had Jorge arrested on little evidence as a bargaining tool against

Thomas. Had the warrant been nothing more than a convenient weapon to use against him? Thomas couldn't believe Fernando had played any part in the conspiracy against Jorge—he doubted he was bright enough to have come up with something as complex. But he had made it clear he wanted Thomas gone from the palace, gone from his Queen.

A flash of red hair ahead caused Thomas to break into a run, but it was the wrong red hair. Theresa turned to him, her face for a moment showing fear before changing to a smile.

"Are you running toward me, Thomas? My, it is a long time since a man was so keen as to run after me."

"I am looking for Isabel."

"She is with Cardinal de Borja and has given instructions they are not to be disturbed. But she did ask me to find you rooms in the palace."

Thomas frowned. If Fernando was playing the strong game, then so, it appeared, was Isabel if she wanted him closer. Thomas felt like a pawn stuck between King and Queen on a board he had no knowledge of.

"Jorge is in prison."

"I was not aware being handsome was a crime. Not yet, at least, but who knows? One of these days it may be. What is he accused of?"

"Murder."

Theresa stared at Thomas for a long time. "Jorge? Murder?"

"Yes, Jorge, murder."

She shook her head. "Any fool knows he is incapable of murder."

"Then the men who took him must be worse than fools, for taken he is, and Fernando signed the warrant. I should be tracking down the true culprit instead of standing here."

Theresa touched his shoulder. "It is late, Thomas, and you are tired. I understand why, now. Let me show you your rooms. Sleep, recover. Jorge is going nowhere and the morning will bring a freshness to your mind."

"All my things are in the tent." Even as he spoke the words, Thomas recognised them as a weak excuse. He wanted to be close to Isabel, if only to offer what little protection he could. Whatever he might discover in the city, it was here, in the palace, that decisions were made on whether men lived or died. Theresa was offering him the opportunity to be among all of that, and he would be a fool to refuse.

"You can fetch your things tomorrow. Is there anything you must have tonight?"

Thomas thought of what little lay in the tent and shook his head. There was his leather satchel of physician's instruments, and a small bag of gold coin hidden in a hole dug beneath one of the blankets. He would be glad not to have that hole beneath his hip all night long. Theresa was right, he was tired. Beyond tired. His head ached and he should have eaten the food offered him on the terrace.

Theresa touched his face. "Come, Thomas, let me show you to your rooms. I can see how exhausted you are. Come."

He shook her touch away. "I have to help Jorge."

"And you will. In the morning once you have rested. I will tell Isabel you have accepted her generosity and see if she can find time to talk with you tonight, but it is late so it may be tomorrow."

"Jorge," Thomas said again, then allowed Theresa to take his hand in hers and lead him away like a child. They followed wood-panelled corridors scented from the beeswax used to polish them. Passed rich tapestries which would never have been allowed in the palace that sat on Al-Hamra. As they passed windows, Thomas glanced out at a city bathed in the last of an evening light that masked the corruption beneath. The bulk of the cathedral—in reality little changed from the original Islamic mosque—sat square between four streets. People strolled in search of some pleasure, private or public. The chitter of swallows honeyed the air and a warm breeze drifted in, smelling of the river and dry grasses.

"We are here," said Theresa, stopping outside a solid carved door. "Isabel says you must stay as long as you want. You know it is her wish that you stay forever. It is mine, too."

Isabel had been offering him a place at her court, at her side, long enough. Thomas had always turned her down, but as time passed he wondered if he had been wrong to do so. He wondered, if he had accepted her offer sooner, would his life have been simpler, and would the woman he had married still be alive? It was impossible to know, and Thomas had finally accepted a truth Lubna would have wanted him to accept. It was time to move on. Not to forget, for he could never forget her, but to allow his life to stutter into motion once again.

"You can go in," said Theresa. "There is nobody inside waiting to attack you."

"Are you sure?"

"I am certain, for am I not out here with you?" She laid a hand over his. "Rest, Thomas. Sleep. If Isabel asks for you, I will come and fetch you."

"Yes," Thomas said.

"Yes what?"

"Yes, I may try to sleep, but come for me if Isabel calls."

"I will." Theresa hesitated, then, as if there was some new complicity between them, she lifted herself on tiptoe and kissed the corner of his mouth before turning away.

Thomas watched her go, filled with tumbling emotions and urges, then opened the door and entered a fine outer chamber furnished with dark wood chairs and a table. A wide window looked across the river and the clatter of the still-turning waterwheels drifted in. He heard a child laugh and wondered if it was one of Isabel's. Juan perhaps, though it had sounded more like a girl, so perhaps Juanna, or even Catherine.

He explored to discover a bedroom with a wide bed, a canopy supported on sturdy posts. Another door led to a private privy large enough to accommodate a table with a marble sink and a metal bath set in the centre of the room, but he ignored everything but the bed. He undressed and pulled the covers over himself. He stared at the patterned underside of the canopy, knowing he would be unable to sleep. Too many thoughts raced each other through his head.

The next thing he knew, a hand was shaking him and he opened his eyes to find Theresa leaning over him, the sight and scent of her raising a sharp arousal in him.

"Isabel is waiting for you next door," she said.

"She what…?" Thomas sat up, only remembering his nakedness when he was half out of bed. He pulled the covers back to cover both his nakedness and arousal.

Theresa laughed. "Too late, Thomas. I saw everything, and am pleased to see the effect I can still have on a handsome man."

"A dream, that is all. Can I get dressed in private, or do you want to watch that as well? Is Isabel really next door?"

Theresa nodded, a smile on her lips. "I will leave you in peace to dress. For now."

As he pulled on clothes that needed washing, Thomas tried to gather his thoughts so he was prepared when he saw Isabel. How much could he tell her? he wondered.

CHAPTER ELEVEN

Thomas entered the main room unsure of what manner of welcome he would receive. A small table was laid with food, and glasses awaited the pouring of wine. Theresa moved to leave the room, but Isabel raised a hand.

"Stay. It would not be seemly for me to be alone with Thomas."

"You may wish to talk privately, Your Grace."

"I have no secrets from you. Go and lie on his bed if you want, but stay close." Isabel looked around before choosing a plain chair with no ornamentation, no doubt taken deliberately. Isabel seldom did anything without a purpose. Thomas pulled out the closest chair and sat at the table, waiting.

When Isabel said nothing, sitting silent with hands in her lap, he said, "You said you wanted to speak with me."

"I did." She looked up at him. "Tell me, what did you and Fernando talk of after I left?"

"Very little, Your Grace." Thomas knew he could not tell her of her husband's threats, nor his feelings toward her.

"Call me by my name, Thomas, as you know you

should." She gave a small laugh and looked around. "You will have to use my name if we are here in your own rooms in the palace. These are yours for as long as you wish. Word will spread among the servants, no doubt, but I care not. Let my husband hear them and worry what we might be doing."

A flush caught at her cheeks, and Thomas did not believe he fully understood her anymore. There was a brittleness to her he had not seen before. Was the relationship between her and Fernando as bad as it appeared to be? If so, what was the reason for it? Thomas knew Fernando had always taken mistresses, knew Isabel must be aware of his infidelity, but a king and queen were considered above the rules of their subjects. At least that would be Fernando's take on the matter. What about Isabel? But there were more pressing matters he needed to talk about first.

"Do you know why Fernando signed the order for Jorge's arrest?"

"I did not even know he had done so until you came to us, let alone what his reasons could be. I would have Jorge released, but cannot go against my husband. It is not my place. Fernando could free him if he wished, but it appears he does not want to. I have sent word he is to be watched. Protected."

Thomas opened his mouth to say something about the way Fernando had reacted to him after she'd left, then closed it again.

"What were you about to say, Thomas?" Isabel leaned closer, reached for his hand and he allowed her to take it. He glanced at the open doorway to the bedroom, but Theresa was not visible. "I know you fear for Jorge, but trust me when I say he will come to no harm. Did Fernando explain why he acted as he did in signing the warrant?"

"He claims there is evidence, but if there is, it is made up."

"Was Jorge with you at the time?"

Thomas glanced away, felt Isabel's fingers tighten around his.

"I see," she said. "But you believe his innocence, as do I."

"He cannot have done what he is accused of, but..." Thomas sighed hard. "There is something I do not understand, and I need to uncover it." He glanced at the window, still mirror-black with the night beyond, and knew nothing could be accomplished until morning.

"It fills your thoughts, does it not?" said Isabel. "Concern for your friend?"

Thomas nodded. "Above all else."

"As it should. It is what defines a man, what defines a woman, their concern for those they love. It is why I continue to offer you a place at my side, Thomas." Isabel smiled. "See, I even honour your wish by not using the honorific you so hate, *Sir* Thomas."

He scowled.

"I will pray for him," said Isabel, "and pray for you too. Perhaps we should both pray in the chapel. I could ask Cardinal de Borja to join us. A man who might be Pope should have the ear of God, should he not?"

"Theresa said you were with him earlier. Who is he?"

Isabel laughed, melting some of his tension. "You do not know? Oh, Thomas, how can you know so much yet be ignorant of so many important matters in the world?" She smiled. "He knows of you, though. We talked about you and I think he wants to see you in private. Rodrigo is assisting me in the matter of the mariner Columb and his plea for funding." Isabel released her hold on his hand, as if talking of this Cardinal had reminded her of the forbidden nature of their touch.

Thomas heard Theresa moving around on the bed, the rustle of her clothing, and wondered what she was doing.

Isabel nodded, her mouth firming into a line. "Columb has let it be known both France and England will fund him if Castile does not." Isabel jabbed at the tabletop with a finger. "I will not allow that to happen. I will find the money for his venture as soon as this war is ended."

"Whenever that might be."

"You know it will be soon. If Fernando would only do what I tell him, it could end this year."

Thomas wondered if it was the war that they argued over, but thought it not the only matter.

"The year is over half gone," he said.

"It could still end this year. You do not need to know how, but I am sure of it. I take it you saw the town we are building when you travelled from Granada?"

Thomas nodded.

"I have named it Santa Fe. It will be where we launch our attack from when the time comes."

"Then definitely not this year," Thomas said. "It looked little more than a few huts, and those barely standing."

"It will get better, and bigger, fast," said Isabel. She settled in her chair. "Now, I ask you again, what was your conversation with Fernando about?"

Thomas examined her face for some sign of anger, but saw none.

"It was a conversation between men."

"Ah. His mistress, then."

"What was said must remain confidential."

"So it was about his mistress, was it? Castellana Lonzal." She gave a short laugh. "He thinks I do not know, but how can I not when she has a house in this city? A house he visits often. She is there now, right under my nose." Isabel tilted her head to one side. "Does he do it to humiliate me, do you think?" She raised a hand. "No, do not answer, for I know what you will say. You do not understand why a man could do such a thing, do you?"

Isabel waited, watching Thomas, but he said nothing because he had nothing to say. He also knew words were not what she needed, even if her words had provided information he had not possessed until that moment. It was a name he had heard before, but only part of it. Señora Lonzal, spoken by the servant when Thomas saw Eleanor. He didn't know if it was a common name, but it was too much of a coincidence not to be the same woman. A shiver ran through him that he tried to hide. Fernando's lover owned the house where Eleanor was staying. Had he and this Castellana Lonzal made love in the same bed as he and Eleanor had? The thought sent more than a shiver through him.

Isabel lifted a hand to tuck a loose strand of hair behind her ear. She was dressed casually for a queen, in a dress no more showy than the one Theresa wore.

"It does not matter, Thomas, for I know what you would do. I know you would never betray your wife. Know you never did. But you are not celibate, are you?"

Thomas again kept his own counsel. How could he not? This was not the Isabel he had come to know over many years, not the woman he had grown to love. This was a woman on the edge of anger, a woman scorned, a woman shamed. Except Thomas didn't know if such was true. He vowed to ask Theresa how many others knew of Fernando's infidelities.

Isabel reached for her glass of wine and drained it.

Another first for Thomas to witness. He stood and refilled the glass and she smiled, touched his wrist with two fingers, then withdrew them.

"No matter," she said, as Thomas retook his seat, though both her manner and the steel in her voice told him it did matter. "Now tell me what you intend to do to free Jorge."

It took half an hour, and all the while he spoke, Isabel's eyes tracked his face as if seeking something, though what it might be he had no idea. Or feared to imagine what it might be.

When Isabel eventually rose to indicate the end of their conversation, she offered her hand. Thomas raised it and set his lips against the back, holding them a moment longer than he should, but there came no pulling away, only the faintest of smiles from her.

At the door, Isabel hesitated, turned back. "Ask Theresa to explain the ways of the world to you, Thomas, for you are far too innocent."

Thomas had no idea what she meant, but when he entered his bedroom, he found Theresa stretched on top of the covers. He was pleased to see she was fully dressed, afraid of what he might have done if she had not been. She had chosen the side Thomas didn't sleep on, and he wondered if she knew that, or was it no more than coincidence?

"Isabel hurts," Thomas said as he lay on his side of the bed. "I wish I could heal her, but I can't."

"She does. She has much to be hurt about, but Fernando is only a small part of it. She needs friends around her now, so more than likely you help her." Theresa smoothed the covers of the bed between them. "This is a fine bed. Most comfortable. Even for two people. I like that you can lie beside me even if we are both fully clothed." She smoothed the covers again, this time her fingers tracing his side. "Though that could be remedied soon enough."

"And if the servants discover us when they come to clear the table?" He was aware it was not a rejection of her offer, for offer it was, and he wondered what was happening to him. Eleanor two nights before. Theresa tonight…?

"You could close the door. I believe it even has a lock." She laughed suddenly at the expression on his face. "Oh, come, Thomas, I promise to behave myself if you will. I want to talk to you before you go to sleep, and this is a good place to do it. If the servants come and we are out there, they will talk just the same. Go and close the door." She clasped her hands over her chest and laughed. "Is it better if I do this, so I cannot touch you?"

Thomas shook his head. He was tired and confused and unsure what Theresa wanted. Feared what he wanted. His uncertainty came from this woman who attracted him, who had always attracted him. A woman he had once almost submitted to, would have submitted to had Mandana not burst in on them and knocked Thomas out cold.

He sighed and rose, closed the door. Theresa was right, the bed was extraordinarily comfortable. Thomas had not been aware such comfort could exist in the world.

"Does Isabel sleep in a bed like this?" he asked.

"I am sure you would like to know, wouldn't you?"

"I am happy where I am for the moment. The powerful are dangerous companions."

"They make better friends than enemies."

Thomas stared at the ornate drapes above their heads, then said, "When did your husband die?"

"He has been in his grave these last two years. He was a pig. A boar. A fool. I had nothing to do with him for years and am all the better for being free once more." Thomas felt the bed move as Theresa rolled on to her side. She propped her head on one hand and stared at him. "Now tell me—did Fernando really tell you about his mistress?"

"He did, though until Isabel spoke it, I didn't know her name." Thomas felt no need to hide the secret from Theresa. No doubt she knew about it already. Despite her familiarity with everyone in the household, she remained a servant, and servants talked among themselves.

"Castellana Lonzal." Theresa rolled the words around in her mouth like a tasty morsel. "She is attractive, I admit, though older than most women Fernando takes to his bed. Which means she must be exceedingly wicked and willing. She has been a conquest of his for longer than most, so he must have some feelings for her. That or she has a hold over him of some kind."

"Does he take many mistresses?"

"Oh yes. Many, many mistresses. Though mistress is not the right word for most, who are nothing to him. A single night or less. Two, perhaps. Young women seeking favour or attracted to power. You know how power attracts, don't you, Thomas?"

"How would I?"

Theresa sighed. "You are not going to let me seduce you, are you? You know you have power over me if you wish it."

Thomas rolled his head so he could see her and Theresa gave a smile so coquettish he almost laughed. An attractive woman who looked younger than her years. A woman who, if he asked, would submit willingly to him. All he had to do was give a sign. Even as he was drawn to her, an image of Eleanor, so recently naked beside him, filled his mind and he knew what his answer would be tonight, and all the nights to come.

"I am tired and have much to think about."

"That is a no then, is it?" There was no rancour in her voice, more amusement than anything.

"It is for tonight." Wondering why he had to qualify his answer.

"You should accept Isabel's offer of a place in her court. She could do with someone close who talks sense. You are Sir Thomas now, a man of rank. An important man." She smiled, laid her hand against his chest. "A man of power. People know who you are. And we can always find you some clothes that match your rank instead of these desert robes you insist on wearing."

"I wear them because they are comfortable."

"Exactly." Theresa rolled away and rose to her feet. She smoothed her dress over her hips. "Do not think too long or hard on these matters that concern you. You need to sleep. You are starting to look unwell."

CHAPTER TWELVE

As soon as Thomas had visited Jorge, he made his way to Lawrence's house. He would have gone there first, but didn't want to rouse the man from his bed two mornings running. Jorge had looked as if he hadn't slept at all, though fortunately he claimed to be unmolested so far. Perhaps Isabel had made good on her promise and sent word he was to be protected.

Lawrence was in his office, a large room set against the even larger building attached to the rear of the house where his indexes were stored. Thomas loved words, but wondered how it must feel to be Lawrence whose life consisted of nothing but words. Did their presence whisper in his mind at every hour of the day and night, or was the man truly as calm as he appeared to be?

Lawrence looked up as Thomas entered, a smile on his face as if he had been expecting him, which he probably had.

"I have found a few things out, one in particular you will want to know, the others not so much." He tapped a small stack of papers, no more than six sheets.

Thomas pulled up a stool and sat. "Can I?" He reached for the papers and Lawrence nodded.

"I have other information to follow up on, too, but need to go out to confirm it. I have to look at the actual documents to be sure."

Thomas leafed through the sheets, but they meant little to him. Brief notes only, not the content of the documents themselves. A contract of sale for the house Cortez had bought five years before. Another note, freshly made, recording a new claim for compensation from the city for the burning down of the house and its neighbours. A third document concerned a marriage, one of the names familiar from his conversation with both Isabel and Theresa the night before, though both events now felt more like a dream than reality.

"This name," he said, tapping the paper, "Castellana Lonzal—why is she here? Both Isabel and Theresa mentioned her last night."

"Are you aware she is Fernando's mistress?"

"I am now. How many others know?"

"It is hardly news." Lawrence put down his pen and raised his eyes to meet Thomas's. He twisted in the chair, and Thomas wondered how long he had been working, and whether he had foregone his usual morning routine to offer help. If so, Thomas was grateful. "Does the Queen know about her?"

"Isabel told me the name last night, and then when she had gone, Theresa confirmed it."

"Last night? How late last night?" Lawrence made a crude gesture which involved cupping his hands over his chest and lifting an imaginary weight. "Theresa is one of Isabel's closest confidantes, so if she knows, then the Queen knows. You are a fortunate man, Thomas. Two beautiful women who want you. One for your mind, the other your body."

"Is she truly Isabel's confidante? She always seems to know everything, but she is of low birth, and the Queen has many other women of position around her."

"It is why Isabel trusts her. Noble women seek advancement or favour. A queen can never trust their words. Theresa wants nothing more than to serve. Have you bedded her yet?"

"It is none of your business."

Lawrence laughed. "So you have! Was she as good as she looks like she would be? Sometimes it is not the most handsome women who are the best between the sheets. I like the merely pretty like my Laurita."

"No, I have not bedded her. You are a pig, do you know that?"

"Of course, but I revel in my station in life and accept all my failings."

"Embrace them, more like," Thomas said, and Lawrence lifted a shoulder as if to indicate he was only doing what most men would if allowed. "Theresa and I talk, that is all."

"Then you are a fool. Ask Jorge. How is he doing, by the way?"

"Isabel has made it clear he is not to be harmed, and so far he is untouched other than what the Hermandos did to him. How long it will last I don't know. Men are locked in that prison because they refuse to accept any commands, let alone the command of a woman."

"Except Isabel is loved by all, both high and low equally. And her judgement is said to be harsher than that of her husband. Jorge will be safe, for a time at least." Lawrence reached out and took the single sheet of paper from Thomas. "You say you saw this woman in the palace?"

"I believe so. Isabel has several such around her."

"Like bees to honey," said Lawrence.

Thomas opened his mouth to tell Lawrence he had also been to her house, where he'd met the girl he had once loved, now a grown woman, then closed it. For some reason he didn't want to disclose anything about Eleanor, unsure how he felt about the situation. The hours he had spent in her bed had brought back memories, but the longer he was away from her, the more reason told him what they had done was wrong. If only he could explain to himself why, he would be happier.

"And men?" asked Lawrence. "Have you seen men in the palace as well? A tall, good-looking man? Probably dressed as a bishop or some such?"

Thomas searched his memory and nodded. "I think so. He was talking with Isabel and these women the day before Cortez was killed."

"Rodrigo de Borja," said Lawrence. "He visits Spain occasionally. Visits now because he wants something. The man was born in Valencia but lives in Roma, of course. He is a Cardinal. Rumour has it he could well be the next Pope."

"Isabel was with him last night, before she came to me." Thomas ignored Lawrence's knowing smile. "The next Pope? Isabel also said that. Is the current one ill?"

"Not as far as I know, but Popes have a habit of getting sick mysteriously fast and dying even faster. De Borja is a clever man. He is a Spaniard, so of course he is." Lawrence gave a smile to indicate the joke he was making. That the two of them knew only Englishmen were clever. "I am not surprised he was there with the women. He is a ladies' man. Even more so than Jorge, I hear."

"Jorge is faithful to Belia these days, despite what he

pretends. And if this de Borja is to be Pope, isn't his being a ladies' man an obstacle to such?"

Lawrence laughed. "Oh, I love your innocence, Thomas. I should try to sell you the Roman bridge so you can set a toll on its crossing. You will make your fortune, I promise."

"What does any of this have to do with that piece of paper?"

"I don't know, not yet, but something is nagging at me. Some memory I cannot quite place, but I will. I know I will." Lawrence stood, gathering the papers to himself, snatching the others from Thomas's hand. "I go now to seek out more." He came around the desk, stopped. "Oh, and this last one will interest you. It tells of the marriage of Jorge's sister, the name of her husband, and where she lives these days." He handed the sheet of paper across. "You can keep that, it is a copy. All the details you need are there."

"She lives in Cadiz," Thomas said. "Where is Cadiz, exactly?"

"You don't know?" said Daniel. "I thought you knew everything."

"Not this. I know the name, but not the location. Is it far?"

"It stands a little east of where the Guadalquivir empties into the western ocean. It is an important location for commerce."

"West of the narrows?" Thomas asked.

"Of course, and from what I hear tell, the wind never stops blowing. Does your piece of paper say exactly where she lives?"

"It does not, but it says she owns a trading business."

"A woman?"

"She married a mariner—I think you told me that. Something to do with the sea, Lawrence says. Did you say he was older than her?"

"That is my memory. I never knew his name, though. Does any of this paperwork state it?"

"Magellani, according to the marriage document. Bartholomew de Magellani. Does it mean anything to you?"

"Nothing at all, though it sounds as if he is not of Spain. Italia, perhaps? There are many mariners in Italia, that crazy friend of yours for one."

"Lawrence found a certificate of death, too. He died shortly after they went to Cadiz, inside two years. It seems Beatriz took over management of the business. Apparently she is good at it."

Daniel smiled. "That sounds like Beatriz. I wonder if Adana does not take after her a little. They are both strong willed. I expect it is why she is still a spinster and not married yet."

"I am waiting for the right person," said Adana, who had been sitting at the table beside her mother the entire time, listening to the conversation. "Are you going to see her, Uncle Thomas?"

He had given up trying to stop her using the term uncle, amused she did it as frequently with him as she did Jorge, who was in fact her uncle. Or perhaps not. Talking with Beatriz might help confirm that.

He looked at Daniel. "How far is it?"

"I have sent weapons there on occasion. Six days by cart, quicker for a man on a horse. Even quicker if you take a galley from Sevilla to Sanlúcar."

"Ten days there and back," Thomas said. "It's too long a time to leave Jorge languishing in a cell."

"Not if it means you can free him," said Zanita. "If you do not go he may be locked away for months."

"Beatriz might know of Jorge's origins, but who is to say that information will lead to his freedom? I am better off spending my time here tracking down the real culprits."

"Miguel and Lawrence are doing that for you, are they not?" said Zanita. "It does not have to be you all the time."

He knew she was right, but it didn't sit well with him. He also knew that the man who had approached Jorge to sell him information about his mother might be important. If his information had been genuine, and not simply a ruse to steal money, then it was possible Beatriz would know who Jorge's real mother was. That information felt important. But ten days was too long.

"If you go, Uncle Thomas, can I come with you? I would like to meet my aunt." Adana looked at her mother, ignoring her father, no doubt expecting a flat refusal.

"I am not going. I have told you why, but I will send a message through Lawrence. Beatriz might know something to help Jorge."

He was a dozen paces from the house when Zanita called him to a halt. She came close, her face serious. Thomas saw there were lines he hadn't seen before, but she continued to be a handsome woman.

"I thank you for your decision. Adana is looking for something she cannot find here in Córdoba. She seeks excitement, and it is unseemly in a young woman."

"To be honest, I did consider going. I even considered taking Adana. Perhaps it would do her good. You can't wrap her in linen cloth her entire life."

"I know, but it is hard, and we fight more than we used to. She is bored, and I understand why. She cares for the children, but she has twenty years now. She should be married with children of her own. I fear she will do something stupid one day. Lie with a man and get with child. She is strong willed and getting more so."

"Perhaps when this is all over, Jorge and I can accompany Adana to Cadiz to see her aunt. Jorge would like to see Beatriz, I am sure."

"And Adana would be safe with you if you decide to go."

Safe. Now he was safe. He remembered the time when no woman was safe from him. Old, young, married, single. He had been wild. Now he was old, and safe. He couldn't decide which was the worse.

"What does Daniel say?"

"Daniel will agree with me, because I am her mother and am meant to love her, to protect her the more. And if I say she can go with you, he will trust my word."

Thomas let his breath out. "Nothing is decided. Jorge's name has to be cleared first. Tell Adana she will not be going anywhere soon." He wondered how Adana would take the news. She had opinions, and was never afraid to air them. Just like Jorge.

"Beatriz is in Cadiz," Thomas said. "I sent a message with a list of questions. With luck we might get an answer in a day or two." He sat beside Jorge on the narrow cot in his cell. It was a dour place and stank from some nearby cesspit. "I thought of going there, but dismissed the idea. I think I upset Adana."

"Why?"

"Because she wanted to go with me to see her aunt."

"No, why did you dismiss the idea? If Beatriz knows something that might help, you should talk with her."

"I told you I sent a message through Lawrence. Though how long it will take to get there, and how long to receive an answer, I have no idea. Less time than the journey, in any case. I would like to know how you came to be an Olmos, and she is the most likely to know. It occurred to me the man who approached you might really have known who your mother was. What if he died to protect that secret?"

Jorge stared into space, and for a moment Thomas thought his incarceration had addled his wits. Then he turned to meet Thomas's gaze, his own sharp and bright.

"Do you think it important, who my mother is? Surely it can't be connected to what is happening now, can it?"

"I don't know what is important and what is not until I know it. The message to Beatriz will have to do for now." Thomas waited a moment, then said, "Adana wanted to come with me."

Jorge frowned. "Why?"

"Zanita tells me she is bored. She seeks excitement."

"Not that she is likely to find it with you."

"Not that I would ever offer it. Her coming would have made the journey longer and harder, which is another reason a message is better. I did tell Zanita once you are proven innocent, perhaps we can go together to see Beatriz. We could take Adana with us."

"I would like that. So would she. All I have seen her do since we came here is look after the little ones and help her mother. I remember her as a girl of spirit. She had to be, to escape from Mandana alongside you." Jorge looked down at his hands. "Who knows, she might even find herself a husband. Someone important. Someone rich."

"Her father is rich," Thomas said.

"And he is her father. Adana needs a man of her own, a household of her own." Jorge frowned. "I notice she didn't even try to tease you anymore. She never stopped when we were here the last time."

"She was younger then."

"All the more reason to tease you now, but I expect she realises you are too old for her. No doubt it is why she doesn't bother anymore. I have a fondness for Adana, perhaps because of her spirit." Jorge pushed at Thomas. "Now, go and find the evidence to prove who is behind this plot. I want to get out of this hell-hole. I am afraid, Thomas, afraid for my life."

CHAPTER THIRTEEN

Thomas returned to Daniel's works to question him again about any memory he had of Jorge coming to their family, but there was nothing new and Thomas left the house with a sense of despair. He was acutely aware of the passage of time, aware that whatever trail there might be was rapidly going cold. He was no further forward and Jorge remained the only suspect.

Standing on the old bridge with a strong south wind rippling the surface of the river, he knew he had to return to the house where Eleanor was staying. He needed to ask questions about her friend, Castellana Lonzal. Was it coincidence Fernando had mentioned her to him, or did the woman have some connection to what was happening? Even the presence of Eleanor made Thomas suspicious now, and he was not sure he wanted to see her again. He trusted no-one and nothing other than himself and Lawrence. Miguel too, perhaps, though what use a constable of the Hermandos fresh to the city could be was doubtful.

He slapped his own face, to the surprise of a passing

woman, and walked toward the city fast before he could change his mind.

"The Countess has gone," said the same servant, his pleasure at being able to tell the news clear on his sour face.

"When?"

"This morning, early, in the company of Señora Lonzal."

"Where?"

"That is none of your business."

"What about Yves?"

"Gone too."

"When will they be back?"

"Even if I knew, do you think I would tell you?"

Thomas wanted to punch the man. Instead he turned away and worked his way through crowds that thinned as he approached the city wall. He called at the Hermandos' office, but Miguel had not been seen that day, so he went on to where Cortez had died. What remained of the three houses had collapsed into the extended cellar Cortez had built beneath them, but the baker remained open and appeared to be doing a good trade. Thomas waited until there were no more customers, then entered.

The woman he and Miguel had spoken with glanced up and smiled. She held a quarter loaf out to him.

"Good bread."

Thomas fumbled for a coin and bought the bread with no intention of eating it.

"Have you recalled anything else about what you saw?"

She gave an impression of thinking about her answer, but Thomas knew it was nothing but pretence.

"No more than I told you."

"You didn't see any other men?"

She shook her head. "I saw only the man I told you of. If

you find him, send him back, I would like to look on his face again."

Thomas held another coin out, letting her see the soft lustre of gold.

"Are you sure you saw no-one?"

The woman stared at the coin. "I will say I did if you want me to."

"What I want is the truth."

"Then no, it is as I told you. The handsome man, that is all I saw that day."

Something in the way she said it sparked a thought in Thomas. "That day? Did you see anyone the day before, or the day after? Or any of the days since?"

The woman indicated the street with her hand. "As you can see, there are always people passing one way or another."

"But you know most of them, don't you?"

"Most. It is why that man stood out." She glanced at Thomas's closed fist where the gold coin nestled. He opened it so she could see it.

"You saw someone else, didn't you?"

"Two men, neither young nor old. Well dressed, clearly from money."

"When?"

"Two days after the fire."

"What were they doing?"

"Nothing. They stood on the street where Alonso's house had been and stared at the ruins."

"Two days after the fire?" Thomas felt disappointment. He wondered how many people had come to look at the ruined houses. Scores, no doubt.

He put the gold coin on the counter, from where it disappeared without the woman seeming to move.

"And they were here the day before the fire, too, with four other men."

Thomas stared at her. She smiled in an attempt to appear coquettish.

"Only now you say this?"

"Strangers pass by on this road all the time. Am I meant to wonder what each of them is doing here?"

"Can you describe these two men, or the other four you say were with them?"

"I thought I already had. Neither young nor old, and well dressed."

"How tall? Taller than me?"

She looked Thomas up and down, raised her shoulder. "A little shorter, I would say. One of them anyway. The other was shorter still by a few inches. And the four others were shorter again. Skinny. I tried to sell them a pie but they refused. I heard them talking and it was not the language of Castile they used."

"French?" Thomas asked, thinking of Eleanor, thinking of his son, Yves. A man not young nor old.

"Not from there, I would recognise it, but similar in some way. Italia, perhaps, I could not say for sure. Though later when all six were together, at least two of them spoke Castilian."

"You saw and heard a lot, my thanks."

"Some days the whole world passes my doorway."

"Do you know the name Daniel Olmos?" Thomas asked.

"The sword-smith? Everyone in Córdoba knows that name."

Thomas placed a second small coin directly into the woman's hand, surprised at the softness of her skin. "If anything else comes back to you, send a message to him, addressed to me."

"I would if I knew your name." She closed her fist around the coin.

"Thomas Berrington."

The woman laughed. "So you are the Queen's lover?" She looked him up and down and shook her head. "It is a strange world we live in, indeed it is."

"Does the entire city believe I am bedding Isabel?" Thomas asked as he entered the courtyard of Lawrence's house. For once Laurita was with him, and it was she who answered.

"Of course they do. The truth is difficult to hide in this city."

Her voice was soft, sultry, and when she smiled she was transformed from ordinary into something almost exquisite, and he saw why she and Lawrence had stayed together all these years.

"Are you any further forward?" Thomas asked Lawrence, who shook his head.

"I go to search again later, but have nothing you don't already know. Try me again this evening."

"Did you send the message to Beatriz?"

"Of course, already it wings its way south. At least I hope it does. Sometimes birds are brought down and eaten. Not much meat on them, particularly these birds, but it happens. If there is no response in another three days, I will send the message again."

Thomas set the quarter loaf on the table between them. "A gift."

"I can think of better gifts," said Lawrence, "but our thanks anyway."

Laurita gave the bread a squeeze and nodded. "Fresh. We can eat it tonight before it goes stale."

"I have another two names for you to add to your search. Castellana Lonzal and Eleanor, Countess d'Arreau."

"I know Castellana Lonzal," said Lawrence. "She has a fine house here in the city and extensive holdings in El Carpio. The other name means nothing to me. It sounds French. Who is she?"

"She was once my lover, a long time ago."

Lawrence laughed. "You have a past?"

"Don't we all?"

"But you, Thomas? Is she handsome? Do you wish to find her again, is that why you ask me?"

"I have found her again. I—" Thomas broke off. To tell Lawrence or not? He thought not, which is why he surprised himself when he said, "I spent two hours in her bed the night before Jorge was arrested."

Lawrence punched him on the shoulder. "By all the gods, you are a source of constant surprise to me. There will be nothing in the records about her if she is French, though. Why do you want me to look?"

"That I do not know."

"Are you going to see her again?"

"That I also do not know."

Events were in Lawrence's hands now, so Thomas could think of nothing else to do but return to the prison to sit for a while with Jorge and try to calm his fears. Both Jorge's fears and his own. But when he heard the cell door lock behind him, his fear only increased. He could only imagine how Jorge must feel under the constant pressure of incarceration.

"Adana came to see me," said Jorge.

"Here? Was that wise?"

"When have you known Adana take the wise course of action?"

"What did she want? I expect she still blames me for not taking her to see her aunt."

"She does, but she will forgive you. She needs more to her life than living at home with her parents." Jorge reached out and patted Thomas's leg. "Now, when are you getting me out of here? Do you know any more than you did?"

"A little, but I'm not sure if it helps or not. I went back to Cortez's house and asked questions. The baker woman says again it was you she saw."

"They took me and made me stand in front of her and she said I was the man. I admitted I bought pastries from her, but that does not make me a murderer. I said they should arrest her for being a poor baker, but I don't think they found it amusing."

"She also says she saw two men the day before the fire, and saw them again a few days afterward. The first time they were in the company of four others. Short men, of Italia I think."

"Like the man who approached me? I knew he talked strangely. It makes sense now."

"Was he short?"

"You saw him, you tell me."

Thomas thought of the corpse in Daniel's tumbled-down house and nodded. "Yes, he was short. Do you think him involved in some way?"

"It was he who told me to visit Cortez. What if it was nothing more than a ploy to have me there moments before he was killed?"

"You said you hammered on the door and got no answer, so Cortez must not have been there."

"Or was already lying dead in the cellar."

Thomas stared at the wall beyond Jorge. Men had carved their initials into the soft stone. Someone had carved an erect penis and a pair of breasts. Perhaps even the same man. Thomas didn't want to think of what else he might have done in this small room.

"You went there early, you said?"

"Shortly after dawn. I left the silver for that man, expecting him to be at Daniel's old house. When he didn't turn up, I went to Cortez's house because he'd told me Cortez had information I would be interested in."

Thomas thought it through. "Cortez was already dead," he said. "Someone went there in the night and killed him, then set a candle burning. I have seen it done before. A trail of oil, or powder, and something gathered around it to start a fire. When the candle burns down, whoever set it is long gone. The cellar was full of wooden shelves and paper, no wonder it burned so fiercely. Except..."

Jorge stared at him, waiting as Thomas put the pieces together in his mind.

"Except Cortez wasn't dead. Badly injured, perhaps unconscious, but he must have woken to discover the world ablaze around him. He crawled into the corner where we found his body. He was looking for an escape, but there was none."

"It is a horrible way to die," said Jorge.

"All ways to die are horrible, but you are right, some are worse than others. I wonder if he was aware enough to choose the papers that were beneath him on purpose or not."

"Has Lawrence found anything out about them?"

"A little, and he is searching for more. I asked him to add two other names to his list. One is Fernando's mistress, and the other is mine."

"You don't have a mistress, Thomas. One night of passion does not make your lovely Eleanor your mistress. She is a Countess now, remember. Though you are also loved by the Queen of Castile, so who knows what strangeness there exists in the world? Why did you ask Lawrence to look into them?"

"Because Fernando threatened me and mentioned this Castellana Lonzal in the same breath. I am curious if the two events are connected. Whether this woman is connected to why you were arrested."

"You have a twisted mind, do you know that?"

"I thought that was a good thing in this endeavour."

"Likely so. I haven't been idling away my hours here either. We are let out once a day at noon to walk the walled courtyard. They call it a courtyard, but it sits next to the cesspits and the floor is half mud." Jorge waved a hand. "But that isn't important. What is important is I have been talking to some of the other prisoners."

"Is that wise?"

"I thought so. Who better to ask about a man who offers information in exchange for money and then has no intention of providing it? Who better to ask who might want to kill Cortez?"

Thomas stared at Jorge. "What answer did you get?"

"None as yet, but it has only been a day. I will hear something soon, I am sure."

"Or someone will slip a stiletto into your back."

"I am not without resources." Jorge leaned across and patted Thomas's leg.

CHAPTER FOURTEEN

As the day slipped into evening, Thomas crossed the Roman bridge. A fierce heat continued to blanket the city in a fetid somnolence. Miguel was not at the main Hermandos building so Thomas tried the old offices, but he had not returned there either and nobody knew where he might be.

As he made his way toward Lawrence's house to see if he had discovered any new information, Thomas wondered how Miguel managed to keep his job. He found both men sitting at Lawrence's table beneath the orange tree, papers spread in front of them. They greeted Thomas and Lawrence called for another chair, which Laurita brought. Thomas watched her return to the house, wondering if she ever made her own choices, or if she even wanted to. He believed he knew the answer.

Thomas sat in the third chair and leaned closer to look at the papers.

"Here, read them if you want." Lawrence pushed the documents around with his fingers. "For all the good they will do. There is too much information, and I have no idea whether any of it is relevant or not."

Thomas scanned two or three sheets, some of the names familiar, most not. He glanced at Miguel.

"Have you discussed these papers?"

"I know less than half the people shown, but like Lawrence, I see some connections."

Lawrence shuffled the pages, picked one up. "Here is a record of a marriage between Rodrigo Lonzal and Castellana Baltieri dated the year of Our Lord 1454. They were married in Valencia, but it seems they moved to Córdoba within a year or two."

"And its significance is?" asked Thomas.

"Lonzal changed his name," said Lawrence. "He is now Rodrigo de Borja, the man rumoured to be the next Holy Father. Castellana Baltieri is of course Castellana Lonzal. She has kept his name all these years."

"Are they still married in the eyes of the law?"

Lawrence raised a shoulder. "Who knows? I haven't found all the documents yet, but what I can tell you is that Castellana Lonzal and her son were two of Cortez's best clients for more than fifteen years."

"Is that why he was killed?"

Lawrence shrugged again. "You tell me. Castellana Lonzal is an influential landowner in the area, and friend to both Isabel and Fernando. More than a friend to Fernando, as he admitted to you, not that it is a secret from anyone. Castellana will have enemies."

"It is nothing but rumour," said Miguel. "People are always jealous of those with connections."

"Fernando admitted it to me." Thomas glanced at Miguel. "I went to see the baker woman again today. She told me of two men who were outside Cortez's house the day before the fire, together with four others. The two were there again two days later. You might like to make enquiries and see if you can find anything out about them."

Miguel offered a nod.

"Rodrigo de Borja is staying at the palace," said Lawrence. "You must have seen him, he is not a man easily overlooked."

"Once, briefly. He was..." Thomas stopped, gathering his thoughts, making links and discarding them. "He was with Isabel and this Castellana Lonzal. Also..."

"Who else?" Lawrence's eyes were sharp on Thomas. "It might be significant."

"Theresa was there, as well as another woman. I didn't know her name at the time, but discovered it later. Her name is Eleanor, Countess d'Arreau, the woman I asked you to search for this morning. When I told you she was once my lover." Thomas glanced between the two men, made a decision, changed it, then changed it again. "She was once my lover."

"And still is, you said. Is it a pleasure you will be repeating?"

"You know as much as I do about that."

The humour drained from Lawrence. "You are mixing in powerful company. Be careful. This de Borja gives every appearance of being a benign presence, but benign men do not rise to the position he has. I hear he has come to petition the support of Isabel and Fernando when the time comes."

"What time?"

"When the current Pope dies, of course. Isabel would like to see a Spaniard as Holy Father. It is said de Borja was influential in having their marriage approved. Did you know she and Fernando are first cousins?"

"I didn't. Is it significant?"

"I doubt it, only interesting." Lawrence leaned closer. "Be careful of this de Borja. He is dangerous. The word is that men have died around him in mysterious circumstances."

"Do you think he might have wanted Cortez dead?"

"It is possible. If all Cortez's work had been destroyed, nobody would ever know of his marriage to Castellana Lonzal. But I doubt de Borja would get involved in anything so blatant or dangerous. Not that it would stop him setting someone else the task."

"Are we any further forward? It doesn't feel like it to me. If anything we are worse off."

Lawrence reached for another slip of paper. "There is also this. Their marriage contract gave reference to another document so I went in search of it, though it took some time. I suspect a copy of this was also held in Cortez's cellar." He handed the second sheet across.

The document was written in Spanish, and two names leapt out at Thomas. The name of the child was Jorge Lonzal, and the mother shown as Castellana Baltieri. Thomas peered at the words, and a date written in the manner of the Romans. It took him a moment to calculate a number he understood. It was dated the 13th of May 1453, and also gave a place of birth: Valencia.

Thomas gave a laugh. "Is this genuine?"

Lawrence offered a nod.

"Jorge claims he has no idea what his birth date is," Thomas said. "Now I can tell him. The year sounds right, but surely Valencia is a mistake?" He kept hold of the slip of paper as he looked at Lawrence. "Has someone mixed up two of the documents you have here?"

"The documents do not lie. Do you see the notation in the bottom corner?"

Thomas glanced down, nodded.

"It relates to this." He handed another sheet across. "Jorge has a brother, legitimate this time. His name is Gabriel. Gabriel Lonzal, and he lives with his mother on their estate in El Carpio."

Thomas realised Lawrence had uncovered the information Jorge had paid money to a dead man for. The name of his mother. It had to be her, who else could it be? And if Castellana Lonzal was his mother, did that make Rodrigo de Borja his father? Except her name had been noted as Baltieri, not Lonzal. Did that mean Jorge was born before they married? Was that the reason he had been given up? There were too many loose threads, and Thomas wanted time to tease at them before saying anything, but he knew Lawrence would have made the connections too.

"Gabriel Lonzal is a troublemaker," said Miguel, unaware of the tumult of thoughts in Thomas's head. "A man of privilege who believes it places him above the law. I have come across him before, but he is too well-connected to arrest or even give a slapping to."

Thomas set the records of birth on the table. He picked up a cup of wine and drained it.

"Is there anything else?"

"Are you wondering about a divorce?"

Thomas nodded. "That, and any mention of who Jorge's father is."

"He is a bastard more than likely," said Lawrence. "No worse for that, but not acknowledged by his father. If Castellana even knew who his father was."

"Why would she not?"

"She was, as near as I can work out, barely fifteen years of age when Jorge was born, which means she must have conceived him when she was fourteen."

“You know as well as I do girls of fourteen get married. They have children, too.”

“Of course. Except because no father is shown, it more than likely indicates Jorge is illegitimate. Like I said, it’s not his fault, but not everyone will be as understanding as you or I.” He glanced away from Thomas. “What about you, Miguel? What is your opinion of bastards?”

Miguel said nothing.

“Could de Borja be Jorge’s father?” Thomas said. “Oh, but he would love it if I told him his father might be the next Pope.”

“I would say not,” said Lawrence. “Their marriage is recorded for all to see. Their son Gabriel is recorded for all to see. It would be no matter to add de Borja’s name as Jorge’s father, no matter at all. So I would say it is unlikely.” Lawrence stared at Thomas, waiting.

“Is any of this connected to what is happening to Jorge?”

“Could be. Could be not. That is your job, Thomas. Yours and Miguel’s. I just deal in paper. You need to make the connections, talk to people. Accuse them if you want. Though perhaps not de Borja. I hear he is leaving soon in any case.”

It seemed to Thomas that the coming of de Borja so recently before Jorge was arrested, and his leaving shortly after, might hold some significance … if only he could see what it was.

“Everyone believed Jorge dead. His mother, this Castellana Lonzal, must have given him away to the Olmos family when he was barely a few months old.” He looked up from the papers he still held in his hand. “No reply from Beatriz?”

“Not yet, but there is a good wind from the south today to speed a bird on its way.”

“Then let us hope it arrives tomorrow. I need to know

how Jorge came to be part of the family he thought was his." Thomas shook his head. "If it is even relevant. He is a palace eunuch, for God's sake. He lives among the Moors. He is my friend and known as a friend to Isabel and Fernando. Jorge is not dangerous and has no enemies."

"All men have enemies, even someone as loved as Jorge. You need to find out who they are."

"I should talk to his mother, his brother too, this Gabriel." He met Lawrence's eyes. "Why give one son away and not the other?"

"I told you, because he was born out of wedlock, which makes me sure he is not de Borja's. Jorge is their weakness. They gave him up to a family they were sure would kill him, or sell him as a slave to some rich man with dark perversions. He would disappear into the cesspit of Córdoba and never be heard of again. He was meant to die."

"Why?" Thomas raised his voice. "Why one son and not the other?"

"There are many reasons, but I suspect it is because of whoever Jorge's father is. Either he is someone of immense importance who didn't want his seduction of a young girl known about, or Castellana was raped and wanted rid of the evidence."

"He was a baby. Why not simply kill him? Leave him on a hillside for the wolves or bears? It happens, you know it does."

"But not in this case. You tell me the people Jorge thought his parents were awful. Perhaps being given to them was an even worse punishment than being eaten alive by wolves."

"Which would mean she hated the child," Thomas said.

"It would." Lawrence searched through the papers on the table, pulled another free and held it out to Thomas. "This is where you will find Castellana Lonzal's house in El Carpio. She has an estate beyond the city where she grows olives, fruit, whatever turns a profit. And turn a profit she does. She is one of the wealthiest women in the region. A strong woman by all accounts, so you need to be careful."

"And her son?" Thomas asked. "Her other son, this Gabriel?"

"I told you, he is trouble," said Miguel. "When you decide to visit her, come for me first and we will go together."

Thomas didn't bother looking at the paper Lawrence had handed him. "I know where Castellana Lonzal lives in Qurtuba. I have been in the house. It is where Eleanor is staying."

"What is a Countess of France doing in Córdoba?" asked Lawrence.

"That I do not know. Strangely enough, neither of us raised the subject." Thomas frowned. "If Castellana Lonzal gave up Jorge in Qurtuba, why did she then come to live here fifteen years ago? Do you think she was looking for him?"

"Again," said Lawrence, "that is your job to find out."

"And if she was, why? To save him, or destroy him?"

Lawrence said nothing. Miguel shifted on his chair as if impatient to leave. When Laurita came out carrying a tray holding bread, cheese and fruit, Thomas made his excuses and rose.

As he walked toward the palace, he barely noticed his surroundings. His mind was somewhere else, chasing down possibilities, but by the time he entered the ornate gates, he was no further forward.

CHAPTER FIFTEEN

"Where have you been? She wants you." Theresa was waiting for Thomas when he entered his rooms. She tugged at his sleeve. "Come, now, before she loses patience. She wants you to eat with them."

"Them?" Thomas glanced down at himself. "I should change."

"There is no time, you will have to go as you are. She asked for you earlier, but you could not be found. She may never talk to you again if you let her down." She pulled at his arm once again and Thomas allowed himself to be led into the corridor.

"Who else is with her?"

"You will find out soon enough. Do I have to tell you everything? You are a grown man, Thomas, surely you can find some things out for yourself."

When they reached the wide terrace, it was to find Isabel sitting at the head of a table with her children and Fernando, as well as a handsome man Thomas almost failed to recognise as the same one he had seen days before. De Borja was no longer dressed in the crimson robes of a cardinal, but as an ordinary man, and the sight of him after the conversation with Lawrence sent a shiver through Thomas.

"At last, Sir Thomas." Isabel rose from her chair and offered a hand to be kissed. At the other end of the table, Fernando looked up and nodded, but gave no indication whether he welcomed the sight of Thomas or not. The child Isabel glanced at him, but he was not Jorge so carried little interest. Juan was another matter, shifting in his seat as he tried to control himself.

The sight of de Borja, tall, lean and handsome, made Thomas uneasy. Lawrence had hinted at some unknown truth, and the sight of the man brought an idea more firmly into Thomas's mind.

"I do not believe you have met Cardinal de Borja, have you?" Isabel re-took her seat and waved for a servant to bring another chair. It came almost at once, to be set at the table between Juan and Isabel, almost opposite de Borja.

"No, we have never met, but I know you by reputation, Your Eminence."

The man offered a nod. "And I you, Sir Thomas. Isabel speaks of you often." He gave a smile. "Prince Juan, too. I believe you are some kind of hero to him."

"I fixed his leg, Your Eminence, nothing more."

"You are among friends here, Sir Thomas, call me Rodrigo. As I believe you call both the King and Queen by name."

"Only if you stop calling me Sir Thomas. It is not an honour I sought or deserved."

Another nod. "Agreed."

Thomas glanced at Isabel, who had watched the conversation as if observing two scorpions circling each other.

"You will eat with us, Thomas?"

"Thank you, Your Grace."

"If you are going to call the Cardinal Rodrigo, you must do the same for me."

Thomas felt awkward, different, the presence of de Borja a weight on him, blanketing his actions.

"I will try to remember, Isabel." Even the uttering of her name, once so easy, felt forced. "But I need to ask you something and it would be best done between yourself and Fernando."

"We have no secrets from Rodrigo, none at all. You can speak freely here. As long as it is suitable for the children to hear, of course."

"It concerns Jorge, so perhaps not."

Isabel smiled. "Are your children here? Your son must come to play with Juan again."

"They remain in Gharnatah. As for Jorge, he continues to languish in prison here in Qurtuba."

"As he should if the charges against him are true," said Fernando.

"I cannot believe Jorge capable of any action that would result in his arrest." Isabel's hand moved to cover Thomas's before she stopped herself.

"Oh, he is capable enough," said Fernando. "I remember when he rode with me to rescue Juan. He killed men that day. And from what I hear he has killed another here in our city. An innocent man this time."

"Perhaps it would be best to discuss these matters without the children after all." Isabel clapped her hands and asked for Theresa to be sent for. While they waited, she ate a small portion of meat and a single green bean.

"I understand you are here for the talks between Castile and Al-Andalus." De Borja filled the awkward silence with an easy charm, which overrode the implied insult of

Thomas being part of the heathen party. "How do the negotiations go?"

"I am sure Fernando can tell you that far better than I can. I am only here because my master knows of my relationship with Castile, nothing more. I have to show my face once or twice a week. Others carry out the negotiations." He glanced at Fernando. "Such as they are. And I thank you both for offering me accommodation in the palace. I am getting too old to sleep on hard ground."

"You are not old, Thomas," said Isabel. "And you are always welcome here, you know you are. You should have come to me sooner."

"You have more important matters to think of than my welfare."

"Isabel is like all good rulers," said de Borja. "She thinks of the small matters as well as the large. It shows her humanity, and is only a small part of why her subjects love her as they do. She tells me you know this mariner, Columb. He is one of the matters pressing on her mind at the moment. What do you think of his claims? Are they madness or not?"

Thomas tried to turn his mind to an answer that might satisfy the man, then made the decision to reply honestly.

"I thought him a lunatic until this last year."

"And now?"

"I too am interested in your opinion," said Isabel. "Speak your mind, Thomas."

"His claims carry some truth," he said. "I believe him wrong in his calculations by some measure, but if he sails west, he will not fall off the edge of the world as some claim. He will find land, though not the land he is looking for."

"Why not?" De Borja's voice had lost its softness, his eyes sharp on Thomas.

"I have examined many documents, both old and new, and maps made by Northmen who I believe have already found a new land to the west, but it is not the Indies. It is a land we know nothing of. Columb's calculations underestimate the size of the world." He returned de Borja's gaze. "Or are you like your colleagues and do not accept that the earth is as a pebble spinning in space?"

"I make up my own mind. I agree we live on a sphere, but have given no thought to how large it is or what lies beyond what we already know." He gave a smile. "I have more than enough to think about without adding such matters. Isabel says you are one of the cleverest men she knows, so I am content to take your word until someone convinces me otherwise. You believe there is an unknown land?"

"Either that or an ocean bigger than we can comprehend. Given the funds and permission, Columb will either sail to his death or discover a land and people we know nothing of."

"Which do you think more likely?"

Thomas was surprised to discover himself warming to de Borja. He was unlike other men of God he had known, with an open mind and less certainty in given doctrine.

"If asked to gamble on the odds, I would wager on him living to return."

"Another land," said de Borja, and Thomas could see his mind working through the implications. "Another land for Spain and a new people to fall under God's grace."

"Or another land for France or England," Thomas said. "I know Columb has spoken with both nations."

"He threatens us," said Fernando. "He thinks we can be bullied into backing his wild claims."

"If Thomas believes them, they may not be so wild." De

Borja glanced up as Theresa came on to the terrace, something in his eyes changing. They softened, as Thomas had seen Jorge's do in the presence of a beautiful woman.

Theresa took the children, one hand in each of hers, and led them away with promises of sweet cakes and games.

Once they were alone, Isabel said, "I thank you for your efforts, Rodrigo." She turned to Thomas. "Now, tell us what you are really here for."

"Have you come in search of a pardon?" asked Fernando. "If so you will be disappointed. The law must take its course."

"Even if Jorge is innocent?" The words were directed at Fernando, but Thomas watched de Borja. There was no reaction, and he wondered about the information Lawrence had discovered.

Fernando said, "I have been informed the evidence against him is sound." He glanced at Isabel. "I know you like him, my love, but I believe him guilty as charged." His gaze returned to Thomas. "He will be tried, and he will be executed."

"Explain the evidence against this man to me," said de Borja, the words directed not to Fernando, but Thomas.

"A life was taken, certainly, but not by Jorge, despite the weight of evidence to the contrary. A scribe died, his records completely destroyed by fire. A witness claims she saw Jorge in the roadway. She identified him when he was taken there by the Hermandos. I admit the evidence points to his guilt, but he didn't do what he is accused of."

"Was he not with you?" asked Isabel. "You are always together. It is strange to see you here without him."

"He says he was with his family—Daniel Olmos the sword-maker."

Fernando nodded in recognition of the name. "And was he?"

"No," Thomas said.

"And still you believe him innocent of the accusation?"

"Of course I do. I cannot believe otherwise. He is my closest friend."

This time Isabel's hand completed its journey and patted Thomas's. "You have friends in us too, Thomas." She cast a warning glance at Fernando. "What can we do?"

"Perhaps I can make a suggestion?" said de Borja, and all eyes turned toward him. He smiled, a picture of affability. "Suppose this man—Jorge, you say his name is?"

Thomas nodded.

"Suppose this Jorge is released into Thomas's care. He will be responsible for his friend's actions while he is free. You say you trust this man?" De Borja stared at Isabel, making it clear whose opinion he valued.

"I would trust Thomas with my life. I have trusted him with my life, and with those of my children as well. He has proven himself loyal time and again."

Fernando's expression was sour, but he held his counsel. What he might say later, when the two of them were alone, was a different matter.

"And you, Fernando?" ask de Borja.

Isabel glanced at her husband.

"You know my mind on this. If it was up to me, the answer would be no, never."

"I may be able to offer a solution. Have this man brought before me and I will talk to him. I believe myself a better judge of character than most. If I think him guilty of the charge, he will be returned to prison, if not, he is to be given over into Thomas's custody." He glanced between King and Queen, his offer one which took the decision out of their hands. “One of you, of course, will need to sign the order, but I am happy to help you make the decision.”

Isabel stared at Fernando, waiting until he nodded. It was a way out of the deadlock, one he appeared grateful to accept.

“But not tonight,” said Isabel. “I wish to talk more with Thomas. His life has been torn apart and rebuilt, and I would hear more of it.” She glanced at Fernando. “All of it.”

CHAPTER SIXTEEN

Thomas came to a halt in the doorway of Jorge's cell and stared at the woman who knelt in front of his cot.

"What are you doing here?"

Belia turned, her face impassive. "Was it not you who sent a message I was to come? How could I not? You did not tell me Jorge was a prisoner, but I knew something must have happened." She continued to sit on her heels, Jorge's hands grasped in hers. "Something, but not this!"

"Did you come alone?" Thomas considered the distance, a hard ride for anyone. It was an indication of her fear that she had made the journey.

"Do you think I would leave your children in the care of that woman? Of course I am not alone. Will and Amal are here, as is Usaden. He refused to allow me to travel alone, or I would have done so."

Thomas knew when Belia referred to 'that woman', she meant Helena—the concubine who had once been his lover; the woman who was Will's mother, not that she ever showed the slightest maternal instinct.

"Where are they now?"

"The children are with someone called Theresa. She said she knows you. We went to the palace, assuming you would both be there. Usaden has gone to what he was told is your tent on the riverbank. He does not hold with palaces and says he will be more comfortable there."

Thomas knew he would have to talk with the man who was once a Gomeres mercenary, and who since the fall of Malaka had been in Thomas's employ. Usaden's skill with sword and knife might be needed before events were concluded.

"How did you know to come here?" Thomas asked.

"That woman told me where Jorge was being held." She looked from Thomas to Jorge, then back. "Why was he arrested?"

"He is accused of murder."

Belia laughed. "Then they do not know Jorge."

"If I didn't know him, the evidence would convince me, but I am working on getting him out. It is good you are here, now I can spend more time on my investigation."

"I have not come to be his nurse-maid. I will help you, Thomas. I brought money. It can be used to make Jorge's life more comfortable."

"I have money, and much has been done already."

Belia looked around. "This is meant to be comfortable?"

"This is better than he would have had otherwise."

Belia made a dismissive sound. Thomas knew her well enough now, but sometimes she still scared him. There was something strange, other-worldly about Belia that resisted analysis. Her true nature was as smoke that could never be grasped. Except, of course, by Jorge. The two were devoted to each other.

"We need to talk." Thomas looked at Jorge. "Alone."

"We have no secrets." Belia unconsciously mirrored

Isabel's words of the evening before, except in this case, Thomas knew them to be true.

"What I have to say is secret even to Jorge. He might want to hear it between the two of us first. He can tell you whatever he likes afterward."

"Belia stays." Jorge reached for her hand. "She is right, we have no secrets. We have had none in the past nor will we have any in the future. Whatever you have to say, you can say to us both." He leaned forward and kissed her mouth.

Thomas looked between them and knew he was beaten. He ran through in his mind what he wanted to tell Jorge, then stopped. He would tell him everything, because he didn't know what was important and what was not.

Thomas sat on the end of the bunk, his shoulder touching Jorge's. He waited until Belia rose to sit on the other side of Jorge.

"Have you heard from Beatriz yet?" asked Jorge.

"Who is Beatriz, one of your lovers?" There was no edge to Belia's question. Thomas knew this was one of the reasons he had wanted to talk to Jorge alone.

"Beatriz is my sister," said Jorge. "I must have told you about her."

Thomas waited for a chance to continue, knowing the pair could carry on this way for hours. When they remained silent, he re-gathered his thoughts.

"Nothing yet, but I have not seen Lawrence today. He said less than a day for the bird to get to Cadiz, the same to return. With luck her answer will be waiting for me."

"I wonder what she is like now? She must have…" Jorge's eyes turned distant as he tried to work it out "…over forty years."

"I am hoping when she replies, she will remember the

woman who brought you to the family. You are not an Olmos. You are a Lonzal."

Jorge shook his head. "I have no idea what you are talking about."

"Of course you don't, Lawrence only told me yesterday. He has discovered a record of your birth."

"Who is this Lonzal? Are you telling me she is my real mother?"

"I believe so. Lawrence and Miguel have been working hard and uncovered a record of her marriage and your birth." Thomas took a breath, trying to decide which to tell Jorge first, though he knew it made little difference. Both revelations would come as a shock. "You have a brother a year apart in age, and—"

"Who is the older?" asked Jorge, his brow creasing.

"I … what difference does it make?"

"I would like to be an older brother to someone. All the people close to me are older than I am." He glanced to one side. "Apart from you, of course, my love."

"Do you even know how old I am?" asked Belia.

"Why, are you older than me after all?"

Thomas ignored them, knowing they were on the cusp of disappearing into their own world again.

"If it makes you happy, you are older than your brother by a little over a year. What might be more important is that your mother kept him after she gave you away."

Jorge's head snapped up and his mouth fell open. "She abandoned me? Is that how I ended up in that sorry excuse for a family?" He shook his head. "No, I loved most of them, but not my parents." He laughed. "Except they were not my parents, were they? It makes sense now. Everything makes sense."

Thomas allowed Jorge a little time to absorb the information. He wondered if he could have done so himself, but didn't know the answer.

"Why did she give me away? Did she give me away? Perhaps I was stolen and even now she hunts for me."

"That is what I intend to find out. All of it. Lawrence is looking hard for me."

"Do you know who she is? Where she lives?"

"I have an address here in Qurtuba, another a few leagues beyond the city. I went to the house again, but she wasn't there. I intend to ride to her estate near a town called El Carpio."

"She has an estate?"

"She does."

"Is she wealthy?"

"She is."

"You said you visited her house again. Did you know of her before? Have you already seen her? Why didn't you tell me?"

"Do you remember when I told you I had been with Eleanor?"

"Eleanor is my mother? That cannot be!"

"No, of course she isn't your mother, but she is staying at the house of the woman we believe to be your mother, Castellana Lonzal. Who was married to Rodrigo de Borja."

"Another name I have never heard of."

"He is a friend to both Isabel and Fernando, a cardinal in Roma, and rumoured to be the next Pope. He is staying in the palace at the moment."

Jorge stared at Thomas for a long time, then began to laugh, shaking the flimsy cot all three were sitting on.

"I am the son of the Pope?"

"He is not Pope yet." Thomas felt a strange sense of

annoyance, but could not work out why. "And I said he *might* be your father. It is more likely he is not."

Jorge shook his head. "Sometimes I wonder which of us is the more mad, me for thinking you are going to save me, or you for believing everything Lawrence tells you."

"Would you rather I did nothing?"

"Of course not. If you are going to visit this woman, I should come with you. Do you think I would know if I met her, would I feel some familial connection? You can ask Isabel to release me. Do whatever you need. Bed her if you must. She would grant me a pardon then, I am sure." Though his face showed he doubted Thomas's abilities as a lover.

"I already have," Thomas said.

"You have bedded her?" Jorge stared at Thomas. "No, of course not. You asked her. So when do we leave?"

"There is someone you have to talk to first. You are to be taken to the palace to meet him and he will decide whether Isabel grants you freedom or not. I promised I would vouch for your good behaviour."

"Are you sure that was wise?"

"Would you rather stay here?"

"How do you intend to honour such a promise when you know you cannot?"

"I will help him," said Belia, and Thomas was relieved, knowing she had a far better chance of ensuring Jorge's good behaviour than he ever did.

"When we reach the palace, you need to be careful, because the man I am taking you to will decide whether you can be freed into my care or not."

"You have already told me that. Of course I will be careful, and honest, and..." Jorge waved a hand in frustration "... and whatever you tell me to be."

"What I did not tell you is that the man is Rodrigo de Borja."

Once more, Jorge stared hard at Thomas. "My father is to decide my fate?"

"We don't know if he is your father."

"But he may be."

"It is a possibility, no more. Lawrence is seeking more information." Thomas glanced at Belia and rose to his feet. "I have to take him to the palace now. Come with us, I will arrange a room for you. If he is freed, you can share his bed tonight."

"If not I will sleep here, on the floor if necessary."

"They will not allow it."

"They will if I pay them enough."

Thomas could see from Belia's expression that argument was pointless, so allowed her to believe what she would.

"Will there be guards?" asked Jorge.

"I expect so—it is the royal palace, after all, and you are accused of murder. No doubt de Borja will have brought men of his own to protect him. Do not do anything to make them suspicious. They trust me to get you to the palace and return you to the prison if need be."

"I will not come back here," said Jorge, his face serious. "Do you know this place is full of murderers and thieves?"

Thomas could think of nothing to say, but Jorge could.

"Which can be useful." He searched his clothes until he pulled out two crumpled pieces of paper. He glanced at them before handing one to Thomas. "Here, take this."

"What is it?"

"A list of men who are capable of killing Cortez." Jorge smiled. "I have been working too. Who better than men in prison to tell me who is capable of carrying out a murder? I asked around and a few men got in touch with me and told me what they knew." He glanced at the list still in Thomas's hand and shook his head. "Thank you very much Jorge. You are welcome. I should keep this other name to myself, but here, take it as well. It is a man well known for placing children with families. Perhaps he placed me."

Thomas and four burly Hermandos escorted Jorge across the bridge to the palace, where he was handed over to the care of four other guards. Belia stood patiently beside Thomas until Jorge was out of sight.

"Can this man really free Jorge?"

"I believe he has the power to do so. He is important, and both Isabel and, more importantly, Fernando will do as he says. I only hope Jorge behaves himself and tries nothing stupid."

"You are talking about Jorge, remember," said Belia.

"As long as he doesn't ask him straight out if he is his father. Gods, I hope he isn't that crazy."

Thomas escorted Belia to his own rooms, then went in search of Theresa to ask if another room could be found. When he eventually found her, it was also to discover his own children with her, and he knew he could not simply abandon them immediately as Will came across to embrace him, Amal toddling along behind, holding her arms out to be lifted up.

It was late afternoon by the time Thomas found time to cross the city in search of Miguel to show him the names Jorge had given him. Theresa had promised to find a room close to Thomas's for Jorge and Belia, and if not for the guard stationed outside in the corridor, they might almost believe they were free to roam at will. She also agreed, with little sign of reluctance, to look after his children until he returned.

Miguel did indeed know the three men identified as capable of killing Cortez, but not the name of the other. He tapped the piece of paper.

"Each of these is capable of murder, no doubt, and I know where to find them. We should do so first thing tomorrow. Very early tomorrow, before dawn. You will come back here then, Thomas?"

"Why not now? The sooner, the better for Jorge."

"Because these men will not be where they live until the small hours."

"At dawn, then?"

"An hour before dawn."

As Thomas left, he tried to shake himself out of a sense of unreality. Everything he had ever believed about Jorge's past had been shattered. He wondered how Jorge must feel. Even more confused, no doubt. And then he wondered how the conversation with de Borja was progressing. Or was it finished already, and Jorge consigned back to the gaol?

The streets were busy. The citizens of Qurtuba had come out in numbers to eat, drink and find what pleasure they could, illicit or otherwise. Thomas firmed his shoulders and walked through them. He felt alone, unloved and frustrated. He passed an inn where tables and chairs were set across the corner of a small square, all of them occupied. Laughter and loud conversation filled the air, but it failed to touch him. He was tempted to seek out Eleanor and take some comfort in her arms until he remembered she had gone with Castellana Lonzal to her estate.

His thoughts turned to Theresa, recalling how she was with his children, and he wondered when his morality had slipped its moorings. How could he think of bedding one woman one moment and another the next? He should ask Jorge. If he could.

Theresa was in Thomas's rooms with the children when he returned, but left almost at once. He watched her go, then let his breath loose. Will seemed taller than he recalled, but Thomas doubted he had grown in the month since he had seen him. He was starting to believe his son might get to be as tall as his grandfather, the Sultan's general Olaf Torvaldsson, who was the tallest man Thomas had ever known.

He went to one knee and embraced the boy, feeling the strength in him.

"Where's Amal?"

"Over there, silly Pa."

Thomas looked where Will pointed. He had missed Amal, curled on her side, asleep on a small bed, as tranquil as her mother had been. Thomas experienced a violent surge of loss running through him and hugged Will all the tighter.

"Pa," gasped Will in complaint, and Thomas laughed, wiping his eyes quickly so his son didn't see his tears. He picked the boy up and carried him through to his own wide bed and flung him on top of the covers, making him laugh. The sound loosened something in his chest.

"What have you been doing all day?" Thomas sat and rubbed Will's belly, bringing another laugh.

"We've been with your friend, the lady, and then she went off, and when she came back Isabel was with her, and we went and played with Juan and Cat."

"Prince Juan and Princess Catherine, you mean, don't you?"

"Do I? Juan and Cat. She likes Amal. Dressed her up like a lady. Me and Juan had a fight."

"He's too big for you to fight now."

"I know. I won because his pa wasn't there."

"You are meant to let a prince win, you know that, don't you?"

"*Morfar* says never let anyone win. Usaden says the same. Do you want me to look weak, Pa?"

Thomas shook his head. "No. You didn't hurt him, did you?"

"Not much." Will gave a huge yawn, the journey and excitement of the day catching up even as he tried to fight sleep. "Can I stay with you tonight?"

"Go and sleep in my bed now. I have something to do first."

Will let out a sigh so loud, Thomas had to stifle a laugh.

"You always have something to do, Pa." He squirmed up the bed and slipped beneath the covers. "Why is that?" Already his eyes were starting to close.

"I am a busy man, I suppose," Thomas said. "Lots of people need me."

"So do Amal and me, remember."

Thomas sat on the bed until his son drifted into sleep. He kissed his brow, then went through and kissed Amal. He sat in the well-appointed main room, staring out at the palace gardens without seeing them, and tried not to think of going to find Theresa. He felt the tug of something without being able to understand what it was. Not lust. Not love. Not even memory. Whatever it was grew stronger and he rose, ready to submit, and would have if a soft knock had not sounded on the door.

Thomas crossed the room and flung the door open, expecting Theresa to be standing there, not sure what might happen if she was. Instead it was Jorge who stepped across the threshold and wrapped his arms around Thomas without saying a word. After a moment, Thomas returned the embrace, his mood changing as he felt a wave of love for the man he held, knowing it was reciprocated.

Jorge finally released him, held his shoulders and stared into his eyes.

"Thank you, Thomas."

"For what?"

"For having me set free." He smiled. "I like that de Borja, he reminds me of me in some ways. Perhaps he is my father."

"You didn't ask him, did you?"

"Of course not. Do you think I am an idiot?"

Thomas glanced past Jorge. "Where is Belia?"

"She is waiting in our room for me. Preparing herself, she said. It has been some time since we have lain together and she is impatient, as am I, to correct that situation. So no offence, but now I have said my thanks, I must attend to her."

"Tomorrow I want you to tell me everything you spoke of with de Borja."

"What if it was a private conversation?"

"Was it?"

"No. But it might have been. All right, tomorrow we will find somewhere to sit and drink like we used to and I will tell you everything. Though there were no great revelations in what we spoke of. He was searching me out, I could tell, and I suppose I must have passed whatever test he was setting. We spoke of you, as well. You and Isabel." Jorge smiled. "I told him there was nothing to be concerned about. Your friendship is purely platonic. I think I set his mind at ease."

Thomas drew Jorge into a last embrace, despite his doubts about his efforts to help.

"Just try not to get into any more trouble."

"Me? I have no idea what you mean."

When Jorge had gone, Thomas picked up Amal and set her in the bed next to her brother, then he climbed in beside them both, comforted by their scent and their warmth, which drove the demons from his mind, for the moment at least.

CHAPTER SEVENTEEN

A pre-dawn chill had descended on the city by the time Thomas and Usaden made their way toward the Hermandos' office next to the city wall. Mist rose from the river to wreath the buildings in strange, shifting patterns. Thomas had waited as long as he could before going to wake Usaden, but found the man already standing outside the tent; still, patient, as if he could stand there until the end of time. He had said nothing when, nor spoken since Thomas had told him what he wanted him to help with.

Thomas's dog Kin padded along beside them. Usaden had brought the dog together with Belia and the children, brought him now on their quest. Kin had proven himself in the past and no doubt would do so again in the future. The three of them stood in a small square while Thomas stared at a house which stood proud, defiant. It was almost on their route, and something had drawn Thomas here. Perhaps the hope that Eleanor had returned, but the house was dark, closed up.

Usaden asked, "What are we doing here?"

"This house is where Jorge's mother lives. Together with another woman. One I used to know well."

"I thought Jorge's mother was dead."

"His real mother."

Usaden shrugged. Most men would be curious, but not Usaden. He took little notice of anything unless he had to fight it, could eat it or drink it. He pretended he cared about nothing, but Thomas was beginning to understand him a little better. He believed Usaden did care about some things, but chose not to show what they were. He only hoped he and his family appeared somewhere on that list.

"I assume at some point you will want to talk to her when she returns? Jorge certainly will. I hope she is ready for that encounter."

"I will, and so will Jorge now he has been freed."

A fresh wave of yearning rose through Thomas, one he believed only visiting Eleanor again might assuage. He wondered why he had not made more effort to see her again. Their first raw coupling had been all haste and yearning and sweat, cataclysmic, wrong and right at the same time. Thomas didn't know how to deal with such raw emotion. Perhaps a second encounter would be softer, would remind him of the love they had once shared. Jorge would understand. Jorge would have advice. Good advice, no doubt, though Thomas was unsure if good advice was what he wanted to hear.

Usaden continued to wait, and Thomas buried his doubts deep and turned away. They had men to rouse from their beds and questions needing to be answered. Thomas's unease changed to excitement. On this morning, he might discover the answer to the puzzle of Cortez's death and return to sleeping the afternoon away. Perhaps sleeping it away beside Eleanor.

The first man they went to leapt through an upper window and broke his ankle on the cobbles outside. He tried running, but was easily caught by Usaden, who would have caught him injured or not. Miguel dispatched the man in the company of another Hermandos constable Miguel had brought along. They moved on, through the northern city gate to a shack that appeared to be losing a slow battle with the elements, sinking into the ground stone by stone. By now a pale light was beginning to fill the air, but its source remained hidden. A pack of feral dogs snapped and snarled at a pile of rubbish hard against the city wall, and the three men gave them a wide berth. Kin ignored them.

"Who is this one?" Thomas asked.

"The name Jorge gave you is Antonio de Parma," said Miguel, "but that is likely only the one he uses for now. He is not the kind of man to keep a name for long, not once it becomes associated with the slightest guilt."

"So he could be the one?"

"As could the last, who was not, or the next."

As they approached the hut, a crashing sound erupted and de Parma left by the simple expedient of running through the rotten back wall, emerging among a spray of wood. Usaden set off in one direction with Kin, Thomas and Miguel in the other. The man was faster than the previous suspect, but then he had the advantage of both ankles working. De Parma sprinted upslope, heading for the rocky summit of a low hill. He would have escaped, but Kin was too fast for any man. He caught a leg and brought him down as Usaden arrived to throw himself on top of the man on the ground. Thomas arrived in time to see the pinned man pull a dagger and he set his foot on his wrist, making no effort to be gentle.

"Well, this is more promising," said Miguel, looking down at Usaden, who continued to sit on de Parma's chest.

"The last one ran as well, remember," Thomas said.

"But not so fast. This one is strong enough to have killed Cortez."

De Parma spat. Usaden wiped his face, then continued the movement to punch the man on the nose, which spouted blood. Usaden got to his knees and waited as Miguel and Thomas lifted de Parma between them.

Thomas looked toward the city wall a half mile distant. There was nobody in sight.

"We should question him out here. We can be more persuasive than in your cells."

"A fine idea. Me and your friend will hold him, you start. I am supposed to have rules."

Thomas laughed and hit de Parma, this time on the ear, little more than a slap.

"I will kill you!" De Parma's accent, not entirely of Spain, softened his curse.

"You can try, but in case you cannot count where you come from, there are three of us and only one of you." Thomas drew a short knife and turned it in his hand, as if trying to work out how it had appeared there. He held it up, the tip close to de Parma's right eye. The man tried to pull his head away, but Usaden twisted his fingers tightly through his hair and held him firm.

"He clearly knows nothing," said Miguel. "You might as well kill him now so we have no need to worry about his threats."

Thomas nodded and touched the knife to de Parma's eyelid, pushing hard enough to draw a bead of blood.

"You cannot kill me! It is against the law." All his bluster was gone. Fear showed as his eyes scanned Thomas, finding nothing of mercy there.

Miguel laughed. "I am the law, which well you know, and this man is Thomas Berrington. You may not have heard the name, though half of Córdoba has. He is friend to Queen Isabel and the King. He can do whatever he wishes. Thomas is above the law."

"It is true, I am." Thomas applied more pressure. "Miguel may be the law, but I am above the law. Tell me who your master is."

"What master?"

Thomas smiled. De Parma knew something. He was involved in some way.

"Did you kill Cortez or only set the fire? One will get you hanged, the other will result in the loss of a hand." Thomas had no idea if he spoke the truth or not. He suspected setting the fire that killed Cortez was as good as killing him, but he also suspected de Parma didn't know that. "Or you can walk away from this encounter and we will say nothing of it. Unless everything was all your idea. Then I will kill you." Thomas glanced around. "Out here. We will put your body in that excuse for a hut and set it alight like you did to Cortez. That would be justice."

"I did nothing. All I did was set the fire-fuse and leave them to their work. I will leave this city, too. I have had enough of this place in any case. It stinks."

"You can go home to Italia," Thomas said, pleased when de Parma nodded.

"Yes, yes I will."

"But first you have to tell me who is behind this." He withdrew the tip of the knife, but left it in view. "Who gave the order, and who accompanied you?" He didn't bother asking why Cortez had been killed. De Parma was not the kind of man to have been told such, nor the kind of man who would care if he had.

"I never met the others, only the two men of Roma."

"Is that why they chose you? Because you are known to set fires and you speak their tongue? That is true, is it not?"

De Parma nodded. "It has been a long time since I used the tongue of Roma, and they spoke too fast for me to keep up. I managed one word in ten, that is all."

"They were bought men?"

"Yes. Paid for. I had nothing to do with the killing, only the fire." He gave a tiny smile, sly, touched with pride. "Those papers will have burned fast. Too fast for a man to escape from, even if he wasn't barely conscious." He tried to turn his head toward Miguel, but his hair was still held tight.

"You left Cortez down there to burn? Who paid you?"

"The men of Roma. Gold coin, gone now." De Parma smiled, showing rotting teeth. "Gone, but not wasted."

"Who gave them the order?"

De Parma shook his head. "How am I meant to know that?"

It was Thomas's turn to smile. "I don't care how you know it, only that I am sure you do. You know more than you say, don't you? There would have been word put on the street asking for the best fire starter in Córdoba. You would have heard that and found out where the word came from."

"I cannot."

"Why not? If you leave Castile you will be beyond punishment. We will not punish him, will we, Miguel?"

"Not if he tells you the name."

"See?" Thomas stared into de Parma's eyes until he saw the last remnant of resistance turn to acceptance of his fate.

"If I tell you, I can never return to Roma, or anywhere in Italia."

"Do I look as if that is any of my concern?" Thomas flicked the tip of his knife to cut a shallow line along de Parma's cheek. As he did so, he was aware of how much his humanity had fled with Lubna's death. Her softening influence had faded into a dark memory. He knew if Miguel asked, he would kill this man without hesitation. He would, after all, be doing the world a favour. Perhaps de Parma saw something in his eyes because he began to nod his head, over and over, as if once started, he couldn't stop.

"The priest," he said. "The priest gave the order."

"Name?" Thomas asked.

"I do not know a name, only a house."

"Where?"

De Parma named a small square familiar to Thomas and Miguel both. Miguel released the man, who rubbed at the back of his head. He put a hand to his cheek where the cut had already stopped bleeding. Thomas knew exactly how to cut a man so as to inflict either maximum or minimum damage.

"Can I go?" He looked around, as if unable to believe his luck.

"You can go," said Miguel. "But if either of us sees you in the city again, you will be arrested and thrown into a prison you will never surface from."

De Parma looked toward the hut he had made his temporary home, a distant speck now, and turned away. There was obviously nothing there he wanted. He began to walk up the hillside.

"You should have killed him," said Usaden, watching the man walk away. "I can still do it if you want me to."

Thomas watched de Parma's retreating figure. "No, leave

him. Do you think he is telling the truth?" he asked Miguel.

"I believe so. There is only one man who lives in that square who has a reputation for being willing to do whatever anyone asks, and his is the name on the other piece of paper Jorge gave to you."

"Is he really a priest?"

Miguel nodded.

"Is he an important priest? A bishop perhaps, or an archbishop?"

"No, a priest is all he is, but a man with connections."

"Would one of those connections be someone far more exalted?" And when Miguel frowned, Thomas said, "Rodrigo de Borja? He is in the city at the moment. I have seen him in the palace, spoke with him only yesterday."

"I believe they once spent some time together, or that is what the man claims. Why? Does de Borja know something about this matter?"

"Oh, I am beginning to think he does."

De Parma's figure was tiny when Usaden said, "Are you sure you do not want me to kill him? What if he tries to warn the priest?"

Thomas gave a shake of his head. "Let him go. He wouldn't be that stupid."

Usaden showed no indication whether he agreed with the sentiment or not, but fell into step as they began to walk toward the city gate. Kin ran ahead, ran back, over and over. Thomas wondered how he might arrange another meeting with the man who might be the next Pope, and if he did, how long he would survive the encounter. But first he had another priest to interrogate.

Thomas wanted to go to the priest's house directly, but Miguel said no. "We have to talk to the third man first."

"We already have the fire starter," Thomas said.

"And this other may know more. You told me the baker woman saw four men outside Cortez's house the day before he died, and she confirmed the same to me when I asked her. De Parma said he met with two men of Roma, so there must have been another man there. Whoever those men de Parma dealt with are, they would have spoken to others in the city before finding those willing to do their work."

Thomas wasn't sure he agreed with the logic, but nodded. The third house was almost on the way to where the priest lived in any case, and with luck the third man would know nothing at all and they would waste barely any time.

The house was narrow, with only a single storey that squatted between two higher buildings used as warehouses, both shut up at that time of day. The sun had risen by now, but the streets remained in shadow. Miguel knocked on the flimsy door, but there was no answer. When he knocked a second time, harder, the door opened a crack, unlocked, and he pushed at it, glancing at Thomas.

"Perhaps he has nothing to steal and never locks it."

Usaden waited in the street with Kin as Miguel and Thomas entered what looked to be the only room, which meant they found who they were looking for at once. Unfortunately, mostly for him, the man lay on a narrow cot with his blood soaking it red. Thomas pushed past Miguel, who had stopped dead in the doorway, and knelt beside the body. There was no need to check for a pulse. The man's belly had been sliced open, his throat cut for good measure. The blood was fresh, still sticky.

"He was killed within the hour. If we had come here

first, he might still be alive."

Miguel shook his head. "Do not put the blame on us, we did not kill him."

"I was not." Thomas felt a roiling sense of events turning to chaos, of chasing an enemy he could not see who was always one step ahead. An enemy with no face and powerful masters. He knew if Miguel had agreed to come in search of these men when Thomas asked the day before, they would still be alive. "Who did kill him?" He feared de Parma might have doubled back and come here, until he realised this man had been dead even as they questioned him.

He went into the street to stand beside Usaden. When Miguel joined him, he said, "We need to wake everyone in the street to find out if they saw anything."

"Agreed, but I need to report this man's death first. I will send constables as soon as I can." Miguel looked in both directions. "But it is a thankless task. Few people actually live here, and it is not an area where they proffer information to the Hermandos willingly."

"Can't you do it later? We have to go to the priest's house first, he may be in danger as well."

Miguel took a moment to think about it before shaking his head. "I cannot. It is my job to report the death, but I can tell you where to find this other man."

Thomas noted an address in a more salubrious part of the city, then watched Miguel leave before falling into step beside Usaden. After a moment, he tapped his shoulder and began to run. The two of them raced through streets just starting to come alive, drawing stares from people setting up stalls, others going to work.

They found the door of the priest's house open like the last they had visited, and Thomas was afraid of what they would discover inside.

CHAPTER EIGHTEEN

It took them longer to find the body of the priest, but only because the house was larger, well-built, with rooms over three well-appointed floors. When they did find him, they also found his attacker, and Thomas experienced a wave of weakness that made him lean against the wall.

The priest lay on his back in a curtained bed. He was naked, and like the previous man, his belly had been opened, but not his throat. He had died more slowly, and no doubt in searing agony. Whoever had killed him had been seeking information, and Thomas wondered if the priest had given it up or not.

Another figure lay curled into a corner like a discarded rag, also covered in blood, a knife grasped in his right hand. Even with his face turned away, Thomas knew who it was, but not how he could be there. Jorge was meant to be guarded day and night.

"Is he dead?" asked Usaden. "It is Jorge, isn't it? Shame, I liked him."

Thomas realised it should have been his first thought to check, annoyed at himself for not doing so. He staggered to where Jorge lay. He turned him on to his back and plucked the knife from his hand, tossed it toward Usaden, who made no attempt to catch it.

Thomas touched Jorge's chest, ignoring the spray of blood that drenched his clothes—not the coarse ones he had worn in prison, so he had changed before leaving the palace—and waited for a heartbeat, relieved when he felt a thump beneath his palm.

"He lives." He expected no answer from Usaden and received none. "Come and help me so I can find out where he is hurt."

Usaden knelt on the other side of Jorge and between them they sat him up. His head lolled, and as it did, Thomas saw a gash on the back of his skull and parted the hair to examine it more closely. It was deep, but not deep enough to account for the quantity of blood that covered Jorge.

"The knife," Thomas said, "is there blood on the blade?"

Usaden nodded.

"Enough to account for the priest?"

Another nod.

"Fuck!" Thomas sat on his heels. He glanced around the room, trying to make a decision even as he knew there was only one that could be made. The inevitable one. The wrong one.

"Miguel mustn't know about Jorge's presence here," he said. "Go fetch him while I get Jorge back to the palace."

"I don't know where Miguel is, nor know the city well enough to find him. You go. I will take him." He offered a tight smile. "And if anyone comes here, you know I am the better able to fight them off."

"Nobody is coming," Thomas said.

"Jorge didn't do this to himself."

"Can you prove it?" Thomas waited, but Usaden had no

answer, just as he had no answer himself. How much evidence did anyone need?

"Go," said Usaden. "You fetch the constable."

"I cannot."

"This is not like you."

Thomas started to object, then held his answer inside. Usaden was right. This was not like him, but he had never experienced a situation such as this before. He had lost people, and he had killed people, but this was something entirely beyond anything he knew how to deal with. Jorge was his other half. Utterly different, yet he completed Thomas, just as Thomas completed him. His mind skittered and slid, searching for purchase, some kind of certainty, and finding none.

"We will both take him away from here," he said.

"You cannot. If you are caught, you will be implicated alongside him. Go fetch Miguel and I will take care of Jorge." It was a lot of words for Usaden, but none of them wasted.

Thomas rose to his feet. He looked around the room with no idea what he was looking for. Then he uttered another curse and left the house. As he walked through streets growing busy, he barely saw the people he pushed past. He thought about Jorge. Thought about whether he was capable of doing what he had seen in the priest's room. And then, the thought he had pushed away only for it to force its way back into his mind until he had no option but to allow it entry: what if Jorge was guilty of what he was accused? Despite all Thomas's trust, his belief in his friend, despite the impossible notion of Jorge killing a man in cold blood, he knew he had to consider the possibility. Jorge had no alibi for either murder. Worse, for the second he had been discovered in the same room as the victim, with a bloodied knife in his hand.

Thomas needed to know if there was any possible reason why Jorge might want these men dead. What did they know that was such a threat as to make him take a knife to them? He had concentrated his efforts on proving Jorge innocent ... but what if he was guilty?

Thomas shook his head. No—not Jorge. The idea was impossible. De Parma had told him men of Italia had killed Cortez. Perhaps they had killed the priest too. Thomas had to return to his task, to double his efforts to clear Jorge's name.

By the time he found Miguel and returned to the priest's house, it contained only one body. Usaden and Jorge were gone, and Thomas felt relief wash through him.

"Carlos Mendoza," said Miguel as he stood at the foot of the bed, staring at the body.

"Is he an important man?"

"Not anymore, clearly, but he was by connection to others, by what he knew and did." Miguel grimaced. "He is distantly related to Archbishop Mendoza, who in turn is close to both Isabel and Cardinal de Borja. So Carlos is not important in himself, only important in the relationships which link him to others." Miguel approached the bed and stared at the blood-soaked sheets. "When did this happen?"

"He died after the other man, so recently. Perhaps only moments before we arrived."

"You saw no-one?"

When Thomas hesitated, Miguel turned to him, a frown creasing his normally smooth brow.

"Did you?"

"No, I saw nobody." Thomas knew he had stepped across an invisible line, and put himself beyond the law. He had betrayed Miguel's trust. It hurt, but not as much as telling the truth would have hurt.

He took a pace closer to the body. "Did he have a position in Qurtuba?"

"Nothing he could boast of, but it did not stop him trying. He worked in the Church library. A position no doubt found for him because it meant he could do as much or as little as he wanted, and from what I hear it was as little as possible."

"Why was he killed, do you think?" Thomas asked.

"You know as much as I do." Miguel looked down at the dead man. "I never liked him, not that our paths crossed often, but he was a pompous bully. There have been complaints made, mostly from women, but I was warned not to do anything about him. He is protected."

Thomas turned at the sound of footsteps on the stairs. Miguel nodded him to one side of the open door before taking a position on the other. The footsteps approached without hesitation, and a moment later a short woman entered the bedroom, carrying a tray of fruit, which she dropped with a crash when she saw the violated body of the man on the bed. Thomas wondered if he should have untied his legs, but decided it would have made little difference.

The woman opened her mouth to scream, then noticed Miguel and let an even shriller cry loose. Miguel grabbed her and dragged her from the room. Thomas followed, closing the door behind him.

"Who are you?" They mirrored their actions with de Parma, Miguel holding the woman while Thomas asked the questions.

"I work for Father Mendoza."

"Doing what?"

"Everything," the woman said. "I make him his … his

noon and evening meals." A sob shook her ample chest and she fought to hold herself from breaking down entirely. "Every morning I buy whatever is fresh in the markets. I get it on my way here, then I clean the house. I cook his midday meal and set him a cold plate for supper."

"What time did you leave yesterday?"

She shook her head, but only to give herself time to think. "A little after sunset. Sometimes it is earlier, sometimes later, but usually near that time. He likes to have the evenings to himself. To pray, to consider God, he says." She met Thomas's stare. "What happened to him?"

"Someone came into the house and killed him." Thomas made no effort to soften his words. He wanted to see her reaction, but it was clear she knew nothing of the matters that had happened that morning. "Does he have enemies?"

Her head shook. "None I know of."

"Have you seen any strangers watching the house? Any callers you would not expect?"

Another shake of the head. "Only the Italians. Men of Roma, Carlos said, but he was expecting them." Another sob shook her. "What am I to do now? I am too old to find another master. I have been with Carlos thirty years."

Thomas noted she used the priest's first name now. "Tell me about the men from Roma. How many?"

"Four. They were well dressed, well spoken. The Spanish of one was excellent, the others not so much. I only saw them briefly when I let them into the master's study. They were still there when I left."

"Last night?"

"Four, no, five nights ago. But they can have nothing to do with what happened to him, they were friends. I was asked to put food and wine out for them all."

"Do you know what was discussed?"

"How would I?" But something in her reply gave the lie to her words, and Thomas was too impatient to be gentle.

"Do you listen to all his private conversations, or only this one?"

The woman tried to step away, but Miguel, despite not appearing to do so, held her firm.

"I … Sometimes, when I am working, cleaning, carrying water to his room, tidying his papers, I pass the door and a little conversation can be heard. I do not press my ear to it. What I overhear is purely an accident, nothing more."

"In this instance, five days ago, what did you accidentally overhear?"

"They asked if he had found the man they were looking for."

"What man?"

"I only heard one name. Olmos. They said his name was Olmos. I know Daniel Olmos, the sword-maker, but so does everyone in Córdoba, so it cannot be him. It is not so common a name, but I expect there are others."

"And what was your master's reply?"

"He told them he had found everything they were looking for, but the information would cost more than agreed because it involved people in high places."

"And you heard all this in passing?" Thomas said.

"I was passing a lot that evening. Master had left his papers in a mess and the floors in the hallway were dirty."

"What time did they leave?"

"They were still in there when I left. There was much laughter as I passed the door on my way out. I was asked to bring wine for them so I assume their business was finished."

"How did your master seem the following morning?"

"No different than usual. Perhaps a little cheerier, so

those men must have agreed to pay him what he asked." She glanced along the corridor, back to Thomas. "Not that money will do him any good now. Who will prepare him? He should be buried today, before sunset. There will be much to arrange. I would like to do it."

"Has he family?"

"None. I am all he has."

"Tell me where you live in case I have more questions." Thomas made no effort to memorise her instructions, knowing Miguel would.

Outside, Miguel said, "You do know she will steal everything she can."

"Is it theft if those things no longer belong to anyone?" Thomas recalled the time he and Jorge had done exactly the same from the house of a dead man with no relatives.

"It is still theft."

"Then go back inside and arrest her." Thomas let his impatience show. "Or wait and catch her on the way out. Will she prepare her master, do you think?"

"I expect so."

"Then she honours his memory. Allow her to take whatever she wishes in order to honour her loyalty."

Miguel wanted Thomas to accompany him to the Hermandos' offices, but instead he pleaded a prior engagement, letting Miguel believe it was with the Queen. As he made his way toward the palace, he ran through the scant information the woman had provided and felt a spark of hope. Men from Roma, the same as de Parma claimed had recruited him. And the men had been with Carlos Mendoza five days ago. The day Cortez had been murdered. The day Jorge was arrested.

He wondered why de Parma was still alive when everyone else involved was dead. Unless his death had been planned, but they had reached him before the killers. Thomas knew there were too many questions still to be answered. First among them was how Jorge had come to be lying unconscious in a dead man's bedroom, with a blood-stained knife clutched in his hand. And where he was now.

CHAPTER NINETEEN

When Thomas returned to the palace, he went directly to the room Theresa had obtained for Jorge and Belia. As he expected, Jorge lay on the bed. What Thomas did not expect was for him to be naked, and Belia leaning over him. For a moment Thomas stopped in the doorway, believing he had interrupted an intimate moment, then realised his stupidity. Belia was examining Jorge, two fingers running across his skin as she searched for injuries.

"Has he said anything?" Thomas came to stand beside her, watching her work, impressed at her skill and diligence.

"He has not stirred." She glanced at him. "How long was he unconscious?"

"I can't say for sure, but no longer than an hour."

"An hour! What if they broke something inside his head?"

"Then there is nothing we can do about it." Thomas knew if that was the case, there were techniques he had used before, but they were dangerous, even if they might become necessary. "Help me roll him over." He slid his hands beneath Jorge and waited until Belia decided to help.

Thomas parted Jorge's hair and leaned close. The blow had broken the skin, but Belia had cleaned it and the blood had stopped flowing. A dark bruise was starting to spread from the wound.

"I made a tincture and forced it into him," said Belia. "I sent the children away with your friend, the red-haired woman."

"Isabel?"

"I thought her name was Theresa."

"You are right, my fault. What tincture?"

"Yarrow, comfrey, a few other herbs, mostly for the wound, but internal as well. I do not like that he is not waking up."

Thomas rolled Jorge on to his back again, unconcerned by his nakedness. He had seen him thus a thousand times before and hoped to see him a thousand more. He lifted an eyelid, looking for wide pupils, relieved when he found them normal, shrinking to pin-pricks when he brought a candle close.

"I need to talk to him, to find out what he was doing in that house. He was meant to stay here." He turned to Belia. "Did he say anything to you about going out?"

She gave a shake of her head. "He was next to me when we fell asleep, gone when I woke. It is not like Jorge to rise without waking me. He makes so much noise, and he grumbles. He told me your friend the Queen had released him to your care, and this is what comes of it."

"You have no idea why he went out—he didn't discuss it with you?"

"We were otherwise engaged last night. Where did you find him?"

"In the house of a priest. What did Usaden tell you?"

"That there was a dead man. I assume Jorge was involved in some way from the state of his clothing. I sent them to be burned and washed him twice over." She glanced at Thomas. "Do not worry, the children saw nothing. I sent them away before I did anything, and Usaden will not speak of it."

"No, I expect he won't. Where is he now?"

"With the children."

"He is not much of a nursemaid."

"He said something about it being time for Will's training, and Amal likes to watch. They also took your dog with them." She smiled, the expression strained. "The servants do not like it being indoors, so I think Usaden sets it loose to annoy them."

Thomas wondered if Belia knew his friends better than he did.

"Does anyone else know about Jorge?"

"Not as far as I know. Not even your red-haired woman." She gave an enigmatic smile. "She is pretty, isn't she?"

"Is she?" Thomas stared at Jorge. His chest rose and fell in a slow rhythm. Thomas waited, watching, but Jorge's eyes failed to move beneath their lids as they would in a dream. He feared the blow to his head might have done more damage than could be survived. He wondered if he would be forced to drill into his skull to release the pressure. It was a dangerous procedure, but he had carried it out before. Some of the patients had even lived.

"He survived that sword wound last year, thanks to you," said Belia. "He will survive this as well. I know you—you do not like your patients to die."

Thomas glanced at her to see if she was smiling, but her

face was set, closed down, and he knew she was trying to hold her emotions in check. She and Jorge had been lovers for four years now, and Thomas had no expectation they would ever part. Belia was strange, unapproachable to many, and he was unsure he fully understood her himself, but knew Jorge did. They were completely unsuited, but then he supposed so had he and Lubna been.

The thought of Lubna drew him into the past, then further to bring Eleanor to mind. The girl who had been stolen from him was now a grown woman his own age, a Countess, and here in Qurtuba. Together with Thomas's son. He let his breath go in a long sigh as crazed images danced through his mind, only slowly becoming aware of Belia tugging at his sleeve.

"Did you sleep at all last night?"

"A little, but not long. There is too much to do."

"Then you need to sleep now. Go to your room, call that woman if you want, but what you need more than anything is rest. I will come for you when Jorge wakes."

Thomas knew Belia was right, but as he walked the wood-panelled corridors, he also knew he would not take her advice. Instead he found his way to the wide terrace which looked across the gardens, hoping to find Will, Amal and Usaden there. What he didn't expect was to also see Isabel, Fernando, and the man he believed might be connected to his troubles: Rodrigo de Borja.

They sat at a metal table with glasses of wine and small plates of delicacies, shaded from the sun by an awning while they watched Usaden work Will and Prince Juan hard in the sunshine. Isabel clutched Amal on her lap. She looked up as Thomas hovered in the doorway, unsure whether to interrupt until she smiled and waved, offering him no choice. She lifted Amal up to him and Thomas took his daughter, who seemed to weigh nothing, and sat her on his hip.

"Will fights good," Amal said in Arabic, the only language she spoke, and Thomas was aware that would have to change soon. The language of Castile would soon become a necessity. Amal was young enough to absorb language like a sponge, and he wondered if he ought to teach her a little English as well.

"What did she say?" asked Isabel. "Sit, Thomas, take a little wine with us. It is very good. A gift from Rodrigo."

"She said Juan fights well," Thomas said. He didn't want to sit, but knew he had no choice. Amal wriggled as he did so, wanting to go down, and he set her on her short legs and watched as she went to where Kin lay in the shade with his tongue lolling.

"So does your son," said Fernando, no inflection in his voice.

"Usaden has been training him a long time, Your Grace." Thomas decided to use the formality with de Borja present. "As I am sure you have been training Juan."

"Perhaps I should steal the Moor from you." Fernando smiled, though nothing showed in his eyes.

"You can try, but Usaden is his own man. Even if I were to order him, he would take no heed of me." Thomas turned his head at a movement. Amal was dragging Kin down to the grass, her fingers clutched in the fur at his neck, the dog taller than she was. Thomas watched, unconcerned, knowing the pair were devoted to each other. He would trust Kin with her anywhere, at any time, and knew the dog would sacrifice himself for Amal if need be.

"I like your hound, too," said Fernando. "Where did you get him? Are there more like him?"

"I found him," Thomas said. "He's not really mine, just as

Usaden is not mine." He was aware of de Borja following the conversation, as though trying to judge the play of relationships between Thomas, the King and the Queen. Now the man who was likely to be the next Pope reached over and poured wine for him.

"Try this and tell me what you think. Isabel has told me a great deal about you, Thomas Berrington, and you intrigue me. I like your friend Jorge, too, so decided to place him in your care. He is welcome to join us, his woman too if she wishes. And you and I must talk again before I leave Córdoba. I enjoy talking with intelligent men who have mysterious pasts."

"Oh, my past is not so mysterious."

"Isabel claims otherwise. She tells me you keep much to yourself, as if knowledge is worth more than gold. Speaking of which, I have given some thought to your advice regarding Columb. He also speaks of gold, and of new converts to the one true faith. Have you really changed your mind about him, Thomas Berrington?"

"Thomas has also spoken with me about Columb's plans," said Isabel, her eyes on Thomas. "Rodrigo and I have been discussing his request."

"Do not set too much store on what I think, Your Grace."

Isabel reached out and slapped Thomas on the arm, offering a frown so exaggerated, he laughed, and as he did so, he caught de Borja's frown.

"Tell Rodrigo what you believe, for we have discussed the matter, amongst a great many other things. You used to believe him mad, did you not?"

Thomas nodded. He reached for the fine crystal goblet and took a swallow of wine. It was indeed good. Very good. Perhaps the best wine he had ever tasted.

The clash of steel on steel came distantly from where

Usaden fought against both Will and Prince Juan, who was beginning to flag. Unlike Will, who was taller than Juan despite being five years younger. He took after his *morfar*, Olaf Torvaldsson, and was relentless.

"I changed my mind about his ideas," he said, in answer to Isabel's question.

"Why?" asked de Borja.

"As I said to you two days since, I have taken some time to study a number of texts, consulted maps made by north-men, and I decided there is a land west of us. At least, I hope for Cristof's sake there is, otherwise he and his men are doomed."

"Which is what I fear." Isabel leaned a little closer. "If I agree to fund his expedition and it never returns, I will be sending scores of men to their deaths."

Like the men you send into battle against the Moors, Thomas thought, knowing he could never voice such heresy in her presence.

"Cristof would go willingly. He considers the risk worthwhile. Worth the potential reward." He was aware that de Borja had noted the informality between them, despite Thomas being careful in his speech.

"He tells me there will be gold. Much gold."

"He does not know that." It was Fernando who spoke. "I say send him packing. Let someone else throw their money away. He demands a great deal."

"Three ships," said Isabel. "He claims three ships are enough." She smiled at her husband. "And I know you like to gamble as much as the next man."

"Unless that man is me," said de Borja. He laughed before turning his attention back to Thomas. It was as if a bright lamp had been directed on to him, and Thomas saw how the man had risen to his current position in the church, would no doubt rise to the very pinnacle. "Tell me true, Thomas—I may call you Thomas, may I not? We are all friends here." And when Thomas offered a nod, de Borja continued as he had at their last meeting, "And you must call me Rodrigo."

"It is not my place, Your Eminence."

De Borja stared at him for a long time. Nobody else spoke.

Thomas saw Amal running behind Kin, laughing wildly as she tried to catch his tail. Kin could leave her behind in an instant, but did not. Thomas wished for a life less complicated. For it to be him and Will and Amal. That he might find someone who could take Lubna's place, because he had come to realise he needed that. Lubna would wish it for him. She had set a need for companionship and love in his soul.

When he thought of Eleanor, he knew she was not the companion he sought. Knew, had they not been parted all those years ago, they would have torn themselves apart in the end. Their love had been brittle with the lust of youth and little more. With the realisation, Thomas felt his body relax. Eleanor was not the one. She never had been. But he wondered if someone closer might not be.

De Borja was still waiting.

"What is it you wish to know, Rodrigo?"

The man smiled, but it was no expression of victory, rather that of a friend, a colleague. Thomas warmed to the man even as he continued to suspect he had some deeper knowledge of what had happened to Jorge. But if he did, why free him? He thought of the possibility de Borja was Jorge's father and tried to find some similarity in their faces, and failed. De Borja was handsome, yes, but Jorge was more than handsome.

De Borja, unaware of his thoughts, asked, "Is it your opinion that Columb is right?"

"No, he is wrong. But wrong in the right way. His calculations are not correct. He believes the world smaller than it is, but there is land to the west. Just not the land he is expecting to find."

"And you know this how?"

"I have studied documents."

"Approved documents?"

"They are openly available in the libraries of Gharnatah."

"So not approved."

"Knowledge is always approved." Thomas expected de Borja to show displeasure, but there was none, and once again he felt his respect for the man grow.

"You know that is not the case." De Borja waved a hand. "But no matter. I am aware you are not of Castile. You are English, Isabel tells me. And is England not also a Catholic country? I can see you wear a cross at your neck like a good Christian. So I will listen to your argument and advise my friends accordingly."

Why me? Thomas wondered. It made no sense, but he went along because he wanted to get closer to de Borja. Close enough to find out what he was planning. Close enough to discover whether he had any involvement. Close enough to clear Jorge's name. He touched his own neck, reassured to find the crucifix he had taken from the dead man hidden beneath his clothes. For some reason he preferred de Borja not see it, at least for now.

"We should talk in private," de Borja said. "Man to man. With no-one to witness heresy should any be spoken. Sometimes it is necessary when discussing new ideas. Would you be willing to do that for me, Thomas?"

Thomas nodded, aware he had little choice.

"Later today, then," said de Borja, the matter decided in his own mind. "I leave Córdoba soon, so it is best we talk this afternoon. I will ask for a private meal to be prepared." He glanced toward Isabel, and Thomas saw the man was fully aware of where the power lay. "Can such be arranged?"

"Of course. I wish I could join you, for I trust Thomas's judgement above that of almost any other, but I know I cannot. I will ask Theresa to organise it."

De Borja was about to say something else, but at that moment Juan ran up to his mother, full of excitement to tell her about what Usaden had taught him. Amal came bounding as fast as she could with Kin, and Will followed her on to the terrace, his face red and dripping sweat. Usaden stood off to one side, barely breathing, as if made of stone.

"I look forward to it," Thomas said, watching Isabel as she whispered into Juan's ear, making him laugh. He experienced a wave of unreality, and wondered what the boy who'd left England at thirteen years of age would make of the man who now sat among these people. Men and women who ruled the world. He would not have believed it, he knew, just as he scarcely believed it now.

CHAPTER TWENTY

"I don't like it," said Belia. "He should have woken by now, but he has not even stirred." Her eyes met Thomas's. "Is there nothing you can do?"

"Not yet." He sat on the edge of the bed while Belia perched with Jorge's hand clutched between her breasts. Under normal circumstances that alone would have been enough to wake Jorge. Enough to wake any man. "If he is no different the day after tomorrow, I will decide then, but most likely all he needs is time."

"I still do not like it."

"Neither do I, but at the moment doing nothing is the best treatment." Thomas felt Jorge's pulse, which was strong and slow. "He has not been dreaming, has he?"

"Nothing. He lies like..." Belia cut herself off, not wanting to finish the thought. She took a breath which trembled into her. "Do you have the tools you need if you have to operate on him?"

"I don't, but I can get them soon enough." He didn't tell her that Daniel would be able to provide most of what he needed, once it had been sterilised. A narrow metal punch, and something to drill a hole with. He stood, looking down on them both. "I need to go out again."

"Then you will have to take the children with you, or find someone to look after them. I am not leaving Jorge's side."

Thomas nodded. It was inconvenient, but he knew they were his to care for even if he could not take them where he wanted to go. He would have to find Theresa and trust in her good nature. He might even need to promise something, and was starting to wonder if it might not be a false promise. After his realisation that lying with Eleanor had been a mistake, something had stirred within he had not felt for over a year. The sensation was unfamiliar, but not unwelcome. Time heals, people said. Thomas had not believed their words even though time had healed his pain many times over the years. The loss of his mother, the loss of Eleanor, his abandonment after the Battle of Castillon, a score of times before and since. The loss of Lubna had seemed one trauma too many, but what people claimed was true. Time did heal, whether a man wanted it to or not.

He couldn't find Theresa, which was perhaps for the best. Instead he took Will, Amal and Kin across the river to Daniel's house. Zanita was overjoyed to see them, even his dog, and more than happy for them to stay with her until Thomas returned. Even before he left, Amal was sitting on the floor between the youngest two, babbling away in Arabic, which they laughed at, and Will was talking to Xever, almost twice his age but no taller, about fighting. Thomas worried his son thought of little else, and knew he had not been attentive enough. Nor present enough. That, he promised, would change. Just as soon as he cleared Jorge's name. Which was what he needed to do.

Thomas crossed back into the city. As the walls enfolded

him, they brought a sense of suffocation. He wished he had never agreed to come to Qurtuba, but even as he wished it, he knew a refusal would have been impossible. Abu Abdullah, Muhammed XIII, Sultan of Gharnatah, no longer wanted to kill him, but instead kept Thomas on a leash, ready to do his bidding.

Thomas went first to Lawrence only to discover he had made no further progress.

"I have gone as deep as I can and there is nothing more to find. You have all the information available in the records." He was sitting outside again, and Thomas wondered if he had been doing any work other than that he had asked of him.

"Have you heard from Beatriz?"

"Nothing. Perhaps the birds did not arrive. It happens. I will send another this afternoon."

"Has Miguel been to you?"

"Why would he?"

Thomas started to turn away, suppressing a flare of anger he knew was unfair. Lawrence had done everything asked of him. If there was nothing to be found, then he couldn't conjure information from thin air.

"Thomas."

He blinked and turned to find Lawrence looking at him with concern. "Sorry, I am tired."

"Exhausted is what you are. If there is anything you need of me, or you find out more and want confirmation, come back. Or if you need my blade, you know I am with you." He smiled. "Like the time we went after Mandana. Those were good days, no?"

Thomas was not so sure, but Lawrence's words calmed his unease and he nodded before turning away. Rodrigo de Borja had said they should talk after noon, so Thomas made his way to find Miguel in the Hermandos' offices. He wanted to ask him if he had made any progress on the death of Carlos Mendoza, but it was Miguel who questioned him.

"When you went to Mendoza's house," he said, "did you see anyone else? Anyone leaving the premises?"

"Nobody." Thomas hoped Miguel would not hear any lie in his voice. "Only the dead priest."

"There was someone else there," said Miguel. "There was blood on the floor in one corner, and a knife nearby. Whoever killed Mendoza would have blood on themselves as well. I questioned the neighbours, but they saw nothing, only you and Usaden entering the house."

"It was early in the day," Thomas said. "I didn't notice the blood, I'm afraid. Have you investigated further?"

"A little. Mendoza's house has been searched and a number of items found, some of them relating to Cortez."

"The two men were linked? That would make sense. What items?"

"Documents relating to adoptions Mendoza had made, others that appear to be threats to expose people. It seems Mendoza did more than just place children, he sold them as well." Miguel's expression was sour, and he had no need to explain to Thomas what the children might be sold for. They both knew depravity ran close beneath the surface of society.

"Do you think they approached someone too powerful for them?"

"The information I have all relates to minor individuals, but I intend to keep digging until I find something."

"Then you need to be careful too. Cortez and Mendoza are both dead. Whoever killed them will not baulk at killing a constable."

"I can take care of myself. Has Lawrence found anything out?"

"Nothing new. You should take what you have found to him, he will be able to make connections nobody else can. I will come and find you later. I have an appointment I cannot get out of."

Thomas left Miguel and walked toward the palace with a roiling sense that events were beyond his control, that actions were happening hidden from him. He wondered if he could attempt to question de Borja, to see if he was involved or not. Care would be needed, for the man was hugely influential. Thomas would have preferred Jorge to be with him, but that was impossible. Unless he had woken.

When Thomas entered the room, he found Belia asleep, her body twisted awkwardly, her head resting on the bed beside Jorge, who continued to lie as a man dead. Only the slow rise and fall of his chest gave any indication of life. Thomas checked him, turned his head to examine the wound, and wondered whether tomorrow he would have to open his skull. It was looking increasingly as if pressure was building within, and would need to be released. Thomas had conducted the procedure only a few times before, and not always successfully, but if it was Jorge's only chance, he would attempt it again. The more time passed without him gaining consciousness, the more likely it became he would have to put him in even more danger. The longer Thomas did nothing, the greater the risk of permanent damage, even death.

He left Belia undisturbed and stalked through the corridors to find de Borja. The day had put him in a foul mood, and Jorge's lack of recovery made it only worse. He caught sight of Theresa, who stopped and waved to him, but he ignored her, not sure if he could trust himself. His body had cheated him with Eleanor, hungry to re-discover something he believed lost, but had never been. It was why he ignored Theresa, a woman he had almost succumbed to once before, a woman he was increasingly drawn to. There were too many women in his life. Too much temptation.

He found de Borja on the terrace where he had left him, alone now, and wondered if the man had been there the entire time. There were worse places to pass a warm afternoon. He stood to welcome Thomas, a smile of welcome on his handsome face. Thomas studied it as he approached, trying once more to find some familial resemblance between him and Jorge, and almost succeeded. It seemed today was the time for fathers and sons, a message of blood that could not be ignored however much a man might wish it.

As though reading his mind, de Borja asked, as he shook his hand, "Where are your children, Thomas? You should have brought them, they are welcome here. I like children. They are still innocent."

"You said this was a conversation between the two of us. Besides, they are being looked after by Jorge's family." The words spoken so glibly, words that hid a dozen meanings and a dozen lies.

"I took the liberty of ordering food for us both, as well as wine. Something cooler, I thought. Have you been busy?"

"I have." Thomas hesitated, then decided it was better to launch straight in before the man could distract him with soft words. Already he felt himself drawn to him, put at ease. Only one more reason to believe Jorge could be his son. "Do you know the Countess d'Arreau?"

"I believe we were introduced by Isabel recently, and I have seen her around the palace on occasion. She is a handsome woman."

"And her son?"

"Not so handsome, but strong. She told me he is a credit to his father."

"His father is not his father," Thomas said, and saw de Borja smile.

"A riddle. I like a good riddle. Is there more?"

"It is no riddle," Thomas said. "Eleanor loved another before she was torn from him. She was promised to the Count, but did not love him."

"It happens often enough, I am sure. I assume you know who the father is. Does it have any significance? I met the Countess only briefly, but I liked her. She struck me as a woman who knew her own mind, knew what she wanted from life. A strong woman."

"I knew Eleanor when she had sixteen years." Thomas watched de Borja's eyes, caught a flash of something, but didn't think it was surprise.

"Are you telling me you are Yves's father?"

"You know his name?"

De Borja waved a hand. "She must have mentioned him. So, are you his father?"

Thomas nodded.

De Borja surprised him by laughing and clapping him on the shoulder. "Do you intend to take up your relationship again? You could do worse. Much worse. You honour me with your confession, Thomas, and I thank you." He smiled. "I expect Isabel has told you all about me, too, has she not? That I have lain with women, as you have. That I have fathered children both in and out of wedlock, as it seems you have. But I always loved the women. Always. Do you love Eleanor still?" De Borja tilted his head to one side, his gaze holding Thomas.

For a moment, Thomas was too stunned to speak. De Borja was confessing his sins to him. His weaknesses. Was it this which endeared him to people, this openness, or did he only speak this way to Thomas because he knew he could? That it did not matter what he confessed because Thomas had no position outside the palace?

"Isabel didn't mention any of what you say to me, but I assume she knows you well enough."

"Of course she does, and loves me still."

"And when you are Pope?"

"If I am Pope. It is not decided, and there is a current incumbent I pray lives a long and holy life."

Thomas made the decision to take a risk. "When you are Pope, will these failings come back to haunt you, or are you taking measures to ensure they don't become public knowledge?"

De Borja smiled. "I see Isabel is correct, and you are a most clever man. But you see, everyone knows what I am. Popes are not meant to father children, but almost every one does. Perhaps in the past it was different, and perhaps in the future it will be different again, but for now it means nothing. It may even prove I am a better man for having known women, that I understand the temptations other men have placed on them." He leaned back in his chair as servants brought platters of food and two bottles of fine, pale wine, their sides beaded where they stood in a bucket of iced water.

"Even if you submit to the temptation?"

De Borja laughed so hard he spilled a little of the wine he was pouring. "Oh, I like you, Thomas. Isabel knows you so well, does she not?" His attention was that of a hawk on its prey, and Thomas felt layers of himself being peeled away. "It is not temptation if you have never submitted. But you already know that. You are a man who has submitted, are you not? Who was the first woman you lay with? Was it Eleanor?"

The question was too personal, but Thomas answered anyway. There was something about de Borja that made whatever he said acceptable.

"It was a girl in England."

"Isabel told me that is where you are from. What was her name?"

"It strikes me Isabel tells you too much. Her name was Bel. Bel Brickenden. She was pretty, and I still owe her a penny."

De Borja smiled. "What is a penny?"

"A coin. Not so small, nor so large. It was what she charged."

"Ah, I see. There is no sin in that, though there may be in your not paying pretty Bel what was her due."

"She told me I could pay her later," Thomas said. "And then she died."

De Borja's eyes locked on his, a softness in them, perhaps an understanding.

"How old were you?"

"A month shy of thirteen years."

De Borja's eyes widened a little. "That is young for your first time."

"How old were you?" Thomas asked.

"Not as young as you. I was fourteen."

"Do you remember her?"

"Of course I do, as I know you remember pretty Bel Brickenden, and I recall to this day everything we did. She was older than me by some years, and taught me much." He smiled. "I believed I loved her, but know now it was not love but lust. Is that how it was with you and Bel?"

Thomas nodded. "And Castellana?"

"Ah, Castellana. You know about her, do you? Did Isabel tell you?"

"No, another friend here in Qurtuba. Another Englishman."

"It sounds almost the same, does it not? Córdoba, Qurtuba? Is that what you call it in Granada?"

Thomas smiled. "Yes, that is what we call it in Gharnatah. Where I live among the Moors. They are my people now. I am no longer a man of England."

"Except you would prefer a different master, I hear." De Borja leaned closer, picked up his glass and sipped from it. "Drink, Thomas, while it is still cold. Isabel says she has offered you a post at her side. Is that what you want? To be more than at her side? You can tell me—confess if you prefer to call it that—whatever lies in your heart."

"Has Isabel confessed what lies in hers?"

De Borja only smiled and Thomas saw the truth. This man would never betray a confidence, however large or small, however trivial.

"You had a child with Castellana? Or more than one?"

"We did, but only the one. Gabriel is his name. A good name. We married in Valencia. She had already had a child by another man, but she was young, so very young, and gave her first born away."

Thomas stopped in the act of reaching for his glass of wine. "Another man?"

"I believe that is what I said. We are being honest, are we not? Yes, we are."

"Do you know this man's name?"

"Of course ... but it is something I will not reveal to you

without good reason. Why do you ask, Thomas, is it idle curiosity or something else? When you came here you looked ready for a fight. Something worries you, I can tell. What is it?"

"Many things worry me. If we are speaking the truth, I will tell you this. I told you I am father to Eleanor's son, but I never saw him, did not even know if the child she carried was girl or boy. I met Yves for the first time here, in this city. He is a man now, full grown. And I am not sure I much like him."

"We do not have to like our children, but still we love them, do we not?"

"I love those I have now. This one … I am still making up my mind."

"And his mother? Do you still love her?"

"You said yourself sometimes we confuse love with lust."

De Borja laughed. "Oh, Thomas, I do like you. We are so much alike beneath the skin. I believe I did love Castellana once, but like you, that was long ago. We are both different people now. As you and Eleanor are different people." De Borja let out a sigh. "A girl you loved and no longer love, a son you do not even like. No wonder you have things on your mind. And you are investigating a murder. A murder your closest companion is accused of."

Thomas felt the threads of truth and lies run across his skin like a physical presence. Now was the time to speak or he never would. He reached inside his shirt and drew out the crucifix he had carried since taking it from a dead man. He held it out toward de Borja, intending to tell him the tale, intending to tell him that Jorge was Castellana's son. He hoped the revelation would shake some truth from the man. Instead, de Borja reached out and snatched the cross from Thomas, jerking so hard the leather thong snapped.

"Where did you get this abomination?"

Thomas stared open-mouthed at him, feeling the world tilt off-kilter again. The truth, he told himself. All that matters is the truth.

"I took it from a dead man."

De Borja frowned. "It is not yours?"

"I never wear a cross."

Again a frown. "Are you aware of the meaning of this symbol? This abomination of our Lord?"

"I thought the fashioning well done, even if fashioned of base metal, but no, to me it is a crucifix."

"You asked me who the father of Castellana's first born was and I said I could never tell you, and then you show me this." De Borja took a breath, for once his placid demeanour lost. His eyes met Thomas's. He glanced away, came to a decision and looked back at Thomas. "The man who was the father owned a crucifix exactly like this." De Borja examined the metal more closely. "It might even be this one. This dead man, was he tall, handsome?"

"Short, and ugly."

"One of his men, then. I heard he has fashioned these objects and gives them to those he recruits."

"Recruits?" Thomas was confused, the conversation taking a turn he had not seen coming. "He has an army?"

"Yes, an army. He claims it is a holy army, but he is wrong. A holy army would not want to attack me, would not want to attack the Church." De Borja held the cross out for Thomas. "I am sorry, I broke the thong, but it can be tied again. Who was the man you took this from?"

"He approached Jorge offering information in exchange for money. The name of his mother."

"He does not know it?"

"It is a long story, with more twists and turns than the

tracks on the Sholayr, but even though the man is dead, Jorge now knows who his mother is. The woman you were married to. Castellana Lonzal." Thomas watched de Borja's eyes widen. The food, the fine wine, lay ignored on the table. The warmth of the sun barely touched either man. The world had shrunk to the space between them.

"Inigo…" said de Borja.

Thomas frowned. The name was familiar, one Lawrence had mentioned, if only he could recall in what context.

"Who is Inigo?"

"He is Jorge's father. Inigo Florentino. And his greatest wish is to kill me with his own hands. To kill Castellana too, perhaps even his own son. He hates us all."

"Jorge's father wants to kill him?"

"There are few he does not want to kill."

"Then perhaps he has succeeded, because Jorge lies in the palace even as we sit here, and I fear he is dying." Thomas's voice broke, his pain too much to contain.

De Borja sat upright. "Then I must see him, must pray over him. If he is Inigo's son, I will be able to tell. I will forgive him the sins of his father that he may live."

CHAPTER TWENTY-ONE

"He could be Jorge's father, even if you say he is not," said Belia. She and Thomas sat on either side of Jorge on opposite edges of the bed. "He has that same handsome nature that goes deeper than beauty, that same spirit. Is he truly a Cardinal?"

Thomas nodded, two fingers resting on Jorge's neck, the steady beat of his heart almost hypnotic. The light in the room was golden as it captured the last of the setting sun and seemed to magnify it. The day was drawing to a close, a long day filled with more revelations than Thomas knew how to make sense of.

"He did not seem surprised when he came in," said Belia.

"Far less so than me. What on earth were you doing?"

"I thought it fairly obvious what I was doing."

"Why? Jorge is unconscious."

Belia gave the faintest of smiles. "Why not?" She held a hand up as Thomas opened his mouth to speak. "I started out washing his body, but then when he responded, I thought…" She let her breath go, the smile coming again. "I thought it might do some good. Might shake him out of his slumber."

"Perhaps if we had not come in you would have succeeded. Perhaps I should leave so you can try again."

"No, stay. I feel safer with you here. In case anything goes wrong. Why did he pray over Jorge? Did you tell him he does not believe in any God?"

"I did. And de Borja said it didn't matter, because God believed in him."

"Is that what he told you when you were whispering outside the room?"

"No, that was something else. He told me if I wanted to know more about Jorge's father, I must ask his mother. This Castellana Lonzal. He said it with a certain emphasis, as if it was an order rather than a suggestion, as if the information was important. He told me the name of his father, and that he hates everyone, but gave no more details."

"Is this man, his father, the one trying to accuse Jorge?"

Thomas recalled where Lawrence had mentioned the name Inigo Florentino. "It makes some sense. He was in contact with Cortez. He wanted him to search for Jorge, I believe, but for what purpose I am not longer sure. I would assume a father seeking his son would want to renew their relationship, but de Borja seemed to imply he was as likely to be seeking him put in order to kill him." Thomas shook his head. "I wish he would tell me more, but he says I have to ask Castellana Lonzal."

Belia glanced at the prone figure on the bed. "Are you going to visit her?"

"I would prefer Jorge to be with me when I do."

"Perhaps he will wake by morning and you can take him with you. Or that man's God will answer his prayers. You do not believe in God either, do you, Thomas?"

"You know I don't. Do you?" He was aware they had never spoken so intimately before, something about their care of Jorge, something about the strangeness of the day conspiring to loosen Thomas's normal restraint.

"My Gods are strange," said Belia. "Far too strange to even attempt to explain them, even if I could."

"I would like to know."

"There is little point. They cannot be defined or described. They are as much within me as without."

"Do they come from where you come from?"

Belia laughed. "Ixbilya? No. I was born there, but my father was not. He brought his Gods with him and passed them down to me." She pursed her mouth as if she tasted something sour. "Why are we talking of Gods, Thomas? There must be much else to discuss. Tell me what you have done today while I slept the hours away. Have you made any progress in clearing Jorge's name?"

"I thought I had, but now I am more confused than I have ever been."

"Why?"

"I more than half believed de Borja was Jorge's father, and he wanted him dead."

Belia stared at Thomas. "And now you know who his real father is, and he wants him dead. Why would a father want his son dead? A son who is now a grown man?" She shook her head.

"There are many reasons. Fear of being found out, of being shamed. Fear of the child wanting something due him. Fear a child will do something to bring disrepute on the family name. Something like murder."

Belia must have heard the strain in his voice because she reached across Jorge's still figure and grasped Thomas's hand in hers. Their joined hands lay on Jorge's chest and it felt like the completion of something, the three of them, and Thomas shivered.

"You should marry again." Belia laughed. "Well, not marry perhaps, but it is well past time you lay with a woman again."

"I have."

Belia grinned, something she did rarely. "Who? The red-haired woman? Not the Queen!"

"Neither."

Belia squeezed his hand. "I am teasing you, Thomas. Jorge told me you have found your first love again. It was almost the first thing he told me after he said he still loved me. As if I did not know, despite his talk of other women."

"I am not Jorge."

"No, you are not. Did he talk to you about children?"

Thomas frowned. "Will and Amal? We talk of them all the time, as I do with you. You know I am still not sure about being Will's father, but I grow more certain as the days pass. I see something of myself in him."

"Not Will or Amal. About our child. Jorge's and mine."

"He has said he wished he could set seed in you, yes. In fact..."

"What? Can you repair him? Tell me you can, Thomas." She squeezed his fingers tight.

"No, I cannot fix him."

"He wants a child with me and has a plan for it to happen. Not directly, of course, but it would be almost the next best thing. Has he talked to you of it?"

"Have you ever known him to withhold even the slightest thought to himself? So yes, he spoke of it to me."

"And what did you say? I understand what your reply

would have been when Lubna lived, though I asked her as well and she told me she had no objection, just so long as you did not enjoy yourself." Belia laughed. "I told her I could make no promises, but now you are a free man."

Thomas stared at Belia, at Jorge, and felt his world tilt even more out of balance. A sense of dizziness washed through him which he put down to tiredness. He needed to sleep.

"Come for me if he wakes. Come for me at once."

Belia's eyes were on him, so dark, so mysterious they seemed to bore into his very soul, to lay bare every secret it harboured. Thomas turned away, angry with himself and his many weaknesses.

Everything might have been all right if Theresa had not been sitting in his rooms watching over Will and Amal, returned from Daniel's house and both of them asleep in the small bedroom set to one side. When she rose, Thomas feared she was about to come to him, grateful when she stayed where she was, smoothing her skirts. He didn't know what he would have done if she had.

"Have they been behaving themselves?"

"They are sweet children," she said.

Thomas couldn't stop the laugh that escaped him. "Will is a sweet child? Are we talking about the same boy?"

"I am. He is like his father. He can fight like a demon, but holds no grudge afterward. Isabel's children like him, too. It is a pity you are not someone important enough for a match to be made."

Thomas had not been aware of her moving, but all at once she was standing far too close.

"I must sleep," he said. "I thank you for your help. I am sorry, but I may need to call on you again tomorrow. Or I could take them across to Daniel's house again. Yes, that would be better."

Theresa laid a hand on his chest, the distance between them even smaller. "I am available any time you need me, Thomas. You know I am. For you I am always available."

When Belia came into his room in the dark of night and shook him awake, Thomas was glad to discover he was alone. His head had been so muddled, he could barely recall his refusal of Theresa's offer. His dreams had been filled so strongly with images of her, he had to reach out to the bed beside him to ensure it was empty.

"Jorge is awake," said Belia. "He wants to see you."

Jorge sat at a small table, eating a plate of sauced meat with rice. He waved a hand for Thomas to sit, while Belia perched on the side of the bed. Instead of doing as Jorge wanted, Thomas felt his neck, put a finger beneath his chin to turn his head.

"I am fine," said Jorge. "Hungry is all. Starving. How long have I been asleep?"

"Did Belia not tell you? Now stay still and let me finish, or I am going back to my bed." He saw a smile flit across Belia's lips.

"I need to tell you something."

"When I am done. Now behave, for once."

Thomas took a candle and moved it in front of Jorge's eyes, pleased to see his pupils react. He parted his hair to examine the wound. It was beginning to heal, the bruise now purple, the gash starting to form a scab.

"Does your head ache?"

"Only at the back, and it itches like mad. They came at—"

"Later. Do you have pain anywhere else? Or feel dizzy? Sick?"

"I am perfectly fine. Now sit and let me tell you what I know."

"What were you doing there? Are you mad? And with a dagger in your hand! The same dagger used on Mendoza. You must be mad."

"My only madness was in thinking I could take care of matters on my own."

"You were meant to stay in the palace. I promised Isabel and you made me break my promise."

"She will forgive you, she always does. I know I should have waited, but it was too good an opportunity to put an end to all this, so I went to see him on my own. I am sorry."

"What did you find out?" Thomas was still angry, but curiosity pushed it aside for the moment. "Did he tell you who the killer is?"

"He was already dead when I got there." Jorge pulled a face. "Well, as good as dead. Two men were still working on him when I arrived. I turned to flee, cried out, but there was another man I hadn't seen. I was sure I was about to die, just like the priest. I was sure I was dead. One man held me and the other hit me with something."

"The hilt of a dagger, it looks like."

"Well, you would know, wouldn't you? It hurt like crazy and I must have passed out, but I came awake and they were still there. They were talking and I lay still so they believed I was unconscious. They said something strange, 'The man from Roma said do not kill the eunuch.'" Jorge's eyes were bright, his face flushed, the words tumbling out too fast in his haste to tell the story. "Were they talking about Rodrigo, do you think? Is my father a killer? Have I found him only to discover he is a murderer and wants me dead?"

"De Borja is not your father. Besides, they said not to kill you."

"You told me he might be." Jorge frowned. "Belia told me you think that woman Castellana brought me to Qurtuba and left me with that sorry excuse for a family. You told me they were married. That I have a brother."

"They were married, which might mean de Borja is not innocent in any of this, though I drank wine with him yesterday and he seduced me with soft words." Thomas glanced at Belia. "Your father is a man by the name of Inigo Florentino."

"An Italian?"

"I don't know. I should have asked de Borja more about him, but I don't think he meant to even tell me the name. I shocked it out of him when he saw this." Thomas withdrew the cross, the thong now retied. He was aware he had grown used to its presence, but had no idea why it should comfort him as it did.

"I don't understand—he told you because you showed him that?"

"He told me your father wore one just like it. For a moment I think he believed it the same cross. It had some meaning for him. Not a good one. De Borja hates your father, and your father hates de Borja."

"Why?"

"That I don't know either, but Castellana gave birth to you and then gave you away. She did so because she was marrying de Borja and I suspect both wanted no evidence of her mistake. It wouldn't make sense for her to give one child away and keep the other, unless de Borja made her do it. She would have been barely a woman when you were seeded in her belly. I can see how de Borja might hate your father for taking her innocence. I can also see how your father would hate de Borja for stealing someone he regarded as his."

"She is still my mother?"

"Of course she is. Lawrence found some papers linking Inigo Florentino to Cortez. What if Cortez was blackmailing people himself, and also through Mendoza? What if they tried to blackmail your father and he struck back?"

"Is it because he is ashamed of me?"

"We can't decide anything yet, or assume anything. Men have died, but for what purpose I don't yet know."

"But you will, Thomas, I know you will. You have done this before and you will do it again. Damn it, I'm hungry." Jorge stuffed more food into his mouth and spoke around it. "What time do we leave in the morning? It's already morning, isn't it? I am not tired so we can leave now if you want, once I have finish this good food. And..." He glanced toward Belia. "No, that can wait. Let me get dressed."

"I don't even know where this Castellana Lonzal lives," Thomas said, "only the name of a town. We need to go to Lawrence and Miguel before we set off on some wild chase." Thomas stared at Jorge until he stopped eating. "Why did you go to that priest Mendoza on your own?"

"One of the prisoners told me Mendoza would know about my past after I explained it to him. How I was abandoned, handed over to another family." Jorge shook his head. "One man told me that is what Mendoza does. What he has done for years. He places orphaned children, not always with good intent. It is astonishing how prisoners talk so openly amongst themselves. It's not such a bad life in prison, you know, not nearly as bad as I feared it would be. Not that I want to go back there, of course."

"You gave me his name, knew I would be going there shortly after dawn. Why did you sneak out, putting yourself in danger of being arrested again, when you knew I would be going to the man?"

"Because some things are best discussed in private."

Thomas stared at Jorge, wondering if he had missed some sign of damage to his brain after all.

CHAPTER TWENTY-TWO

Thomas smiled as he watched Kin bound ahead of their small party, revelling in his freedom from the constraints and foul air of the city. The hound raced through long grass, bounced off bushes, then ran full tilt into the wide Guadalquivir where he seemed to instantly regret the decision. Kin was a hunting dog. Tall, lean, built for speed, but less so for swimming. His legs were too thin, his chest too deep. He flailed in the water, coughed when he swallowed some, eventually managed to pull himself ashore where he shook vigorously, almost disappearing in the spray. Thomas laughed. He saw Usaden almost smile. Jorge rode a little ahead, lost in his own thoughts, almost certainly considering the coming meeting with the woman who lay at the end of their journey.

Almost two days had passed since Jorge woke from his coma and Thomas listened to his story of why he had gone to Mendoza's house. Jorge had demanded they travel to El Carpio at once, but Thomas said no. He wanted to ensure he was at least partially recovered. Jorge pointed out it was not as if his brain was the most important part of his anatomy, but still Thomas insisted.

He had gone to Miguel in the Hermandos' offices while he waited, wanting to know if there had been any progress in the search for the men seen in Cortez's street, but there was nothing new.

"Too much time has passed since the event," said Miguel. "My masters want me to move on to other matters. I am pursuing it in my own time, but they are probably right. Men come and go. Men hired to kill a man and burn his house to the ground will have come into the city and left soon after the event. But I continue to try, Thomas. I will not give up."

"And the priest, Mendoza, any progress there?"

"One night-worker said he saw a man approach the house shortly before dawn, but he had his back to him so he did not see his face. He said he was tall and slim." Miguel smiled. "If you had not been with me and your friend not restricted to the palace, it might describe you both. I will keep digging into that mystery as well, though. There was another person in that room, and I would like to know if they were the killer or another victim."

"So would I," Thomas said, relieved Jorge had not been identified a second time. "This watchman saw nobody else? A group of men?"

"Only the one, why? Do you know something else? Was there evidence you found that I missed?"

"Nothing. You know everything I do." Thomas watched Miguel for any sign of suspicion, but saw he believed him. He felt bad at deceiving the man, but not as bad as if he'd told him the truth.

Jorge had said the men who attacked him spoke of a man

from Roma, which might implicate either de Borja or Inigo Florentino. The problem was, Thomas liked de Borja and found it hard to believe him involved. Which was all well and good, except it meant he was no further forward in exposing the true culprit. The journey to see Castellana Lonzal seemed a distraction. She might know something, but would it be relevant in any way? Thomas was not convinced.

They had set out at dawn, and once again Thomas had left his children in Theresa's care. He thought she might have offered some objection, but she had shown no reluctance, if anything the opposite. Thomas worried she was growing used to being a replacement mother for them. A position she would no doubt like to make permanent, as well as other positions she had mentioned while teasing him.

Toward noon, the town of El Carpio appeared ahead, perched on a low hill, still an hour's ride away. Thomas had led them across the Roman bridge when they left Qurtuba, knowing there was no crossing point if they stayed north of the Guadalquivir. Castellana Lonzal's estate was beyond the town, extending along the rich valley land for several miles. They rode through the main street of El Carpio and for once Jorge did not ask to stop to eat or drink. Thomas considered it a sign of nervousness at the prospect of meeting his real mother.

When a track led toward a walled entrance to a substantial house raised above the river, Thomas called them to a halt and they stripped out of their clothes. He had ensured they had all brought something clean to wear before they approached Castellana Lonzal. Thomas was sure Jorge would have made sure he had something suitably flamboyant, so was surprised when he pulled on conservative hose, trousers and jacket. Usaden simply replaced his fighting clothes with a less dusty set. Thomas dressed in a similar manner to Jorge and they set off again, watching to see if anyone had observed their approach. Men and women worked the fields, which stretched as far as the eye could see, mostly well-tended olives, but here and there were stands of cork oak, vines, and even a large field of mulberry, though how much silk it might yield was questionable. Its presence struck Thomas as a rich woman's vanity. He glanced toward Jorge to see his face was serious and knew he was nervous. He didn't blame him.

The track passed between two weathered stone columns without anyone coming to ask their business. Thomas began to wonder if the servant in Qurtuba had lied to him and Castellana had not returned to her estate. He knew he should have gone to the house again to check before leaving, but could not bring himself to do so. He wondered if Eleanor was also regretting their foolish coupling. She had sent no message, made no overture she wanted to meet again. Already the images Thomas carried of her in his head were fading, the old as well as the new. If their love had been so intense at the age of seventeen, should it not remain so at the age of forty-eight? Or was that nothing but the fantasy of a young man? Whatever the reason, Thomas was aware of a change in himself. He had held her memory inside him for years. Meeting her again had shattered those memories. It felt like a liberation.

As the three of them rode on, one or two field-workers paused to watch before returning to their labour. Nobody called out. Nobody questioned their presence.

"I want you to do the talking," said Jorge, bringing his horse close to Thomas's. Even Kin had stopped his lunging runs and trotted obediently behind Usaden, almost like a normal, well-behaved dog.

"It is you who needs to introduce yourself."

"I want to see what she is like first."

Thomas smiled. "Whatever she is like, she is your birth mother. You can't change that."

"But I can ride away without her knowing who I am."

Thomas glanced at Jorge. "How could you? Besides, she might be wonderful and you will fall in love with her instantly, and she with you."

"Yes, that might happen." Jorge sat a little straighter and stared ahead as the roadway rose to a tree-shaded terrace set along the front of the house, an inner courtyard visible beyond. A flag flew from a circular tower to one side, the coat of arms unfamiliar, but most were to Thomas, each family claiming their own. A fine carriage had pulled up in front of the wide entrance archway and Thomas wondered if the woman they had come to meet was planning to leave. It was only as they dismounted and tied their horses to a waiting post that anyone confronted them. A man came from the courtyard, a sword in his hand. Behind him came six others, each of them also armed.

"State your business." His voice was curt, used to being listened to and obeyed without question. Thomas studied him. His features were shadowed with a confusing familiarity that pulsed in and out of focus. This, he knew, had to be Jorge's half-brother. Not as handsome, nor as tall, but the resemblance could make him no other. And even less handsome than Jorge, it still made him good-looking, someone women would welcome the attentions of. He also had a position, which would no doubt help.

"I am friend to Eleanor, Countess d'Arreau." Thomas tried to make his voice sound half as arrogant as the man who confronted them, but found it difficult, for he was exceptionally arrogant.

"That is not stating your business. What do you want?"

"I would speak with your mother." Thomas allowed a little steel to enter his voice. He glanced to one side to ensure Usaden was prepared, but knew he would be. "The Countess sends me with news for her."

The man laughed. "Then she has no doubt delivered it herself, for she arrived here yesterday. She made no mention of any news, so you can turn around and go back to wherever you came from." His eyes scanned them, but appeared to find nothing to concern him. A mistake, Thomas thought, but one he might never become aware of.

"I can't do that. It is Castellana Lonzal my business is with, not you." He watched as the man's companions spread out to either side, their eyes measuring the opposition. Only seven men in total, but Thomas would prefer not to fight anyone today unless he had to. He hoped Usaden felt the same way.

"I told you, my mother has no appointments today. This is your last warning." He took a step closer, his companions matching him. Thomas didn't reach for his own weapon, was pleased to see neither did Usaden, though he knew it would appear in his hand faster than the eye could follow when needed.

He briefly studied the other men and considered they might be a problem. Four held themselves like trained soldiers. The others were not, but neither was Thomas, though he had fought like one often enough. Castellana's son he dismissed, recognising a bully when he saw one, knowing he would be the last to attack, and only when assured of victory. That still left six men against their three. Two if he did not count Jorge.

Thomas let the world of humanity leach from him, to be replaced by a sharp cold.

Then a woman appeared behind the men and Thomas let his breath go. He recognised her from that first glimpse in the palace all those days ago, when Jorge was considered only wicked, not guilty of murder.

"What is going on, Gabriel? Who are these men, and why are you confronting them?"

"They look like brigands, Mother."

Castellana Lonzal pushed past her son until she stood between the two groups. Close to, she was more handsome than Thomas's distant glimpse of her had suggested. She was tall for a woman, with rich pale hair and a slim waist. Her clothing was testament to her wealth, as was her confidence. Her eyes met Thomas's and he saw a flare of something, perhaps respect, perhaps fear, more likely nothing more than recognition, just as he had recognised her. Then she turned her attention to Jorge. It took a moment before a frown appeared on her brow, and Thomas knew she was experiencing the same strange unbalancing of the world he'd had when he first looked on his own son. Finally realisation came to her and she opened her mouth to speak, but nothing emerged.

"They must leave," said the man Thomas now knew was Gabriel Lonzal. Despite being the younger half-brother of Jorge, he appeared older. Not as tall as Jorge, but still taller than most men, he had broad shoulders and shared his mother's pale hair, but there was a weakness to the way he held himself despite his bluster. It was easy to be brave when six men stood behind you.

"No," said Castellana, "I have a mind to admit them. But these two only." She indicated Thomas and Jorge with a curt wave of her hand. "The dog stays outside with the other. He can attend to their horses."

Usaden raised an eyebrow but said nothing.

"I was expecting you, gentlemen," she said. "Eleanor warned me you might visit, and here you are. You must be Thomas, and I assume you are my first-born son." She turned and walked past the line of unmoving men. As she did so, she gave a single order: "Let them pass."

None of the men moved, so Thomas walked around them, knowing they would not attack now, and if they did Usaden would be on them in a moment. As he entered the wide courtyard shaded by fragrant orange and lemon trees, he became aware Jorge was not with him and turned back. Jorge stood unmoving beside Usaden. Thomas raised a hand and beckoned him to follow, but he stayed rooted to the spot. Gabriel Lonzal raised his sword in a mock threat and Jorge flinched, took a step back.

Usaden leaned close to him and said something. Jorge nodded, firmed his shoulders and walked directly toward his brother. Gabriel stepped aside at the last moment, perhaps more afraid of his mother's wrath than he was of them.

"Idiot," Thomas said as Jorge reached him. When he turned back, he saw Castellana Lonzal standing in a doorway at the far end of the courtyard, waiting for them. She remained there as they approached, then turned and entered a deep room that led to another terrace. This one looked across a bluff to the river, which had carved a wide loop for itself, the force of water unstoppable over the aeons.

Castellana led the way to a table set with chairs, but remained on her feet. She studied Jorge, showing no indication of approval or not. Nor any sign of acceptance.

"It is you then, is it?" she said.

Jorge looked at Thomas, who shrugged. She was not interested in him.

"What do you want? Money? An acknowledgement?" When Jorge continued to say nothing, she turned to Thomas. "Is he simple?"

"Far from it. He is afraid."

"I apologise for Gabriel. He meant nothing."

"Oh, I think he did, but it's not him Jorge is afraid of."

"He is afraid of me?"

"Of himself. Of what he feels in your presence." A movement to one side made Thomas turn his head. He expected to see Gabriel come to watch the encounter, but instead Eleanor stood there, her eyes on Thomas. There was no sign of Yves. Something coiled inside him, some want he had thought silenced only for it to push itself forward. Did it mean they had unfinished business?

"Why?" said Jorge. A single word, but Castellana knew what he meant and let her breath go in a deep sigh. She stepped to one side and reached for the back of a chair, as if unsure of her balance.

Eleanor came further into the room, concern on her face, but stopped again.

"I want nothing from you," Jorge said, and Thomas was relieved to hear his voice sounded almost normal. "All I want to do is talk. To know why you abandoned me. Why you gave me up."

"I was…" Castellana put a hand to her head, touched her hair. Her features reflected his, not a mirror image, but as if viewed through a shifting mist. Her eyes were the same colour and softness as Jorge's. Her mouth the same, but her nose different.

So engrossed did Thomas become in studying the likeness, he was startled when Eleanor touched his arm.

"We should leave them to talk." She gripped his wrist and tried to pull him away.

"No, stay." It was Castellana who spoke. "I need you with me, Eleanor. And he probably needs you with him, too. You are Thomas, aren't you?" And when he nodded, she said, "Eleanor has told me all about you. It seems it is time for sons to discover their parents, is it not?" She glanced at Eleanor. "Send for food and wine. The good wine, for this should be a celebration." She clapped her hands together. "Yes, a celebration. And send something out for the Moor, but no wine for him." It was a petty thing to do, and Thomas wondered how much it revealed of her true nature. She turned her attention back to Jorge. "I do not even know your name. It is stupid, I should at least know your name."

"Jorge."

Her lips thinned. "So they did not change it. Jorge…" She rolled the word in her mouth, tasting its familiarity. "It was my father's name."

Thomas felt a shifting in the room. Eleanor had left, but would return soon, and he knew he would have his own decision to make. Life had grown complex.

Castellana sat, indicating the chair next to hers. She turned to face it as Jorge took the seat. She reached out and grasped his hands and Thomas saw tears gather in her eyes. Then Jorge returned fully to himself. He smiled and lifted her hands to his lips, kissed the back of each, his magic returned, his mother captured in his presence. Jorge drew her closer and put his arms around her shoulders and held her while she sobbed. Only when her tears finally ebbed and stopped did Eleanor return, and Thomas knew she had been waiting for the moment.

"They will bring the food and wine." She took one of the chairs and stared at Thomas in expectation, though of what he did not know, and tried not to even think of.

"You say I share your father's name?" Jorge reached out

and ran his thumb across his mother's cheek to wipe away the track of a tear. "Tell me about my father. Tell me how you met, how you fell in love." A smile. "You did fall in love, didn't you?"

Castellana showed no acknowledgment. It seemed as if she had fallen into her own despair.

"Tell me everything," said Jorge. "And then, when you are done, Thomas will tell me what else I need to know."

CHAPTER TWENTY-THREE

Jorge sat beside his mother while she talked. Her tears had dried, but her voice trembled as she spoke with a suppressed emotion. Was it shock at the sudden appearance of a son she had abandoned over thirty years before? Thomas wondered if she had ever taken any interest in him after abandoning him. Was that why she had come to live close to Qurtuba? If so, had she believed Jorge dead, as his own family had when he was carried away by the Guadalquivir? Whatever she thought, she had clearly decided to be brutally honest, holding nothing back.

"I was young," she said, once the servants had poured wine and laid small plates of olives, pork and veal on the table. "I had barely fourteen years, your father a few years more. The three of us were close. Me, Inigo and Rodrigo." Her eyes caught on Jorge's face, captured by what she saw.

"Inigo Florentino?"

Castellana nodded.

"Do I look like him?"

Another nod. "Oh yes. You could be him, if he had lived."

"He is dead?"

"He was dead before I married Rodrigo."

Thomas frowned. Was Castellana's claim true or false? And if true, why did de Borja seem to believe the man alive?

"What happened?" Thomas asked the question. He wondered how the two friends had fallen out. Was it over a beautiful woman? It would not be the first time, nor the last.

"He was sent away."

"Who by, his family?"

"That is the story I was told, but I did wonder later if it was true or not. Rodrigo told me when his family discovered Inigo had set a child in my belly, they sent him away to Roma."

"What did you believe later?"

Castellana gave a wave of her fingers, a flick of almost dismissal. "I believed the same, even after Rodrigo asked to marry me. It should have been Inigo, but Rodrigo was handsome too, and ambitious." Her mouth tightened. "Too ambitious for me, in the end."

"Are you sure this Inigo Florentino is dead? How do you know?"

"Rodrigo again, of course. We are no longer married, but when he comes to Castile we always meet. He is a good friend to the Queen." Her eyes lifted to meet Thomas's. "As good a friend as you are, I hear, and a better friend to Castile. When Rodrigo moved to Italia, he made enquiries. Perhaps he wanted to mend the rift between them. I have a letter from him somewhere with everything laid out. Inigo had set himself up in business as a merchant, a trader. It is said he did well for himself and then, on a journey to Tunis, his ship was lost in a storm, together with all hands. Rodrigo wanted me to know. He knew I still thought of Inigo." She glanced from Thomas to Eleanor, then back. "You do not forget your first love, do you?"

Thomas knew he had other questions to ask of de Borja. Clearly the man wanted to keep knowledge that Inigo Florentino remained alive to himself, but to what end? Did he want to protect Castellana?

"Why did you give Jorge up?"

"I could not keep him, not once Rodrigo asked me to marry him. He could not be seen to accept another man's child. Nobody knew when he asked me, of course, only him and me. He took me away from Valencia, where we all lived, and brought me here to Córdoba. Rodrigo arranged everything. There was a priest and he took the baby away." She looked toward Jorge. "You had only six weeks when you were taken. My breasts ached with unshed milk for a month after they took you. I did not even know you were given to a family in the same city until much later, and by then it was too late. I paid the priest to find you again. He claimed to have tried, but I suspect he did no more than take my money and tell me lies."

"What did he say?" Thomas asked.

Her gaze remained on Jorge as she replied. "He told me Jorge was dead. Carried away by the river and lost. He had found his family, though, a brother who carried a broken leg, and a man and woman I did not ever want to meet." Her chest hitched and she wiped a fresh tear from her eye "I thought you dead, my sweet boy."

Thomas listened for the truth or the lie in her words, but could not decide what lay there.

"Why did you return to Qurtuba if this is where you gave him up?"

"Why do you think?" she snapped. "It was years later, fourteen years and Rodrigo was long gone to make a name for himself in Roma. I had Gabriel, who I dearly love, but there is never a love like that of a mother for her first born.

I had lost two men I loved, father and son both, so I came to look for the one I believed was still alive. I never re-married after Rodrigo left so I was a free woman. I could do whatever I wished, and I thought Gabriel young enough to accept an older brother then." She glanced toward the doorway. "Less so now, I suspect."

Thomas believed the same based on the man's greeting of them.

"What happened?"

"I found the priest who gave Jorge away and asked him to try to find him again. Córdoba is a large city, teeming with life, and I knew I would not find him without help."

"Was the priest Carlos Mendoza?"

"It was."

"Tell me what he discovered." Thomas knew the answer, he had worked out the timelines for himself, but he wanted to hear if Castellana Lonzal would tell him the same thing.

"He took months. Jorge had disappeared into the cesspit of Córdoba's slum, but eventually he tracked down the family with the help of another man, a scribe he said. He came to me with the news I did not want to hear. Jorge was dead."

"How?"

"You should know how." Castellana's voice took on a sharpness.

"Should I?"

"He was carried away by the Guadalquivir after his brother fell from the old bridge and broke his leg. A search was made, but no body was ever found. I believed him drowned, just like his father. I liked to think the mighty river had carried him into the sea so they could lie side by side."

"Have you had dealings with Mendoza since?"

"None, though I have with the other man, the scribe. I have used his services since. He is efficient and charges little."

No, he wouldn't charge much, Thomas thought, because the information Cortez held was worth far more than the making of it.

"Alonso Cortez," Thomas said, rewarded when Castellana nodded. "Are you aware he was murdered, and his house razed to the ground?"

For a moment her eyes widened, then she shook her head. "I was not. I heard talk of a fire, but did not know it was where he lived."

"Even though his house was owned by Inigo?"

Castellana stared at him. She shook her head. Opened her mouth, then shut it again.

"No," she said at last. "That is impossible. Inigo is dead."

Thomas had no idea when the document he saw had been written, that part had been burnt away, but he took a risk anyway. "Is he? How can he own a house in Qurtuba if he lies on the bed of the sea? How did Cortez not tell you this? He must have known who Jorge's father was."

"I never mentioned Jorge to him, ever. All the work he did for me related to trade, land contracts, property. He did not know about Jorge."

"Of course he did. You told me he worked with Mendoza to track him down. I never met the man, but I don't believe he was stupid. He would have worked the connection out. Did he come to you wanting the information kept quiet? The only thing I don't understand is why he waited so long."

Castellana rose to her feet, her body sharp with tension. "What are you accusing me of, sir?"

"Nothing, I am trying to unearth the truth."

"The truth is what I have told you." Castellana swung around as a servant entered with a tray of food and wine. "No! Take it away!" She flung her arm out, almost crashing the tray from the woman's hands. Castellana clenched her fists and appeared to make an effort to control herself. For a long time she stared at the floor, then raised her head and looked at Thomas. "I want to talk to Jorge alone. Go with Eleanor. I will send for you when we are done."

"I haven't finished asking you questions."

"Yes, you have."

Eleanor led Thomas to a side-room furnished with elegant couches, chairs and a small table already set with wine and two glasses. A wide window looked out across the Guadalquivir and Thomas walked across to watch the slow progress of the river. He heard Eleanor moving around, heard her approach.

"Did Castellana tell you about Jorge?" he asked. He expected her to come to stand beside him. Instead her arms snaked around his waist and closed over his belly. Her breasts pressed against his back. Her scent enveloped him, washing away the doubts that plagued him.

"Some time ago, when I came to Córdoba. But like her, I thought him dead. Why would I not?"

"When did she tell you?"

"At the end of summer, so a little more than a month."

"What did she say?" Thomas flinched as Eleanor's fingers began to play with the tie of his breeches. He knew he should stop her, but his will had drained away like water into dry soil.

"She told me she believed her son dead. I do not think

she would have told me anything about him, but I made a confession to her, just as I made my confession to Rodrigo."

"De Borja?"

"Yes."

"What did you confess?" Eleanor's fingers had almost completed their work and began on the next stage of her seduction. In the distance men on horseback rode along the river's edge. "Is that Gabriel and Yves?" Thomas asked. Another group of four riders appeared, staying a hundred paces behind the pair.

"They have become the best of friends. The very best of friends." Eleanor tugged Thomas around and held his face in her hands. "I want you to undress me as I have undressed you, and then I want you to make love to me, but slower than we did the last time. I want you to mean it this time."

"I meant it last time."

"That was all rush and the ache of memory. I want this to be with the man you have become. You must have improved your abilities with women by now." She turned her face up so he could kiss her, and then when it was done she took his hand and led him to another door he had not seen, beyond which lay her bedroom.

A long time later, Thomas lay beside her, watching a line of sunlight mark the minutes as it crept across the floor.

"Now, that was better, was it not?" said Eleanor. She lay on her front, her skin damp with sweat, her hair disarranged.

"What did Castellana say to you about Jorge?"

She slapped his belly with the back of her hand. "Questions. Always questions. Why do you want to know everything?"

"Because he is my friend, and he is only out of prison on de Borja's word. He is accused of murder and not yet proven innocent. Fernando would have him hang, I am convinced."

Eleanor smiled. "But not Isabel." She kissed his chest. "Have you lain like this with her?"

"Of course not."

"She wants you to, you know. I heard the way she said your name when we saw you in the palace."

"Was that before or after Castellana told you about Jorge?"

"Stop it."

"I will if you answer my question."

Eleanor rose up and straddled him. "I will answer when we are finished for the second time, while you recover for the third."

The line of sunlight fell across Thomas's foot, marking the passage of an hour. He glanced at the window, judging the lateness of the day. Eleanor once more lay on her front while she played with the hair on his chest, touching the scars that few others knew about.

"Now?" Thomas said.

Eleanor sighed. "Will you stay the night with me?"

"I can't. I have to return to Qurtuba."

"I like how that name sounds when you speak it. All right, but promise me one more bout and promise to make it the best yet and I will tell you anything you ask."

"Anything?"

"Anything."

"What did you confess to de Borja?"

She slapped his chest. "Anything except that."

"When did Castellana discover Jorge was still alive?"

"Recently, and by accident. She said that Fernando told her, let slip your name and the name of your companion when they were lying as we lie now."

"So she is his mistress? I heard him boast of it, but was not sure. He is not a handsome man."

"Neither are you, unlike your friend. It is a shame he is a eunuch or I would try to seduce him."

Thomas laughed. "I think if you did, you would have a surprise. He remains half a man."

"You know this?"

"It was me who made him what he is, so of course I know it. But don't distract yourself from your answer. How did she know Fernando spoke of her son? Jorge isn't so unusual a name, and I'm sure Fernando will have mentioned him."

"She told me he did, more so I suspect to boast about the potency of his own. She said the name sparked some curiosity, so she went to the man who placed Jorge. She had looked before and been told he was dead, now she wanted confirmation. What she got instead was a shock. The son she gave up was alive and here in Córdoba." She tried to pronounce it as Thomas had and laughed when she failed. "Here in Córdoba with a man named Thomas Berrington. A man I once loved."

Thomas turned his head and kissed her, laid his hand on her lean flank. "Do you not still love me?"

"I am making up my mind. We are different people, are we not? And you are yet to convince me of your skills as a lover. I have a mind to ask the eunuch to join us."

"He would no doubt enjoy the challenge, but he is faithful to his woman these days."

Eleanor rolled on her side. She gripped his wrist and encouraged his hand to explore further.

"He has a wife?"

"Something like that."

"But he cannot give her children."

"No."

"I am too old to have more children, Thomas. Too set in my ways to marry again. You do not expect that, do you?"

Thomas laughed. "No, I don't expect that. How did Castellana feel about finding her son again?"

"She was angry."

"Angry?"

"It is why I am surprised at how she is treating him in the other room."

"Will they wonder where we are?"

"Castellana will know what we are doing."

"So will Jorge. Why was Castellana angry?"

"She told me she had forgotten all about him until Fernando made that stupid remark. I think once she would truly have taken him back into her household, but not now. She is a wealthy woman, and her son jealous of his own position." She rolled on to her back and pulled Thomas on top of her. "Clearly she has changed her mind if what we both witnessed is genuine."

"Do you think it was?"

"I think nothing, Thomas. Now stop talking and prove yourself to me as the man you once were."

"Why could we not stay the night?" Jorge rode beside Thomas through the soft light of the last hour of the day, the sun a giant orb hovering above the horizon ahead of them. "I wanted to stay."

"And Eleanor wanted me to stay, too," Thomas said.

"Would that have been such a bad thing? She is a handsome woman. One whose body you are already intimately familiar with. Is that what you were doing while Mother and I talked?"

"Mother now, is it? Eleanor doesn't want me other than as a toy to play with. I will not allow it again." Thomas rode on for a moment in silence before realising Jorge had managed to distract him from what he wanted to know. "What happened when you met Gabriel?"

"My brother Gabriel?"

"Half-brother."

Jorge waved a hand in dismissal at such an unimportant distinction. "He doesn't like me. I believe he thinks I have come to steal his fortune. An elder brother, more handsome, more clever. Well, more handsome anyway, and I know people far better than he does. I don't like those men he had with him. I overheard two speaking and their accents are almost exactly the same as those men who attacked me."

Thomas slowed. "Could they be the same men, do you think?" He was thinking of what Eleanor had told him, of Castellana's anger, and Gabriel's malice.

"How can they be? Not that I would recognise them if they were. They don't look much like the men I saw in the moment before I was hit. Besides, why would they be all the way out here? What did you do with Usaden?"

"He's gone back to the city with Kin. I think they got tired waiting for us. Kin is more his dog than mine these days."

"Except Kin doesn't know that. Did you send them back? Why?"

Thomas sighed. "In case we did have to stay the night. I wasn't going to have him sleep in the stables like some servant."

"Where would you have slept, Thomas? With your lover?"

Jorge had done it again, changing the subject.

"Does Gabriel know who his father is?"

"I expect so. Mother doesn't appear to hold anything back, does she?" Jorge smiled. "I like her. That is good, isn't it? I may not have. There is no guarantee I would, but she is clever and sharp, and I like her a lot."

"I am pleased."

"So am I." Jorge glanced around, no doubt barely seeing anything, unlike Thomas, who was aware of the group of riders who had been following them for some time. "Gabriel doesn't like me and I don't think he ever will."

"You must be losing your charm."

"No doubt that will be it. It is a shame I don't have a sister, I am far better with women than men."

"Even if she was your half-sister?"

"I did not mean I would—"

Jorge did not finish what he was about to say because at that moment the men following them kicked their horses into a gallop, and Thomas said, "Ride. Ride fast!"

CHAPTER TWENTY-FOUR

There were six men riding hard after them, Gabriel and four of his companions, and a sixth who Thomas thought might be Yves. What he didn't know was the business they had with him and Jorge, other than the obvious. Gabriel had made it clear he didn't like the idea of having a brother.

Thomas steered his horse closer to Jorge and shouted, "Do you think you can fight your brother?"

"Why?"

"Because that is who is behind us." Thomas glanced back. "And they are gaining." Their pursuers had good horses, and he and Jorge were riding mounts borrowed from Daniel, not intended for speed. It had been something Thomas had not considered when selecting them.

Jorge slowed and it took Thomas a moment to notice. When he did, he pulled his horse up and turned to see Jorge waiting as the men bore down on him. Thomas cursed the affability Jorge thought could win over the entire world. Despite Gabriel showing no love for his brother, Thomas didn't believe he meant him any harm. Even so, as the group reached Jorge they surrounded him and words were exchanged.

Thomas encouraged his horse toward them. As he approached, one of the riders came out to meet him.

"This is none of your business." His voice was soft with the accent of Roma and Thomas experienced a moment of fear. Two men of Roma had attacked Jorge, the same as the men who the fire starter de Parma had described.

"Did Rodrigo de Borja send you, or are you here without his orders?"

"Who?" Which only confirmed Thomas's suspicion de Borja could be involved. No-one from Roma would be ignorant of the man's name. He wondered how he could take the information to Isabel, and if he did whether she would do anything with it. And then the man said, "Stay out of this fight, it is nothing to do with you."

"Jorge is my friend. Of course it is to do with me."

"Gabriel says he is not going to kill him, but he has to be taught a lesson." The man laughed. "He's going to show him who rules here. Who will inherit."

Thomas leaned to one side to look past the man and confirmed that the sixth figure was indeed Yves. He sat astride his horse to one side, as if distancing himself from what was about to happen. Thomas rode toward the man, pushing past when he turned his horse in an attempt to block his path. He took care in case he attempted to strike out, but he did not, which surprised him. He almost wished he had, because it would have been the excuse he needed. He wished Usaden was with them, but believed he could handle these men without him. If it came to that.

Jorge and Gabriel had dismounted and now faced each other. Thomas slid from his own saddle and patted the horse's rump to send it cantering away. It would return eventually, and if not these men had horses he could take if he needed one.

"What is going on here?" He spoke to Gabriel.

"Not your business. This is between me and my brother." Gabriel let his distaste show in the way he spat the final word. "He needs teaching a lesson, and I am the man to teach it to him."

"Is that why you had him arrested? Why you framed him for a murder he didn't commit?" Thomas glanced to where the other men had dismounted. They formed a loose circle around him and Jorge, all except Yves, who continued to hold back. He looked back at Gabriel. "Is that why you brought these men to Castile? To kill an innocent scribe so your brother would be arrested? Are you afraid he will steal your mother's love?"

"I know nothing of any killing." Gabriel smiled, and in it Thomas saw something of Jorge, but it was a distorted reflection, all the amiability of Jorge twisted to hate. "I won't hurt him too much. I only want to teach him a lesson so he never returns. Mother does not need distractions, not at this time."

Thomas stepped between Jorge and Gabriel. "Then you will have to fight me first."

Gabriel allowed his eyes to track Thomas from head to foot. "That will take all of ten heartbeats."

Thomas smiled.

"It's all right," said Jorge. "I will fight him."

Thomas turned his head to see his expression. Set, determined, and he saw Jorge needed to do this, win or lose. And no doubt it would be lose. He only hoped Gabriel didn't hurt him too badly.

"You have only just recovered from a blow to the head."

Thomas thought it worth trying wise advice, but expected Jorge to ignore it, as he always did.

"Which only proves how hard my head is."

Thomas knew he was beaten and stepped aside. "No weapons. Gabriel, remove your sword and any other blades you have. Jorge, do you have anything?"

Jorge held his hands out to show they were empty. The sword he had brought remained tied to his saddle.

Thomas glanced at the other men. They were starting to lay odds on how long Jorge would last. None of them bet on him winning the fight.

"Nobody interferes, regardless of the result," Thomas said.

Two of the men nodded, those of Roma, which surprised him. He wondered who the others were. They were less well-dressed and he suspected estate workers. Gabriel must be confident to have brought only the two trained men with him. Thomas didn't want the fight to take place, but knew Jorge was determined. He had something to prove, though exactly what Thomas wasn't sure. Maybe it was nothing more than anger at the way Gabriel had treated him, dislike for his half-brother, or simply a chance to vent his anger at events he had little control over. Whatever it was, the scuffle would soon be over, just as Gabriel claimed, just as the men were betting on.

Thomas studied them with care without making it obvious. He wanted to know if Gabriel's defeat of Jorge would make them want more. He wasn't concerned, but he didn't want to harm anyone. It was too fine a day for death or injury. A year ago, still weak from his self-inflicted exile in the Sholayr mountains, he would have been less sure of his own ability. Now, after months training with Usaden, Thomas had no doubt at all.

As if the thought of Usaden had transmitted itself through the air—something Thomas would have dismissed at one time, but now was not so certain—the man himself appeared on the ridge of a low hill to the south. Nobody else noticed his presence, each engrossed in Gabriel and Jorge circling each other. Only as Usaden came close did one of them see him and pass the word. Jorge and Gabriel had still not thrown a punch, and Gabriel stepped back as he saw the Gomeres mercenary slide from the saddle and come to stand beside Thomas.

"Am I too late?"

"It hasn't started yet."

"Good, I am curious as to how Jorge will fare."

"I am sure you know the result already."

"Perhaps I do."

"Were you hiding your man away on purpose?" asked Gabriel. "Waiting for him to join you so you could attack us?"

Thomas made a show of looking around. "Three of us and six of you? What are you worried about?"

Gabriel shook his head with all the bluster of a bully, and Thomas saw he was sure of the men he employed. No doubt they too were skilled, but nobody was skilled in the same way as Usaden.

"Are they going to fight or not?" asked Usaden to Thomas, ignoring Gabriel.

"Doesn't look like it. We should return to the city and find out what this man is hiding."

"We are going to fight!" Gabriel appeared on the edge of losing his temper. It was clear events were not working out the way he had expected.

"Then do it," said Thomas. "We are late already. At this

rate it will be tomorrow before we get back. Hit him and get it over with."

It was the taunt Gabriel needed. He turned fast toward Jorge and swung a wild blow at his head. Had it connected, Jorge would have been instantly felled, but it didn't connect. Instead Jorge ducked, just enough for the blow to sail harmlessly over his head. He snapped out a punch of his own, which thudded into Gabriel's chest and sent him staggering back a pace. Anger flared bright and he came at Jorge again, using both fists, but once more Jorge avoided each strike, each time landing his own in retaliation. Not enough to cause damage, barely enough to hurt, but enough to stoke Gabriel's anger, enough to demonstrate Jorge's skill.

Thomas watched the soldiers start to argue between themselves as two tried to take back the bets they had made. Usaden watched the fight with narrowed eyes, his shoulders swaying with tiny movements each time Jorge struck.

For a time nothing changed, except both men started to sweat in the late afternoon heat. Beyond them the river ran, wide and slow. Olive trees studded the land as far as the eye could see, and smoke hung in the air where pruned wood was being burned. Then Jorge grew tired of the pretence. The next time he struck, his blow thumped hard against Gabriel's ear, and he went to his knees.

"Kick him," Usaden said, the words too soft for anyone but Thomas to hear.

Jorge waited while Gabriel shook his head, breathing hard, then as he lifted himself to his feet, Jorge hit him again, square on the nose before he had time to raise his fists. He fell flat on his back. Not unconscious, but perhaps feigning such in an attempt to prevent further humiliation. Which was when the four men drew their swords, and Usaden smiled.

"Nobody dies today," Thomas said.

He took a step back, his eyes on the two men of Roma, judging them the most dangerous. He caught a glimpse of his son as Yves mounted his horse and rode away. He was disappointed at his cowardice.

Gabriel rolled over and got to his knees. Jorge examined the knuckles on his hand. He shook them as if they hurt, then went to where he had left his robe and picked it up. He returned to his brother and offered his hand.

Gabriel stared at it, blood dripping from his nose on to the dry ground. Jorge waited more than long enough, but when Gabriel continued to ignore his offer, he shrugged and turned away. He went to his horse and pulled himself into the saddle and rode away without a backward glance. Thomas looked around, saw his own horse standing on the hillside and whistled loudly.

"I will stay a while until you have both left," said Usaden. His weapons remained sheathed, even the ones nobody could see. Thomas knew it would take no time for them to appear if needed.

"I don't think they want to fight anymore," he said.

"I know. It is a pity, but cannot be helped if they are cowards. All the same, join Jorge first and then I will follow. Kin is around somewhere, but I told him to stay where he was."

Thomas went to fetch his horse, which had been distracted by a particularly succulent patch of grass, though to him it looked as dry and brown as all the rest. He took the reins and lifted himself into the saddle, then followed Jorge, who was two hundred paces ahead. One of the men of Roma was helping Gabriel to his feet as Thomas passed. He leaned down to stare at his bloodied nose, which did not appear to be broken, which was a shame.

Thomas spurred his horse into a canter and caught up with Jorge. "I know you fight better than you used to, but when did you learn to do that?"

"You are not the only one spending time with Usaden. You should pay him more for all the extra work."

"Or perhaps you should. Why have you never listened to me the way you've listened to him? I could have shown you how to fight."

"Not as well as Usaden can."

Thomas admitted Jorge had a point.

"Gabriel is afraid of you," he said.

"He thinks I may worm my way into my mother's affections and take half his inheritance."

"You should have told him you are already wealthy."

"I would have, but you always tell me it's meant to be a secret. Can I spend some of the money now?"

"Perhaps. As long as you have a story to explain where it came from if anyone asks."

"I will tell them you gave it to me, of course," said Jorge.

"Then I will have to make up a story."

"Tell people Isabel gave it you as thanks for showing her how a man can truly satisfy a woman. Everyone believes you are bedding her so it is a perfect excuse."

Thomas shook his head, knowing Jorge was conjuring up random thoughts to amuse himself. Besting a man in a fight could do that.

"Or your mistress from France," said Jorge. "I expect she is rich, isn't she? Not as rich as Isabel, but you share a mysterious past that would explain your wealth."

"I'm not so sure Isabel is wealthy," Thomas said. "This war is fearsomely expensive."

"Except she is going to win it, and soon, and then all the riches of Al-Andalus will be hers."

Yes, Thomas thought, she is going to win the war. And what then? She had already asked him to serve at her side. In what capacity had never been made clear, but the request always came, and he expected it would do so again. He had always refused in the past, but now everything was different. Gharnatah was not his city anymore. Muhammed wanted him dead, and Helena lived in his house, tainting the air with the glory of her presence. He would have thrown her out, but knew he could not, for she would always remain Will's mother whatever else she had done. Threads of loyalty and family held him tight, cutting into his skin with an invisible pressure he could not ignore. He wondered if Jorge felt the same.

"Why did you take so long to hit him?" Thomas asked.

Jorge smiled. "I wanted to see how good he was."

"And?"

"Not as good as me."

"Clearly."

"He is my brother—my half-brother—so we should have been more evenly matched, don't you think?" Jorge glanced at Thomas. "His father is de Borja, isn't he?"

"That is what Castellana claims, and I see no reason for her to lie."

"She was lying about something. Did you see that before you went to bed your lover?" Jorge laughed at Thomas's expression. "Or did you think I would not know? I could smell the sex on you, and am pleased at it. You are wound too tight, Thomas. My mother lied even more when you weren't there, as if she thought me stupid."

Thomas shook his head. "I thought she sounded like she gave honest answers."

"I don't know which were lies and which were not, yet.

She is good at lying or I would have known." He gave a loud sigh. "This Rodrigo de Borja, why would he want me dead?"

"If he wanted you dead you already would be. If he wants anything, I believe it is for you to be accused of a murder you didn't commit."

Jorge waved his hand as if the difference was a petty matter. "Why that, then? What benefit does it bring him?"

"Or what hate does he hold against you?" Something occurred to Thomas and he stared at Jorge. "Or what hate did he carry the man who was your father?"

Jorge smiled. "Oh, that's easy. My father took Castellana's innocence before de Borja could, and I am the living proof."

"Except he doesn't want her. Isabel told me de Borja is going to be the next Pope. She says she will make sure he is appointed. His life will be in the Lateran Palace, and he will rule over the Papal states and every Christian in the world. What would he want with a woman he was once married to but hasn't seen in years?"

"I don't know that yet," said Jorge

"Perhaps you should ask him to his face. He was still at the palace when we left. Stand in front of him and ask him what makes him hate you enough to have you arrested. I thought he was behind everything, and then I thought him not. Now I am simply confused."

Jorge stared ahead to where the smoke of the city stained the horizon, the sun dropping fiery through the haze.

"Perhaps I will." He smiled. "I don't like it when you are confused, Thomas. It worries me."

"Me too."

CHAPTER TWENTY-FIVE

Will lay soft against Thomas's chest as he sat in a chair, feet on a low table, and stared through the window across the dark gardens. Servants were once again walking the ground lighting lanterns, their passage marked by the long tapers they used, which danced like fireflies. Beyond lay a greater darkness beyond the city wall, punctured here and there by farmhouse candles. Amal lay asleep on a cushion on the floor and Thomas knew he should put her to bed, but was too lethargic.

He thought Will had gone to sleep, but he wriggled, digging an elbow into an unfortunate place to make him wince.

"Pa," he said, and waited.

"What is it?" Thomas was pleased Will was full of questions, but some days he had more questions than could be answered in a year. Still, what was one more? And Will's questions were often interesting. Or if not interesting, at least quirky enough to bring a badly needed distraction.

"Is Theresa our new ma now?"

Thomas tried to sit up, but Will was too heavy to allow it.

"No, of course not. What makes you say that?"

"Because she is here looking after us all the time, and I know she likes you."

"You do, do you? How?"

"She talks about you all the time." Will blew his cheeks out. "*All* the time. Talks about you with Isabel, too."

Thomas smiled. "You mean the Queen of Castile, don't you?"

"Yes. Isabel."

"Theresa is not your new ma. She is helping me until I can prove Jorge is innocent, that is all."

"It would be all right if she was. Me and Amal have talked about it and she can live with us if she wants to."

"What about what I want?"

"She is pretty," said Will. "Not as pretty as Ma, but different pretty. And you need someone to look after you now Ma's gone. Isabel says so, too."

"She does, does she?"

He felt Will nod.

"Where did you go today, Pa?" Will's voice had grown as soft as his limbs, and Thomas knew he would not remember whatever answer he gave. "You took Usaden with you. Were you going to fight?"

"Usaden wanted to get out of the city."

"I like it here," said Will. "Isabel says we can stay as long as we want. Forever, she says." Will twisted so he could look up at Thomas. "Can we, Pa?"

"What about our house in Gharnatah?"

"Isabel says she will destroy Gharnatah. Except she cannot say it right. I tried to tell her how, but she only laughed at me, but I am teaching Juan and little Isabel and even Cat. I like Cat. She is only little, but she is clever."

"Cat, is it?"

Will nodded and settled down on Thomas's belly. "So where did you go?" He never forgot his original question, however much he distracted himself. It was a trait Thomas approved of.

"We went to see Jorge's ma."

This time Will sat up and turned all the way around. "Jorge's got a ma?"

Thomas laughed. "Of course he has. Everyone has a ma."

"Even eunuchs?"

"Of course. Eunuchs cannot be fathers, but all people are born of two parents."

"Like you and Helena borned me, and you and Ma borned Ami?" said Will.

"Yes."

Thomas watched Will think about it for a moment until he had it straight in his head.

"So who is Jorge's ma? I thought she lived in Qurtuba before he met you, but you rode off to the south."

"Were you watching us?"

"From the tower," said Will. "Me and Juan. He said you were probably going to war. Juan says he knows all about war. Were you going to war, Pa?"

"Jorge did get into a fight, but no, we were not going to war."

Will laughed. "Jorge got in a fight?" He laughed again. "Jorge doesn't get into fights."

"He did today."

"But I saw him when you came back and he had no bruises. What did you really do, Pa?"

"I told you." He eased Will from his knee, knowing he

had spent too long being comforted by the presence of his children. "Time for bed now. Wake Amal and take her through with you, I will send Theresa to sit over you."

"Where are you going, Pa? Out again?"

"I am going to talk to Rodrigo, and then Isabel."

Will frowned. "Why can you call her Isabel and I can't?"

"Because you might forget and say it to her face."

"I do. Me and Ami both do and she doesn't mind." He thought a little longer. "I don't think she minds."

"What about Fernando?"

Will laughed and gave a mock shiver. "No, we always call him King, or Your Grace. That's right, isn't it, Pa? But we don't know what to call the other man so we call him Rodrigo, because that is what he said we should do. I like him. He's funny, like Jorge's funny. Except he says he has nothing missing between his legs."

Thomas almost dislodged Will from his lap in shock. "You asked him that?"

"I did. He laughed so hard I thought he might wet himself. Then he said yes, he had everything still intact, and laughed again. I like him."

Thomas went in search of Theresa to ask her to sit with the children until he returned. He found her in the small room close to the royal wing of the palace where she slept and lived her life of duty. As usual, she wanted a reason from him.

"You are out of luck, Thomas. Rodrigo left this morning. He is on his way to Sevilla, and from there takes ship to Roma. I doubt we will see him in Castile again until after he is elected Pope." She cocked her head to one side, her eyes sharp, knowing. “But Isabel is still awake. She doesn’t sleep long these days. She tells me there is too much to plan.”

“Are you saying I should talk to her?”

“I don’t know what you wanted to talk to Rodrigo about. Will she be able to offer you advice? Or perhaps you would just like to talk to her, as I am sure she would with you.”

“Yes,” Thomas said, without indicating which of her questions he might be answering. “Can you ask if she will see me? And can you sit with the children?”

“I can.” Theresa touched his arm, a fleeting contact before she turned away.

Thomas waited, staring at one of the ornate tapestries, trying to work out how its makers had created something so complex, so beautiful. When he heard footsteps, he turned, expecting Theresa. Instead it was Isabel who approached, alone. She offered a smile.

“I wanted to talk with you anyway, Thomas, but thought my rooms might have too many ears.” As if she already knew what troubled him. “We can go to the terrace, or even your rooms. Theresa will be there, will she not, so I will have a chaperone. Not that I need one with you.” She waited for Thomas to indicate agreement or not. Waited until he nodded and offered his arm. She lay her hand on it as they made their way in the direction he had come from.

“Theresa tells me you are not sleeping well,” Thomas said.

“It is none of Theresa’s business how I sleep. Besides, there is a great deal for me to do.”

Thomas tried to hear some judgement in her voice, but found none.

Theresa was sitting in the chair Thomas had used when he held Will. Her eyes were half-closed, but as they entered, she stood abruptly, smoothing her skirts, and gave a tiny curtsey.

"There is no need to be so formal amongst us three," said Isabel. "Thomas and I have matters to discuss. You can stay if you wish, or go sleep in his bed. I am sure I am safe with him."

When they were alone, Isabel sat in the chair Theresa had been using, and Thomas pulled another close so they were facing each other.

"What is it you want of me?" she asked.

"I thought it was you who wanted to talk to me?"

"I do, but there is something you wish to say, isn't there? And then you can tell me what is happening with your friend Jorge, and what this business is that takes up so much of your time. And finally I do have a question to ask of you."

"Is it the usual one?" Thomas said.

"Possibly."

He was about to say that she already knew his answer, but he was no longer sure of what it might be. Instead he cut straight to the most important matter.

"How long have you known Rodrigo de Borja?"

"Ever since I was a girl. I used to worship him. I still worship him. In a few years I may need to worship him in an entirely different way, but it will be good to have a Spaniard as Pope. By then this country will be reunited, and we will need friends in high places." She stared at her hands while she spoke, but now she lifted her gaze to meet his. "Did you enjoy your dinner with him? He is a pleasant companion, is he not?"

"He has the ability to make people like him. He made me like him. But what I have discovered makes me like him less when I am away from his influence."

"You must explain yourself. If anyone else spoke those words, I would have them expelled from my presence."

"This is to do with Jorge," Thomas said.

Isabel nodded, an indication for him to go on.

"You know de Borja was married to Castellana Lonzal?"

"Of course. It is one of the reasons she is welcome at court. She visits often, and is a pleasant companion. Her son less so, but he rarely comes with her."

"Do you also know that in the eyes of the law, they are still married?"

"I did not, but if between him and myself such a small matter cannot be resolved, then nothing can be. Is it relevant to what happened to Jorge?"

Thomas took a breath, unsure where to start, how to start. Unsure of Isabel's reaction. There was no reason for her to care about Jorge's past, or even what was happening to him, other than through his friendship with Thomas. Even that might be expecting far more than he had any right to. He tried to draw the scattered information he had into a rational order.

Isabel must have seen the uncertainty on his face because she said, "Did I not have him freed from prison and allowed here under your stewardship?"

"You did, and for that I thank you."

"Has he been behaving himself?"

"More or less."

"So tell me what is on your mind."

"Jorge is accused of murder. Possibly two murders by now."

"I know of only the one, what is the other?"

"A priest by the name of Carlos Mendoza."

"The name is not familiar. How was he killed?"

"Badly. It is not something you need to hear about, but

he was the individual who placed Jorge in the care of those he always considered his parents. I believe that single act, thirty years ago, is the reason Mendoza was killed, just as the first death was to cover up some knowledge of the adoption. Someone doesn't want anyone to know who Jorge's real father is."

Isabel stared at Thomas for a long time, her expression set. He waited, aware she was thinking about his words.

"I know Castellana's son is Rodrigo's," she said at last. "Are you trying to tell me Jorge is also his son?" She held a hand up to stop Thomas's reply while she gave the idea consideration. "They are handsome in the same way, I see that, and they share an ability to make people like them without seeming to make any effort. But Rodrigo has never made a secret he is the father of Gabriel."

"According to Castellana, Jorge's father is another man, not de Borja. A man believed dead and now not dead. Like Jorge was once believed dead and was not."

"You don't suspect de Borja in any of this, do you?" And when Thomas made no reply, "You do, don't you?"

"Does the name Inigo Florentino mean anything to you?" When Isabel gave a shake of the head, Thomas continued, "Castellana, de Borja and he were friends in Valencia. All three of them were close friends until Inigo set a seed inside her and the friendship shattered. Rodrigo wanted nothing to do with another man's son and arranged for him to be adopted here, in Qurtuba. The man who arranged the adoption was killed five nights ago. The man who handled the paperwork was burned to death in the cellar of his house. I believe Rodrigo has to be connected in some way to both events."

"You will need to explain yourself very carefully to me if you intend to make such an accusation against a man I have known all my life. Without Rodrigo's efforts, my marriage to Fernando would not have been sanctioned. He has done much for both Castile and Aragon, much for the reunification of Spain. Is that why you accuse him? Because you do not want that to happen? Is that it, Thomas? If so, then know that if you pursue this baseless accusation, you are turning your back on my friendship and protection both." Her face was set, eyes cold, and Thomas saw her as those who displeased the Queen of Castile did.

"Do you think I would risk your friendship on a whim? I have followed the logic, as you know I have done in the past on such matters and not been wrong. His involvement makes sense. He will not have been directly involved, but there are men here from Roma, men I believe carried out the killings to throw the blame on Jorge."

"Why would Rodrigo do such a thing? What advantage is there in it to him?"

"That is what I have to ask you. Is there anything you know—anything at all—that would offer even a slight confirmation of my suspicions?"

"None. None at all. I am aware Rodrigo has the failings of other men, but that does not make him evil, and only an evil man could do what you accuse him of. I cannot believe it. I refuse to believe it." Isabel rose, her body stiff with tension. As she turned, Thomas also rose and gripped her wrist. He saw her part her lips in preparation to cry out, to call guards that would no doubt be nearby.

"Give me time, Isabel," Thomas said. "Let me chase down the information I have to a conclusion. If I am wrong, then I am a fool and you deserve to dismiss me from your presence forever. But if I am right ... then I may be saving you and Castile from the threat of destruction."

Isabel stared down at his fingers laced around her wrist, but made no move to pull away.

"Rodrigo is no threat to me or Castile. He has given nothing but aid to both in our fight against the Moors. A fight you seem to have now taken a side on, Thomas." She pulled free. "Because of our past friendship—which you are determined to toss to the winds—I will allow you one more day to uncover the true culprit. Who is not Rodrigo, I tell you that now. If you cannot discover who is behind this by the morning of the day after tomorrow, then you will be banished from the city and Jorge returned to prison to await execution."

"If I am to do that I need Jorge with me," Thomas said. "Allow him to leave the palace and I will find your proof." Thomas thought his words brave and foolhardy.

"I heard my permission is not required. That you both rode away from here today. But I will order it. The guards will let him pass, you have no need to sneak around together." Isabel would not meet his eyes as she spoke, and the moment she finished, she stormed from the room.

Well, that could have gone better, Thomas thought, and then Theresa strode from his bedroom and slapped him hard across the face.

"Idiot!"

Thomas couldn't disagree.

"I have to start now. Tonight. I need to find Miguel and discover if he has found anything out. Can you—"

"He is a strange one, that man."

"You know him?"

She offered a smile of pure innocence. "He set his sights on me when he came to Córdoba, but I rejected him. He is pleasant on the surface, but something felt wrong beneath it, and I heard he often visits the whorehouse. He is ambitious, though. Too ambitious is what I heard, and unpredictable. He goes off on his own instead of asking for help."

"Will you watch the children for me?" Thomas asked, trying to work out exactly what Theresa was trying to tell him, or even if it carried any significance.

"It would serve you right if I said no. But yes, I will stay with your children. It is time you began to spend more time with them, Thomas. Do you know what Amal did today? She called me Ma!"

Thomas saw something in Theresa's eyes, a glitter of unshed tears, and wondered how his life had come to this. Today he had spent an hour in the bed of a woman he didn't love, did not even like, while the woman in front of him offered both love and security. Theresa was right, he should leave matters alone. Except he knew he could not. How could he? Jorge was his closest companion and he would never abandon him, even if it meant a permanent break with a woman he admired, and perhaps even loved.

CHAPTER TWENTY-SIX

Lawrence was not pleased to find Thomas knocking on his door in the middle of the night, but came downstairs when he heard the desperation in his voice.

"Apologise to Laurita for me, but I need you now. Go put some clothes on."

"You come here to wake me after disappearing for days and expect me to help?"

"I do."

Lawrence shook his head. "I should make you go upstairs and apologise yourself, but she'll only hit you with the chamber pot so best you don't. Wait here." Lawrence cursed. "I don't suppose I'll be lucky enough to find you gone when I come back, will I?"

Thomas waited beneath the orange tree, too impatient to sit. He needed to be doing something so paced, muttering under his breath until Lawrence returned.

"What do you want at this ungodly hour?"

"Do you know where Miguel lives? I went to the Hermandos' office but he's not there."

"I do, but he won't be any more pleased than I am at being woken. What do you want with him?"

"To find out what he's been doing these last days."

"Working on your behalf, I thought. You cannot doubt him, Thomas. He has risked his position to help you."

"Do you know when he came to Qurtuba, at least?"

Lawrence gave Thomas a strange look, and he knew he was pushing too hard.

"Six months ago, I believe. Why?"

"That is what I intend to ask him when we find him. You will help me? I may need a man who can use a sword."

Lawrence didn't ask the reason why, simply leading Thomas through a maze of alleys toward the river. Usaden appeared from the shadows and fell into step beside Thomas.

"Is he with you?" asked Lawrence.

"He's a friend."

"Glad to hear it. Has it occurred to you Miguel might have other calls on his time?"

"Indeed he may, but I heard something tonight that made me wonder what he might know that he is keeping to himself. I was told he is ambitious enough to try to solve this mystery himself, to hold on to information we need to know. I also did something stupid, even for me."

Lawrence slowed, came to a halt. "What?"

"I told Isabel who I believe is behind these crimes."

"Someone important, I assume?"

Thomas nodded. "Rodrigo de Borja."

Lawrence let his breath go. "God's teeth, Thomas, could you be a bigger idiot?"

"I know. But I have to find out if I am a wrong idiot."

"Of all the men you might accuse, he is the one who

cannot be touched. You would be better to accuse Fernando. At least Isabel doesn't like him. She adores de Borja."

Miguel's small house was on the far side of the river among a clutch of other new buildings, with even more being thrown up by the day. Qurtuba was growing, spreading its stain across the countryside like a fetid growth. The glassed windows were dark, but Thomas knocked hard, then knocked again when they remained dark. Eventually a wavering light showed as someone approached, but when the door opened it wasn't who he expected. Instead a pretty woman stood with a candle raised, a robe clutched around herself. It seemed Miguel had found a woman after all. Her eyes went from Thomas to Usaden, before resting on Lawrence.

"What do you want? If you are looking for Miguel, he is not here."

"I tried his offices," said Thomas, "and they told me he had gone home. Are you his wife? He told me he wasn't married."

"Housekeeper, and I've barely seen him for a week." She closed the door hard.

When Thomas raised his hand to knock again, Lawrence said, "He's clearly not here."

"Don't you think a man might ask his housekeeper to lie for him?"

"She might be a housekeeper, but she's more than that as well."

"Where is he then? Theresa told me he visits whores—is he there, do you think?"

"Almost certainly. I heard that about him also." Lawrence shook his head. "Though if I was him, I'd be in bed with the housekeeper. She was exquisite."

"Now you sound like Jorge."

"Good, because Jorge makes sense when he talks about women. Come on, then, if you must see him."

They crossed the old bridge again and passed through the open city gate to emerge beneath the wide cathedral. As Lawrence turned aside and began to ascend narrow alleys, Thomas knew where they were heading: to a row of houses where interior walls had been knocked through to make an extensive space on the lower floor, with smaller rooms set above. It was a house Thomas had visited years before when he was searching for Abbot Mandana.

"How long has he been going to the whorehouse?" Thomas asked.

"As long as I've known him."

"He said nothing to me about whores."

"It's not the kind of thing most men boast of, nor something they are going to volunteer in casual conversation. 'Oh, do you know I fuck whores at night instead of doing my job?'" Lawrence glanced at Thomas in the dark. "You should bed that nurse who has doe-eyes for you, she's pretty enough, and willing I'd say."

"Why is everyone so concerned about my love life?"

"Has Jorge been nagging you as well? Good. We need to get you back in the saddle."

There was no need to knock at the door when they reached the house because it stood ajar. A man almost as wide as the doorway stood outside in the street, but a nod from Lawrence was enough to gain them entrance. The last time Thomas had been in the house, an older woman held court. Now she was gone, replaced by a much younger and prettier version who appeared to know Lawrence well enough to make Thomas wonder how.

"Is Miguel upstairs?" Lawrence asked.

"With two girls. He claimed to have come into money."

"Can you send a message we are here to see him?"

"He's been up there a while now so he'll be finished soon enough. Why don't you wait, or if you have the money, pick a girl?" She glanced at Thomas and Usaden, but showed no concern. "They are all willing and skilled. I expect they can show you a few things you've never experienced before."

Having lived with the ex-concubine Helena for almost a year, Thomas wasn't so sure of her claim, but thought it better not to say anything.

"We will wait in the street," said Lawrence.

"Suit yourself."

"I might stay," said Usaden.

Outside, Lawrence said, "Has he got enough money? These are the best girls in the city and they don't come cheap."

"I expect we'll find out when we see how soon he rejoins us. Does Miguel have to pay, do you think?"

"Not the full rate. I expect he offers them protection."

Thomas felt a sense of betrayal. He had liked Miguel, trusted him. He walked to the end of the street and looked both ways, aware of the passage of time and Isabel's deadline. Three men stood at the end of the alley that ran down toward the river, and Thomas tried to make them out, something in their stance sparking a sense of familiarity.

"What have you found?"

Thomas turned to discover Lawrence had come to join him. "I'm not sure. I thought I recognised those men, but it's too dark to see them clearly."

"We should walk down and get a closer look. We've nothing better to do until Miguel's finished."

Thomas nodded, but as they descended across the cobbles, one of the men looked up and said something to the others.

They turned and walked away, heading to the entrance of another alley. As they turned to enter it, a lantern highlighted their faces for a moment and Thomas recognised them. They were three of the men who had been with Gabriel at the fight. He broke into a run, leaving Lawrence behind. The men also started to run. By the time Thomas reached the corner, they had disappeared and the alley was empty. He heard the distant slapping of boots on stone, but it faded even as he listened.

"Why did you chase them?" Lawrence came to a halt beside Thomas.

"I am sure they were the men who were with Jorge's brother today."

"Then they were probably on their way to the whore-house, the same as everyone else around here."

"So why did they run? Do I look so frightening?"

"Sometimes you do, but not tonight, I admit. Maybe they didn't want anyone to know where they were going."

"Perhaps." Thomas stared along the dark alley before turning away. Four men, but more than likely not the four men he was looking for. "We should get back in case we miss Miguel."

As they reached the top roadway, Usaden came toward them.

"Not enough money?" asked Lawrence.

"He has gone," said Usaden.

"Miguel? Where to?"

"If I knew that I would tell you. I paid for one of the whores as an excuse to get upstairs, but when I got there, the man you seek was gone. He had been gone a while. He must have slipped out the back way or the house madam would have told us."

"What's he playing at?" Thomas said. "Does he know

something and wants the credit for himself? Is that why he's been hard to find the last few days?"

"It's possible," said Lawrence. "If he left a while ago, he's no doubt on his way back home, so we should try there. Or do you want to leave it until morning?"

"Let's do it now. Unless you want to get back to your own bed? I'm sure we can take care of Miguel between the two of us."

"I might as well come along. Laurita will be in a foul mood because I left her, so I'm better staying out until dawn, at least." Lawrence grinned. "Besides, it's always fun when we make up."

They followed the upper road toward the cathedral. As they approached it, Thomas glanced down to where the old bridge crossed the wide river and saw the men he had seen before, their number now grown to four, and this time Miguel was there too. They appeared to be arguing, though no words reached Thomas. The four men stood across the roadway while Miguel had his back to the city, his hands moving to make a point. One of the men stepped forward and pushed at him, and Miguel struck back, hitting him across the cheek. In the blink of an eye the others were on him, but instead of using fists or swords, they pushed him to the edge of the bridge and hoisted Miguel off his feet.

"No!" Thomas began to run, already knowing he was going to be too late.

Miguel fought hard, but he couldn't stop the men. With a final effort, they threw him over the edge of the bridge. One leaned over, then straightened, and all four started back toward the city. As Thomas reached the bridge, they stopped, hesitated, then turned and fled in the other direction.

Thomas reached the spot where the fight had occurred

and leaned over the low parapet. It was too dark to see a body, only the silver foam of water running across the rapids. Had Miguel landed in the water to be carried away, exactly as Jorge had been carried away as a boy? Thomas wasn't sure, but the spot where he stood could be the same place Jorge claimed his brother Daniel had fallen from.

Usaden reached him first, Lawrence coming along behind, not running fast now.

"See if you can find them," Thomas said, pushing Usaden away along the bridge. "Follow them if you do and tell me where they go, though I suspect I already know the answer."

When he had gone, Thomas waited for Lawrence to reach him.

"Can you climb?" he asked.

"Not unless I have to."

Lawrence's answer came as no surprise, and Thomas knew what he had to do. He stripped out of his robe and pulled his boots off, knowing the descent would be easier with bare feet. When he sat on the parapet, Lawrence grabbed his shirt.

"You will kill yourself."

"Probably, but I need to find out what has happened to Miguel." Thomas looked along the dark bridge. "Go to the Hermandos' office this side of the river, it's closer, and bring men and a rope. If I find him, he might be hurt, and we'll need it to get him up."

"We should both go," said Lawrence. "Then you can use the rope to get down."

"And if he is hurt?" Thomas pushed at Lawrence. "Go fetch them. I will be all right, I've climbed worse places than this."

But after Lawrence had taken his reluctant leave, Thomas wasn't so sure he had. His only hope was that if he fell, the distance might not be enough to kill him. He swung himself over the low wall, feeling for somewhere to plant his toes. When he found nothing, he lowered himself further until only his fingertips stopped him falling. He wasn't sure if he could pull himself up even if he wanted to. Then he found an anchor point and dug his toes in and began to descend.

He found Miguel at the bottom of the buttress. He was alive, but would not remain so for long. A rock had crushed the side of his head and blood flowed like spilled wine into the water. Thomas pulled his own shirt off and wrapped it as tightly as he dared, afraid of causing more injury through the broken skull.

Miguel groaned and his eyes opened. He tried to smile, but only one side of his mouth was working.

"Sorry, Thomas," he said, the words slurred. "I wan—wanted to arrest them for you."

"Did they kill Cortez?"

Miguel's eyes closed and his breath stilled. Thomas felt his neck, found no pulse, but Miguel was not quite dead. He had something else to say.

"Baker woman ... heard the two men tal—talking." He went silent for a long time, his eyes still closed. The flow of blood from his wound lessened, but Thomas knew it was not thanks to his attempt to bind it, merely because Miguel's body now contained less blood. "Saw them. Heard names." Miguel's breath left him again and Thomas leaned close, his ear against the young man's mouth as he summoned his last reserves. He spoke the names, garbled and distorted, but Thomas recognised them.

Gabriel and Yves. The two men seen in Cortez's street the day before the fire, and two days after, were Jorge's half-brother and Thomas's own son.

CHAPTER TWENTY-SEVEN

By the time the group of Hermandos managed to retrieve Miguel's body, Thomas had been arrested as a suspect in his death. Had Lawrence not been present he would no doubt have been thrown into the same prison he had only recently freed Jorge from. At the Hermandos' offices, Thomas was acutely aware of the passing of time. Already the first hints of dawn greyed the eastern sky. By the time he was released, day was coming and the streets were starting to grow busy.

"I thank you for your help," Thomas said to Lawrence, who looked tired.

"You could have told them you are friend to the Queen yourself. You would have been released the sooner had you done so. It was not my place to say it."

"They wouldn't have believed me. It was better coming from you, a man respected in this city. Are you going back to Laurita?" He glanced around, pleased to see Usaden had joined them when they came from the Hermandos' office. Thomas hoped he had returned with news of the men who'd killed Miguel.

"I will stay until we find out what happened. Let's go

somewhere to sit and talk about what we know. Everything is different this morning, isn't it?"

"Daniel's house is close." Thomas stepped back as three men emerged from the Hermandos' building and marched into the distance.

"They are off to tell Miguel's housekeeper, I expect," said Lawrence. "And ask her what she knows. We should have gone there first."

"We can go later. The Hermandos will make a mess of whatever they ask. I will send for Jorge to talk to her. He will tease out what she knows, but I suspect there isn't much." Thomas cursed his own stupidity. "Miguel was a fool, but a brave fool. Did he think he could arrest four men on his own?" He saw Daniel's works ahead, the braziers being encouraged into fresh life, men moving about selecting materials and discussing the day's labour to come. A dense river mist drifted along the street, swirling around their legs as they walked.

"At least he gave you those two names," said Lawrence. "Are you sure they are who you think?"

"Gabriel is a common enough name, but how many Yveses are there in Qurtuba? Combine the two together and it is clear who they are. I wish I'd had this information before we rode to Castellana Lonzal's estate. Miguel should never have kept it to himself." Thomas turned to Usaden, who had remained silent the entire time, waiting his turn. "Did you follow those men?"

Usaden shook his head. "But I saw signs. They had horses on the edge of the city and went east, but you already know that. They are almost certainly the ones who were with Jorge's brother."

"Then they have to be involved—Castellana and Gabriel both." And Eleanor? Thomas wondered. "I believed them, and trusted Miguel." Thomas glanced at Lawrence. "We need sharp minds to tease out the truth. I'm not sure mine is working anymore."

Daniel met them on the way from his house to the works and turned back. The household was already awake, children on the floor, Adana in her role as carer.

Thomas went to Zanita. "I want you to go to the palace and ask Jorge and Belia to come here. I have work for them both. Isabel has agreed to allow him to leave the palace."

"They won't let me in, you need to go yourself."

"They will if you tell them I sent you." Thomas hoped he spoke the truth, and eventually Zanita agreed to try. Lawrence and Usaden sat at the wide table and began picking at remnants of food. After a while Adana rose and began to prepare more.

Thomas searched the floor until he found what he was looking for and brought a handful of coloured wooden blocks and laid them on the table-top.

"What are we building?" asked Lawrence.

"These are the people we know about." Thomas pushed one of the blocks, bright yellow, into the middle of the table. "This is Jorge."

Lawrence laughed. "I like it, though the resemblance needs a little work."

Thomas scowled and moved the other blocks. "De Borja is black. Castellana and Gabriel white. Miguel is the brown one." He arranged them to one side, close to each other, before reaching for a red block. He stared at it for a long time before setting it near the others.

"Isabel and Fernando?" asked Lawrence.

"Eleanor and Yves," Thomas said, letting out a sigh.

"Why?"

"Because Yves was at El Carpio with Gabriel and also

with him in Cortez's street. Eleanor was with Castellana, both at her estate and in her house in the city. They know each other, which may make them involved too, or it might only be their sons who are working on this accusation against Jorge. It would help if I knew how long they have known about him." Thomas took four more blocks and set them between the yellow one and the others. He tapped each in turn. "Cortez, de Parma, Mendoza and Miguel."

Lawrence reached out and moved a block. "Miguel might be a victim, but he isn't the same as the others." He shook his head. "I have known the man only a few months, but always believed him different to other Hermandos. More honest, but foolhardy. Today he found himself in the wrong place at the wrong time."

"Agreed, Miguel's not involved." Thomas set the block representing him to one side, but left it on the table. He reached for another, this one unpainted.

"Who is that? Is that Isabel now?"

"This is Jorge's father, Inigo Florentino," Thomas said. He didn't set the block down yet because he didn't know where it belonged. He tapped the block on the table, thinking. "Castellana claimed he was dead, but de Borja told me otherwise."

"You are sure he lives?" asked Lawrence.

"His name was on one of the documents Cortez was clutching when he died. It was you who showed it to me. According to Castellana, he died many years before that paper was drawn up."

"I have seen too many documents these last weeks to remember every single name on each." Lawrence stared into space for a while before nodding. "The partial letter, yes? His name was on it, together with Jorge's, but neither of us thought of following up on it. It was not a name known to me, and as soon as Jorge's name was mentioned, Miguel said he had been told to arrest him."

"It has to be the same man. We should find it again and see if knowing he is Jorge's father allows us to make a better job of deciphering what little there is on it. Do you still have it?"

"I have everything," said Lawrence. "I'll find it when I go home. Which I hope will be before too long."

"Does Castellana truly believe him dead, or did she lie? Jorge said she hid the truth from him—was that one of the truths she hid? And if so, why?"

"He might be irrelevant," said Lawrence. "If Castellana's son was seen at Cortez's house that must mean he is involved in some way. He could even be the instigator of all this. He set Cortez and Mendoza to searching for his brother because he feared what he might want. And you said you saw those four men with him."

"I saw four men—whether they are the same men who killed Cortez, the same men who killed Miguel, is not certain yet."

"How many men like that can there be?" said Lawrence.

"If they are the same, and they are working for Gabriel, how did he find out about Jorge?" Thomas recalled what Theresa had told him. "Of course, his mother heard about him from Isabel. Theresa told me she talks of me often, and will no doubt have mentioned Jorge as well. The story of a handsome eunuch is a good tale to tell."

"If it is Gabriel, why all the convolution? Surely it would be simpler just to kill Jorge."

Thomas tapped on the table with his fingers as ideas circled each other in his head. "Perhaps Isabel also told Castellana my story too, of what I did to Mandana and Guerrero after they killed Lubna. She would have enjoyed showing me as a man who took his revenge. She would have enjoyed telling the tale in front of Fernando to remind him, too."

"They would have had you killed as well," said Lawrence.

"Would they? I am a difficult man to kill, even more so with Usaden at my side." He glanced at the Gomeres, who showed no indication he had heard or cared.

"Don't forget your dog," said Lawrence. "I heard he saved your life in the high mountains."

"I suspect he wanted to save his own life more than mine, but save us both he did." Thomas stared at the blocks as he tried to make sense of what he knew and what he didn't know. There was still too much of the latter. He pushed some of the blocks around, but it was nothing more than distraction. He knew he needed sleep, knew he could not afford to sleep.

"Who has the most to lose, or the most to gain?" said Lawrence.

"Or who has secrets they don't want revealed?" Thomas said.

"Let's take them in turn. Start with Jorge."

"Jorge's an open book, you know he is."

"I thought so until recently, now everything he believed true has been scattered to the winds. His parents aren't his parents, he has a brother he didn't know of, and … and a past. They are all relationships we need to tease out."

"There's something there, certainly, but I don't know what yet." Thomas set the unpainted block down, away from the others. "It is still nothing but confusion to me. There is no connection I can see, so let's follow the trail. Castellana is his true mother, agreed?"

Lawrence nodded, waiting for Thomas to continue.

Adana set fresh bread, fruit and meat on the table, then

sat as if she wanted to be involved. Thomas knew she had listened to their conversation, but wasn't sure what she could contribute.

"And Gabriel his half-brother, agreed?"

Another nod.

"Gabriel does not like Jorge," said Usaden, "but that does not mean he wants him dead."

"Would he try to stop someone else who did want him dead?" Thomas asked.

"That I do not know."

"I wasn't with you when you went to El Carpio," said Lawrence, "but I know Castellana is a wealthy woman, and until recently Gabriel believed he was her only son. What happens now? Does Jorge have a claim on her wealth, or not?"

"If he's her first-born son, he has a claim," Thomas said. "Not that he would ever press it."

"Except neither Castellana nor Gabriel know that," said Lawrence. "So they are still suspects."

"Perhaps. Except I saw Castellana with Jorge and she loves him. I suspect she's regretted having given him away every day of her life since. Jorge said she was lying about something, but I am sure it wasn't that."

"Perhaps we should all ride out there and confront them. Usaden said those men who killed Miguel went in that direction. We can chase them down. Fight them. Bring them back to be judged." Lawrence smiled. "It is a long time since we rode together after evil men, Thomas. I miss the excitement."

"We're both getting too old these days. Apart from which Isabel has given me a deadline. There is no time to ride out there, but you are right, those men need finding. We should send a message to the Hermandos and tell them everything we know."

Lawrence touched a few of the wooden blocks. "Once we discover what it is we know. Go on, Thomas, talk about the others. Does de Borja have the most to gain and the most to lose? The biggest prize in Christendom? He was married to Castellana and Gabriel is his son."

"Which he doesn't deny. He claims his past is an open book and I believe him. Besides, he might be Gabriel's father, but he's not Jorge's, so where is the connection?"

"Unless someone out there believes he is Jorge's father? Does that change anything?"

"One more bastard among a list of others?" Thomas said. "De Borja makes no secret he has fathered children. He makes no secret of his failings. He claims it will make him a better Pope because he understands the temptations put before a man. Claims it makes him better than those who have not had to fight them."

"I don't think he ever fought very hard," said Lawrence.

"No, maybe not."

"What about these?" Lawrence touched another block. "Eleanor and her son? They are connected to Castellana, but not to de Borja. Are they nothing more than a distraction? We should take them off the table, surely?"

"We can't. If what Miguel told me with his last breath is right, my own son was with Gabriel in Cortez's street. It is a stretch to see them involved, they are not even of Castile, but leave them where they are for now."

"You know who this is, don't you?" Lawrence pushed the unpainted block around on the table-top.

"It has to be Jorge's real father, this Inigo Florentino who was dead and is not dead, if that remnant of a letter is to be believed."

"Paper doesn't lie," said Lawrence. Thomas was not so sure, but Lawrence's life was built around paper, so of course he believed it.

"I wonder if this Inigo Florentino is a rich man?" Thomas said. "An important man?"

"No doubt Uncle Jorge would like everyone to think so," said Adana with a smile.

"What would Uncle Jorge like everyone to think?" The man himself entered the room, followed by Belia and Theresa, together with Amal. "That he is the handsomest man in the world? Well, that is self-evident. What do you want with me, Thomas? This is an ungodly early hour to be woken."

"Where is Will?"

"With Daniel. He wanted to know how to make a sword. Will, that is—I think Daniel already knows. So what do you want?"

"Miguel's dead."

Jorge reached for a chair and sat. "How?"

"Thrown from the bridge by the men who were with Gabriel when you and he fought."

"Then we need to find them and kill them."

"I want you and Theresa, or Belia, to go and talk with Miguel's housekeeper to find out what she knows, if anything."

Jorge shook his head. "I don't know what you're talking about. Knows about what?"

Thomas realised he had jumped ahead too fast, so told Jorge of Miguel's attempt to solve the mystery and how it had led to his death.

"I liked him."

"So did I, so we need to honour his memory and find out what he was doing."

Jorge noticed the blocks on the table and frowned. He reached out to pick one up and Thomas slapped his hand.

"Leave them where they are." He pushed the block representing Miguel closer to Jorge's, pushed the unpainted block, the unknown person, to make a triangle between the three. "I want you to go to Miguel's house and use all your skill to find out what his housekeeper knows. I suspect she was his lover, so there will be something even if she's not aware of it." Thomas tapped the unidentified block. "We need to know who this is, and she might offer some clue. She is going to be distraught. Her employer and lover has been killed, but I know you can do it. Take Belia or Theresa to help."

"Theresa," said Jorge. "And isn't the unknown man Mendoza? The prisoners more or less told me he gave the orders. In which case the puzzle is solved. He set the trap and was caught in it himself."

"Then ask Miguel's housekeeper about him. If you're right she will know the name." Thomas glanced at Theresa. "Will you go with Jorge?"

Theresa nodded. "You should come with us. You are the man with the questions."

"You know what I'm like, I frighten people."

"I will come," said Lawrence. "The three of us should be able to manage together. I know Miguel's housekeeper a little so she will trust me, but you do all the talking, Jorge. I'm not bad at it, but I've seen you in action."

After they had gone, Thomas pushed the blocks around without purpose. They seemed stupid now, contributing nothing. They were nothing but inanimate lumps of wood. People were too complex to be represented in such a way, with all their emotions and prejudices.

Zanita moved around him, clearing the table but leaving

the blocks where they were, and then Adana cried out, a loud wail that sounded as if she was in pain, but when Thomas turned, he saw it wasn't pain but joy as a woman entered the room with Daniel right behind her.

"Look, everyone. Look who has turned up on our doorstep. I told her she had just missed Jorge, but he'll be back soon. Zanita, we need to prepare a feast. Our entire family is together again. Beatriz has come home." Daniel touched the shoulder of the pretty girl at the woman's side. "And this is her companion, Sama."

When Thomas stood to greet them, he looked into Beatriz's eyes and saw she had something more than a reunion on her mind. She had come in response to his message. Her coming, rather than the sending of a reply, told him her words could not be risked to the care of a pigeon.

CHAPTER TWENTY-EIGHT

"I told Sama we were coming to Córdoba to see Jorge," said Beatriz, "but that is only a small part of the truth, as I am sure you know."

Thomas had brought Beatriz across the river to his rooms in the palace, wanting to avoid the distractions of Daniel's house until later. At first, as they entered into the gilded interior, she had been quiet, clearly unsure of herself despite her position in Cadiz. Thomas's rooms were less ornate, and she began to relax as they sat facing each other with morning light streaming through the window.

"Have you come to tell me the missing piece of the puzzle?" Thomas asked.

"I don't even know what puzzle you speak of, or if what I know or don't know will help, but I admit I have held secrets too long. If their revealing can help Jorge then I will tell you everything."

"You know who Jorge's father is, don't you?"

Beatriz nodded, but her gaze darted away as something beyond the window attracted her attention. Her eyes widened at the sight of Isabel and Fernando. They faced each other, and appeared to be arguing.

"You move in exalted circles, Thomas Berrington. Is that who I think it is?"

"If you think it is the Queen and her husband, then yes."

"Why not call him King?"

"Because it is Isabel who rules here. Isabel who will rule once Spain is reunited."

"You know them both well enough to call them by name?"

"Everyone knows their names."

"But not everyone uses them. Do you call her by name when you speak with her? Do you call her Isabel?"

"Sometimes. When we are alone."

Beatriz shook her head at the wonder of it before turning back to Thomas. She firmed her shoulders, as if needing to gather her courage.

"I saw who brought Jorge to our family, and I have met his father, but that was only recently."

"Inigo Florentino?"

"That is the name he gave me, though it took some time before I discovered who he really was. He came to me in Cadiz. At first I thought him no more than a trader, even if he was the most handsome trader I have ever met. And with such a sweet tongue on him. Had I not looked as I do and been ten years younger, I might have asked him to dine with me."

"You are a handsome woman," Thomas said.

Beatriz laughed. "I know what I am. I look like Daniel, not Jorge. But this man … ah, he looked like Jorge. I might have guessed if it had not been so long since I saw him last. He had barely thirteen years when I believed him dead."

Beatriz stared into space for a time. Outside a voice was raised in anger, but Thomas didn't take his eyes off her.

"When did you discover he was not?"

Beatriz shook herself as if coming back from some distant place. "When this Inigo came to see me. He stayed several days, but it took two before he told me his true reason for being there. I should have been disappointed he did not want to trade with me, but the news he brought was so thrilling I did not mind. He told me Jorge still lived."

"When did he tell you he was his father?"

"Another day later. The man holds secrets to himself like others hoard gold. Even then he did not reveal everything, but I could work out what he did not." Beatriz let her breath loose in a long sigh. "Is Jorge handsome?"

"The most handsome man alive," Thomas said.

Beatriz smiled. "Is he married? Does he have children? I know nothing of him and would know everything. He was such a sweet child, but wicked too."

"He is still both of those things. He's not married, but as good as. He lives with a beautiful woman by the name of Belia. They have no children. Jorge will never father children."

"Why not? Even before he was taken by the river Jorge was no stranger to the ways of love. Girls his own age, women far older, everyone loved Jorge and he loved them back. I am only surprised he did not plant a child in anyone —is that why, he cannot?"

"He cannot now because he is a eunuch."

Beatriz stared at Thomas. "A eunuch? I do not understand. How can Jorge be a eunuch?"

"It's a long story and one he should tell you himself. Can you wait until you see him?"

"If I must." Beatriz shook her head. "No, I must, I know I

must. How long will Jorge be on this errand you sent him on?"

"I don't know. Tell me what you know of Inigo Florentino, and then we will return to Daniel's house. No doubt Jorge will have returned by then. He wants to see you too, I know. He has fond memories of your care." A thought occurred to Thomas. "I am remiss, are you hungry? Shall I send for some food and wine?"

"Nothing. I am sure Daniel and his wife will feed me when we go there." Beatriz took a breath and told Thomas about Inigo Florentino. "As I said, it was two days before his real purpose was revealed. I think if I was a different kind of woman he would have come into my bed if I had asked, because he wanted information from me. He asked about a boy. A boy by the name of Jorge."

"How did he find you?"

Beatriz waved a hand. "Stop asking me questions and I will tell you everything I know, but I need to start from the beginning. Which is with a woman by the name of Castellana Baltieri—"

"Who is now Castellana Lonzal."

"Let me tell you in my own way, Thomas. Keep your questions for after, or I will get distracted and forget something. It began with a woman by the name of Castellana Baltieri and a man by the name of Rodrigo Lonzal, as well as this Inigo—so yes, you are right, and I will get to that. Inigo told me they were the best of friends until Castellana set her sights on him. He was from a less well-off family, he told me. Not poor, but not wealthy like Lonzal. Except Inigo was—still is—the most handsome of men and Castellana, though young, was advanced. Like Jorge, I suppose." She laughed. "No wonder he is like he is. She wanted Inigo, and he wanted her. I have no need to explain the details, I am sure a man such as you knows how such things happen.

"When Lonzal found out he flew into a rage. Castellana's family had promised her to him. It was a marriage of equals, a marriage to cement two dynasties together. All of that would be destroyed by another man's child, so Lonzal took command.

"It started with a beating, and then he hired men to kill Inigo. That is what he claims. Whether it is true or not I cannot tell. What I did see was his hatred of this man. Inigo would see him dead. Has wanted him dead ever since he was expelled from Valencia, for that is where they all lived." She held a hand up as Thomas opened his mouth to ask a question and he closed it again.

"Why did he leave? Is that what you were about to ask me?"

Thomas nodded. The story Beatriz was relating had a ring of truth to it. The kind of tale told over and over between men and women, between lovers and rivals.

"You need to know how powerful this Lonzal was. How powerful he has become. Inigo told me who he is, who he has become. He is Cardinal Rodrigo de Borja, and rumour is that when the current incumbent dies, he will be the next Pope in Roma. But I am getting ahead of myself.

"Inigo left Valencia and became a mariner. A number of years later he was on a ship caught in a storm and it went down with, so everyone thought, all hands lost. Except Inigo found his way to shore with half a dozen others, but it was the coast of Africa. He told me he stayed there a long time, and then moved to Italia. He ended up in Roma and saw Lonzal there. He recognised the man and remembered his hatred of him. The man who had ruined his life. It was as he told me this I saw the spark of madness in his eyes.

Inigo's hatred has turned a fine mind into one obsessed with revenge. Revenge and redemption.

"Inigo had no idea he had a son. He knew Castellana was with child, but children can be scraped out of a woman when they are not wanted, and I think he believed that is what had happened. Then, he said, something strange occurred. He joined a group of religious men set against de Borja. Not because he carried any great belief, but it suited him because it allowed him to spy on de Borja and plan his revenge. He had discovered that the child Castellana carried had been born, and then given away, here in Córdoba. So Inigo sent messages asking for anyone who might know something of the boy. He even knew his name was Jorge. But, like everyone else, he was told the boy he sought was dead. This news might have been what turned his mind. I am sure he thought of nothing but how to destroy de Borja."

"Why did he come to you if he thought Jorge dead?" Thomas asked.

"Because the people he originally paid to find him found something else here in the city. They were men, Inigo told me, who dealt in secrets. Men who made their living extracting money from those who did not want their secrets laid out in the open. Men who listened and searched for anything they could use. One of the men had placed Jorge with our family. I saw him brought as a babe of no more than three months. I was handed Jorge by my mother, who kept the money this man gave her, and the rest of us never saw any of it. I raised him myself. I loved him, wickedness and all. And then everyone thought him dead. Until you came here. The story Inigo heard is you pursued an Abbot and brought him to justice. Is that true?"

"Abbot Mandana," Thomas said. He could tell Beatriz

more about the man later, but didn't want to interrupt her now she was coming to the core of her tale.

"Castellana lived in Córdoba then, together with her second son. She had become a companion of Queen Isabel, who regaled her with the story of this mysterious surgeon who could also fight like a demon and would never give up. A man by the name of Thomas Berrington, Inigo said, and his companion Jorge Olmos." Beatriz stared hard at Thomas and he watched as tears gathered in her eyes. "When he told me that, I almost fainted. My Jorge lived. And when Inigo heard it, he knew his son lived."

"How? He would not know Jorge's name, would he?"

"Because of the men he paid. Castellana paid men to make Jorge disappear. Without knowing it, Inigo paid the same men to find him. They must have been laughing at how easy it was to extract money from them both. Except whatever the cost, Inigo considered it worthwhile. He knew his son lived. Which is what brought him to me. He traced me as the person who'd raised Jorge and he came to find me. He wanted to know all about his son. Wanted to know everything I could tell him. And then..." She sighed and ran a hand through her hair. "Then he said he would kill them all."

Thomas stared at her. "All? Jorge as well?"

"No, of course not Jorge. But the others. This de Borja, the men who took his money. He told me they had to suffer his judgement. It was then I knew how crazy he was. He hid it well, but it is there, barely beneath the surface."

"And Castellana?"

"I think he still loves her, not that she will ever want to take him back, not if she values her own life, or that of her second son."

"When did Inigo come to you?"

"Three months since. He revealed to me that Jorge still lived and I wanted so to see him again. I almost came before when I heard Daniel had done well for himself. Such news spreads, even as far as Cadiz. I should have come sooner. If I had, two men might still be alive and Jorge would be out of danger."

"I should not have told you anything about that, but I was desperate."

"As you should be. As I was when I received your message. I wrote one to send back, but realised I had to tell you what happened face to face."

Thomas laughed. "Lawrence, the man who sent you the message, told me pigeons were small birds. You would have needed an eagle to carry your news."

"Does it help Jorge?" asked Beatriz.

"I don't know, not yet. I need to work through what you have told me. Did Inigo say where he was going after he left you?"

"He said he was coming here. He was coming to Córdoba to take his revenge."

CHAPTER TWENTY-NINE

Daniel's house was in chaos when Thomas and Beatriz arrived. Thomas took Jorge's arm and attempted to lead him outside, only for Jorge to pull free to embrace the woman he had always believed was his sister. Beatriz held Jorge at arm's length, her eyes tracking him: his height, his beauty, his strength, clearly unable to believe what she saw … what he had turned into. Then she embraced him again, tears in both their eyes.

To one side, Adana stood next to Beatriz's companion, Sama. They seemed to have formed a friendship in the short time they had known each other. Thomas saw Zanita's gaze on them both, her face expressionless. Then Daniel entered the room and gave a great shout as he saw Beatriz, and the embrace between two became an embrace between three. Thomas waited to intervene, knowing making an attempt too soon would result in a rebuff, leaving it too long would waste valuable time. Then he glimpsed Theresa sitting in a chair near the far door and crossed to her.

"Were you there?" he asked. "When Jorge spoke with Miguel's housekeeper?"

"I was, though she is far more than a housekeeper. Jorge is good with women, but it was fortunate I went with him."

Thomas looked around. The level of sound in the room had risen even more, as everyone started to talk at once.

"I need you to tell me if she knew anything about what Miguel was doing." He would have preferred to ask Jorge, but knew he might be another hour at least. He appeared to have forgotten he was free from prison only with Isabel's permission. Thomas experienced a sense of the world turning around him while he stood at its centre, an onlooker incapable of affecting anything.

"I don't think she knew everything he was doing, but enough, perhaps." Theresa gripped Thomas's shirt and led him across the room. They skirted the group gathered around Beatriz and left through a rear door which led to an area of untended scrub that ran down to the river bank. Thomas followed Theresa to the water, where the air was a little cooler. So much had happened to Thomas since waking, it seemed it should be evening instead of still an hour shy of noon.

When Theresa turned to him, he was uneasy at what he saw in her eyes. There was a hunger, a want he didn't think he could satisfy, was even capable of satisfying.

"Did Jorge do all the talking?" he asked.

"Of course. He led her gently to what he wanted to know. He got her talking about how she began working for Miguel, and then he worked his magic so she told him everything. He made her laugh, then he made her cry, then he soothed her tears. You know what Jorge is like. Women love him."

"Yes, I know what he is like. How did he broach the subject of money?"

"With tact, and she was happy to accept. I think she feels

it her due."

"What did she know?"

"She definitely knew he was doing something he shouldn't. She even said she tried to tease it out of him and warned him to stop. Their life together was good and he threatened to destroy it. He has destroyed it now in any case, hasn't he?" Theresa gripped Thomas's wrist, lifted his hand to her shoulder, which rose and fell with each breath.

"The money will help," Thomas said. "She is pretty enough. Perhaps she will find another master."

"Yes, she is pretty, but pretty doesn't heal a broken heart."

"Tell me what you heard beneath her words."

Theresa released his hand, but kept her own on his shoulder. "As I said, she knew he was doing something, but not what. He was often out in the small hours. Neglected his work. She was concerned he might lose his post, but when she confronted him, he told her there was nothing to worry about even if he did. If what he was working on came to fruition there would be a promotion."

"I take it she asked him what it was?"

"She did, but he told her she didn't need to know, not until everything was settled."

"It's not much to go on."

"She also heard your name and Jorge's mentioned. She thought it in connection with the work he was doing, but couldn't be sure."

"Miguel wanted to prove himself by solving this crime on his own. Had he succeeded he would be lauded. But he didn't succeed. All he managed to do was get himself killed."

"He disappointed you, didn't he?"

"I liked him. Trusted him. So yes, he disappointed me. Did she tell Jorge anything else?"

"She knew about Miguel's whores, but most women do, don't they?"

"You're asking the wrong man."

Theresa rubbed her thumb across his shoulder. "Oh, I wish you loved me like I love you, Thomas. You are a rare creature indeed. One of a kind."

"I'm not sure that is a good thing to be. Did she mind about his whores?"

"I don't think so. Some women are grateful."

"Did she love him?"

Theresa raised a shoulder. "She may have, but I would say more likely she was used to him. Often that is enough, is it not?"

"Is it?"

"See, there you go again. You cannot be as innocent as you pretend, it is not possible. Are you going to go back to your Eleanor?"

"What else did Miguel's housekeeper say?"

"Nothing."

"No names, no faces? Other than mine and Jorge's, that is?"

"Not that I heard, but you should talk to Jorge because you know what he is like. He can suck the very soul from a woman and leave her grateful."

Thomas laughed. "Perhaps you should turn your attentions in his direction then."

"I would be tempted, but he already has a woman, and she scares me. I would never cross Belia."

Nor me, thought Thomas. What Theresa had told him didn't feel like enough, but he was probably the wrong man to know whether it was or not. He and Lubna had never had secrets. At least he'd had no secrets from her, and now it was too late to know whether she had withheld any from him. The thought of his dead wife crashed a wave of loss through him that Theresa must have seen, because she pressed against him, her arms circling his waist, her body soft against his, and she held him. Nothing more. No words. No attempt to kiss his mouth or let her hands stray. Thomas stood without moving, waiting for the moment to pass, as he knew it eventually would. The crushing sense of loss came less often than it did, and he had grown used to it. He knew this moment would pass, as had the ones before.

He held Theresa's shoulders and eased her away. Only then did he press his lips to hers.

"Thank you."

She made no reply, letting him hold her a moment longer before turning away and walking toward the house. Thomas wondered if she was disappointed in him, but knew he could do nothing about it if she was. She attracted him, but it wasn't an attraction he wanted to take action on. Why, he was not quite sure. Perhaps he wasn't ready yet. He wondered if he ever would be. It certainly wasn't because of Eleanor. The lapses in her bed had brought his youth back, but waking beside her had washed it all away again. He had felt old and corrupted. They were neither of them the people they had once been. It wasn't surprising, but it was, perhaps, a disappointment.

A movement caught his attention and he glanced up to see Jorge emerge from the house. He walked past Theresa with the exchange of a few words.

"Beatriz finally let me go," he said with a laugh. "She has captured Daniel now and keeps moving between the children, wanting to touch every one of them. It is going to take some time because now they are running around to confuse her. She has already told Adana she can return to Cadiz with her."

"What did Zanita say to that?"

"I think she knows it's right for Adana."

"And Daniel?"

"I will talk to him. He wants Adana to be happy. She needs more than to be a maid for this house."

"Theresa told me what she heard when she went with you to Miguel's house, but I need to hear it all from you."

"Tell me what she's already told you so I don't need to repeat anything."

"Tell me anyway. Assume I know nothing."

"That won't be hard. All right … let's walk. There's an inn at the end of this road somewhere, I passed it on my way back. I need wine and food, and we'll be away from the others in case Beatriz decides she wants to hug me some more. We can talk as we go, if you want."

"Isabel has given me a deadline to prove your innocence."

"I hope I will never be innocent. But if you mean of these crimes, then good. How many days?"

"Until dawn tomorrow."

Jorge slowed. "Can you do it?"

"Tell me what you heard beneath the words of Miguel's woman. Theresa heard the words, you will have heard the heart of them, so tell me. Did she love him?"

"Once, I'm sure, but no longer. Not that it matters. In most relationships love is the first thing to be lost. You and I are fortunate individuals, Thomas, and you will be again. It is in your nature."

Thomas gave a shake of his head. "It never was, why should it be again? Lubna was … different to anyone else I ever knew."

"Even Eleanor, your girl of France?"

"That was a long time ago and in another world. I have

learned a lesson—that you can't always discover what has been lost."

"Yet here she is, close by and available."

"We have both changed too much. We can never recover what we had. We are different people. I tried, but even as I lay with her I knew it was wrong."

"Did she think so too?"

"I don't know, but I suspect she did, despite her words of encouragement. Tell me what Miguel's housekeeper knew. Theresa said she was aware he was doing something, but didn't know exactly what."

"Of course she did, but she didn't want to know. She cared for Miguel when he came home and tried to ignore everything else. So we are no further forward."

"Not with Miguel, but while you were with his housekeeper, Beatriz and I spoke. She told me your father came to her. He asked about you."

Jorge stopped walking despite the fact the inn lay only a score of paces ahead.

"When were you going to tell me?"

"I am telling you now. I haven't had much chance yet."

"And why did she tell you rather than me?"

"Because I was there, and I asked. It is why she has come to Qurtuba. To tell me who he was, and what he has done."

"I thought she came to see me and Daniel."

"She has, but she also wanted to confess things that couldn't be put in a message."

"I already know who my father is," said Jorge. "The man who lay first with Castellana. Inigo Florentino." Jorge started to walk again, rubbing his palms together at the prospect of food and drink. He raised a hand to attract the attention of a serving girl, not that the gesture was necessary, because her eyes had already been drawn to him. He took a chair at a table far enough from the other patrons for their conversation to remain private. "A name is not enough, though, I want to know more about him."

"Beatriz told me he came to see her."

"Then I need her to tell me everything about him. Is he handsome? Clever? Charming?"

"All of those, she told me. Plus angry."

Jorge frowned as he ordered wine and small dishes of food. "Why angry?"

"He came in search of you," Thomas said.

"I make him angry?"

"No, not you. His anger is directed against de Borja. Perhaps Castellana too, but mostly de Borja I think. He believes he took Castellana from him and forced her to give their child up."

"You know this how?" Jorge poured dark wine from a jug into their cups.

"It's what Beatriz worked out and passed on to me. Ask her and she will tell you it all. You may hear more in her words than I do. She said he paid Mendoza to find out who you were lodged with when you were given away, and paid him later to track you down. He also wrote a letter to Cortez, which Lawrence has a scrap of."

"He was searching for me?"

Thomas nodded.

"Because he wants to find me, or wants to get rid of me?"

Thomas saw that Jorge had gone to the crux of the matter. Was Inigo in search of a lost son, or was he looking to remove an embarrassment, or even wanting to destroy him to punish Castellana?

"That is the question we need an answer to most. I intend to visit Castellana again and be less gentle this time. She may be in danger from Inigo, but she may also be involved. If she has discovered his interest, she might want to remove the threat you pose to her. Or it is de Borja who wants to cover up his action in forcing you to be given away. He appears unconcerned about Castellana and his other women, but giving a child away into a fetid slum would taint even him. I don't know all the connections yet. I would prefer to know why everything has happened before going to see Castellana."

"Then find the connections, and fast. How long did you say Isabel gave you?"

"The connections aren't here," Thomas said. "They're with de Borja, your mother or your father. One of them is on their way to Sevilla, another is close enough to question again. I heard she has returned to the house in Qurtuba, which will save me a few hours. I want you to stay here."

"I have to be there, Thomas. She is my mother, after all. If you mean to question her, I need to be there to provide a moderating influence."

Thomas stared at Jorge, trying to decide whether to agree to his request or not, knowing he had to.

"Both of us, then, together with Usaden."

"Are you expecting trouble?"

"It is always best to be prepared. I have to talk with Castellana again if only to warn her she could be in danger. I also want to question Gabriel, and Yves if he is there, to find out why they were outside Cortez's house."

"Will knowing everything prove me innocent?" asked Jorge.

"If not, we may have to ride from here as fast and as far as we can. We will send a message for Belia to bring the children."

"I don't like the idea of running," said Jorge, "but I like the idea of being executed even less."

CHAPTER THIRTY

Thomas stood outside Castellana's house in Qurtuba with Jorge and Usaden beside him. The afternoon heat made it difficult to draw breath as he waited for some sense of exactly what he wanted to do to come to him. He had intended to ride out to El Carpio, but considered it worth trying the house here first. It would save them several hours of riding if she had returned. Confronting Castellana was a risk, but he could think of no other way of finding out what he needed to know. No other way to prove Jorge innocent. Beatriz had provided the clue when she told him Inigo Florentino was searching for his son. Now Thomas had to find out how much Castellana knew, and whether Inigo's search had triggered her to act. If it was not her, Thomas hoped she might know who.

"It will go easier if you stay outside," he said to Jorge.

"Which is why I have no intention of doing so."

"I can get answers faster if Castellana is afraid of me. You won't want to watch me do that."

"Do you intend to hurt her?"

"Of course not, but she has to believe I will. Her and Gabriel both."

"Do what you want to him, but spare her. Promise me that and I won't interfere." Jorge smiled. "However ferocious you look." Jorge stared at Thomas. "Just promise me you won't kill him."

"Even if he is behind everything that has happened to you?"

"I cannot believe he is. He is an oaf and a bully, but we share the same blood. Try not to spill too much of it."

Thomas waved a hand and Usaden ran off to the end of the street. He would work his way along the back of the houses until he found a way in. Thomas was sure he would succeed. He didn't bother announcing their presence. Instead he tried the gate, surprised when it opened. Had it not, he knew Jorge would be able to pick the lock.

The shaded courtyard was empty, as was the ground floor, and Thomas wondered where the servants were as he climbed the ornate staircase. He recalled the last time he had ascended it in Eleanor's company. He regretted his actions that day and since, regretted them even more now, ashamed of his weakness. He should have known it was impossible to re-capture his youth.

As he reached the upper floor, Eleanor appeared, as if conjured by his thoughts. She drew a robe tighter around herself. Thomas wondered if everyone was sleeping the heat of the afternoon away.

"Have you come for me again?" She tried to stop him passing, but Thomas pushed her aside. She came after him, pulling at his sleeve, but he ignored her.

"Hold her and wait here," Thomas told Jorge before opening the door next to the one Eleanor had emerged from, relieved to find he had guessed right. Castellana was starting to sit up, covering her breasts with one arm, and Thomas looked away even as he spoke.

"Put something on. I want to talk to you."

"I am in no state for company, sir. Leave now or I will call out."

"Call all you like." Thomas turned back so she could see he didn't care whether she was naked or not.

Castellana let out a piercing scream that echoed through the house. A moment later came the sound of shouting and scuffles, and then everything went quiet. Thomas smiled. Usaden had found a way in.

"It appears my companion has taken care of whoever you have out there. Get dressed." Thomas turned away again. He heard the sound of bedclothes thrown aside and then rustling.

"What is it you want of me?"

"The truth."

"I told you the truth the last time you came."

It was awkward talking with his back to her, so Thomas turned around and stared at Castellana. She was dressed in a long cotton robe belted at the waist, clearly naked beneath it and not caring he knew.

"You told me Inigo Florentino was dead. When did you learn he was not?"

He saw a moment of surprise cross her face before she managed to control herself.

"It was not so long ago. The man who placed Jorge in this city came to me to tell me Inigo had been in touch with him. I did not want Jorge to think he could go looking for his father. Does he know he lives?"

"Of course he knows."

"Does he know what kind of man Inigo is?"

"You tell me—and I want to know everything this time."

He nodded at the bed. "Sit if you want, we might be some time. I want to know everything. No secrets, no protecting anyone."

Castellana looked as if she was going to stay on her feet if only to defy him, then thought better of it and sat on the edge of the bed, one hand curling around the upright.

"Are you keeping me here deliberately? Are you going to ravish me like you did Eleanor?"

"I hadn't planned to, no. Would you like me to? I have another man out there who might be willing. A Moor. You know what heathens the Moors are, don't you?"

"Eleanor told me how it was for her." She sighed as if disappointed.

Thomas knew she was trying to goad him and ignored her, but he did approach closer, pleased when he saw her flinch.

"Or should I ask Eleanor to come here so you can abuse us both together?" asked Castellana.

"You appear determined to have someone abuse you. I met Eleanor when we let ourselves in. She didn't appear concerned at my presence."

"Her son is here too. Your son." She smiled. "Did you think she wouldn't tell me? Eleanor and I have become the best of friends. As our sons have become the best of friends."

"Tell me about Inigo."

Castellana smiled as if she knew things Thomas would never think of asking, things she would never reveal unless he did. He wished she wasn't Jorge's mother, because he would be the man to strip her mind of every withheld secret. Thomas knew he would have to manage on his own.

"I know you are not going to hurt me," said Castellana.

"Don't be so sure of it."

Castellana laughed. "Jorge told me about you. He said you are a good man, and good men do not torture innocent women."

"What about guilty women?"

All Castellana did was offer a smile.

Thomas turned away and went to the door.

"Bring me Gabriel," he called out, pleased when he saw Usaden move away. "Wait—where's Jorge?"

Usaden stopped long enough to say, "Talking to your woman."

"Do you know where Gabriel is?"

"Of course." Usaden started off once more and Thomas returned to Castellana's room. He stood too close to her, trying to cast his mind into that cold place it went in battle, but failing. Eleanor was right—he was a good man, and good men didn't torture women, innocent or otherwise.

"Do you know how much trouble you are in?" asked Castellana, her voice as calm as if they were discussing the latest fashion in dresses.

"I am always in trouble. I have grown used to it by now."

Usaden appeared, dragging Gabriel beside him without effort. He had a grip on his shoulder that looked as if it hurt. Thomas took over and dragged the man inside the room. Usaden turned without a word, closing the door as he left. When Thomas released Gabriel, he circled his arm as if trying to ease a pain.

"What is going on, Mother?"

"This man wants answers of me and thinks I will give them if he hurts you."

"Well he is wrong."

Gabriel tried to look brave, but Thomas recognised a bully when he saw one and knew his first punch would change things. He decided he might as well get started and pushed Gabriel against the wall. He pressed an arm across his throat so he had to rise on tiptoe. He glanced toward Castellana, who was watching without any show of emotion, so Thomas punched Gabriel hard in the stomach. He gasped, almost going to his knees as he tried to draw breath into his lungs. Thomas let him drop to the floor, then kicked him in the side of the head, picking his spot so he caught him on the ear. He knew it would bleed profusely without doing much damage.

When he turned back, Castellana had paled. Gabriel staggered to his feet, one hand pressed against his ear. Thomas knew Castellana would talk now so he grabbed Gabriel and tossed him out into the corridor for Usaden to take care of.

"Inigo was here," Castellana said, "but left this morning at dawn."

"Here? Why was he here?"

"He wanted to see me again." She shook her head, pursing her lips. "And he wanted to know where Rodrigo was headed."

"Had you seen Inigo before, since he was exiled?"

"Of course. He visits now and again when business brings him to Castile, which is not often. He is as virile and handsome as ever, but his hatred makes him a dangerous man."

"His hatred of de Borja?"

"Of course."

"And you? Do you hate him, too?"

"Rodrigo? No, I love him. I love them both." She gave a sly smile. "We all three of us loved each other once." The smile came again, a softness to it now. "Together."

Thomas stared at her. "You were … too young," he said.

"I had thirteen years. Is that so young? I was curious, we

all were. It is an age when the young change and seek to experiment. I am sure you did also, did you not?"

"This isn't about me. Could Jorge not be de Borja's son as easily as he could be Inigo's?"

Castellana gave a shake of her head. "No, he is Inigo's. If you ever meet the man you will see it at once, but I pray neither of you ever do, for Inigo is different. His beauty has turned bad inside. His mind is no longer sound."

"And yet you let him into your bed."

"How could I not? He would have taken me whether I wished it or not. But I did wish it. Mad he might be, but he is still the best lover I have ever enjoyed. I can never refuse him."

"You told me he was dead," Thomas said.

"Which was true, once. Imagine how I felt when he came to find me, not here, but in El Carpio."

"When was this?"

"Two years ago."

"Did he tell you why he came to find you?"

"Because he still loved me, he said—is that so strange?"

Thomas looked at Castellana. No, not so strange, he thought. She and Eleanor both shared the kind of beauty that age did not lessen. Perhaps it was as much in the mind as in the body, but wherever it resided, she was a beautiful woman.

"And he continues to hate Rodrigo," said Castellana. "Enough to kill him, I am sure, which is why I went to him in the palace, to warn him. You saw me with him, you must have because I saw you. I was with Eleanor and the Queen, and then I was with Rodrigo." The way she spoke, Thomas knew exactly how she had been with Rodrigo.

"What did he say when you told him about Inigo?"

"He told me not to worry, it was being taken care of. And

then after, he had papers for me to sign. A declaration of divorce backdated thirty years. He said it would be unfortunate if it was discovered that a new Pope possessed a wife and family he had abandoned years ago. I expect he is travelling the country doing the same with a dozen other women, though whether he is bedding them too I don't know."

"Did you sign the papers?"

"I was offered no choice."

"I assume you don't love him anymore?"

"Of course not."

The tale Castellana told sounded far-fetched, but Thomas heard a truth in the way she told it. He brought a chair and set it before the bed. This time when he came close, Castellana didn't flinch.

"When we spoke before, you said Inigo and Rodrigo were friends. Why?"

"Because they were, and the truth is harder to explain. Besides, I cared not whether you believed me. All I wanted was to see Jorge." She lifted a hand and wiped at her eye, but Thomas saw no tears.

"Did you send Gabriel after us?"

"I didn't even know he followed you, so no. What did he want?"

"I'm not entirely sure, but I suspect it was a need to confirm to himself who was the more important son. Who was the more loved."

"Did he get an answer?"

"He fought Jorge. He might have hurt him by using those men against him if the rest of us hadn't been there. As it was, Jorge won the fight."

Castellana suppressed a smile. "Gabriel always believes he is stronger than he is. Usually there are others who save him from himself. But he is my son, and I love him. Of course I do."

Thomas heard little conviction in her voice. "And Jorge?"

She shook her head. "Rodrigo made me give him away. I tried to forget about it. I was young, and within a year Gabriel was born. I believe I had forgotten him until you turned up on my doorstep."

"Inigo is looking for Jorge. Why? Does he wish him harm or to reunite with his son?"

"I didn't even know he was looking for him. If I had, I would have offered to help. Jorge still joins us together."

"You never remarried?"

"I have enjoyed the love of two men, both of whom can never be equalled. I knew if I took another husband, he would never live up to what I once had. By then I did not need a man, I had made my own way in the world." She stared at Thomas. Her confidence had returned, but still she frowned. "Two men who I believe are about to become one. I will lose one or the other, and know which I would prefer to lose."

"De Borja is untouchable," Thomas said.

"Inigo doesn't believe that. Or he doesn't care. It is where he has gone now, to kill Rodrigo while he is journeying back to Roma and vulnerable. He took those men with him, the ones he left with me."

"Inigo sent them here?" Thomas was puzzled.

"To protect me, he said. Also to search for any information relating to Jorge. I suspect their true purpose was to report on what I did. To report on whether I betrayed him to Rodrigo."

"Four men and Inigo? It's not enough."

"He has other men as well. He boasted of a small army."

Thomas saw he had been wrong about almost everything.

"I thought Jorge's arrest was an attempt to punish me." He shook his head at his own arrogance. "It had nothing to do with me, did it? Was de Borja behind it?"

"Not Rodrigo, but someone else. Someone who hates you even more than Inigo hates Rodrigo."

Thomas tried to think of who it might be, or was Castellana only taking her own revenge on him?

"Are you going to tell me who?"

"Do I need to? Who can hate you that much?"

"I don't know. Almost everyone who hates me is dead at my hand. The only other person I can think of sits on the throne in Gharnatah, and I can see no connection to him in this business."

Castellana laughed. "You are so close to the truth, and yet so wrong."

"Tell me who!"

"A man who sits on another throne, one not half a mile from this house."

Thomas shook his head, not believing her, but believing her.

"He hates you more than any man can hate, because his wife loves you more than she loves him. God knows why, you are no great catch, are you?"

"Fernando," Thomas said, and he saw Castellana smile in victory at his confusion and pain.

CHAPTER THIRTY-ONE

Thomas found Theresa sitting in her room close to the royal chambers. She glanced up and smiled, but stayed where she was, waiting for him to go to her.

"I need to see Fernando."

Something in his voice made her frown and she rose to her feet.

"You are out of luck. He has ridden to see Rodrigo off. He said he might accompany him overnight before returning. You know what he is like, always wanting to do whatever shows him in a manly light."

"I had forgotten de Borja was leaving so soon."

"He is on his way to Sevilla. He will stay there a few days, then take a ship to Roma." Theresa smiled. "It is going to take him over a week to complete a two day journey, because he wants to bless as many of his flock as he can."

"How many men does de Borja have with him?"

"How am I meant to know that?" Theresa came closer. Too close. "Does it matter?"

"He will have taken a dozen at least, won't he?"

"I don't know, Thomas, but Fernando took eight, so if

you are worried about brigands, they will be safe enough. I expect de Borja may have others of his own as well, plus the priests. There were a lot of priests gathered to accompany him."

"He will be perfectly safe then, won't he?"

Thomas saw Theresa smile.

"What about Isabel?"

"She ate with the children and now she is working. Do you want me to ask if she will grant you an audience?"

Thomas didn't know if he wanted that or not. He would prefer to have a discussion with Fernando first to judge his involvement before saying anything. If he was brave enough to say anything at all. Castellana had scattered so many accusations, he didn't know which to believe and which not.

And then he made the decision that might change everything. Might end the life he knew, or start a life he wasn't sure he wanted.

"Yes, go and ask if I can see her."

"And afterward? Shall I wait in your room?" Theresa smiled so innocently Thomas tried not to laugh, glad she could lighten his mood.

"I won't be staying, I have to get back to Jorge."

"He has rooms here as well."

"Not tonight. By morning he may be back in prison, and I won't allow that."

"Thomas Berrington, the saviour of the world." Theresa rose on her toes and brushed his lips with hers, then she was gone, only her scent remaining. Thomas sat in the chair still warm from her body and tried to think about what he wanted to say to Isabel. When Theresa returned, he still hadn't decided, but rose anyway before he could change his mind.

Isabel looked up from where she sat behind a large table,

papers scattered across its dark-stained surface. The fingertips of one hand were marked by ink, and strands of pale red hair had come loose to hang across one cheek. This is her domain, Thomas thought. She looked content.

"Theresa said it was important." She smiled, and in that small gesture his decision was made. He could never tell this woman anything other than the truth. He owed it to her. Owed it to himself and to Castile.

"Here..." She pushed a large sheet of paper toward him as he approached. "Tell me what you think of this."

He leaned across the table and looked at the drawing. It showed a series of straight-lined roads, square blocks representing buildings of different sizes.

"Where is this? I don't recognise it."

Isabel laughed. "Of course you do not, because it does not exist yet, other than as a filthy camp. When it does, I will call it Santa Fe. It will start to be built this year, ready for next."

Thomas looked at the plan. He knew where it would be built, and what it represented. It was more than roadways and houses. It promised the end of the life he had known for almost thirty years. When he looked up, Isabel was staring at him in the same way Theresa had only a few moments before, and he almost groaned, not sure if he could do what he'd come here for after all.

"Tell me what troubles you, Thomas. I see it on your face, I see it in the way your body holds a tension. Is it so hard to say the words you want to speak to me?"

He wanted to look away, but made himself return her stare.

"I need to tell you something, and once I do you might banish me from your presence forever."

"You know such is not possible, whatever you say."

"You haven't heard what it is yet."

"There is nothing you can say that will make me not want you at my side. I have asked you often enough, and you know I will ask again. Now, if you wish. Will you—"

"Not yet." He turned away, unable to look at her any longer. He walked to where chairs were set before a cold fireplace. There was less lamplight there and he welcomed the shadows. He watched as Isabel came toward the chair nearest his, her footsteps small and lithe. Her body was sturdier than it had once been, but he barely saw the signs of ageing. As he was sure she didn't see them in him either. As he hadn't seen how Eleanor had aged, he thought, before dismissing her from his mind as irrelevant on this night.

"Tell me what pains you, Thomas."

"Theresa tells me Fernando is accompanying de Borja."

"She speaks true, but what has that to do with why you are here? Unless it is Theresa herself? If it is, you know you have my blessing, both of you. I love Theresa as a sister, and would see her happy. I know she has feelings for you."

"It is not Theresa. It is Fernando. I…" He pushed a hand across his head, clutching at a handful of hair. "I believe he wants me dead. And not only me."

Isabel laughed. "Why would he want you dead?"

"You have to admit he doesn't like me."

"If he wanted everyone dead he didn't like there would be a stack of bodies a mile high. I am sure your own would be almost as tall. As would mine."

"I mean what I say." Thomas wanted to communicate a truth to her, this woman that spun threads of want and fear through him. He leaned forward, closing the gap between them to a shared intimacy she didn't withdraw from, as he knew she would not.

"I thought you had come to tell me you have your proof that Jorge is innocent, not this."

"He is innocent, but my proof is not here. My proof is stalking Rodrigo de Borja with the intent to kill him. Fernando rides with de Borja, but I don't know which side he supports, or what he will do. Did Castellana Lonzal tell you Jorge's father had returned to see her—a man by the name of Inigo Florentino?"

"She did not."

"She claims she told de Borja."

"She may well have done, but not me. Is there any relevance to what happened to Jorge? Do I need to have this man hunted down?"

"Inigo Florentino is Jorge's father. He started looking for him two years ago, an act I believe has triggered everything that has happened since. That has ended in the false accusation against Jorge. But even more important now is that Inigo hates de Borja, and is hunting him down. He intends to kill him and I don't know whose side Fernando is on."

"Fernando is a friend to Rodrigo. Everyone is a friend to Rodrigo. He has known Fernando longer than he has known me. I do not know this other man, but trust me, Rodrigo is safe." Isabel sat back into her chair. "Why would Jorge's father want to kill Rodrigo?"

Thomas laid out what he had pieced together. Inigo's love of Castellana, his exile from Valencia and deep hatred of de Borja for stealing Castellana from him. And then his discovery he had a son he never knew about. A son that de Borja had forced Castellana to give away. He watched Isabel listen to his words, but was unable to tell whether she believed him or not.

When he had finished, she stared at the empty fireplace

for so long he thought she was trying to conjure up a way to dismiss him. Then her eyes rose to meet his.

"I know Jorge is not guilty of what he is accused. How could he be? If you had told me Rodrigo was his father, I would have more easily believed it, but this other man? Are you sure of what you claim? And what has Fernando to do with any of this?"

"Nothing perhaps … or everything. I came here tonight to confront him only to discover he has ridden out with de Borja. I am afraid of what he intends."

"Fernando would never harm Rodrigo, I have already told you that. As for this other man, Fernando will kill him in an instant."

"There are others with him, men of Roma who want to see one of their own family as Pope rather than de Borja."

"You know that matter is not settled, nor is it certain he will even be considered. There is already a Pope who I pray will reign for many years yet. And when he does die, there will be a vote."

"I understand all of that. But if Rodrigo is dead, he can hardly be considered. And if he is disgraced, he will not be appointed."

"There are other candidates."

"None so qualified. None so suited. You told me the same yourself not so long since." Thomas stared down at his hands before looking up to meet Isabel's gaze. "Do you love your husband?"

"That is an impertinent question. If anyone else had asked me it, I would be calling the guards to have them thrown out."

"A simple 'Of course' would have been answer enough. I hadn't expected you to, of course. Royal marriages are rarely matters of love."

"You are not making this any better for yourself." Isabel rose and walked to a bell-rope. She grasped the end, but did not draw on it yet. "I loved Fernando with all my heart, even before we were married. You should have seen him then. He was magnificent. Handsome. Brave. Courtly."

"People change."

"Of course they do. And circumstance forces change on them. Power changes people."

"Not you."

Isabel's laugh carried not a trace of humour. "Oh, you know so little. Of course I am changed. Just as you are changed. Just as Fernando is changed." She released her grip on the bell-rope and returned to her chair. She smoothed her skirts over and over as if trying to brush a stain from them. "I do not need to give you an answer because you already know the truth, but it does not matter. I am Queen of Castile and Aragon, and Fernando is King. Next year Santa Fe will be built. It will look out on Granada and the city you call home will fall to Castile. Go tell your Sultan that, because I don't want you in my presence anymore."

She glared at him. He saw anger in her, but also a deep sorrow, and he caught the sheen of unshed tears in her eyes.

"An accusation against my husband is an accusation against me. It will not be tolerated. Not from anyone. Go, Thomas Berrington. Take your children with you, take Jorge, take everyone who reminds me of you. Take Theresa and Eleanor and your son—yes, I know about your son—and go to set up a harem in your infidel city while you still can, but be gone from my presence. I cannot bear to look on your face anymore."

CHAPTER THIRTY-TWO

Thomas knew he should leave the palace and ride after de Borja immediately, but as he returned to his rooms, he staggered with exhaustion and had to reach out to a wall to stop himself from falling. When he entered the room, Theresa rose from the chair where she had been waiting and came to him.

"Not now," he said.

"It is all right, Thomas. You need to sleep." She took his hand and led him to the bed, removed his outer clothes then lay beside him. Thomas barely noticed as a roiling darkness enveloped him.

"Wake me at dawn," he managed to say, before allowing the darkness to take him.

The dark remained when he was shaken awake to find Theresa pushing at him and Isabel standing at the foot of the bed. He shook his head, sure he must still be dreaming.

"Get dressed," said Isabel. "Fernando has returned, and some of what you told me is true, so get dressed and do what you are best at."

Thomas threw the covers back, not caring Isabel saw him as he reached for his trousers.

"Is he badly injured?"

"I do not mean that. He has confessed everything to me. You were both right and wrong, but Fernando needs to tell you himself. I will wait for you where we spoke before." She gave a nod to Theresa and strode from the room.

"What did you say to her?" asked Theresa. "What have you done now?"

"Not enough."

He finished dressing and followed after Isabel, wishing she had allowed him a little more time to sleep, but his exhaustion had softened, and by the time he reached the wide chamber where Fernando sat in the chair Thomas had recently used himself, his mind was sparking into life.

Fernando remained sitting, staring into the cold fireplace. Isabel came to Thomas and touched his hand, took it briefly in her own, a bold statement in front of her husband.

"I will leave you to talk in private, but if you need me afterward, send a message. There will be a servant in the corridor."

Thomas looked at her face, saw the bruises of exhaustion beneath her eyes, and knew she too had barely slept. He glanced at the window, but it was a dark mirror with no hint of dawn. He lifted her hand and kissed the back of it. Isabel nodded, as if agreeing to something, and then she turned and left the room.

"She likes you better than me." Fernando sat near the cold fireplace in the ornate chair built more to impress than offer comfort. His voice was masked, as if he needed to control himself, and Thomas knew this conversation had not been volunteered by him. Isabel, the commander in their relationship, had ordered it, and he had no choice but to obey.

"Do you hate me so much?" Thomas walked to the fireplace, but didn't sit in the other chair drawn up. Instead he stood with his back to the grate so Fernando had to look up at him.

"With every fibre of my being. Did you not know?"

"I suspected, but hoped it untrue. And Jorge, why did you involve him? Surely you, a king, could have sent an army to kill me and no-one would question your action."

"I could have, yes. But I would prefer to kill you with my own hand." Fernando's lips thinned in what might have been a smile. "I have tried once or twice."

"I am aware you have, but I am the better of us."

Fernando surged to his feet, his body tense. "Are you, damn it? Are you? I think not. We can go outside now and take swords to answer the question once and for all."

"You would like that, wouldn't you? And when I kill you, I will be torn to pieces by your guards. It would be some kind of justice, I suppose, but we would both be dead. So no, I think not. Tell me why you plotted against Jorge. Was it no more than to punish me? To put me in a bad light with Isabel?"

Fernando shook his head, a deflated figure. "It was not my idea. Not my idea at all. It was your woman who came to me with the proposal." He straightened, as if recovering some of his normal arrogance. "Or rather, she came on top of me." He smiled. "Several times as I recall, then she whispered a plot into my ear."

"Make sense, man." Though Thomas feared Fernando was about to. "I have no woman anymore."

"That is not what she says. She says she was yours, and still will be if you will have her. Of course, it didn't stop her sharing her body with me. A fine body it is, too. You are a fortunate man to have known her when she was young, lithe, and even more willing. Though experience counts for much, does it not?"

"Eleanor?"

Fernando grinned. "Of course Eleanor."

"All of this is her idea?" Thomas shook his head, confused.

"Of course not. Eleanor is a friend to Castellana, another fine woman who has pleasured me often, but so far not the two of them together. That delight is only a matter of time, I expect. They are both women with strong appetites."

"Stop boasting about your cock and tell me what you know!" Thomas snapped, angry at the man. Angry at his infidelities against Isabel.

"I should have you thrown out, but that would only make Isabel angrier with me. It is only because of her I agreed to see you. It is only because of her I will answer you."

Thomas waited, watching emotions play across Fernando's face. For a moment, he felt like Jorge must, seeing the man's thoughts reflected in every gesture, and even before Fernando began to talk, Thomas knew at least some of what he was about to say was a lie.

"Your woman was sent by Castellana. She asked to see me a month since, to ask my help. Inigo Florentino had been to see her, she said, making threats."

"Against Jorge? Why?"

"Not Jorge. Not everything is about you, Thomas. The threats he made were against Rodrigo de Borja, the man she was once married to."

"Is still married to, it seems," Thomas said.

Fernando waved a hand in dismissal. "Such matters are easily fixed. You have spoken with Castellana, have you not? What did she tell you of Inigo?"

"What she told me is my own business. I am still waiting to hear what yours is." Thomas had no wish to show his hand to Fernando, who he was sure would change his story to match the facts already told to him.

"Florentino hates Rodrigo," said Fernando. "Hates him as much as anyone can, Castellana says." A glance of the eyes away then back, as if Fernando was aware he might have indicated deception. "I have no great love of the man, unlike my wife, but he is a good Spaniard and a good Christian and I would not have harm come to him. Castile will be the stronger when he sits on the Papal throne. Which is why I rode south with the man, why I left a few of my own guard with him. He has his own men, of course, but not enough."

"Where would Inigo find enough men to attack him?" Thomas asked.

"Men are easily bought, you should know that. How much do you pay that African?"

"Wouldn't you like to know, but there is no point offering Usaden more. He is not interested in money, only in friendship. What has this tale to do with Jorge's arrest?"

"He also told Castellana he was searching for his son."

Thomas waited, aware not enough had been revealed.

Fernando paced away to the far side of the room and stood with his hands crossed behind him. Thomas continued to wait, watching the tension in the man's shoulders.

"He wants Jorge dead," said Fernando eventually.

"Why?"

With his back still to Thomas, Fernando raised one

shoulder in a shrug. "I received all of this information at second hand, so I can only relate what Castellana passed on to me. She said Florentino is mad. His mind holds only hatred for everyone. De Borja, me, Castellana, Jorge, even you."

"Me? He doesn't even know who I am."

Fernando turned around, a smile on his face. "Oh, but he does. Isabel talks of you all the time." He scowled. "She talks of you far too much, and I have told her such, for all the good it does. She will have told Castellana of you, and no doubt Jorge too, though she would have had no reason to suspect he is her son. I have no idea how Florentino made the connection, either, but it seems he did."

"He has been searching for him for years," Thomas said. "Lawrence has found paperwork relating to the search. Inigo paid Cortez to find out what he could. Whether he knew Jorge had been abandoned in Qurtuba or not or he sent searchers out throughout the land, I don't know, but search for him here he did. Now you say it is because he hates his son?"

"That is what Castellana told me."

"If it is Inigo who wants to harm Jorge, why was it you who signed the warrant for his arrest?"

"Again, Castellana asked me."

"You could have refused. It was a false charge, you must know that."

"The Hermandos told me otherwise. Besides, why would I refuse? I bear Jorge no particular ill will, unlike you, but his arrest hurts you, does it not?"

Thomas stayed silent, and Fernando laughed.

"I know it does. Of course it does. But do not concern yourself, I know what ire I will bring down on my head if I bring harm to either of you. Once this matter between

Florentino and de Borja is settled, an arrangement can be made. You will agree to go away and never return, and Jorge will be freed, but only after you have proven you can stay away from my wife. Half a year perhaps, possibly a year."

"I will consider your words, but I want to ask if your promise is true. You will release Jorge unharmed?"

Fernando offered a brief nod. "Eventually. If you give me your promise."

"And if I do not?"

"Then he dies. Whether at the end of a rope or in that prison makes no difference. A month or two at most, that is all he will have left if you refuse me. What say you, Thomas Berrington? Yes or no?"

"I say nothing, not until Jorge is released. I do nothing until Jorge is released."

"Not good enough." Fernando looked to one side, his head nodding as he worked through some internal thought. "There is another possibility."

Thomas waited, knowing the man would tell him soon, knowing Fernando did not like being in his company and would want this meeting ended.

"Inigo Florentino," said Fernando.

"What about him?"

"I would prefer he did not kill Rodrigo de Borja. For the sake of my wife."

"Then send soldiers. Stop him."

"I could … but where is the advantage in it for me?" Fernando met Thomas's eyes and smiled.

"Do you think I care about the death of a man who may become Pope? I am a heathen, remember. I might even welcome it. What benefit does it bring you to have de Borja dead?"

"A Spanish Pope, is that what you are thinking? It is what

Isabel wants, I know, and perhaps that in itself is reason enough. It is not only Inigo who wants him dead." Fernando smiled, his eyes bright with some measure of victory. "Your lover..." He rolled the word softly across his tongue, "...she too wants him gone."

"Eleanor? Why?"

"A century ago there were Popes in Avignon. France would like to see them returned. So would she. As would I. Avignon is far closer to Aragon than Roma. It is a place I could exert influence on. And if that idiot Columb does manage to survive and discovers new lands, then the Holy Church will be the one to exert its influence, not kings and queens."

"You're an idiot," Thomas said.

"Says the man who follows my wife around like a faithful hound. Who are you to call me idiot?" Fernando stepped closer and punched a finger against Thomas's chest. "None of this was my idea, but I have grown to appreciate the cunning of it. I will support neither side, for there is no advantage for me to do so, nor any disadvantage whoever wins."

"What is to stop me going to Isabel and telling her all of this?"

Another jab to the chest. "Because of Jorge. I can have him thrown into prison again simply enough, or worse. His entire family can be arrested."

"Only if you order it. And if you make that threat, what is to stop me killing you, here and now?"

"Because you will not. We both know why."

"There is no-one in this world more important to me than Jorge."

Fernando sneered. "I always suspected you lay together. Do you do so every night? Does that whore of his join you?

And when your wife was alive, did you—"

Thomas hit him. He wasn't sure whether Fernando had intended to goad him into it or not. He barely considered his action, nor regretted it.

Fernando staggered back, but managed to stay on his feet. He clutched his nose, which streamed blood. As he opened his mouth to shout, Thomas raised his fist again.

"Don't call the guards."

"You are a dead man, Thomas Berrington. You are all dead men now."

"Where was de Borja when you left him?"

"How far do you think you will get before I send my soldiers after you? Give yourself up and save me the effort."

"Where did you leave him!"

Thomas waited until he saw acceptance come to Fernando. Perhaps he was seeing the implications for himself, the judgement of a wife who may or may not know the extent of his treachery.

"He was at Posadas, where he intended to stay the night. It is no distance, but he has many followed with him and is in no rush to return home."

"How many men did you leave with him?"

"A dozen. What are you going to do?"

"I am going to do what you won't. Stop Inigo killing de Borja. And then I will return to Qurtuba so you can pardon Jorge. I know you can do it. You will do it. And then I will tell you my decision, but not until I am sure Jorge is a free man."

Thomas saw Fernando wanted to offer some objection, but he didn't give him the time. He turned and left the room. He was half way back to his own rooms when Isabel stepped from a doorway.

"What are you going to do, Thomas?"

"How much did he tell you?" Thomas was sure she must know of Fernando's lovers. Did she also know of his treachery?

"Some. Not all, I am sure, but enough. Are you going to tell me the rest?"

"Even if you don't want to hear it?"

"I must hear it. Will you tell me, Thomas?"

"Not tonight." He studied Isabel a moment. "Is Jorge to be arrested at dawn?"

"If he remains in the city. Pressure is being brought, not just from Fernando."

"And if he isn't in the city?"

"Ride fast and far then, but return to me when it is done. You know what I will ask, and this time I will demand a different answer. I spoke rashly before. I know what my husband is and should not have allowed your words to anger me. It is time you came to me, Thomas. Your world is about to end, and there is a place for you beside me at court." She turned and walked away. Thomas watched her until she was gone from sight, then left the palace, crossing the river toward Daniel's house.

CHAPTER THIRTY-THREE

They rode out from the city at dawn—four men and a dog. By the time the sun rose, the city was no more than a dark stain behind, and the good road ahead allowed for fast travel. Kin roamed far and wide, often disappearing but always returning. Thomas had no idea if the dog was looking for something or merely revelling in his freedom to run. He suspected the latter, and couldn't blame him. He felt the same himself. All the plotting, the deceit, the greed and hatred had tainted his soul.

He wondered, when this day's work was done, whether he might go back for Belia and the children, and then keep on riding. Where, he had no idea, only that there was nothing for him in Qurtuba anymore. Fernando had made that more than clear. Nothing in Gharnatah either. There had to be somewhere, though he wondered if that was true. Could any place be better if the problem was within him, not without? Perhaps he should ask Columb to take him on his voyage west. Death or discovery. The exploration of new lands.

He jerked in the saddle as he felt himself slipping sideways and knew he had almost drifted into sleep.

"How many men will this Inigo have with him?" Lawrence brought his horse close to Thomas. Usaden rode to one side on higher ground. Jorge was ahead, claiming to be scouting.

"The four from Roma that I know of, but no doubt he will have recruited more. Fernando told me he claimed to have an army."

"De Borja will have many around him. Four, even forty men, will not be enough."

"Most of those with de Borja are priests, not soldiers."

"Mandana's monks made good soldiers," Lawrence reminded him.

"These are not Mandana's monks."

"Inigo has a head start on us."

"Most likely, which is why we won't slow until we find either him or de Borja."

"And if Inigo has forty men or more? Are we enough to protect de Borja?"

"We will have to be."

Lawrence smiled. "I like a man with confidence. You do know Laurita will never forgive me if I get killed, don't you? I should have told her I was coming with you, but then…" He shrugged. "She would have detained me, and I knew you wanted to leave as soon as possible. What did Fernando say to you? I thought he might have sent men with us, or even come himself like he did when we chased after Mandana."

Thomas considered how much to tell Lawrence before deciding on the truth. He liked the man, and he had been instrumental in seeking out information about Cortez's activities.

"I think he would prefer I get myself killed on some pointless escapade."

"Isabel would kill him if she thought he had anything to do with it. But try not to get yourself killed, I have grown to like you." Lawrence gave a laugh. "Even Laurita says she likes you, and she likes nobody—not even me, sometimes."

Thomas gave a shake of his head. "Dying is something to worry about another day, once this one is done. More than likely we may all be dead and it won't matter one way or the other."

"I would prefer not to be dead."

"So would I." Thomas lifted in his saddle as he saw a group of men ahead on the roadway, eight of them on horseback, but they were riding toward Qurtuba rather than away. "If that's some of Inigo's recruits, then the deed is done."

"Only eight?" said Lawrence.

Usaden had seen them too and ridden down to fall in at Thomas's flank. Jorge also slowed so all four came together. Even Kin stopped his roaming and waited for them to catch up.

"We should attack them before they attack us," said Usaden.

"And if they are nothing more than travellers?" Thomas could make out their clothing now. There was no sign of anything that marked them as fighting men other than the way they held themselves and the way they rode.

"What if they mean us dead? Though there are only eight, so you may be right and we can wait and see."

They waited.

The lead man saw them and spoke to his companions, but nobody drew weapons as they came on. The lead rider raised a hand in greeting and Thomas did the same.

"How far to Córdoba?" the man asked. He was Spanish, with the look of a mercenary about him. Easy in the saddle, with a sharp gaze.

"You'll be there before noon, sooner if you ride fast."

"We are in no hurry. Where are you and your companions headed?"

"We are looking for Rodrigo de Borja. Do you know the man?" And when the man shrugged, Thomas asked, "Have you seen a large party headed to Sevilla?"

"Possibly. We have seen many people, but I don't know their names. How would I recognise him?"

"He'll have a lot of priests with him, and likely a gilded carriage, and they will be travelling slowly."

"In that case we passed them this morning as we set out from Peñaflor. I believe the party spent the night there. We had to sleep on hard ground because all the inns were full."

"It is good for the soul," said Lawrence, and the man glanced at him for a moment before returning his steady gaze to Thomas.

"Is there a good whorehouse in Córdoba?"

"I am the wrong man to ask. Try him." Thomas nodded toward Lawrence and rode on.

Thomas knew of Peñaflor from previous journeys he had made between Córdoba and Sevilla. It sat on the northern bank of the Guadalquivir and straddled the main roadway west. If de Borja's party was moving slowly, they would catch them on the far side before sunset. As the thought came to him, he realised he had forgotten another question, perhaps more important than his first, and turned back.

"Keep riding," he said to Jorge, "I won't be long." He encouraged his horse into a gallop and soon caught up with the band of men.

"Are you coming with us to the whorehouse?" the leader asked, laughing. "I like your hound."

"He's not for sale. Have you seen any other men on this road?" Thomas fell in beside the leader, impatience burning inside, knowing he had to hold it in check. "Say a group of between half a dozen to a score, possibly more?"

"We have seen men the whole time we have been travelling. Some groups that size, certainly, at the lower end anyway. I assume you mean men travelling west?"

"I do."

"We passed two groups, one of four, the other six. I thought there might have been trouble with the smaller one, but they passed at a distance from us. I would guess they are looking for somebody, but if so it wasn't us."

"Where was this?"

"Early morning today, so a few hours' ride. They will be further on by now, I expect."

"Were they moving fast?"

"Not fast, no. Like I say, they were looking for somebody. You cannot do that when you ride hard."

"My thanks." Thomas turned his horse and encouraged it into a gallop. His companions had moved out of sight, but as he crested a low rise, he saw them ahead.

"They passed a band of men a few hours ahead," he said as he fell in beside them.

"Florentino?" asked Lawrence.

"He wouldn't know that, but it could be."

"You think it is, don't you?"

"When we catch up with them, we can be sure. Eight, possibly a dozen. Is that enough to attack de Borja?"

"You said yourself priests don't fight, so perhaps. If it was me, I'd prefer double that number at least."

By the time they reached Peñaflor, the sun was painting

the rooftops with fire, but they had seen no other groups that might be who they were looking for. Thomas began to hope they were in time to protect de Borja. He was about to push on through the single main street when Usaden pointed to a large group gathered below on the banks of the river. A carriage was pulled up, not gilded but finely polished, with two sturdy mules nearby, unshackled to let them graze.

"What are they doing?" Thomas narrowed his eyes, but couldn't make out what was going on. Some people stood in the water, others were arrayed along the sandy bank looking at proceedings.

"There's one way to find out." Lawrence guided his horse down an alley between two low houses. As they came closer, he laughed and slapped Thomas's arm. "Damn if he's not baptising them!"

Thomas glanced at Jorge, who had spoken barely a word the entire journey, an unusual enough occurrence to cause him concern.

"You should have stayed behind," he said. "The three of us can manage whatever comes."

"He is my father," said Jorge. "My father intends to kill de Borja—the man who freed me." Jorge offered Thomas a stare so filled with anguish it was hard to meet. "What if I am like him?"

Thomas shook his head. "You are nothing like him. You know you are not."

Ahead of them, Lawrence reached the ornate carriage and dismounted. He tied his reins to a wheel and walked toward the small group standing in the shallows of the Guadalquivir. In places he had to push his way through the crowd, which parted reluctantly. Some wore their wet clothes proudly, others were onlookers. Still others waited their turn to be drowned. There was close to a hundred people milling about, which reassured Thomas. Attacking such a large group would be difficult. Not that these people would fight, but they were witnesses. Unless Inigo killed them all, and that would prove almost impossible. Perhaps the man didn't care, his madness against de Borja all consuming.

Thomas tied his horse next to Lawrence's and forced his way through the crowd. Women resisted and men pushed back. Thomas glared until they made space, then went on until he stood ankle deep in the water. A shingle bank split the river along the middle, forming a deeper pool close to the near shore. It was here that de Borja stood up to his waist, hair loose, hands on the head of a woman as he held her beneath the water. Thomas watched, surprised how long she was beneath the surface. When de Borja finally pulled her clear, her face was ecstatic with awe. She had been transformed by the touch of water and man both. De Borja kissed her on both cheeks, then one of his acolytes ushered her away while a young boy was brought forward, not tall enough to wade so he had to be carried.

"We can't interrupt this," said Lawrence, who stood the same as Thomas with his boots in the water. "Never mind Inigo, this crowd will kill us if we try."

Thomas glanced up at a sky which showed not a single cloud. "It's going to be dark soon and he'll have to stop. We can wait. If an attack comes, we'll be here to protect him." He studied those in de Borja's party, seeing that a little less than half were priests or monks, the others servants or hangers-on. Forty people, more or less. None of them would be much use if it came to a fight. The only person there who might be capable and strong enough to wield a sword was de Borja himself.

The man finished with the young boy and looked up. He saw Thomas and waved.

"Come, Thomas Berrington, let the glory of God enter you!"

Thomas remained where he was, and Lawrence laughed. "You know you'll have to go so you might as well get it done with. It won't really change you, you know."

"Better you go. At least you believe."

"Which is why I don't need to. You and Jorge are the heathens. Go on. Then, when we kill men tonight, you will be forgiven by God."

"I would rather not have to kill anyone."

"You know we will have to."

"Thomas!" de Borja called again. "And is that Jorge I see? Now fully recovered, thanks be to God. Let them through."

It was impossible to refuse, but it seemed Jorge didn't want to. He pushed past Thomas and waded into the river, allowed de Borja to grip his shoulders. A few words were exchanged before Jorge was plunged beneath the surface. De Borja raised his eyes to heaven, his lips moving as he spoke a blessing. As Thomas came closer, he could make it out. Latin. He was asking forgiveness for Jorge's sins, which meant they could be there for a while. Though not as long as it might be when Thomas's turn came.

Jorge emerged from the river, shaking his head and sucking in air. De Borja held his face and kissed both cheeks before pushing him away. Then it was time for Thomas to make a decision. He glanced at Lawrence, who grinned. At Usaden, who remained expressionless. And then de Borja had him. Before he was fully ready, the water closed over his head and the sound of the world grew muffled. Thomas opened his eyes, the water muddy from all the feet and the plunging. He glimpsed de Borja's legs before closing his eyes again. Briefly he considered if he felt any different, and decided he didn't. God, if such existed, had not entered him.

De Borja's words were masked by the water and Thomas began to feel a rising panic as the strong hands continued to hold him below the surface. Had Jorge been submerged as long as this? Had time stretched? Had he been only moments beneath the water? It felt like an hour. He began to struggle, felt de Borja's fingers dig deeper into his flesh. Strong hands, as suited a man of power. Perhaps the most powerful man Thomas had ever met. More so than kings and queens. More so than any other man who walked the earth. Not yet, but soon.

And then the pressure slackened and for a moment Thomas remained where he was, at peace, at one with the sound of the river and the velvet touch of water against his skin. It was de Borja who lifted him up, de Borja who held him as he had Jorge, and kissed his cheeks.

"May God go with you, Thomas Berrington." He laughed, as if he knew the words had no meaning for Thomas, but he didn't mind. "What brings you here, my friend? Are you travelling to Sevilla? I would ask you to accompany us, but we will take days to reach the city. As you have witnessed, many people seek salvation in one form or another."

How much to say? Thomas wondered. He decided he had grown to like de Borja too much to lie.

"Do you know that Inigo Florentino is nearby?"

The good-humour left de Borja's face. "That man. I believed him dead, but now I hear otherwise."

Thomas took a breath. "He is on his way to kill you. I expected him to be here already."

"How many are with him?" De Borja showed immediate

acceptance. He spread his hands out. "I have a horde with me, not to mention this entire town."

"Which is why they are not already here, no doubt, but tomorrow you move on. Tomorrow there will be another opportunity." Thomas studied de Borja for a moment. Around them the crowd was thinning, as if they knew the evening's entertainment was over. "You are not surprised, are you?"

"He has been trying to kill me ever since we were boys."

"Is this about Castellana?" Thomas felt a sense of despair at the frailty of men.

"If it was, it would be me wanting to kill him, but I put all such notions behind me long ago. He wants to kill me because he is a man of extremes. When we were all young together, his love was extreme." Distaste showed on de Borja's handsome face. "Then he lost his senses. He believes I took Castellana from him, even though she was never his. He is not a rational man. He considers the entire world against him. Nothing happens he does not turn into an argument, often over nothing at all."

"Has he always been the same?"

"Always." De Borja put his hand on Thomas's wet shoulder. "Come, walk with me. I have rooms in the monastery tonight and want to change into dry clothes before I catch a chill. Bring your friends, too. Even the Moor. If he is with you, I trust him."

"And my dog?"

De Borja laughed. "Yes, and your dog. I like dogs. They are far easier to understand than men and women."

As they made their way toward the building, Usaden approached. "I spent some time looking around while you were swimming. There is a party of men in the hills behind the town. Near forty of them, I judge."

"Inigo's men?" It was de Borja who asked the question.

"I intend to find out," Thomas said. "How safe are you here?"

"The monastery has thick walls and stout doors, and Fernando sent guards to accompany us. Come find me when you return and I will tell you all about Inigo."

CHAPTER THIRTY-FOUR

"The men were here, I saw them." Usaden held the reins of his horse while he stood beside it. Kin had roamed free, but now lay on the hard ground at Thomas's feet. "Not an hour since. They were settled for the night, I am sure of it."

"Did they see you?" Thomas asked, ashamed when Usaden gave him a dismissive glance. "Of course they didn't see you." He stared into the shallow bowl of ground. There was no water, no trees, no shelter of any kind. It wouldn't have been his choice to spend the night here. The land was losing colour as night approached, and some distance behind and below, lamplight showed from the town. A string of lights along the riverbank reflected patterns across the water that danced to the music of the current.

Thomas made his way into the depression, knowing he would have to check, knowing Usaden wouldn't be wrong, but still having to go himself. If Inigo Florentino's men had been here, they were more numerous than he expected, and that worried him. Had they known someone would be watching, or was their moving elsewhere simply the action of careful men?

There was no sign a fire had been built, but in the last of the light Thomas made out depressions in the hard ground. Horses had been here, together with their riders.

"Kin, seek." He watched as the dog scoured the area before catching a scent. He looked back at Thomas, who nodded. "Go find." He broke into a run after the dog as it crested the edge of the bowl. When Thomas reached the top, he saw Kin running away from Peñaflor, not toward it, and he stopped.

"Kin, here!"

"That is the way they came from," said Usaden, coming to stand beside Thomas.

"Then it's the wrong way. Inigo's men came from Qurtuba."

"Other men then. He has brought other men from the west."

"How many does he need?"

"When you intend to kill someone, you can never have too many men," said Usaden.

Jorge joined them. He had walked up the slope rather than run. "What if this is all a ruse to draw us away from de Borja so he's unprotected?"

"He's not unprotected. He has men of his own and eight left by Fernando, or so he claims."

Jorge made a noise of amusement. "And you trust Fernando?"

Thomas didn't want to consider the answer. Not the true answer. Fear and uncertainty itched at his skin, and he wondered if he had made the wrong decision coming out here in search of Inigo. Except he had believed Córdoba was where he would prove Jorge's innocence. Now he knew there could be no proving it. Jorge was accused through an act of spite, of hatred. Only victory would clear his name.

"They have gone to Peñaflor. They are going to attack de Borja tonight." He glanced at Usaden. "How many did you say? Two score?"

"Thirty and seven."

Thomas knew Usaden would have counted accurately. "Plus those we heard of travelling from Qurtuba. De Borja has sixty, but most are priests and hangers-on." He returned to his horse and urged it into a canter as the others fell in on either side. Usaden and Kin to his left, Lawrence and Jorge on his right. Four men and a dog against ... how many? Was Jorge right not to trust Fernando? If he was, they were riding into a fight against almost sixty trained men, all of them seasoned, all of them ready to kill.

As they came out of the bowl for a second time and Peñaflor appeared below, Thomas slowed.

"Usaden, I want you to ride to the far side of town. Keep a look out for Inigo's men. I need to know if they are down there or not. If you see them, don't approach, but come back and let me know. Or light a fire, I'll watch for your signal."

Usaden gave no acknowledgement, simply encouraging his horse into a gallop. Kin hesitated, glanced up at Thomas, then ran after him. He knew where the entertainment lay.

"And what do we do?" asked Lawrence.

"We approach from this side. I can't see any men yet, certainly not two score, but the light is almost gone. Still, we should see some sign if there are that many. If we get close without being challenged, we go to de Borja and protect him."

"Fernando's men are protecting him for now. We should find Inigo and his men and attack them."

"All four of us?" Thomas said.

"You brought the four of us to this fight," said Lawrence. "What did you expect, it would be easy?"

"I can't fight my father." Jorge sat astride his horse a little ahead of them and spoke without turning. "And I certainly can't kill him."

"I don't want him dead, I want him captured." Thomas urged his horse closer to Jorge. "I want him returned to Qurtuba for punishment, so that someone else can make the decision. I am tired of doing the work of others."

Jorge laughed. "Yet here you are, and here am I. The two of us, as it should be." He shook his head. "You are never going to change, are you, Thomas?"

"Tomorrow, perhaps. Tonight we have a man to save, and not just any man."

Jorge laughed again. "I like that you always end up friends with important people. It makes for an interesting life. Just promise me if it comes to any killing, you will do it."

"I promise. But it won't, not unless it's kill or be killed. I promise that as well."

It was a promise he wasn't sure he could keep. If they were attacked, or de Borja threatened, he knew what he would do. He also knew Jorge would fight when the time came. He was no longer the effete palace eunuch he had been, though Thomas couldn't say exactly when the change had come about. He feared it was Jorge's association with him that had caused it.

As they approached the sorry excuse for town walls, with not even a gate capable of being barred because they were deep in Castilian territory, there was no sign of Inigo's band. No indication from Usaden that they were on the far side either. Thomas wondered if he was wrong, if de Borja wasn't Inigo's target and he had moved on, following the river west to Sevilla. Except he knew he was here, had seen the signs. He also knew Inigo wanted de Borja dead. Did he know a better spot from which to mount an ambush? If no attack came tonight, it might mean they would have to accompany de Borja to Sevilla. Once he took ship to Roma, he would be safe. Inigo could have attacked him there, but had chosen not to, pursuing him to Castile instead. Sitting where they were would do nothing to prevent what was coming.

Thomas slapped his horse into a faster pace, hoping Jorge and Lawrence would follow. They were but three men against ten times that number, except Thomas had fought such odds before and triumphed.

When they reached the town, he saw a flare of light on the far hillside. Usaden had found Inigo's men.

"To the monastery!"

Even as he urged his horse to more speed, Thomas saw they were too late. Armed men streamed from the town, others came along the river bank. He reined his horse to a halt and dismounted, recognising the insanity of attacking such numbers. Jorge and Lawrence followed his example. Both looked at him in the flickering torchlight, waiting for orders.

Thomas had none.

"We cannot abandon him, not now," said Lawrence.

"And we cannot save him. Not against these odds."

Jorge pushed him hard, not a punch but enough to send him back two paces.

"I won't allow you to abandon him."

"Where has this come from? You don't even like the man."

"I changed my mind after he prayed for me. He's not like other priests."

"Of course he isn't. This is the man who will be the next Pope, so of course he's not like other priests. But we can't fight all these men." Inigo's force had turned now, making its way toward the monastery entrance where a pitifully small number of men stood in a line. Not even a dozen, and soon they would be fewer.

Jorge shook his head and re-mounted his horse. After a moment, Lawrence did the same. Thomas expected them to turn and ride east toward Córdoba, but instead they started toward the band of men who were slaughtering the meagre group of defenders.

"Fuck it, I've lived long enough." Thomas swung into the saddle and urged his own horse forward, then pulled hard at the reins as a figure came toward him fast, but it was only Usaden with Kin loping ahead.

"Are we going to fight them?" asked Usaden, a shadow of excitement in his voice.

"Looks that way."

Usaden grinned. "Good. I like impossible odds."

As they rode hard toward the milling crowd that was starting to pass inside the stone gates, the meagre defenders having taken the sensible course of action and fled, Thomas felt the familiar cold fill him, and with its coming all fear, all doubt, faded. He caught up with Jorge, who had a sword in his hand.

"Stay back if you can. Belia will kill me if you are injured again."

"No she won't, she likes you. If I die, she will marry you if you ask."

"Try not to die, then. She scares me."

The small army had finally noticed the four men bearing down on them and a group turned to set up a barrier. They were well-trained, holding pikes out to gut the horses and kill their riders, but Thomas had faced similar defences before and knew how to deal with them. He knew Usaden would too, and most likely Lawrence. Only Jorge concerned him, but he couldn't fight and worry at the same time, so he pressed the thought aside as he slid down beside his horse. His boots dragged along the ground for a moment, then he released the saddle and rolled until he was amongst the feet of the soldiers.

He heard a crash, the scream of a beast, and then his blade was doing its work, slashing at legs and groins and bellies as he rolled again and again. Nothing else mattered. Lawrence and Usaden and Jorge were fighting somewhere close by. They might be dying, but all Thomas saw was one enemy to disable or kill, and then another, and another. He had no sense of how many he struck, only that it was easy. There were so many, and everywhere he thrust his blade found a target and there was one man less to worry about. He twisted and leapt and lunged, avoiding knives and swords and the heavy, wicked heads of pikes, which were the worst. He tried not to kill, but sometimes there was no alternative. And then, all at once, he found himself in an open space with Usaden at his side. Kin was there, sides heaving, mouth hanging open.

"Do you think they want more?" asked Usaden, bouncing on his toes.

"How many are left?"

"Well over half, though some went inside the building."

"That's where we need to be then. De Borja's inside somewhere."

A man ran at them, mouth wide as he screamed. Usaden ran him through without appearing to move.

"Why do you want to save a Christian? He means nothing to you."

"I have grown fond of him."

Usaden almost smiled. It must have been the fighting, it

always cheered him. "I suppose I have grown fond of you, too, but do not count on me dying to save you."

"I will try to remember it."

Three men came the next time, all of them at Thomas. Perhaps they considered him an easier target. In which case they had chosen wrong. He sidestepped the first and wounded him in the thigh. The second fell to a dagger thrust in his sword arm, the sword dropping to the ground as he withdrew. The third man screamed as Kin shook his head from side to side, his muzzle buried between his legs.

"That has got to hurt," said Usaden. "I am glad your dog is on our side."

"Your side," Thomas said.

"No—he only follows me because he knows that is where the trouble is, but he is your dog. He, too, would die for you. Are we going to try to save this infidel, then? Or can I kill a few more first?"

"We can do both, I expect. There seem to be enough for that." Thomas glanced around until he saw Lawrence. He was on the edge of the band of men, standing beside Jorge. Both held swords red with blood, but for now they were recovering while attention was on Thomas and Usaden.

Thomas raised an arm and waved toward the side of the monastery, indicating he wanted them to go to the far side and find an entrance. Lawrence nodded and slapped Jorge on the shoulder. When they were gone, Thomas did the same to Usaden. The two of them attacked so fast, so fiercely, that men fell over themselves in their haste to avoid both their blades and their dog.

CHAPTER THIRTY-FIVE

Thomas expected to be challenged, but already the attacking forces were breaking apart. The majority remained outside and appeared to have forgotten their purpose, unless there was a plan and they waited deliberately. If so there was little sign of what the plan might be. A smaller number had entered the monastery. Thomas could hear them ahead, the sound of blades and the screams of dying men. He had no idea where de Borja was, or if he even remained alive.

Usaden walked softly on one side, Kin on the other. What the monks would make of a blood-smeared dog in their midst, Thomas neither knew nor cared. They found a man sitting against a wall in a pool of his own blood. He was alive, but wouldn't be for much longer. He watched their approach with resignation on his face.

Thomas dropped to one knee. "Where is de Borja?"

"I will never reveal my master's location."

"I come to save him, not kill him."

The man tried to smile. "You would claim that, of course. As did the man who killed me."

"Are you in pain?"

"Blessedly not. God is kind to me even at the end, and I will see him soon in heaven. You, on the other hand, will burn in the flames of hell."

Thomas rose and walked on.

"You people have a strange religion," said Usaden. "One that welcomes death as a friend. How do we find this man you seek? The monks will not tell you."

"We'll search every room if we have to." Thomas knew it would take too long, but had no other plan. He supposed he could find a living monk and torture him, but doubted that would yield an answer either. Usaden was right—it was a strange religion that welcomed martyrdom before defiance.

A sudden commotion sounded ahead and they broke into a run, Kin loping ahead to disappear, setting up a raucous barking which made Thomas run faster. They came into an interior courtyard, and as he looked around, he clearly saw the monastery had been built over an older Moorish house. Islamic script still ran around the walls. A group of a dozen men faced away from them, while beyond two figures were preparing to fight.

Jorge and Lawrence had found another entrance.

Thomas glanced at Usaden and gave a brief nod as he stepped forward.

Two men would have died without knowing who'd struck them if Kin had not stopped barking, alerting them to their presence. The two still died, but it took longer, by which time Lawrence had started his attack on the other side. It would have been a bloodbath except the remaining men broke and ran to save themselves.

"Were there any more the way you came?" Thomas asked.

"The street was deserted," said Jorge. "How many alongside the river now?"

"Two score, more or less, not that it matters if we can't find de Borja."

"Oh, I know where he is." Jorge turned and started along a wide corridor.

Thomas ran to catch up. "How do you know? I tried asking, but all I managed to do was to frighten an already dying man."

"You forget who I am. It is not the question, Thomas, but the way it is asked. There were monks huddled together in a small prayer room and they recognised me from the river. It's lucky people always seem to remember me, isn't it? De Borja's at the end of this corridor, and then up two flights of stairs. If we're fortunate, we'll get there before anyone else."

Thomas hoped he was right.

As they progressed, he began to believe his hope might not be in vain. There were few of Inigo's soldiers as they progressed, and those they came across slunk away when they saw the expression on their faces. Only four men and one hound, but they were blood-streaked and savage. Jorge was right in his logic, Thomas thought, if you twisted it a little. It is not the way you fight, but how dangerous you look. And in their case, he knew of no better fighters in the world. Not that it would do de Borja much good if they were too late. As they climbed the first flight of stone steps, he wondered if Fernando had thrown his lot in with Inigo or had seen sense.

They came across the first serious resistance at the top of the steps. Eight men leaned against the walls, laughing and teasing a monk they had captured. They had stripped him of his robes and now two held him while a third used a wickedly sharp knife to carve lines in his pale flesh. None of the wounds were fatal, but the pain had to be excruciating, though the monk's face was set as he held any cry inside. As the soldiers caught sight of the four men, they released the monk, who scuttled away as fast as he could go.

Thomas glanced at Usaden. Each of them knew their role, they had fought together often enough over the years. Thomas attacked without a moment's hesitation. These men had placed themselves beyond any mercy. Whatever fate befell them was a result of their own actions. Thomas had no regrets, not even a thought of regret as he maimed the man attempting to take his head from his shoulders.

When it was done, Usaden said, "You are going soft, Thomas. You should have killed them all."

"I have grown tired of killing."

"Then I hope it has grown tired of you too, my friend."

They went on, leaving five bodies lying on the stone floor. Where the others had fled to was no concern, for they would not be coming back. Bought men had more sense than to die needlessly for a cause they didn't believe in.

There was a larger group at the top of the second staircase, harder men, more skilled, but the result was the same. This time Thomas let his sword go where it wanted, shutting down what little remained of his humanity. He would find it again later when their task was complete. If he remained alive.

De Borja sat on an ornate chair in the room they fought their way into, but he wasn't alone. Another dozen men stood between Thomas and the man whose ambition was to be the next Pope. A tall, handsome man stood behind de Borja's chair. Thomas knew he could be no other than Inigo Florentino—the resemblance between him and Jorge was clear to be seen. One hand held a length of rope which was knotted around de Borja's neck. In the other sat a knife, the blade held to de Borja's throat.

"I heard you coming so thought I should wait until you arrived before I killed him." Inigo smiled. "Of course, you will also die soon after, but at least you will have seen his sorry excuse for a life spilled." Inigo's attention shifted to Jorge and for a moment he stilled, then smiled. "One of you will live."

"Kill Thomas and you will have to kill me, if you want to live," said Jorge.

Inigo stared at him, a frown creasing his brow, then he shook his head. "You would kill your own father, my son?" He studied Jorge a moment longer before seeing the truth. "Very well, but this one dies."

"Why?" Thomas said. Inigo's men stood shoulder to shoulder a dozen paces in front of him. De Borja appeared unconcerned at his situation. Perhaps he was waiting for his God to save him. If so, God would have to work a little harder than he was doing at the moment.

"You don't need to know why. You are here to witness the act, nothing more."

"We will be poor witnesses if you kill us." From the edge of his vision, Thomas saw Usaden moving to one side, so slowly none of the soldiers appeared to have noticed. Most kept glancing toward Kin, the sight of the dog's blood-smeared muzzle frightening them more than their opponents' swords.

"Tell your man to stay where he is," said Inigo. "Tell him now or Rodrigo dies."

Thomas lifted a hand and Usaden stopped.

"You are going to kill him anyway. Why shouldn't we attack you now?"

Inigo laughed. "Have you not seen my men? If you think

you can triumph against trained troops, you are an even bigger fool than Eleanor claims."

Thomas dismissed a moment of doubt. He scanned the men separating him from Inigo and realised what they were. Despite not being dressed in royal uniform, these had to be Fernando's guard. Left to protect de Borja, now turned against him.

"Let him kill me," said de Borja. "Do not sacrifice yourself. My poor life is not worth the cost of yours. Go, Thomas Berrington, and take your friends with you." He inclined his head toward Jorge, as far as the rope and knife would allow. "I cannot believe you are this man's son, Jorge Olmos. Are you Jorge Florentino, I wonder, or Jorge Lonzal?" De Borja smiled, a tiny madness showing deep in his eyes. "Tell them, Inigo. Tell them the truth of what happened all those years ago."

"The truth ends with your death." Without hesitation, Inigo sawed the blade across de Borja's throat. Somehow, sensing the movement, de Borja jerked back and the first stroke ran harmlessly across the rope at his neck, the razor-sharp edge parting the strands so that when de Borja jerked a second time, he was free.

Thomas moved at the same time as Usaden, caught a glimpse of Lawrence to one side, Jorge on the other. De Borja threw himself backward, taking both the chair and Inigo with him. They crashed to the hard stone floor and were lost behind the array of men separating them from Thomas. He took the first man, no longer holding back.

All around him metal clashed against metal. Kin barked and snarled and fought with an abandoned wildness that sat at odds with the animal that allowed Amal to pull his ears and twist his fur, but Thomas knew he would die for him, would die for them all. They were all kin. They were pack, and the pack was under threat.

Usaden worked silently, with a savage fury. Lawrence was fast and strong. Even Jorge drove men backward. His life had been changed, turned upside down, and then turned again until it was barely recognisable. Men died, but none were members of the pack. Fernando would be short a few more guards before this night was done.

Inigo reared up from the melee with his hands around de Borja's throat and Thomas fought like a demon to reach them. Some of the soldiers, seeing the fury set against them, started to turn away. No doubt they had been told there would be no resistance. This wildness was something beyond their experience.

As Thomas broke through, de Borja freed himself and turned to run, but his robe caught under his own feet and he fell hard on his side. Inigo threw himself on top of him. There was a flash of silver as he raised the knife in his hand.

Thomas leapt, knowing he was too late.

Then Inigo gave a high scream and fell to one side. Thomas saw a knife lay in de Borja's hand, and he drew back to strike a second time just as Usaden broke through on the other side and raised his own sword.

"Usaden—no! I need him alive."

Usaden stepped back, turned to look for other targets, but there were few of the soldiers left. Bodies littered the ground, both dead and injured, and Thomas vowed that he would heal none of them.

De Borja rose to his feet, the knife held in front of him. Thomas reached out and grasped his wrist, twisted until the blade fell to the floor.

"I thought you were a man of God," he said. "Show him God's mercy."

"God's perhaps, but never mine. This man has worked against me his entire life. I would see him dead with an easy conscience. At my hand or yours, or your companion's there. I could do with a few like him beside me."

Thomas laughed, the ice that held him in its thrall melting away in an instant. He was surprised he didn't stand in a pool of water so rapidly did it leave his body.

"Usaden works for money, and for me, but he has friends who are equally as good..." Thomas hesitated when he saw Usaden's expression. "Almost as good. They will fight for you if you pay them."

"It is a pity then they are heathens, for that will never be allowed."

"Not even when you are Pope?"

"Everyone in Spain believes I will be, but that sentiment is lacking in Roma. There are others more suited to the position. Better men than me, men who have not sinned as I have done."

"All men sin," Thomas said. "It is how they repent of their sins that matters."

De Borja smiled. "Perhaps I should pay for you to be at my side. A man who makes sense. A man who understands sin."

"I cannot be bought."

"No, I don't believe you can." De Borja gathered his robe around him, pulled at a twist of material that had been cut through. "I thought I would die today at Inigo's hand, but you and your friends have saved me. Even Jorge, who believed him his father."

"He is my father." Jorge came to stand in front of de Borja. "My mother told me he was. She is my mother, isn't she? I do hope so, because I like her. Less so my brother, but my mother yes, even if she lied to me."

"Of course she is your mother. And Inigo is most likely your father. But..." De Borja wiped a hand across his face. "We cannot talk of it here." He glanced to one side where Usaden and Lawrence had lifted Inigo to his feet, grasping an arm each. The man looked broken. "What are you going to do with him?"

"Take him back to Qurtuba for trial."

"He will be executed. Isabel will see to it once she learns of his attack on me. You should have let me kill him."

"And taint your inviolable soul?"

"It would have been a kindness, and I would have prayed for forgiveness. But you are right, and I should thank you for that." De Borja began to turn away, stopped and looked at Jorge. "Do you have time for a brief conversation, my son?" And then to Thomas, "Tie Inigo up, do whatever you want with him, but in the morning I intend to continue my journey to Sevilla. I would welcome your company, you and your friends, if you wish to come. I would feel safer with you at my side."

"I have to return this man to Qurtuba."

"Give it some thought." De Borja beckoned to Jorge. "Now you, come and let me tell you the truth." He held up a hand as Thomas also began to move. "Jorge only. He can reveal to you whatever he wishes afterward, but for now what I have to tell him is for his ears only."

CHAPTER THIRTY-SIX

"What did de Borja say to you, or is it a secret?" Thomas rode beside Jorge in the early light of morning. Mist rose from the wide river and drifted across the banks, sometimes gaining enough density to hide Usaden and Lawrence ahead, where they flanked Inigo Florentino. The man appeared broken, his hands bound with a rope which stretched to Usaden's saddle. Another was knotted at his neck, and this led to Lawrence. Thomas had roughly stitched the wound to his shoulder inflicted by de Borja. There was no sign of Inigo's men. No doubt those still alive had made the sensible decision and fled as fast as they could. Thomas had seen no sign of the four men of Roma who had been with Gabriel, but in the confusion they might have been there and he missed them. Those men he would not hesitate to kill, not after what they did to Miguel.

Thomas thought Jorge wasn't going to answer his question and he didn't press him, assuming he would hear eventually. Jorge wasn't a man to keep secrets long.

Kin distributed his company equally between the two groups, running back to skip and trot beside Thomas for a while before returning to Usaden. Lawrence appeared to be talking to Inigo, but received no response, not that it put him off. Earlier he had said how much he was looking forward to returning to Laurita. They had spent little time apart for years. Not since the battle for Ronda, he claimed. Perhaps he was trying to explain the pleasures of a long relationship between a man and woman to Inigo. Thomas wondered if it was a conversation he needed to hear himself. He still didn't know what to do about Theresa. Or Isabel. At least Fernando's confession meant he could forget any reconciliation with Eleanor. There were already too many women in his life, too many conflicting emotions.

"He told me Inigo could be my father, but it wasn't certain." Jorge spoke without looking at Thomas, the words held in long enough to be released in a rush. As if they needed to be expelled before they could do any damage.

"So who else could it be?"

Now Jorge turned his head. "You know who."

"Not according to Castellana."

"I told you she was lying about something. What if she was lying about this? The claims de Borja made to me offer that possibility. She says one thing, he says another—that it is possible I am his son, not Inigo's."

"So you could be the son of the next Pope?" Thomas laughed as Jorge scowled, the expression sitting uneasily on his face. "Did he tell you how?"

"I don't need to explain the how, do I? Even you managed to father children."

"You know I don't mean that. Did de Borja say any more?"

"Much more."

"And you intend to keep this knowledge to yourself?

Besides, one look at Inigo Florentino and it's more than clear whose son you are."

They rode on for another while. The mist thickened and then faded all at once as the heat of the sun burned the last of it away. Out on the river a heron stood perfectly still as it sought prey. High in the sky three dark vultures circled, also looking for their next meal. Kin decided he had been with Thomas long enough and ran ahead, covering the ground with the abandoned joy of being alive. Thomas had washed him clean of blood in the river. Kin had thought it a great game. Now his fur stood out at even crazier angles than usual.

"What is going to happen to him now?" There was no need for Jorge to state who.

"He will be handed over to the authorities. Fernando, I thought. Then I will tell Isabel what Inigo planned and she will make sure he can't ever try again." He thought about Fernando for a moment, then said, "I still cannot decide if he had anything to do with what Inigo was trying to do."

"What makes you say that?" Jorge rode easily in the saddle, his body relaxed as if a weight had been lifted from him.

"Those men trying to stop us reaching Inigo could have been those left by Fernando. Either Inigo turned them, or Fernando was part of the plot as well."

"Or they weren't his men. Why would Fernando want to harm de Borja?"

"For the same reason he wants me gone from the side of his wife. Because Isabel likes him."

"Likes, yes," said Jorge, "but she loves you."

Thomas made a sound through his nose and shook his head. "Don't confuse friendship with love."

"Nor should you. I would recommend you offer not the

slightest hint of your suspicions to Fernando. If you do he'll have you killed. Keep the knowledge to yourself. Pretend you saw nothing."

"Just as you are keeping hold of what de Borja told you?"

"You knew your father, didn't you? There was no doubt you were his son."

"You forget I have no such certainty about Will being my son. Helena continues to withhold that truth from me. Out of spite, I believe, because she can."

Jorge smiled. "Will is yours. How can you doubt it? I see you in everything he does. He has even started to look like you, and he is getting grumpier the older he gets, so who else's son can he be?"

"He looks nothing like me." But inside Thomas was pleased. He hoped Jorge was right. And even if he wasn't, nothing would change. He loved both Will and Amal with every fibre of his being. Just as he knew Kin would sacrifice himself for him, so he would sacrifice himself for them.

"You should bed Helena again and force her to tell you the truth. You will know then, and I guarantee the experience will be exquisite. She is more skilled than that ancient girlfriend of yours."

"Are you so sure?"

"Young love throws a shade over reality. When you were beside her a few days ago, did you see the woman she is now, a woman your own age, or did you see the girl of, what did you say, seventeen years?"

"I saw both," Thomas said. "People age. She has aged and so have I. Do you think she saw the boy of seventeen when she looked at me? Of course not."

"Helena doesn't age."

"She will."

"If you say so. I take it you're not going to take my advice, good as it is?"

Thomas shook his head.

"I didn't think you would, but a man has to try. How much further to Qurtuba?"

"The same distance it was coming the other way, so you should know the answer."

"In that case I have more than enough time to tell you the sad tale as de Borja related it to me." Jorge laughed softly. "It is a tale of friendship turned to enmity, but mostly of love turned to hate." He glanced toward Thomas. "At first it was only love."

"Who did Castellana love?"

"Both of them, of course."

"Of course?"

"Yes. But even more than that..." Jorge rode on in silence for a time, staring into a distance it was clear he didn't see. "You know I have lain with men, don't you?"

The change of topic surprised Thomas. "So you claim."

Jorge smiled. "I would lie with you if you asked, but I know you never will. It never stops me loving you, though. Our love is deeper than sex."

"If you say so." Thomas was uncomfortable with the direction the conversation had taken, but knew better than to attempt to change it. Jorge would get to his point eventually.

"I have lain with men, but lain with more women, and sometimes I have lain with both together." Jorge glanced at Thomas. "Surely even you can make the connection now, can't you?"

"The three of them?"

Jorge nodded.

"Together?"

Another nod.

"How old was Castellana?"

"Young. Inigo and de Borja a little older, but still young. It is less unusual than you might think."

"But against the laws of God," Thomas said, and Jorge laughed.

"It is also against the laws of Islam, but you know it happens."

"But de Borja wants to be Pope."

"Do you have a point to make?"

Thomas shook his head, frustrated. "Whatever de Borja might claim, you are Inigo's son. You only have to look at him to see that. You have his eyes, his face, his ability to make people like him. Even I like him, despite knowing what he was planning to do. Inigo is your father."

"Yes … I think even de Borja believes that. Which is why he forced Castellana to give me up."

"He admitted that to you?"

"Not as such," said Jorge, "but as good as. You know I can see the truth between people's words, and I saw the truth between his. He wanted Castellana, and then…" Jorge hesitated. "No, wanted her is not quite right. He wanted her, yes, but even more he didn't want Inigo to have her. I believe she loved him the more, and so de Borja forced him to leave Valencia. They all three of them lived in the city at that time."

"I know that."

"Good for you. I suspect the expulsion was not pretty, nor gentle. I also think de Borja might have come close to murder if Inigo had not left." Jorge smiled and shook his head. "He apologised to me, you know."

"De Borja?"

"He told me he was sorry he'd had me given away

without checking where I would end up. He claims had he known, he would have done things differently." Jorge laughed. "He even said he should have placed me in a monastery. Me, a monk?"

"God forbid," Thomas said.

"Yes, no doubt He would."

"You have not turned out so badly, have you?"

Jorge gave the question the time it deserved, which was not much. "I would have liked to still be a whole man, then I could give Belia the baby she so wants."

"If you were you would never have met her. You would never have come to Gharnatah, or met me, or done all the things you have done with your life."

"But I would have had a different life."

"As a monk."

"Yes," said Jorge, "there is that." He gave an exaggerated shiver.

"How much of what de Borja told you did you believe?" Thomas asked.

"Almost all of it. I saw no reason for him to lie because he could have done so easily, but I think he knew I would be able to tell. So his story is true, at least as far as he sees it. But we both know there are many layers to the truth."

"Indeed." Thomas stared ahead to where the man they were discussing rode between Lawrence and Usaden. "None of this explains why Inigo plotted to have you accused of murder."

"That was nothing to do with him. Inigo returned to Qurtuba to kill Rodrigo de Borja. He hates him more than any man has ever hated anyone. De Borja is aware the man has been living in Roma for many years, believes he came there exactly so he could kill him, but couldn't reach him."

"So who wanted you arrested if not Inigo?"

"You already know the answer, once you realise it's not me who is being punished. You have said it already. It is you."

Thomas urged his horse into a canter and rode ahead until he caught up with the others.

"I'll take him for a while," he said to Lawrence. "Take a rest. Go back and ride with Jorge."

Lawrence passed the end of the rope to Thomas and turned his mount without a word.

"Wanting to kill de Borja I can understand," Thomas said in Spanish, knowing Usaden wouldn't understand the conversation, "but why Jorge?"

Inigo turned in the saddle to look behind. He stared back for a long time while his horse plodded along the track.

"He is handsome, isn't he? Is he clever, too?"

"He is."

"Is he cruel?"

"No."

"So maybe he is not my son after all. I assume de Borja told you why I want to kill him?"

"He told it to Jorge, who told it to me. Is it a lie?"

Inigo faced ahead and settled himself in the saddle as if preparing for a long journey, though Córdoba was now in sight.

"I don't know what truth he told you, but suspect it was not the whole of the truth." He glanced at Thomas. "Did he tell you we were all lovers?"

Thomas nodded.

"All three of us together?"

Thomas nodded again.

"So he told you the truth in that. Did he claim to be Jorge's father?"

"How could he? You only need to stand together to see who his father is."

Inigo smiled. "Yes … he is handsome, isn't he?"

"Did you pay Cortez to find him?" Thomas asked.

"I did. I wanted to know if he still lived, but it was the worst decision I ever made. It almost killed my son." He glanced back once more, then toward Thomas. "Cortez found him, did you know that?"

"I have my own man who is good at digging out secrets."

"Lawrence? Yes, we talked, he told me what he discovered. And you are right, he is good at discovering things people would prefer hidden. As are you, he tells me."

"What happened?"

"The man got too greedy for his own good. He came to me demanding more money or he would offer the information he had uncovered to others."

"Who would want it?"

"Who do you think? De Borja, Fernando, the Queen … Castellana? She would pay handsomely to find the child she gave away."

"She claims to love Jorge."

"Yes, she would, but I suspect she would offer payment to discover where he was so she could kill him." Inigo smiled. "Or have him thrown into a prison and left to rot."

"To protect Gabriel?"

"That, and her position in society. She is a friend of the Queen, mistress to the King. She is wealthy and powerful. Those are not advantages she would want to give up, and news she had abandoned her bastard son to the ravages of Córdoba's slum might destroy her reputation."

"So Castellana is behind Jorge's arrest?"

Inigo raised a shoulder. "I cannot say. I do not know one way or the other, but I suspect she had someone else do the planning. She is a good enough businesswoman, but not as clever as she thinks, though clever enough to be aware of when she needs help. So she will have asked someone else to do it."

"I would suspect Fernando, but he sided with you back there."

"Did he?"

"Those men protecting you were his."

"I didn't know that. I thought they were soldiers hired by Rodrigo who decided to switch sides when they saw how the fight was going. Why would the King want to help me?"

"Because he doesn't like Rodrigo. He thinks the man is too close to his wife."

"We will never know for sure, will we? Those of his men you left alive, if they were his, disappeared like the mist of the night. It is the only reason you captured me. Had I another twenty trained soldiers, the world would be a different place today. Except not for you, for you would be dead. I would have tried to save Jorge, though."

"Then it's lucky Fernando didn't send more. Do you think he did that on purpose? I know he doesn't like a lot of people, and now you no doubt are among their number."

Inigo shook his head. "I hate kings."

"And queens?"

"They are all as bad as each other."

Inigo laughed. "I have decided I like you, Thomas Berrington. You can let me go now if you want to. I mean you no harm, nor the King or Queen or my son. It is only Rodrigo I want to destroy, and doing so would be a favour to Christendom."

"It's not my decision," Thomas said. But he knew it was. Inigo Florentino had come to Córdoba in search of his son, and had found him. Everything else he had done came from his hatred of de Borja—a man it was difficult to hate, but Thomas didn't know what had happened between them. He wondered how he would act if someone stole Will or Amal away from him and gave them away to pimps and murderers. He smiled. He knew what he would do. Exactly what this man riding next to him had done.

Thomas rode close and reached over to untie the rope from the pommel of Inigo's saddle and let it fall to the ground. As he did so, the cross he had worn since taking it from a dead man slipped from within his shirt and swung free.

Inigo glanced at it. "Where did you get that?" He reached into his own shirt and drew an identical crucifix out. His eyes were cold on Thomas. "Did you kill someone for it?"

"No. But someone did." Thomas stared at the other cross, identical in every way, even down to the leather thong. "Was he your man?"

"I sent him to make sure that Cortez didn't take my money and do nothing. How did he die?"

"Like Cortez he got greedy. He wanted to sell Jorge the name of his mother."

Inigo shook his head as if disappointed in a wayward child. "You cannot trust anyone anymore, can you? Who killed him?"

"I don't know, but I am sure it was to hide the knowledge Cortez had discovered. They died close together in time."

"Castellana," said Inigo.

"Do you think so?"

"Not with her own hand, of course, but she is wealthy and the price of killing a man is cheap." Inigo stared at Thomas. "Not that the knowledge will do either of us any good. She is protected, as is her son."

"Only one of her sons."

"That is true." Inigo offered a sad smile. "Will you truly let me ride away?"

"I will."

"You are a good man, Thomas Berrington. Take care of Jorge for me. I would have liked to know him better, but that is unlikely now. I will have to leave this land."

"Will you return to Roma?"

"I have not decided that yet, but I expect so, in the end."

"Do you intend to continue to work against de Borja?"

"It has been my life. Would you have me change now?" Inigo dug his heels into the flank of his horse and rode away north. He raised a hand, but whether in thanks or farewell, Thomas didn't know, only that he felt good about the decision he had made.

CHAPTER THIRTY-SEVEN

"We have to confront Castellana and Fernando both," said Jorge. "She lied to us the whole time, and he hates you even more than we already thought he did. And then we should ride to Gharnatah. We will send Belia and Usaden ahead with the children. There is nothing here for us anymore, and Fernando will come for you directly the next time."

They were sitting in Daniel's house, which for once was quiet. Will and Amal were playing with the other children on the riverbank. Will had made up a game involving sticks and a great deal of shouting, which came only distantly into the room. Zanita and Adana had gone to the market, together with Beatriz and Sama. Some kind of feast was being planned. A double celebration, to mark the safe return of Thomas and Jorge, and the imminent departure of Adana, who would return to Cadiz with her aunt.

The world turned from one day to the next. Everything changed, including Thomas's life, and he didn't know if there was anything he could do about it, or even if he wished to. He wanted to believe Jorge was wrong, but knew he wasn't. He had always known Fernando hated him. He had simply underestimated how deeply that hatred ran. It would mean he could never accept Isabel's offer to be at her side. Such was now impossible.

"He can't be jealous of me," Thomas said. "He knows the most important thing in Isabel's life is Castile and being its Queen. She would never stray. She would never even think of straying."

"And there are more handsome men to choose if she did. Don't forget Fernando's a man who has done a great deal of straying himself, so he no doubt believes other men are like him."

"Except he should know I am not."

"No, we are both men of excellent character, but there are few like us in the world. Don't judge others by your own standards or you will be sorely disappointed."

"We could live in Cadiz," Thomas said. "Beatriz will find work for us."

"Work? I have no wish to work. Besides, we are rich men, and rich men don't work."

"Except our riches sit in our cellar in Gharnatah, and you know Muhammed will not welcome our return."

"Then we will ask someone else to send the gold in secret. I am sure Britto will do it for a small share for himself. There is enough for everyone."

"Not if you keep offering it to people."

"I see you are in a good mood. Go to see Eleanor and get it done with. Tell her you never want to see her again, tumble her again, pledge your undying love, but get some decision made." Jorge smiled. "You never know, perhaps you can marry her and become the Count d'Arreau. That would be a fine reward, would it not? And as your servant I will be expected to wear exquisite garments fitting to my new station in life."

"You will have to learn another language, and you can barely manage your own."

"My tongue has more important work than words. Go see her, Thomas. You will have to at some point, and when you come back, you will be in a better mood and we can talk about where to live and with who."

Thomas rose and walked outside. Not to visit Eleanor, though he knew she was a wound that remained unhealed. He was unsure it ever would heal. He didn't want to tell Jorge of her involvement in what had happened because he barely understood it himself. Instead he went down to the river and sat to watch the children play, comforted as always at the sight of their innocence and simplicity. All of them together. Will and Amal and all nine of Daniel and Zanita's brood. Even eighteen-month-old Lope joined in as Adana perched him on her hip and passed him pebbles to throw into the water, each accompanied by a laugh.

If only we could stay here, Thomas thought, a sense of missed opportunity settling through him, a lost chance at happiness.

Kin came and lay at his side and Thomas stroked the dog's long fur.

Then Adana approached, Lope now in the care of Maria.

Adana knelt in front of Thomas and took his hands.

"Thank you, Uncle Thomas."

He smiled. "For what?"

"For asking Aunt Beatriz if I could return with her. Mother told me it was you and Uncle Jorge who persuaded Father I could go to Cadiz, but mostly you."

"I think she might have that the wrong way around."

Adana shook her head. "No. Uncle Jorge of course told them we could go, but everyone knows what he is like. You are the sensible one. They listen to you more." She leaned close and kissed his cheek.

"When do you leave?"

"After the party, of course. We wouldn't want to miss it. So most likely tomorrow, because Beatriz said there will be much wine drunk." She kissed Thomas's cheek again and rose to her feet. He watched her walk away and smiled. A memory of a younger Adana came to him, of her bravery when they escaped the clutches of Abbot Mandana. They had both been meant to die, made examples of, but Jorge had saved them at the risk of his own life.

Thomas watched for a while longer, then rose. He clicked his fingers and Kin came to pad along beside him. After a moment, Usaden appeared, though he had been nowhere to be seen.

"Where are we going?"

"I am going to confront Castellana."

"You and Kin?"

"I expect he'll tag along. And you?"

"Will there be fighting?"

"I doubt it."

"Then perhaps not." Usaden smiled. "But there might be, so..."

Thomas went to ask Daniel if they could borrow two horses, explaining they needed to ride to El Carpio. "Don't tell Jorge where we've gone," he said. "He'll only want to come, and I need to be harsher than I could if he's there."

Daniel shook his head. "I can still scarce believe he's not my brother. Of course you can have horses, but I may be able to save you a few hours' ride. I had a note from Gabriel Lonzal only this morning regarding the delivery of weapons. He says they will be in the house in Córdoba for three more days, and he wants me to take a sample for him to see. As if anyone needs a sample of Daniel Olmos's work."

"Can I take a sample to them? Two daggers, perhaps?" He glanced at Usaden, who nodded. Daggers were good for close work.

As they crossed into the city and turned into the narrow alleys which would lead them to Castellana's house, Thomas wondered if Eleanor would be there, and what he might do if she was. Jorge was right—some kind of decision had to be made … but not yet. After today was done, he promised himself. After today. Once he had shaken the truth from Castellana and shown his face at Beatriz's party and drunk enough wine to give him courage. Or if not courage, he would accept oblivion.

Kin paced ahead, constrained by the alleys of the city. Usaden was almost equally constrained, not a man suited to narrow streets and fine houses. His natural world was desert sand and open vistas. Sometimes Thomas wondered what he was still doing with him.

"I'll stay out here to keep watch," said Usaden when they reached the small square with Castellana's house sitting on one side. "Shout if you need me."

Thomas nodded and walked through the shaded arch into the central courtyard. He expected to have to hunt for Castellana, but found her eating a midday meal at a table set in the shade. Gabriel sat across from her. The four men of Roma who had been with him at the fight with Jorge sat in one corner, picking at their own food, excluded but also included. So they had not gone with Inigo to kill de Borja after all, and Thomas wondered at their involvement or otherwise. Except he knew these must be the men who had murdered Miguel.

Gabriel rose and put a hand to his waist before realising

he wore no weapon. Neither did Thomas. He had decided to leave both of Daniel's daggers with Usaden. He hadn't come to fight. He hoped he hadn't.

He glanced briefly to one side as the four men rose to their feet. They were armed. Of course they were armed.

Thomas walked to the table, pulled out a chair and sat as if an invitation had been issued. He reached out and pulled the leg from a pigeon and sucked the meat from it.

"I talked with Jorge's father."

"Which one?"

"Both of them. So it's true—you didn't know which of them it was?"

"How could I? Not then, but I only have to look on his face now to know. Not that it matters. I have only one son."

"You failed to get rid of Jorge. He will always be there."

Castellana smiled. "I sent a message."

Thomas saw Gabriel smile and lift a hand, beckoning the four men forward. They came in a line, which was a mistake, and showed inexperience. Thomas waited for them to approach closer before rising to his feet. The man on the left took it as a sign and ran at him. Thomas caught his knife arm and twisted, then threw him across his body so he crashed into the food-laden table, knocking bottles and fine glasses to shatter on the marble floor.

Usaden appeared in the entrance of the courtyard, a blade in each hand. Thomas shook his head to tell him to stay where he was. He wanted to finish this himself. Wanted to banish the ache of frustration that had been building ever since Jorge was first arrested.

The man on the table was barely conscious, so Thomas left him where he was. Castellana retreated to the far side of the courtyard, but remained, almost certainly waiting to see Thomas killed. Gabriel came around the table, but avoided

Thomas, going to stand with the others to make their number back to four.

Thomas knew he had to keep Gabriel alive. The others he didn't care about. He knelt and picked up the knife dropped by the first attacker. Believing the movement made him weak, two of them came forward at speed. Thomas twisted aside to avoid the first blade and used his own to slice across the back of the man's knee. He fell to the floor, gripping his leg as blood pooled beneath him. Thomas expected the other to slow, but instead he struck a savage blow that would have killed Thomas had he not thrown himself to one side. He sprawled, sliding along the smooth marble floor, aware he had been over-confident. He tried to rise, but his feet slipped, and this time all three remaining men came at him. But they had forgotten about Kin.

The dog was a black streak, all instinct and power. He leapt high and took the throat of one man, blood spraying bright in the sunlight. It gave Thomas time to rise to his feet, but he was breathing hard. He glanced to where Usaden stood, still unmoving. No doubt waiting to see if Thomas needed help before intervening.

Two men remained.

And then only one as the last man of Roma backed away. He circled, helped the man on the table to rise as his wits returned. They glanced at the hobbled man and left him where he was before they made their way toward the back of the house, seeking an exit that would not require them to pass Usaden.

Kin growled deep in his chest and stalked them.

"No," Thomas said, unsure if the dog would obey, and for a moment he thought he would not. Then Kin turned his head, gave another growl, and returned to his side, tongue lolling. He looked as if he was grinning.

Only then did Thomas raise a hand to draw Usaden close.

"Fetch her," he said, nodding toward Castellana, who was edging toward a doorway. "Then go close the gates so we are not interrupted."

Usaden ran across and caught Castellana by the arm, dragged her twisting and crying back to the table, which Thomas had righted, together with the chairs. There was little could be done for the spilled wine and food, though Kin began to help himself.

"Leave her alone!" It was the first sign of resistance from Gabriel. Thomas grabbed the man's long hair in his fist and pulled him to the table. He righted another of the upturned chairs and sat him. Then he set the point of his knife beneath Gabriel's chin, exactly as he had done once before.

Usaden sat Castellana and stood behind her, a hand on each of her shoulders.

"Now you will answer my questions," Thomas said, staring at Castellana. "And this time I want the truth. If you refuse, or if I believe you are lying, your son dies." To make his point, he jerked the knife briefly upward so blood ran down Gabriel's neck. It was a harmless cut, but Castellana wouldn't know that, and Thomas doubted Gabriel did either from the wail that came from him as he clutched both hands to his neck to stem the bleeding.

"You have killed him," said Castellana. "You have killed my son!"

"He will be fine. Don't you care about your other son? The one you tried to kill?"

"He is no son of mine. We gave him up, Rodrigo and I. Both of us agreed it."

"What were you afraid of? Jorge has no claim on

anything of yours. Even if he did, he wouldn't want it. He is a rich man in his own right."

"He is no man," said Gabriel, a little of his bluster returning as he realised Thomas hadn't killed him after all. "He is a eunuch. A palace fop."

Thomas held a laugh in check. "A palace fop who defeated you in a fight. What does that make you?" He turned back to Castellana. "Why do you want to incriminate Jorge in murder?"

Castellana stared at him, and Thomas saw her trying to decide whether to lie or not. When she answered, she chose the right path. There had already been too much deception.

"I didn't. It was a mistake."

Thomas frowned. "I don't understand. Those men who failed so dismally to protect you killed Alonso Cortez on your orders, because he held proof of who Jorge's father is."

"We didn't know if he did or not. I wanted to pay him what he asked, but Fernando told me the man would only keep coming back for more."

"Fernando had him killed?"

"No. I didn't have him killed, and Fernando didn't have him killed. I have no idea who did. Fernando had Jorge arrested because I asked it. I wanted him removed, but I did not want him dead. I promise you I did not want him dead." She lowered her head. "None of this was meant to happen. None of it."

Thomas glanced at Gabriel. The man's eyes, that had been watching the conversation, flickered away and Thomas saw who had been behind Cortez's death. Had Gabriel also had Mendoza killed as well? And de Parma? Thomas wondered if Castellana knew the truth, and when he looked back at her he saw she did. She hadn't lied, not directly, but she knew who was behind the deaths. The two men seen in the roadway had been Gabriel and Yves. The four men who killed Miguel were the ones Thomas had just defeated. No doubt Miguel had been getting too close to the truth and had to be removed.

Thomas's fingers curled and he fought an urge to lash out at Gabriel. He continued to stare at him until he met Thomas's gaze, unable to look away from it.

"Did you send the man to Jorge with the message about his mother?"

Gabriel said nothing, but he didn't need to. Guilt was written all through him. On his face. In the way he held his shoulders. In the tension in his body and the tremor in his hands.

"And had him killed when you heard we were going to find him?"

Still no response came.

And then Castellana said, "Gabriel? Did you do what he accuses you of?"

The man flinched. Over thirty years of age and still his mother's voice could make him feel like a boy who had done wrong. And Gabriel had done great wrong.

Castellana saw the truth as well, but her reaction was that of a mother.

"It makes no difference," she said. "Fernando will not allow anything to happen to him, nor to Yves. He did help you, didn't he?"

Gabriel offered the smallest of nods.

Castellana looked around at the spilled food, at Thomas's dog lying with a bone in his mouth, at expressionless Usaden.

"Gabriel thinks he is a bad man, but he isn't."

"And Miguel?" Thomas said, still staring at Gabriel. "Did you have him killed as well?"

This time Gabriel seemed to gather some courage to himself. "That was not me. It was those men. He came close to unmasking their part in everything." His eyes met Thomas's. "The scribe was not meant to die. They were meant to scare him into silence and destroy his records, not kill him. I didn't ask them to kill him. It is Florentino's fault—he sent the men to us."

"But you corrupted them. Both of you turned them to your own ends."

Thomas glanced at Usaden. He offered a nod and the man turned away. He didn't need telling what to do. The four men of Roma would still be within the city and Usaden would track them down. Kin grabbed a last roast pigeon in his jaw and scrambled after him. The job would be done. At least some punishment would be inflicted, some justice achieved. Except those who had been behind everything would escape all justice.

Unless Thomas applied the justice these two deserved.

He thought about Eleanor, and then about his son, Yves. They too were complicit. Could he kill them as well? His own son?

He shook his head. Castellana, not aware of his thoughts, said, "I know. Sometimes events do not take the path meant for them." She sighed, settling into her seat as if the matter was settled. Perhaps, for her, it was.

"Why did they all have to die?" Thomas asked.

"They knew too much." Castellana gave a brief smile. "As do you and Jorge."

"Except we are both protected."

"You, perhaps, but not Jorge." Castellana gave a shake of the head. "While you stand here questioning me, it is already too late for him."

CHAPTER THIRTY-EIGHT

Thomas entered Daniel's house with such force that Zanita almost fell as she turned.

"Where is he?"

"Gone back to his works." Zanita indicated a pile of pots, plates and cups which still covered the table. "Leaving me to do all the work as usual."

"Not Daniel, Jorge. Has he been taken?"

Zanita frowned. "Do you think I would be standing here washing pots if Jorge had been taken? A message arrived and he has gone to the palace."

"A message for me?"

"No, for Jorge. Not everything to do with the palace is about you, Thomas. And where have you been? You missed the party. Everyone wanted to know where you were."

"I'm sure they didn't even notice I wasn't here." He glanced around. "Has Adana gone?"

"The three of them left an hour since."

"I thought they were staying until tomorrow. I wanted to say goodbye."

"Then you are too late."

"Did Jorge say what the message was about?"

Zanita shook her head as she turned back to the pots, clearly considering the conversation at an end, an unsatisfactory one.

Thomas went outside to where Usaden still waited, Kin at his side. Usaden reached his hand into his robe, and when he withdrew it, four crucifixes swung on leather thongs.

"Did you kill them all?"

Usaden said nothing, but Thomas knew the truth. There was little of mercy in Usaden, and the four men of Roma had deserved none.

"Will their bodies be found?"

Usaden smiled.

"After you went, Castellana told me Jorge was going to be arrested again, and now he's gone to the palace. Go back to the tent and take Kin with you. Wash your clothes and yourself in the river, and throw those crosses into it. I'll come and find you later."

"Do you think she wanted to scare you?"

"She knew as soon as we got there we would learn the truth. This is her protection—attack rather than defend."

"I thought you were going to kill them both," said Usaden. "You should. They remain a threat to you as long as they live. She wants you and Jorge gone. She cannot kill you, I doubt she can even ask the King to kill you, but she will do everything she can. No doubt she is riding to El Carpio to continue her plotting."

"Where she knows I can just as easily follow." Thomas began to walk, Usaden at his side. The sun was lowering to the west and long shadows offered welcome patches of shade. Beneath his robe Thomas was sweat-stained and dirty. He wanted to find somewhere to bathe as soon as he was satisfied Jorge was safe. He might even ask Theresa to join him. She had offered to do so in the past, and the generous simplicity of her love promised a safe haven he yearned for.

As they approached the palace, Usaden left to return to the riverside while Thomas went inside, his presence now so familiar the guards barely glanced at him. Was this how life could be? he wondered. A part of this majesty? One of the anointed at Isabel's side? If so, was it something he wanted? He was beginning to believe he might. Beginning to work out how such could come about despite Fernando's hatred.

He hesitated at a splitting of ways, trying to decide the best course of action, then turned toward where his rooms lay. It was also where he knew he would find Theresa.

She sat in a chair where a shaft of late sunlight caught the red in her hair and cast it aflame. She turned as he entered, then rose and came to him. She stopped half a foot away, waiting for something Thomas wasn't sure he could ever offer.

"Have you seen Jorge?"

"He said there was a party. I would have liked to have been invited."

"I didn't go either."

"I would still have liked it. He has gone to see Fernando."

"Did he say why?"

Theresa gave a shake of the head. "He had a message clutched in his hand, but I didn't read it."

As she spoke the words, Thomas realised Jorge would have been incapable of reading the words for himself, and knew he should have found out who had done so, and what the message said. Most likely Belia, and he gave a sharp nod which made Theresa frown, because she had no idea of the thoughts that darted fish-like through his head.

As he started to turn away, she caught his wrist.

Thomas looked down at her hand, waiting for her to say something, but nothing emerged. After a moment, she released her grip and he walked away.

Belia and Jorge shared a room at the far end of the palace wing, but when he got there it was empty. He stood in the middle of the room, unsure what to do. Belia's scent hung faintly in the air, Jorge's too. A decision came to him. There was only one thing he could do. Confront Fernando and stop what was about to happen. Thomas knew he would have to challenge the power of the King.

He went to the long corridor that looked across the gardens and found what he didn't expect to be there. Fernando was with Prince Juan, watching the youth practise with the sword. Thomas's own son was with them. Will faced Juan, while Isabel sat at a distance on the terrace, Amal on her lap as before, her own daughter on a chair beside her. Thomas waited for a moment, his sense of urgency fading as he took in the domesticity of the scene. If Jorge was in danger, then Fernando would not be here.

Thomas noted how tall Will looked where he confronted Juan. There were several years between them, but a stranger would consider Will the older of the two. As well as the more skilled. By far the more skilled, even though a sword was not his preferred weapon. He had already taken after his *morfar* and chosen an axe to swing light and deadly under his control. Except today it was swords. Fernando's palace, Fernando's rules.

Jorge was nowhere to be seen. Thomas descended stone steps and walked toward Isabel, who heard his approach only at the last moment and turned, at ease with herself and the day.

"Pa!" Amal wriggled, and Isabel set her down to run to

Thomas. He scooped her up and kissed her face all over, making her laugh. When he met Isabel's gaze again, she was smiling at his manner with his daughter. He realised he had never seen any affection shown by Fernando to his own daughters. All his attention was focused on his son. Heir to both thrones of Castile and Aragon.

The heir to a nation, and a boy who now fought against Will.

As Thomas watched, he saw how Will hid his own strength and skill. He was going to allow Juan to win again, clever enough to make him believe the victory justified.

When Thomas turned his attention to Fernando, he saw concentration on his face, a need for Juan to prove himself, to be worthy. The youths fought with blunted blades, but they could still hurt. Will would carry bruises later, which Belia would anoint with her lotions.

Thomas sat on one of the steps and perched Amal in his lap.

"Did you like the party?"

Amal nodded and began to babble, some words clear, others of her own construction. Thomas loved watching the way she grew, turning day by day into her own person. He loved how knowledge and skill was absorbed from without to emerge from within. She looked so much like Lubna that his chest ached with the loss of his wife.

When he looked up, he had no idea how much time had passed, only that he knew holding his daughter had calmed him, and that Isabel was staring at him with a hunger that made his skin stipple. He turned away, unable to continue seeing the raw need in her eyes.

Below the terrace, Juan and Will's mock battle drew to the only possible conclusion. Fernando slapped his son on the back and congratulated him. He ignored Will as the loser he saw him as. Will trudged across the perfect grass and climbed the steps to sit beside Thomas.

"You made the right choice."

Will nodded, still young but with an older head on him, a wise head. "It was hard, though."

"Losing is always hard, but it was the right thing to do."

"Not losing, Pa. Making it look like I was losing. Juan is a good enough fighter, but I could have beaten him in the first minute."

"I know you could. But you made Fernando think Juan had the better of you. I am proud." Thomas squeezed his son's shoulder. He glanced at Isabel again, seeing that same hunger still in her eyes, which he knew wasn't for his body, but his soul. He knew she was watching how he was with his children and comparing him to her husband. Even as he recognised the need in her, Thomas knew that he and Isabel had no choice but to act as they did, despite what they might both want.

"Have you seen Jorge?" Thomas asked Will. "I was told he came here, but he's not with Belia."

Will gave a knowing smile. "They spend all their time tumbling." He glanced at Thomas. "Did you tumble Ma as much as they do? I don't remember."

Thomas almost repeated the words he had spoken before when Will had said such things, then changed his mind. The boy was growing older, even older than his years, and sex was a part of life he would learn about soon enough for himself. Will would be a handsome man. Tall and strong. Women would throw themselves at his feet in search of a protector from the troubles of the world. Thomas only hoped his son would make a better job of his life than he had.

"No, not as much." He ruffled Will's long blond hair that

he had inherited from his mother. "I don't think anyone could tumble as much as Jorge and Belia."

"It's how babies are made, isn't it, Pa? How Amal was made? And me?"

"It is." Thomas pushed aside the doubt that he was Will's true father. It became easier each time he did so.

"So why doesn't Belia carry a baby in her belly?" Will laughed. "She should have a hundred babies."

"You know why. Jorge is a eunuch." Though sometimes, even more so recently, it was easy to forget the fact. "He can't plant a seed in her."

"Belia told me you have good seed, Pa."

"She did?" Thomas wished he had followed his first instinct and not acknowledged Will's questions, but it was too late now. "I have you and Amal, and you know we lost Bahja. So yes, I expect Belia is right, I do have good seed."

"You make strong children." Will punched himself on the chest, and Thomas offered a smile tinged with sadness.

"Yes, strong children." He remembered his own question, which remained unanswered. "So you haven't seen Jorge?"

"He went off with Fernando somewhere before I fought with Juan. He knows where he is, you should ask him." He stood up, twisting to ease an ache in his strong body. "Can I take Amal to play with the girls? She likes them, and they like her. I like them too." He smiled. "Little Cat says she's going to marry me one day."

Thomas said nothing. Let the boy enjoy the fantasy until the real world bullied the truth into him. He set Amal on her feet and watched as she walked off hand in hand with her taller brother. His children. Blood of his blood, whether it was true or not. Thinking of Will brought Yves into his mind. He, too, was Thomas's blood. There was no doubt of that. But did it mean he had to like the man? Could he like the man after what he had done? He thought of Castellana protecting Gabriel and wondered if he would protect Yves, because he was his son. Was that enough, or did there have to be more? Would the pair of them change if they spent more time together? And then, that thought led to Eleanor, and Thomas knew they would never spend any more time together.

When he looked up, Isabel was still staring at him, but Fernando was approaching and she would have to stop or he would be even angrier than he already was. Thomas rose and brushed down his clothes, aware there might even be blood on them. Blood on his hands, certainly, even if it couldn't be seen.

"Your children love you so much, Thomas," said Isabel as he approached where she sat.

"As do yours."

She pressed her lips together and tilted her head, as if she didn't believe him. "I try."

"What do you try, my dear? To keep yourself away from my manly charms?" Fernando laughed at his own wit, poor attempt that it was. He spoke too coarsely for company, but perhaps he didn't consider Thomas as such. More likely he wanted to make his claim clear. "What are you doing here?" All humour had gone when he addressed Thomas.

"I came looking for Jorge."

Fernando laughed. "Then you have come to the wrong place. He is back in prison."

Thomas stared at him. Fernando returned the stare, turning it into a challenge, and Thomas's fingers curled into a fist as though he was holding the hilt of a sword.

"He was proven innocent."

"No, you thought him proven innocent, but I have new evidence. Incontrovertible evidence of his guilt. He is to be tried in the morning and executed before the day's end." Fernando smiled in triumph.

And then Isabel was on her feet, standing as if she wanted to insert herself between the two of them.

"You said nothing of this to me."

"It was my decision. Am I not in charge of matters of war?"

"This is not war!"

"Oh, but it is."

"What proof?" Thomas stepped closer to Fernando, pushing Isabel to one side.

"Attend the trial in the morning and you will find out." Fernando turned to leave, but Thomas grasped his arm.

Fernando looked down at his hand. "Do you wish to join him? I can as easily arrange two hangings as one. There are many in this city would be glad to see you dangle, Thomas Berrington."

"Fernando!" Isabel snapped. "What do you think you are doing?"

"My job. What I should have done years ago." He didn't even look at her. He pulled to free his arm, but Thomas maintained his grip, tightening it until he knew it must hurt. Fernando glanced down at their joining. "I have given you warning, there will be no other. Release me now or suffer my wrath."

Thomas let his hand drop away. He watched as Fernando raised his own hand to rub at where he had been held, and then stop, not wanting to show weakness.

"Come, Juan, let me tell you everything you did wrong today so you can improve the next time. Though I think you need better competition than that heathen boy."

It was fortunate Fernando's anger prevented him looking back as they entered the arched entrance to the inner palace, for by then Isabel had taken Thomas's hand and was clutching it to her belly, which rose and fell beneath his touch.

"I did not know, Thomas. I honestly knew nothing of this. Why has he done it?"

Thomas turned away from the empty arches and looked down on her. He tightened his fingers through hers and saw a soft smile touch her lips before she suppressed it.

"You know why. He wants me punished. He wants me gone from your life."

"He knows I would never … we would never … he knows, Thomas. He *must* know."

"He is a proud man, one who sees how you are when I am in your presence. I see it too. I suspect everyone does. Ask Theresa."

"What does he see, Thomas?" Isabel's voice was soft, her gaze avoiding his, but her fingers tightened under his touch.

"If only we had met thirty years ago…" He laughed, making her look up, blue eyes and red hair and a face not pretty, but beautiful to him. "No, I would still have been a commoner, a nobody, and you a princess." He smiled. "You were magnificent then, were you not?"

She gave a little moue. "Am I not magnificent now?"

"Of course you are."

"But yes, I was. People told me so. Men and women. And I would not have cared what you were."

"Yes you would, for even then I lived in Al-Andalus, and I was not a good man. I have never been a good man, but at least now I try a little harder."

"You are the best man I know. Far and away the best. And it would have been different, I know it would." She let loose a deep sigh. "The world would have been different had we met then, would it not?"

Thomas gave a shake of his head. "You know it would not. But the thought is pleasant to conjure with."

"It still can be," said Isabel. "That thought. I play with it now and again, as I am sure you do."

"An impossible dream, nothing more."

"Is it?"

"You know it is."

"What are you going to do about Jorge?" she asked, as if the matter had been decided, a decision Thomas had missed if it had.

"I have no idea. None at all. He is guilty of nothing, but those who are guilty can't be touched or even named. Perhaps the morning will prove his innocence once and for all."

Isabel gave a sad smile. "It is you who is still too much the innocent. For my husband, the matter is already decided. There is only one chance for your friend, but it comes at a cost."

"I am not without resources."

"Not money. A different cost."

"Whatever it takes. If you know of a way, then tell me and I will pay the price, whatever it is."

"There is no guarantee of success."

"I will take the chance. It is the only chance left now."

"Two things," said Isabel, and Thomas knew the point where he had to make a decision had arrived. Here and now. One way or the other.

"Name them."

"I have asked before. I want you at my side. I need you at my side. I need your intelligence, your humanity, and your skill. I saw the way your son fought Juan—he could have beaten him at any time he wanted, and you and he are the same. You are a man who protects people. I want you to protect me."

For Thomas, it felt as if the world faded around them, leaving only the two joined by their hands. A pivot in time. All his life before had led to this moment. All after led away.

"And the other thing?"

"Say yes first."

"Yes, I will be at your side. I will protect you. If your husband allows it."

"I will demand it."

"And the other thing? Whatever it is, my answer to that is also yes."

"Whatever it is?"

Thomas smiled. "My answer is still yes."

Isabel laughed. "I wish now I had been a little more ambitious. A kiss, Thomas. One kiss. Our one and only kiss. Kiss me like you love me. Kiss me as lovers do. One kiss, that is all I ask." She glanced around and giggled. "Out here where we might be seen, yes?"

"Yes," he said. "And you know I love you."

He lowered his face and pressed his lips against the softness of hers. His hand touched the curve of her back and drew her against him, and they kissed as lovers kiss, kissed as he and Lubna had kissed, and when eventually they drew apart, Thomas saw his own tears reflected in Isabel's eyes, and he knew once might not be enough.

CHAPTER THIRTY-NINE

Thomas woke in the deep of night, despite having been sure he wouldn't be able to sleep. Theresa leaned over him and he groaned and tried to push her away.

"She wants you." Theresa shook him again, even though she could see he was awake.

"What for?"

"What do you think?"

For a moment, Thomas was unsure, but knew a summons from the Queen could not be ignored.

"Turn away while I dress." He swung his legs from the bed, but kept the sheet wrapped at his waist.

"Why? I would rather sit here and watch you." She pulled a chair close, a smile on her face.

Thomas was too tired, too worried, to care. He stood and walked past her to where his clothes lay. He knew he should dress in clean ones, but they were to hand, and he pulled them on, aware of Theresa's eyes on him the entire time.

Isabel had returned to where he had left her on the terrace, which was now cloaked in darkness, only a small lamp burning beside her, against which insects crackled as they caught flame. Theresa moved away, but didn't leave altogether. Isabel patted the chair next to hers.

"I have spoken with Fernando."

"Has he agreed to release Jorge?"

Isabel shook her head. "He is determined in this matter. He insists the trial will be in the morning."

"That is idiocy!"

"You have no argument from me," said Isabel. "But it is who he is."

"Does he fear me so much? If so, why not arrest me instead of Jorge? He is an innocent in all of this."

"I tried everything at my command, but all failed. There will be a trial, and if it goes as we both fear, there is one last throw of the dice that might win the day."

"Tell me."

Isabel shook her head. "If needed, you will discover what it is tomorrow. This is not something I consider lightly, for there will be consequences. Plead for him yourself. Speak for him, Thomas." She reached out and took his hand, a light touch this time. "Jorge will not die."

As he returned to his room, Thomas asked Theresa to wake him again at dawn, with no idea how far away that might be.

"It would be far simpler if I just stayed," she said, standing before him, a challenge in her eyes.

"I don't think simple is how I would describe it. Will you do it for me?"

"And who is going to wake me?"

"Find a footman at a loose end, I'm sure he'll be only too happy to oblige."

"Unlike you. One day, Thomas..."

When she was gone, Thomas undressed and lay on top

of the covers, afraid of himself and the emotions that roiled within him. He knew it was the prospect of death, of losing Jorge. All emotion combined to loosen his boundaries until love and loss and lust became the same ravening beast.

He closed his eyes. When he opened them, Theresa stood over him with a knowing smile on her face.

The day was starting to warm as Thomas walked toward the trial rooms, Theresa on one side and Belia on the other. He had not meant Theresa to accompany them, but she had been insistent. Will and Amal were being cared for by a friend of hers, another woman who worked in the palace. This is how it will be, Thomas thought, when I am at Isabel's beck and call. My children will be raised by others. He determined it would not be so, but knew some promises were made to be broken.

A line of men snaked away from the side door of the trial room, each chained to the man in front. The first man in the queue was Jorge. Thomas went to him, but was pushed back by the guards. Belia grasped his hand and squeezed it hard, her eyes on Jorge the entire time.

"You are to be saved!" Thomas shouted, hoping Jorge could hear him.

Once inside, he tried to explain he was there to speak on behalf of the accused, but a clerk scanned a list of witnesses and failed to find his name.

"Only those written here can speak."

"I am his friend. Friend to the King and Queen both."

"Except you are not on the list." The man turned away, his face sour.

Thomas forced a way to the front rank of the viewing gallery, pushing others aside until there was space enough for the three of them, each complaint met with a stare so feral the complainer immediately fell silent.

The chamber grew full, then fuller still. Conversation around them was of the heathen Spaniard who had killed his mother and father, killed his children. Rumours sparked, spreading wildly, and Thomas wondered who had been the instigator of them. He suspected Castellana—or more likely Gabriel. He still failed to fully understand Castellana's actions or motives, but Gabriel's jealousy was a palpable thing that tainted the air around him.

Robed men sat on a platform, waiting for something. Silence fell as two figures appeared behind them and walked to ornate chairs set on one side. Isabel and Fernando took their seats. Thomas had expected Fernando, but not Isabel. Both wore expressions he had seen only rarely before. The faces rulers show to their subjects. They lacked all emotion, closed to scrutiny, giving nothing away. And then Jorge was dragged in. The dragging was unnecessary, but done all the same. He was set in front of the judges and told to give his name, which he did in a firm voice.

"Jorge Olmos."

Fernando sat back in his chair as witnesses were called to state what they knew of the events surrounding the death of Alonso Cortez. Others gave their opinion of Cortez's reputation, and to hear them, Thomas was surprised the man had not already been made a saint. Isabel leaned forward, her small body tense, eyes sharp on the three judges. Her face showed fleeting expressions as each outlandish claim was stated without refutation.

The murder of Carlos Mendoza was also given with more evidence. Thomas wondered how anyone had found out that Jorge was even there, or did they simply not care? Perhaps all deaths in the city were about to be set against him.

Thomas had to force himself to remain where he was,

helped by the iron grip of Belia on one side and Theresa on the other. The air in the trial room was fetid with heat and the stink of a hundred unwashed bodies. Light came through high windows designed to illuminate only the judges and accused. Thomas saw Jorge sweating and doubted it was only from the heat.

At last the litany of false testimony drew to a close, and a clerk rose.

"I call witnesses to speak for the accused."

Thomas rose to his feet. "I speak for him."

The man consulted the single sheet of paper in his hand, as he had done before. "Your name?"

"Thomas Berrington."

The man consulted the list once more. "That name is not here, sir. Take your seat or be ejected."

"Whose name is listed?" Thomas demanded.

"That is none of your business, sir. Sit or leave. The choice is yours."

Thomas opened his mouth to claim the entire proceedings were a sham when a glance from Isabel stilled him. He re-took his seat and the women on either side grasped his hands once more.

There was only a brief discussion before a slip of paper was passed to the clerk. He read it, smiled, then spoke in a loud voice so all could hear.

"In the case of murder against Jorge Olmos, the accused is found guilty. He is to be taken from this court to await execution no later than sunset today." The man slipped the paper into his pocket and reached for another. "Second case…"

As guards gripped Jorge, Fernando rose and swept from the room, a feral grin on his face. He looked toward Thomas to show his victory, to show who his next victim would be.

As he left through a rear door, Isabel also rose to her feet, but instead of following her husband, she turned to the court.

"Gentlemen, you all know who I am." She waited until the three judges nodded, waited as a murmur ran around the room before falling silent. Everyone wanted to hear her words. "This man…" She raised a hand and pointed at Jorge, who was still gripped between three strong guards. "This man," she repeated, "is known to me. No, more than known, he is a friend to me. I am your Queen, and I say he is not guilty of the charges brought against him. Let him free. Let him free now!"

"Your Grace…" One of the judges rose to his feet. "We have listened to the evidence brought against this man and all agree he is guilty as charged, and a heathen to boot."

"Where were the witnesses to speak for him, sir?" Isabel demanded.

"None were listed."

"Then why was that man," she pointed at Thomas, "not allowed to speak in his favour?"

"He was not listed, Your Grace." The man looked at his companions, clearly conflicted over how to proceed. "We have much work to get through today, Your Grace. Perhaps this matter can be raised later?"

"Would tomorrow suit you, sir?" said Isabel. "After he is dead? No! As Queen of Castile, I maintain my right of pardon for Jorge Olmos. It is a royal imperative. Let him go!"

The rising babble of voices in the room hushed at once. The guards holding Jorge looked toward Isabel, looked toward the judges.

The senior judge released a loud sigh and nodded, bowing to the inevitable. "Let him go." He knew there was nothing he could do. "All charges are set aside. He is a free man." He glanced at Isabel. "Though I recommend he leave Córdoba as soon as he can, before more charges can be raised against him." The message was clear. Stay and you die. How many times is the Queen willing to pardon you?

The guards let loose their hold on Jorge. Thomas scanned the faces of the men on the raised platform and knew they could do nothing more. Isabel's word was law. Jorge was a free man, but Thomas knew that also meant the guilty would go unpunished. It was the price of Jorge's freedom. This entire plot had been intended to cover up where true guilt lay. Now it would remain hidden forever. Castellana and Gabriel were close to Fernando, and both protected. Men had died, but there would be no punishment. Not today. Perhaps never.

"Go to him," Thomas said to Belia. "Take him to Daniel's house. He needs family around him now." He turned and started to push through the crowd, but a strong hand gripped his wrist. Thomas turned, intending to fend off an attack, but the hand belonged to Jorge. He drew him close and embraced him, the stink of prison on his clothes and body despite the shortness of his second incarceration.

"Thank you, Thomas." There were tears in his eyes as he kissed Thomas's mouth.

"I did nothing. Your freedom is Isabel's doing."

"Then thank her for me, but I know you mask the truth. She will have extracted a price, will she not?"

Thomas stared into Jorge's eyes, aware of how close he was to this man, how much he trusted him. He nodded.

"It is no more than I am willing to pay. We both know Castile is within months of winning this war. Next year, when the fighting season starts, Gharnatah will fall. It is sensible for us to be on the winning side, is it not?"

"And our lives? Our house and friends? Our wealth?"

"Brick and tile, gold and jewels. The friends will remain. I will do something. I don't know what, but something." An image of Eleanor came to mind, and Thomas wondered if he spoke the truth or not. Wondered if he and Eleanor had ever truly been friends. There had been lust mistaken for love … but friendship? Probably not.

Thomas knew what he must do before visiting Isabel, wondering as the thought came to him whether he would be admitted to the palace ever again. Fernando was likely to have given orders for him to be excluded. He smiled. It would make his new role, whatever it involved, more difficult to carry out. Not that he intended such to stop him. He was Isabel's man now, and no-one had ever accused Thomas Berrington of shirking his responsibilities.

CHAPTER FORTY

"What do you want? You are no longer welcome in this house." Yves stood at the gate, barring Thomas's entrance. He had recovered all of his arrogance and certainty. He had helped plot murder and gotten away with it.

Thomas studied him, trying to find some similarity between them and once again failing. He was tall, but other than that not a single feature gave a clue to the closeness of their relationship, unless you had known Thomas's father. It told him that sometimes blood didn't matter, and he felt better for the thought.

"I want to see your mother."

"She is busy. She wants nothing to do with you anymore. You must know that." Yves started to close the gate, but Thomas blocked it.

"Who is there?" It was a familiar voice, and after a moment Gabriel appeared in the hallway. He smiled. "Ah, I see." He came closer, a swagger about him showing he and his mother had won the day, despite Isabel's intervention. Jorge lived, but that was no issue now for they were free to continue their plotting. "Invite him in, Yves. We cannot let your father stand out in the street like some common man."

"He is not my father." Yves's face showed a sour expression, and he increased his pressure on the gate, but it was going nowhere. "My father is dead."

"That can be arranged if you wish," said Gabriel. "Admit him. It is only a pity his perverse friend is not with him. Let him in." There was command in Gabriel's voice and Yves stepped aside.

Thomas brushed past him, disappointed in his son's weakness. Had his own father felt the same about him? Had he despised what he regarded as weakness, and his mother as intelligence? If so, Yves showed no sign of either strength of body or mind. He was weak and easily manipulated by Gabriel, who waved an arm in invitation and led the way to the courtyard where Thomas had first encountered Eleanor. The adult Eleanor. The changed Eleanor. He had come for a confrontation, but now it seemed as if it would be with these two, not the one he sought.

"Where is Eleanor?" Thomas asked.

"Do you mean the Countess d'Arreau?"

"Don't play games with me, boy. Where is she?"

Thomas saw Gabriel wasn't afraid of him anymore, and he wondered where he had found his courage from, and how? He was a different man from the one who confronted Jorge on the dusty roadway and lost their fight. A different man from the one who cowered with a knife at his throat. Thomas knew Yves had followed them into the room and stood behind him. Perhaps he thought he was hidden, but Thomas saw him clearly in the wide mirror hanging on the far wall. He smiled, pleased when a frown came to Gabriel's face. Then the frown faded to be replaced by a grin.

In the mirror Thomas saw Yves draw a dagger and

approach from behind. Gabriel drew a blade of his own and came from ahead.

"I don't want to hurt you," Thomas said. "Either of you."

"But we want to hurt you," said Gabriel. "And then we will hurt my brother. Your pet Moor isn't here to save you anymore. You are going to wish you'd never meddled in matters beyond your ability to understand. And then you will die."

Thomas wondered if Yves saw this as the moment to prove himself. To prove Thomas couldn't be his father. But he was, Thomas knew the truth, and it would make what was to come all the harder.

Thomas sidestepped Gabriel's strike, then spun and took the dagger from Yves's raised hand. He punched him square on the cheek to send him sprawling to the floor.

Gabriel came at him again, making a better job of the attack than when he'd fought Jorge, but it was all far too easy for a man honed by a lifetime of conflict. Thomas caught his wrist as the dagger descended, pushed Gabriel's arm up through the angle between them and jerked hard. A small, soft sound came as Gabriel's shoulder popped out of its socket, a louder one when he screamed.

Thomas pushed him to the ground and stood on his arm, tired of these two, tired of the world.

"Where is Eleanor? Now!"

"Hellfire, what is all this noise about?" Fernando stood in the doorway, dressed only in his underwear, his feet bare. When he saw Thomas, he grinned and came into the room. "Of course, who else?" He glanced at Yves, at Gabriel. "Did you break his arm?"

"Not broken, merely displaced. It will pop home soon enough, but it will hurt like the fires of hell."

"Serves him right for picking on a better man. What are

you doing here? There is nothing for you in this house anymore." Ferdinand came close enough for Thomas to smell the sex on him, the scent a man and woman make when their bodies merge into one.

"I came to talk with Eleanor." He glanced behind Fernando to where the staircase rose to a gallery, but there was nobody there. "Is it her you have been lying with, or Castellana?"

Fernando smiled. "Do you recall when I told you I would like to lie with both together? You would not understand such pleasures, would you? The perfect Señor Berrington." He punched Thomas on the chest, a familiar gesture, one he had made a hundred times before, and a hundred times before Thomas had restrained himself. Now his restraint was exhausted.

"You think you are better than me, don't you?" he said. "That those pretend fights we've had were not staged. That you could have killed me at any time you wanted."

Fernando shook his head. "The trouble with you, Thomas Berrington, is you are a clever man, and clever men can convince themselves of almost anything." Another punch, harder this time. "They believe they can defeat a superior enemy." Punch. "They believe they know better than those who carry the burden of power." Punch. "They believe they can seduce another man's wife without consequence!"

Thomas laughed. This from a man who claimed to have come fresh from the bed of two women. Admittedly neither had a husband, so perhaps Fernando had some small justification, in his own mind at least.

"It is different between Isabel and me. We are a meeting of minds, not loins."

When Fernando jabbed the next punch, Thomas caught

his fist inside his own. He felt the pressure increase and pushed back harder. Fernando's face reddened, and Thomas was sure his own did the same. From the edge of his vision he saw Gabriel push himself away with his feet, cradling his dislocated shoulder. Yves leaned against the side of the fireplace, all fight gone from him.

"Shall we fight now, Your Grace?" Thomas put as much disdain as he could into the honorific. "Shall we take blades and fight to the death?" He stared into Fernando's eyes and saw doubt flare there, but the man was vain and a bully, unable to back down.

"You are a fool." He jerked his hand away and stepped back. "Take Yves's blade, I will have this one." He knelt and picked up the dagger dropped by Gabriel. It was the larger of the two, of course. Fernando smiled. "Do you know how long I have wanted to kill you?"

Thomas shrugged. "A while, I am sure."

Fernando laughed. "Oh, more than a while. And when you lie dead at my feet, I will go upstairs and screw your first love, and then I will mount Castellana, and then I will return to the palace and screw Isabel. And you will be unable to stop me doing any of it."

"That's a lot of screwing for a man with your reputation." Thomas smiled when he saw Fernando frown.

"What reputation?"

Thomas held his fingers two inches apart.

He stepped aside effortlessly as Fernando struck. Yes, they had fought over the years, and yes, he knew Fernando considered himself the better man, but the hardest part of their fighting had been for Thomas to allow him to believe such. Now all restraint was gone. He might suffer for it in the future, but now, in this room, with the world tumbling around him, he no longer cared.

Fernando turned fast. He was good, Thomas had to admit, but then so was he. The months of training with Usaden had honed the natural skill he had always possessed, and he knew he was invulnerable. Not against all enemies, but against Fernando certainly. And so he toyed with him. He pretended to strike before pulling his blow. He avoided each of Fernando's attacks as if they came from a child.

"Were you part of the conspiracy?" he asked, barely out of breath, an exultation filling his entire body, his mind like crystal. "Or was it your idea in the first place? Did Castellana want Inigo dead? Was he too dangerous to live?"

"You came too close, Berrington. Too close to my wife. A man cannot allow that." Another thrust, another parry.

Fernando glanced around. "You two, help me! Hold him while I pierce his heart." He grinned. "I'd like to see you fix that, surgeon!"

Gabriel would be no help at all, but Yves came forward, perhaps the presence of the King of Aragon and Castile sparking some courage in him. He ran from behind at Thomas, who backed into him, swung around and lifted the youth from his feet and flung him at Fernando.

They went down in a heap and Thomas moved fast to stand over them.

"I'm tired of this charade." He knelt, swept Fernando's dagger to one side, then pushed Yves away. He laid the tip of his own knife at Fernando's throat and applied pressure, pricking the skin. As blood welled, a deep sense of failure rose in Thomas to match it, rising from within. He couldn't kill Fernando. He didn't want to kill him. Once he had even liked the man. Not a lot, he admitted, but he had tried for Isabel's sake. Of course Fernando had been involved. Castellana as well. Even Eleanor. He knew it now, had been seduced by old memories and not seen the truth. They were among the privileged of this world. Small men and women were seen as their playthings. Whatever they did, they did for advancement and wealth, and for pleasure. They would continue to do so because there was no-one to offer punishment, or even judgement. Or was there? Thomas wondered about a possibility.

"I should kill you," he said, his voice harsh, "then go to the palace and bed Isabel like she dreams of me doing. You know I speak the truth. You have always feared it, haven't you? But I won't do either. You will live. Isabel and I will remain friends, but never more than that." He smiled. "Even though you fear she would like it to be more. You wanted de Borja dead because she looks at him the same way she looks at me. He is a handsome man, just like Jorge. A man who will one day sit next to God. Where will you sit, Your Grace, when your final day comes? Bathed by the light of God, or in the flames of hell? Think on it. Act accordingly."

Thomas threw the dagger across the room, disgusted with them, himself most of all.

He went to Gabriel and gripped his wrist, set a foot beneath his arm and pulled hard. There was a loud snap as his shoulder returned to its correct alignment, and he screamed even louder than the first time.

Thomas turned from the room to discover two women at the top of the staircase, both wrapped in a single white sheet that barely covered their nakedness. Eleanor started down the stairs, letting the sheet fall loose so she descended as Thomas remembered her. When he thought of her at all. That was the difference. That was what the last month had brought him. A clarity of thought and emotion. He had loved her once, but that was long ago and far away. Now he didn't even like her, just as he didn't like his son. It was life.

Sometimes things didn't work out. Not everything had to be a pleasure.

He turned and walked from the house into a future that promised more uncertainty than he could ever remember, and he welcomed it.

CHAPTER FORTY-ONE

It was deep midwinter before Thomas and Jorge returned to Gharnatah. Thomas came with a new mission, one assigned to him by Isabel herself. It was a mission he welcomed. Isabel had warned him there would be danger and peril, but when had there not been?

A cold wind blew from the north to greet them, heralding the coming of snow. The house on the Albayzin smelled musty, and Thomas wondered where Helena had gone to, but didn't care. They came into the city late in the day, Jorge uncharacteristically quiet. He had been so for the entire four-day journey. Thomas suspected family was on his mind. His real family and his adopted family. As the city wrapped around them, Thomas felt an easing of the hurt he carried. This was where he belonged. This was his city. His place.

A week after they arrived, Thomas was woken in the night by a hand on his chest. He rolled over, reaching for the blade that always lay beneath his pillow, then stopped. The hand was soft, and a familiar scent enveloped him.

"Wrong room," he said, recognising Belia in an instant.

"No, Thomas, tonight I am in the right room."

He sat up, reaching for a flint to light the lamp, but she pushed him back down. She took his hand and lifted it, laid it against her naked breast. Thomas jerked away as though the brief touch had burned.

"What are you doing?"

"I thought it obvious what I am doing. Am I not beautiful, Thomas?" Her voice was velvet in the dark.

"You are, but you are also Jorge's woman. Again, what are you doing?"

She pushed him across the bed and slid in beside him, her skin hot, her unmistakable perfume filling his senses. "Do you think I would come here without his permission? It is Jorge who sent me. He says it is time he became a father."

"He can never be a father."

"He disagrees. He says you will plant the seed, but the child..." she gave a soft laugh, "...maybe several children if you are lucky will be mine and his." She lay half across him and kissed him as Lubna had kissed him. With love. Her hand traced his belly, drifted lower, as Lubna's hand had often done. Thomas responded even through his confusion.

"This is wrong."

He felt Belia's lips smile where they touched his. "This," and she gripped him, "says it is not wrong. You know I feel love for you, Thomas. Not as I do for Jorge, but we have been friends a long time, and there are many different forms love can take. Do this for me, and do it for Jorge, for I know you love us both. Set a baby inside me. Do it with love, for the world has little enough love. We must make more. Create more.

When dawn came, Belia was gone. Thomas stared at the ceiling and wondered if it had been a dream, but she came again a week later, and again the week after that. None of them spoke of what they were doing, not even Jorge.

And then, six weeks after Belia's first visit, she announced her bleeding had not arrived.

At the turning of the year, Thomas mounted his horse, alone but for Kin, who trotted along beside him as he rode through the open gates of Gharnatah. The snow-capped peaks of the Sholayr lay behind him, and Isabel over a week's ride ahead in Alcala de Henares. No doubt she sat in the cold castle where her youngest daughter had been delivered by Thomas. He would ride to her and measure the welcome. If it was warm enough, he would send for the others, though he knew Isabel and Fernando would be coming to Gharnatah soon enough.

HISTORICAL NOTE

The Message of Blood takes place during the relatively calm period during which Spain made its final preparations to take Granada, which occurred on 1 January 1492—a story which will be told in book 9 of the series, *A Tear for the Dead*.

Rodrigo de Borja (or Borgia) was elected Pope shortly after the events fictionalised in this book. De Borja was a Spaniard, his family coming from Valencia, and returned to visit Spain on several occasions. He was known to be close to both Isabel and Fernando, and was involved in the legalisation of their marriage, because they were cousins and required a Papal dispensation to marry. I have brought de Borja to Spain during the period of this novel for obvious reasons, but as far as is known, he did not visit during 1489–90. However, he did so both before and afterward, so I am comfortable at taking a slight liberty with the timing.

De Borja has often had a bad press, but my readings show him in a kinder light than others, though clearly not a saint. At the time I write about, many Bishops and Cardinals were married or had mistresses. De Borja himself was married young, and is believed to have fathered children while living in Spain, a rumour I have used as a plot device here. He is also said to have been extremely handsome, and of an affable nature. Castellana Lonzal, who becomes his wife in this story, is a fictional creation, but it is no great leap of logic to assume someone like her may well have existed in real life.

The final book of the Spanish phase of Thomas and Jorge's life, *A Tear for the Dead,* will tell of the battle for Granada and their part in it. There will also be a mystery, as always. Expect *A Tear for the Dead* to appear some time toward the end of 2020.

And if you feel a pang of loss with my saying "the final book", there is no need. After a brief hiatus, Thomas, Jorge and the others will return, but this time to England in the company of the seventeen-year-old Catherine of Aragon, when she arrives to marry Prince Arthur, the son of Henry VII. That book will form the first volume in a new phase of Thomas's life and will lead, perhaps a decade in the future, to the William Berrington Mysteries...

REFERENCES

Most of the information on Rodrigo de Borja was taken from the excellent *The Borgias,* by G.J. Meyer.

ABOUT THE AUTHOR

David Penny is the author of the Thomas Berrington Historical Mysteries set in Moorish Spain at the end of the 15th Century. He is currently working on the next book in the series.

Find out more about David Penny and sign up for his Newsletter here:

www.davidpennywriting.com

Made in the USA
Monee, IL
26 October 2020